a YEAR of
FLOWERS

NOVELS BY SUZANNE WOODS FISHER

LANCASTER COUNTY SECRETS

The Choice

The Waiting

The Search

STONEY RIDGE SEASONS

The Keeper

The Haven

The Lesson

THE INN AT EAGLE HILL

The Letters

The Calling

The Revealing

AMISH BEGINNINGS

Anna's Crossing

The Newcomer

The Return

THE BISHOP'S FAMILY

The Imposter

The Quieting

The Devoted

NANTUCKET LEGACY

Phoebe's Light

Minding the Light

The Light before Day

THE DEACON'S FAMILY

Mending Fences

Stitches in Time

Two Steps Forward

THREE SISTERS ISLAND

On a Summer Tide

On a Coastal Breeze

At Lighthouse Point

CAPE COD CREAMERY

The Sweet Life

The Secret to Happiness

Love on a Whim

The Moonlight School

A Season on the Wind

Anything but Plain

Lost and Found

a YEAR of FLOWERS

A 4-in-1 Novella Collection

SUZANNE WOODS FISHER

Revell

a division of Baker Publishing Group
Grand Rapids, Michigan

© 2024 by Suzanne Woods Fisher

Published by Revell
a division of Baker Publishing Group
Grand Rapids, Michigan
RevellBooks.com

Printed in the United States of America

Library of Congress Cataloging-in-Publication Control Number: 2024033380
ISBN 9780800742348

This book is a work of fiction. Names, characters, places, and incidents are the product of the author's imagination or are used fictitiously. Any resemblance to actual events, locales, or persons, living or dead, is coincidental.

Author is represented by Joyce A. Hart.

Cover photograph © Jane Morley / Trevillion Images
Cover design by Laura Klynstra

Baker Publishing Group publications use paper produced from sustainable forestry practices and postconsumer waste whenever possible.

24 25 26 27 28 29 30   7 6 5 4 3 2 1

Contents

an APOLOGY *in* BLOOM

Cast of Characters

Jaime Harper—(age 25) raised in the South, now a floral designer for Epic Events, a wedding and event planning company based in New York City

Liam McMillan—(age 30-something) owner of Epic Events

Rose Reid—(ageless) owner of Rose's Flower Shop in Sunrise, North Carolina

Harrison—(don't ask) artist and neighbor to Jaime in NYC

Sloane—(age 40ish) project manager for Epic Events

Mrs. Zimmerman—(somewhere in her sixties) a critical client for Epic Events (literally and figuratively)

Todd—(age 22) unpaid intern for Epic Events

Floral Glossary

fillers—material used to fill gaps or empty spaces

focal point—the area of dominance or emphasis where the eye naturally travels

foliage—greenery, such as plant leaves

forage—harvesting free material, such as blooming forsythia branches, taken from private properties (*only* with permission, please!)

mechanics—the hidden foundation that holds flowers in place (such as flower frog or chicken wire)

negative space—a planned open space within a design that contains no flowers or foliage

recipe—a set of instructions to prepare a specific arrangement

vendors—sources for flowers (local growers, farmers' market, a wholesaler, or international)

vessels—containers to hold arrangements (such as vases, urns, compote bowls); all kinds of objects can become vessels to hold flowers—mason jars, bottles, crocks

Flowers always make people better, happier,
and more helpful; they are sunshine, food,
and medicine for the soul.
　—*Luther Burbank*

one

*J*aime Harper stepped back to examine the bridal bouquet she'd created for the Zimmerman-Blau wedding. She had to get this bouquet right today. Did it seem balanced? Was anything sticking out? A bridal bouquet was the most photographed floral piece of an entire wedding. Nail it down and everything else would fall into place.

This was the sixth mock-up. All previous ones had been shot down by the mother of the bride. These mock-up meetings were critical steps in the planning process. And Mrs. Zimmerman was a critical customer. She had a way of making Jaime feel like a rooster one day and a feather duster the next.

The Zimmerman-Blau wedding was going to be the highest-profile wedding yet for Epic Events. Sloane, the project manager, reminded her that it was such an important wedding that Epic's owner Liam McMillan was leaving an initial design consultation with a prospective client to be at this flower mock-up with Mrs.

Zimmerman. "Liam asked me to make lunch reservations at his favorite restaurant," Sloane said. "A congratulations lunch," she added, crossing her fingers. "Today's the day." Final approval from Mrs. Z, she meant.

"Let's hope so," Jaime said, but she wondered. She'd been tinkering with the arrangement all morning. Her mind kept wandering, and she had to keep tugging herself back to the here and now. When she was distracted, she missed things. When she missed things, bad things happened. She knew that for a fact. "Do you think it's too, too . . ." Too much? Too little?

Sloane rolled her eyes. "Stop sounding so pathetic."

"I can't help it," Jaime said. She had a better sense of the terrible things that could happen in the world than most people did.

"Hurry and finish and clean up your workshop!"

Jaime looked at her and sighed. "I don't know why y'all are always in a rush."

Sloane turned from the door and winked. "My little Southern belle, have you still not realized we have only one speed? Express."

Jaime listened to the sound of Sloane's staccato heels doing their fast-walk down the hallway. Why did New Yorkers go through life like their hair was on fire? And for what? She got the same results by taking her time.

In the mirror, she examined the bouquet one more time. Was it as good as Sloane said? She hated that her first thought was no, that she never thought her work was good enough. She didn't know what took a greater toll on her sense of well-being—her own self-deprecating thoughts or high-maintenance clients with way too much money. Something was still cattywampus with the bouquet, and Mrs. Zimmerman would notice that indescribable *something* and reject, yet again, the design.

For most weddings, flowers took about 10 to 15 percent of the total budget. Clients were delighted to cut down on costs and waste by letting the ceremony flowers do double duty at the reception space. The welcome arrangement from the ceremony could be reused at the table seating display. Or the bridal bouquet could be put in a vase and used as the sweetheart table arrangement. But there was no such skimping for the Zimmerman wedding.

Flowers, Mrs. Zimmerman insisted, were to be the main décor for her daughter's wedding. She loved flowers and wanted lavish displays to fill every space in the venue, the New York Botanical Garden—a beautiful oasis in the middle of the Bronx. All in all, the flower budget for the Zimmerman wedding came to a staggering sum. That was the reason there was such heightened concern at Epic Events to get Mrs. Zimmerman's approval on the flowers. Sloane couldn't start billing until Mrs. Z signed off, and Jaime couldn't order the flowers without paying a sizable deposit up front. So today was the day. She had to get the mock-up bouquet right today.

She took a picture on her phone of the bouquet and sent it to Liam. A minute or two later, Liam texted back *Subtract*, and of course he was right. He was always right. Jaime had a tendency to jam-pack so that blooms competed for space as they expanded in the heat of the day. What looked to be a perfectly balanced floral arrangement in the cool of the morning would look stuffed and tight by evening. So she subtracted by pulling stems and removing materials, until she thought it thoroughly resembled Liam's recipe.

That man had some kind of superpower in how he could read his clients' minds. He was able to visualize and articulate what the clients wanted even if they didn't seem to know themselves. This was the sticky-floral-tape thought for Jaime: How to put into reality the creation Liam had imagined. That was the secret sauce for everyone at Epic Events—to think like Liam McMillan thinks and execute like he executes. He *was* the brand.

She went over to the mirror again to hold the bouquet low against her belly, the way a bride would. She rotated the bouquet to see it at every angle, examining different viewpoints to make sure it looked balanced. Photographs exaggerated the depth of field, so it was wise to note whatever might jut out.

Everything looked good. Better than good. Jaime exhaled a sigh of relief. Time to stop. Knowing when to stop was critical.

Jaime taped the stems and set the bouquet in water in the walk-in cooler to keep it as fresh as possible for the meeting.

Before closing the cooler, she breathed in deeply the perfume of fresh flowers, letting their scent calm her nerves. Whenever she paused to soak up the fragrance of flowers, she was instantly transported to the sweetest, happiest time of her life. Back in high school, working afternoons and weekends in Rose's Flower Shop in a tiny town in North Carolina with her two best friends, Claire and Tessa. Mentored in the art of flower arranging by Rose Reid, the shop owner, who had the patience and kindness and generous nature to teach the three girls everything she knew. Flowers were the business of happiness, Rose had often reminded them. They brought joy and comfort to people.

Rose Reid had been on her mind all morning. She was the reason Jaime felt as if tears kept threatening. The reason she felt emotionally wobbly. It was hard to squeeze shame back into its box. Even harder to keep it from spilling out again.

When Jaime had arrived at work this morning, a registered letter was waiting for her. Instantly, she recognized the elegant handwriting, the pale pink stationery. She hurried to the workshop and sat right down on a stool, her chest stinging with pain. How had Rose found her? It was the first time there'd been contact between them since that terrible August day. She cringed at the memory she'd tried so hard to forget. Hands trembling, Jaime skimmed the letter once, twice, then read it again more thoroughly. *All is forgiven*, Rose wrote. *It's time to come home.* And then she outlined a plan for Jaime to return to live in North Carolina, to run Rose's Flower Shop.

Run a little flower shop in that off-the-beaten-track Southern town? Was Rose serious? After all that had happened between them, that offer took gumption. But did she really think Jaime would give up all *this* . . . for *that*?

Because *this* included quite a bit. A floral dream job led by a remarkably creative boss. And when it came to Liam, there was potential for romance written all over their relationship. Well, sometimes it seemed to be written all over it. Scribbles, maybe. They had "moments" now and then that made her think something was brewing. She hoped so. Oh boy, did she ever hope so.

Then again, so did most every female who worked at Epic Events. So did every female client.

Jaime closed the cooler door—pushing with two hands because it had a tendency to stick—and grabbed a broom to clean up the stems and leaves and petals strewn over the floor. As she gathered the excess flowers to return to the cooler, she glanced at the large wall clock. An idea had been tickling in the back of her mind for a unique bouquet—a contemporary take on a cascade style. Why not? She had time. Sitting in the cooler were leftover Zimmerman flowers, plus some unusual flowers she'd picked up on a whim this morning at the New York City Flower Market.

First, she began with a dense center: clusters of color for focus. The showstoppers. Café Latte roses, Cappuccino roses, Café au Lait Ranunculus as big as roses. She built intensity by adding pops of color: Black Parrot tulips and Hot Chocolate calla lilies. The black tulips were the color of an eggplant (Mother Nature doesn't make truly black flowers), petals glossy with a dark luster, tops fringed like feathers—hence the name parrot tulips. The calla lilies were a deep chocolate burgundy bloom.

She brought in texture with trailers of creeping fig woven in through the roses. Next came gradients, accent flowers to bridge the colors—mini Epidendrum orchids, ruffly Lisianthus. Then foliage to fill the gaps. A light hand, though.

She stood back to assess. It felt like it still needed more, but she hesitated, thinking of Liam's text: *Subtract!* A phrase from Rose popped into her mind: *"Let the flowers speak."* So Jaime added layer upon layer, letting the flowers do the talking. She stood in front of the mirror, just as she had done with the Zimmerman bouquet, and felt a deep sense of satisfaction.

The door opened and Sloane stuck her head in. Her mouth opened, closed, opened again, then stopped. Her eyes and attention were on the bouquet. "Jaime, it's an absolute stunner." She took a step into the workshop. "It's like an oil painting." Adding in a warning tone, "But . . . that's *not* the bouquet that Liam wanted—"

"No, no. Don't worry. This isn't the Zimmerman bouquet. That's in the cooler."

Sloane crossed the room to examine the bouquet in Jaime's hands.

"Sometimes . . ."

"What?"

"Sometimes . . . I wish I had your job."

Jaime's eyes narrowed in surprise. Sloane was a phenomenal project manager. So smart, so capable. She kept the team on a strict timeline. "I thought you liked doing what you do."

"I do. Sure I do. I mean, if I want my own company one day, this is the best path. But there's just something about flowers."

Sloane bent over to inhale deeply from the bouquet and Jaime understood. There *was* just something about flowers. "I'll tell you *what*! After the Zimmerman wedding, maybe I can teach you some flower basics."

Sloane smiled. "I'll tell *you* what." She liked to mock Jaime's Southernness. "You're on." She tipped her head. "Are those black tulips?"

Jaime nodded. "Tulips symbolize eternal love."

"Get a picture of that one. I want it for my wedding." Sloane rolled her eyes upward. "If Charlie will ever get over his allergy to commitment." They'd been engaged for seven years. She pointed to the large clock on the wall. "I just heard from Liam. They're on their way."

More than on their way. Through the large warehouse window, Jaime could see an Uber pull into the parking lot, followed by Mrs. Zimmerman's white Tesla. She took a few steps over to the large window, watching Liam, her heart humming like a contented cat. She enjoyed observing him unawares. Stolen moments, she thought of them.

"Checking out Mrs. Z's latest ensemble?"

Not hardly. Jaime's eyes were on Liam. He hurried over to open the door on the Tesla for Mrs. Zimmerman. *Such a gentleman.*

Sloane came up behind her to join her at the window. "What's she got on today?"

Mrs. Zimmerman, somewhere in her late sixties, had memorable taste in clothing. Today, she wore an orange pantsuit—radiation, glow-in-the-dark orange—and her hair was hidden under a yellow and purple scarf, its tail resting on her shoulder. Sloane whistled, long and low. "I'm still amazed that the flowers for the wedding are subdued colors."

"She wanted everything in pink, all shades, especially hot pink, until Liam told her that pink was requested all year long."

Sloane coughed a laugh. "He's got her figured out. Mrs. Z wants nothing more than to stand out from the crowd." She gave Jaime a pat on her shoulder and started toward the door.

Jaime was barely aware of Sloane's departure. Her eyes were still glued on Liam. Mrs. Zimmerman was giggling at something he was telling her. Mothers of the brides seemed especially vulnerable to Liam's charms. Maybe it was his thick Scottish brogue. There was definitely something mesmerizing about it. Or maybe it had to do with the way he looked at you when he spoke, as if you were exactly the person he was hoping to see and he just couldn't believe how fortunate he was to find you. She wondered if that characteristic might be true of all Scotsmen . . . or if it was just part of the Liam McMillan magic.

Add to that musical accent his good looks—finely chiseled features, his deceptively casual appearance—and females became captivated. Jaime, especially. If he were tall, he might have been an imposing figure, but his below-average height for a man only added to his appeal. He was so approachable, so inviting. Today,

Liam was dressed in a black merino sweater and olive trousers, Ferragamo loafers. Jaime caught herself calculating how much money his outfit cost—easily between one and two thousand dollars. Right in the range of hers, though everything she was wearing today had been purchased at an upscale consignment store for a fraction of its original cost. It was one of the perks of living in New York City—lots of one-season-wear castoffs.

With that thought, her stomach started turning again. This, she knew, was the core of her insecurity. Pretending to be someone she wasn't.

With a start, she hurried over to the walk-in cooler to switch the bouquets. She pulled at the door with her free hand, but it wouldn't open. "Stupid cooler!" She rued the day she'd bought this cooler. It was a smoke screen—it looked new but broke down regularly. She yanked and yanked, but she'd need two hands to open the stuck door. She spun around to find a place to set the cascading bouquet and there were Mrs. Zimmerman and Liam, staring at her with wide eyes.

two

Flowers don't tell, they show.
—Stephanie Skeem

As soon as the waiter seated them, Jaime cast a shy glance at Liam. "She liked it. Everything." She was giddy. Overjoyed. She felt as if light beams were radiating off her head. An hour earlier, when Mrs. Zimmerman had appeared at the workshop door with a shocked "What's this?" she had marched straight toward Jaime—who stood frozen like a deer in headlights, her heart pounding, her palms sweating. She shot a glance at Liam. His smile fell and he raised a serious brow, as if to say to Jaime, *What have y' done with m' recipe?*

I can explain, she mouthed back, but suddenly Mrs. Zimmerman was circling her, quietly and cautiously, as if she were watching a rare bird on a feeder.

"What is *that*?"

"That? It's . . . a parrot tulip."

"And that?"

"A calla lily called Hot Chocolate. Even its stems are dark."

"Rare, aren't they? This is one of a kind, isn't it?"

23

Well, yes and no. Floral arrangers certainly knew of black flowers, though they weren't commonly used in wedding arrangements. But Jaime sensed what Mrs. Zimmerman was truly asking. Once, after a particularly difficult mock-up meeting with her, Sloane had rolled her eyes and whispered to Jaime, "Nouveau riche," as if that explained everything. Jaime had to google it: "Newly rich. A derogatory term to describe persons who acquire wealth within their generation and spend it conspicuously."

Jaime had never had any money at all, not old or new. But she did understand Mrs. Zimmerman's almost desperate need to "be somebody." So she nodded and said what was true. "Mrs. Zimmerman, I highly doubt any of your friends would be familiar with black tulips or black calla lilies."

Jaime knew that to be true because Sloane had given her the inside scoop to the Zimmermans' social circle. Mr. Zimmerman had warned his wife that not a single friend of theirs would want to schlep into Manhattan for a wedding, and that was the reason Mrs. Zimmerman chose the New York Botanical Garden for her daughter's wedding venue. The opinion of her friends mattered to her greatly. She had high hopes to impress them with this wedding.

Mrs. Zimmerman was beaming. She turned on her heels toward Liam. "Liam, your girl finally, finally got it right."

It was like the sun had come out from behind a cloud. It was like a chorus of angels had started to sing.

The waiter brought some bread and butter to the table. Liam held the bread basket out to her. She shook her head, too excited to eat. Not only did the mock-up meeting go better than she could have expected, now she was having a private lunch with Liam. Just the two of them! She'd assumed Sloane would have joined in as the project manager for the wedding. But she didn't. And she thought Mrs. Zimmerman would also be joining them, but she had lunch plans with her daughter the bride, who seemed as disinterested in this wedding as her mother seemed obsessed with it. Jaime had met the bride only once, at the initial consultation, and was surprised at how bored she had seemed. Bored! By her own wedding.

"So," Jaime said, running a finger around the top of her glass of iced tea, "do you think I can go ahead and put in the flower order?" The flowers should have been ordered weeks ago.

Most flowers came from the Netherlands, the land of flowers. "Such a wee country," Liam often said, yet it provided half of the fresh-cut flower imports to the United States, especially tulips, lilies, and peonies. From Ecuador and Colombia came long-stemmed roses, because the stems grew perfectly straight near the equator. South America was also the source for orchids and anthuriums, and so many other varieties.

Mrs. Zimmerman had insisted on a hard-to-source Café Latte rose. Vanilla-scented, with a copper bronze color and very slight pink undertone, it was definitely a showstopper. But it was also bred and grown on a flower farm in Kenya, and there was only one supplier to the United States. Jaime would probably have to pay express shipping fees to make the deadline.

Liam smiled thoughtfully and picked up his fork. "Aye, order away. Mrs. Zimmerman signed off on yer happy accident, mo leannan."

Normally, Jaime nearly swooned when he called her mo leannan. It was Scottish for "my sweetheart, a term of endearment" (she had googled it). Sadly, he used it quite generously with women. Still, she loved the sound of it.

But calling her bouquet a happy accident popped her giddy-balloon. So she had veered far, far off from Liam's recipe. Why was that so wrong? The original bouquet was waiting in the cooler. She'd followed his instructions to the T.

The waiter interrupted to take their order. Jaime hadn't looked at the menu, so Liam ordered for both of them. After the waiter left them, Jaime said, "Liam, about that happy accident bouquet. I thought I might—"

But she couldn't finish her sentence because Liam's watch buzzed, snagging his attention.

The second half to her sentence was that she had thought she might enter the bouquet in the New York City Blooms to Bouquet competition. Jaime had never thought her work was good enough for that contest, plus the concepts weren't her interpretation. They were Liam's ideas with that special Liam finesse. Today's success gave her a boost of self-confidence. Enough to make her think about entering the bouquet in the competition.

Or maybe it was Rose's letter. In it, she'd outlined a plan for Jaime to run the flower shop—but required winning one of the prestigious flower competitions held around the country. *Just one*, she wrote. *Just to prove you've still got "it."* It being passion, drive, determination.

Jaime had forgotten how Rose loved these contests. Rose considered them to be objective affirmation of a florist's imagination and ambition. She used to enter regional contests on an annual basis, and she won many of them. If she didn't win, she was almost always a finalist, which she considered a win. Plastered on the front window of Rose's Flower Shop were seals of her awards. Claire would tease her by calling it her trophy display. And Rose would blush, insisting it was nothing of the sort.

Claire, full of sass. And Tessa, full of daydreams.

Jaime hadn't thought of those lighthearted moments in the flower shop in a very long time.

"Sorry 'bout that, lass. Now, what were y' saying?" Liam's Apple watch had gone silent for the time being, which meant his attention was turned back to her.

Maybe Jaime was getting ahead of herself. Maybe Liam was right—her design today was just a happy accident. "Nothing," she said, taking a sip of her iced tea. She stopped, mid-sip, surprised by the taste. *Well, I'll be.* Sweet tea? Heavy-handed with simple syrup. She didn't think anyone in New York City knew how to make sweet tea. Just then the waiter brought their meals and Jaime lifted her head and looked around. "Where are we?"

Liam snapped his head up, surprised by her question. "Southern Comfort. Best Southern and soul food in Brooklyn. Have y' never come here?"

No. She'd been in New York City for over two years and had never been to a restaurant that served Southern cuisine. She didn't think there were any. On her plate was a heaping pile of biscuits and gravy. And pickles! Her eyes darted to the bread basket. *Corn bread*. Her favorite. Liam had chosen a restaurant that featured Southern cuisine. And she hadn't even noticed! Just yesterday, she'd had a hankering for a real Southern biscuit—buttery, flaky, fluffy, soft like a cloud. How had he known to pick a place like this? *So thoughtful.*

She held up her glass of sweet tea to clink with his. "A toast to celebrate our winning over of Mrs. Zimmerman."

"A toast t' you, lass," he said, holding her gaze in a way that stole her breath.

Breathe, Jaime. Breathe.

ℓ·ℓ·ℓ

Late in the day, Jaime's mind kept circling back to the Blooms to Bouquet competition. Today was the last day to enter, and the application required a photograph of her work. She asked Todd, the intern, to come and take pictures of the bridal bouquet that she'd made with the excess flowers this morning. Todd had more technical skills than anyone else in the company, and they all relied heavily on him to problem solve. "Send them only to me," she told him. Twice, because as savvy as Todd was with tech, as remarkable as he could be with details that interested him, he was equally poor at listening.

Todd went to his computer to edit the pictures and, not thirty minutes later, forwarded the finished photographs to Jaime. She clicked through them, holding her breath. Todd's backlighting enhanced the arrangement, bringing out certain textural elements that might be overlooked. Even to her self-demeaning eye, the bouquet looked exquisite. Dramatic and captivating. Like Sloane said—an oil painting.

She glanced at the big clock on the workshop wall. One hour left before the deadline for the competition. Could she, should she? She whispered a little prayer, filling out the entry form and paying the fee, but her fingers hovered over the send button.

Why was she doing this?

She pulled back from the keyboard. Why? Well, because floral design competitions had been experiencing a resurgence in the last few years, especially in the virtual world. They were a way to have design work evaluated by the best in the industry, to receive feedback from respected judges.

She wasn't entering the competition because she wanted to run Rose's Flower Shop, because she certainly didn't. No way.

Or did she?

No. Absolutely not. She had everything she had always wanted. This was her dream—to live in New York City, to work for Liam McMillan. Why would she want to change her life?

Because something has been left unfinished.

Her head snapped up. Where did that thought come from?

She looked around her office, as if she sensed someone was there. A shiver went down her back, though of course the workshop was empty.

She shook off that unnerving thought, turned back to her computer, took in a deep breath, and pressed send.

three

A flower's appeal is in its contradictions—so delicate in form
yet strong in fragrance, so small in size yet big in beauty,
so short in life yet long on effect.
—Terri Guillemets

Jaime was hoping to hit the sack early because she wanted to get to the flower market when it opened, but her neighbor Harrison caught her in the hallway. As she went past his door, he burst out of his apartment, just waiting for her to get home.

"Jaime! I need your help."

She should have tiptoed past his door. She usually did. "Hey there, Harrison." She smiled and kept walking, hoping he'd get the hint that she was busy, but he didn't. He never did.

"Jaime, I need another one."

She stopped and turned. "Another Apology Bouquet?" He looked distraught. Puppy-dog sad with droopy eyes. "What have you done now?" Or, more likely, not done?

"My mother's been in the hospital. I meant to go visit, but I—"

"You forgot? Your eighty-year-old mother is in the hospital and you *forgot*?"

"I know, I know. I just get so absorbed in my art." He waved his hands. "Time becomes irrelevant. Please, Jaime. Help me out."

The look on his face! Like he was about to cry. She softened. "I'm heading to the market in the morning. I'll pick up some flowers for you."

"Actually . . . I stopped at a store and bought flowers for you." He scrunched his face up. "I was hoping, maybe, you'd make a bouquet for me to take to my mother tonight."

"Oh Harrison, can't it wait? It's been a long day and I'm worn slap out."

"You're what? Never mind. Please, Jaime. Your flowers always do the trick."

Jaime let out a sigh. She felt like a drug pusher, enabling him to keep neglecting his long-suffering mother. "You have got to stop forgetting about your mother. She's no spring chicken! You're not going to have her around forever. A woman in her eighties deserves a son's attention."

Harrison's face blossomed into a smile. "Don't you worry. I've learned my lesson." He crossed his heart.

That, Jaime thought to herself, was a stray-dog lie. Poor woman. Bless her heart.

She put the key in the dead bolt and turned it. "Go get the flowers and bring them to my apartment." He practically skipped back to his open door. "Bring a vase this time too!" He never returned her vases.

He stopped at his door, his face a puzzle. "A vase? I have an empty pickle jar."

"That'll do. Just make sure it's cleaned out." That's the kind of thing you had to tell Harrison.

An hour later, Harrison left her apartment with the pickle jar full of arranged flowers—the jar was completely covered in satin ribbon, wound and wound around it and tied with a perfect bow.

Jaime couldn't let her work go out the door in a jar with a pickle label on it. He'd bought tight bundles of cheap flowers in plastic wrap, unsold leftovers from a street vendor. Lots and lots of inexpensive carnations, some Japanese iris with petals that looked a little worse for the wear. Two red Gerbera daisies, yellow stock, and a feathery bunch of chamomiles, which Jaime didn't even bother to include. All in all, a truly dreadful combination of flowers.

The bouquet wasn't her best work, the colors and textures were difficult to harmonize, but she hadn't chosen the flowers, she wanted to get to bed, and Harrison's serial forgetfulness of his poor mother didn't deserve another hour of her time. But he left happy with his pickle jar of flowers.

Poor Harrison's mama. Bless her heart.

She didn't mind doing a favor for Harrison. He'd been good to her. He looked out for her, and when he knew she had a jam-packed schedule of events, he would offer to move her car to the other side of the street in the early hours (street cleaners!) so that she could sleep in. Now and then, they'd walk to the laundromat together, and he would carry her laundry. All in all, Harrison was a good neighbor, and everybody needed a good neighbor.

Best of all, he loved hearing stories about her hometown. A native New Yorker, he said it sounded like she'd grown up in a foreign country. When she told him that she'd grown up in a "dry town" (if you had a hankering for a beer, you'd have to drive over yonder to the next county) and that the name of her town was Sunrise, he howled with laughter.

As she lay in bed, looking up at the ceiling, she breathed in the fresh scent left over from Harrison's carnations. Rose used to call them gimcrack—substandard to other choices—but Jaime loved their spicy smell, and as cut flowers, they lasted for ages. She had enjoyed creating the impromptu flower arrangement. It reminded her of slow times at the flower shop. Rose would empty out the cooler and give the girls the leftovers, and tell them they had an hour to create something special. "No rules!" she would say. "Just have at it." After an hour's time, she would judge the arrangements and pick a winner.

Their three arrangements couldn't have been more different. Rose would inspect each one, offering compliments and helpful suggestions. It didn't even matter who won—they oohed and aahed over each other's work and learned so much. Looking back, Jaime benefited from some of the lessons that Rose taught in those friendly contests. Working under a time pressure. Handling flowers that might not appeal to you. Finding ways to not waste inventory.

Rose let them take the arrangements home, and somehow all three girls felt as if they had won. But that was back when they were friends. Before Rose's nephew had changed that.

♈

This kind of a morning was worth getting out of bed at the crack of dawn. Jaime had set her alarm for 4:00 a.m. to arrive at the New York City Flower Market when it opened to professionals at 5:30. Located in Chelsea on West 28th Street, between Sixth and Seventh Avenue, you knew you were close when the air started to smell different. Cleaner, fresher, greener. A gem in the jungle. And if she arrived before 5:00 a.m., she could actually find a parking spot on the street.

The first time Jaime had gone to the flower district, she thought she'd died and gone to heaven. The abundant variety of plants and cut flowers was a horticulturist's dream. So many different smells, blending and mixing, that she didn't even bother separating them in her mind. When she first moved to New York, she'd tried to find a job at the market, but without connections, no wholesaler would hire her. Two years later, vendors knew her by name and set aside buckets of flowers for her. All because of the Liam McMillan magic. Like fairy dust.

Having found the lilacs she'd come for, she treated herself to a cup of coffee and drove to the warehouse. There was less traffic than expected and she arrived before seven o'clock. The parking lot was empty, so it startled her to open the front door to Epic and hear the sound of music. She closed the door behind her and paused. Was that . . . ? No . . . it couldn't be. But it was. Hezekiah Walker! But who would be listening to gospel music? She walked down the hallway and realized the sound was coming from Liam's office. His door was partially opened, and she peeked inside to find him scribbling on the large whiteboard on his wall, singing at the top of his lungs to "Better," a gospel song. Not just singing, he was rocking out! He knew every word to the song. Jaime stared in disbelief. The lyric at the end of the song, "Things are going to get better 'cause God is in control," rose to a crescendo, Liam right along with it. When it finished, she couldn't help but clap.

Liam spun around, a look of shock on his face. "How long?"

"The whole thing." She laughed. It was fun to catch Liam being . . . a regular guy. "What the Sam Hill is a Scottish lord doing listening to Southern gospel?"

Still frozen, he didn't smile or flinch. "'Tis a Grammy winner, I b'lieve."

True. And to think he would know the music of Kentuckian Hezekiah Walker made her fall in love with him just a little bit more. Was that even possible?

"Y' found the lilacs?"

Not so fast. "So you *like* gospel music?"

She thought she saw his cheeks color a bit. "I'm fond o' all kinds o' music."

Yes, but. "Gospel music is a little more . . ."

He waited for her to finish the sentence. When she didn't, he filled it in for her. "A wee bit more Christian."

Ah, there it was. Religion. A subject she carefully avoided with New Yorkers after making some naive assumptions and getting mocked as a farmgirl sap. Ever since, she studiously avoided assuming people approved of a traditional faith. It was right up there with her efforts to retire some Southern phrases that brought ridicule, like *might could* for "maybe." Or *down yonder* for "over there." Or *bless your heart* for "poor you." Liam was the only one in the office who didn't tease her. He smiled at her homespun sayings, amused but not mocking. There's a difference.

He gave her a thoughtful look. "'Tis a good thing, is it not?"

It was. It was a very good thing to be Christian. Jaime had been raised in a churchgoing home. Her mother sent her a monthly postcard with a postscript: *Have you found a church yet?* But she hadn't. She'd looked around for a church when she first moved to New York, but they were so big! Overwhelming. And then the pandemic hit. After the lockdown ended, when she was newly hired by Liam, her weekends became consumed with the pent-up demand for weddings. Sometimes, during wedding season, depending on the scale, Epic had two to three weddings per weekend.

So no. She hadn't found a church yet. But she did think of herself as a churchgoer. She did, the way she thought of herself as a brown-eyed brunette. It was part of her identity, her DNA. And her mother made sure she remembered it as well, texting her Bible verses. Thinking of her mama, she felt a stab of guilt. She did pray! Every morning and every night, like clockwork. That counted for something, didn't it? "It's harder here, in New York City, to keep faith from growing cold," she said.

"Takes a bit more work, I'll grant y' that. So now and then, I find I have t' borrow faith from the lyrics in a song." He lifted his shoulders in a slight shrug. "Surely there are seasons in life when faith can go dormant. But it can spring t' life again. After all, that's what faith is, is it not? It brings new life."

Startled, she didn't know how to respond. She had never thought of Liam as a man of faith. Not that he seemed like a man lacking a moral compass. Liam was honorable and conscientious in his work. Squeaky clean, Sloane called him. But he acted as skittish as a calf about anything remotely personal. She certainly never expected to have a conversation like this one with him.

His eyes were intense, curious, and staring right at her, waiting for an answer. His look became too much all of a sudden. She felt her cheeks flush and her skin tingle, so she lifted the bundles of lilac. "Speaking of life, I'd better get these into water."

ℓ·ℓ·ℓ

Jaime walked down the long hall to the workshop, located at the far end of the Epic Events warehouse. She had designed this room herself when she first started working here. She considered it a serious workplace for a serious floral designer.

A far cry from Rose's Flower Shop in North Carolina.

But would Rose think this was a place for the business of happiness? Or was it just business?

Jaime pushed that thought right out of her head. She had to stop thinking about Rose Reid! That registered letter she'd sent kept churning up old memories, best forgotten.

When Liam had offered the job to Jaime, he promised her space for a dedicated workshop. She'd come to New York City fresh out of college with a degree in horticulture, inspired by an interview with Liam that she'd read in *Martha Stewart Weddings*. She'd been following Liam on social media for a year or two, just as he was making a splash in the wedding world. In the interview, he said that New York City was the place to break into the flower world, because it has a sumptuous floral scene. *Sumptuous*. Who used that word for flowers? Only someone who loved flowers like she did. So she took that advice to heart, along with her from-afar crush on him, and moved to New York City without knowing a soul. Her mother thought she had lost her mind. There were many times during that first year when Jaime thought she'd lost her mind too. She sublet a small furnished apartment in Brooklyn from a friend of a friend of a friend in college . . . a dinky four-hundred-square-foot apartment on the second floor of a five-story building. So dinky that her shower was in her kitchen. On the garden level were two retail shops—a cat adoption agency and a shop that sold crystals and incense. (Mama would have something to say about *that*. Ironically, Jaime never saw a single customer go in or out of the shop.)

That first night in her dinky apartment, Jaime wanted to pack up Tin Lizzie and head home. But she didn't . . . and she couldn't. She had scrimped and saved to give herself a year in New York, and knowing she would wobble, she had written down that promise to herself, dated it, and stuck it in her Bible.

And it was a good thing she did, because the wobbling only got worse. She had absolutely no connections to anyone flower-related in the city, no résumé to speak of other than working in a flower shop during high school, and she ended up with no job offers.

Then the pandemic hit. And boy did it hit New York City. She'd never known what lonely was until that time. Desperate for something to take her mind off her loneliness, she started making flower arrangements in her dinky kitchen. Social media was her only means to advertise (free!), so she created Instagram-worthy arrangements and posted them. She had ten followers, one of whom was a cat from the adoption agency below.

Until one day, when everything changed.

Sharing the second floor in her apartment building was Harrison the artist, a weird-but-nice-but-weird man who painted enigmatic oil paintings. Dramatic, colorful, inscrutable. (She could just imagine what her mama would have to say about Harrison's paintings. "Son? What the Sam Hill were you thinking?") He'd seen her bringing cut flowers from the flower market up the stairwell, and one morning he stopped her in the hallway to beg for a bouquet. "I've done something terrible."

"What?" Then, "No, don't tell me."

But he did. "I forgot my mom's eightieth birthday. The date blew right past me. I got all involved, you know, in my work."

"Can't you just admit you forgot it and tell her you're sorry?"

"Tried that. Didn't work. She's really, really mad at me. Won't even pick up the phone when I call. Jaime, I need your help. My mother loves flowers. And flowers have a way of getting the message across."

Wasn't that the gospel truth? Flowers said so much. Of course Jaime said yes. How could she not? So she made Harrison a gorgeous bouquet, one of her best (if she did say so herself). And his mama forgave him.

But the story didn't end there.

Turned out Harrison had quite a following online, and he posted the arrangement, tagging Jaime, crediting the Apology Bouquet for repairing his relationship with his mother. The post went viral and suddenly she had a steady stream of orders. Seemed like a lot of people in New York City had apologies to make.

It was a start in the flower world, but it didn't pay the bills. Not with New York City rent, not with student loans to pay back. So she nannied for a few families over in Park Slope and Brooklyn Heights. Nanny jobs paid well but left her with no time for flowers, plus the children were incorrigible. Absolutely appalling manners. Coming from the South, Jaime thought children should show respect for those who were older than them, like their nanny. Not the children in New York City. When she told them to call her Miss Jaime, they burst out laughing. Jaime started to seriously consider packing up and moving home.

And along came Liam McMillan.

four

Love is like wildflowers; it's often found
in the most unlikely places.
—*Ralph Waldo Emerson*

*J*aime had been living in New York about nine months
when Liam McMillan saw her Apology Bouquet on Instagram and sent her a direct message, asking to meet to
discuss a job opportunity at Epic Events. At first, she thought some
dark-hearted friend was pranking her. When she realized the DM
had come from him—from Liam McMillan *himself*—she'd nearly
passed out. And then, when they met in person, she had trouble
concentrating. Inside, she was turning cartwheels. He was everything she had imagined him to be . . . and more. More charming,
more appealing, more charismatic.

As they sat down with hot drinks at the coffee shop, he explained that he had found the Apology Bouquet to be quite touching, to think that it had prompted a mother to forgive her son.
"I have a tender spot in m' heart for mams and grannies. They
deserve our attention."

"You are spot-on." As she launched into the backstory of Harrison and his weird art with so many followers, Liam's face grew

increasingly confused. She stopped, midsentence. What could she have done wrong? She'd only been talking for less than a minute.

"Where did y' say yer from?"

"Actually, I don't think I did say. I come from a little mountain town in western North Carolina."

"Appalachia?"

She nodded, a little surprised that he would know the region. She watched his eyes closely to see if there was any pity in them. There often was among New Yorkers. She was a target for mockery. Was his Scottish upbringing so highfalutin? Probably, she thought. His gentlemanly manners, his crisp accent, his ease with fancy-type customers. For all she knew, he might have been raised in a castle.

His eyes took in her face, then quickly dropped to the table. He remained lost in thought for an uncomfortably long moment, almost wistful, before snapping back into professional-employer interview mode. "So tell m' something," he said, leaning forward. "I've noticed y' place an allium in each of yer Apology Bouquets. How do y' keep it from smelling like . . . ?"

"Like an onion?" She could barely keep a smile tamped down. More cartwheels! He must be following her on Instagram if he'd seen more than one Apology Bouquet. "Add a few drops of Clorox bleach." She snapped her fingers. "Takes that onion smell away." It was a trick Rose had taught her. Alliums belonged to a genus that included onions and garlic. The very name means cultivated garlic. Adding an allium—just one to an arrangement—was Rose's touch too. They added a delightful surprise. The round purple bloom resembled a lollipop on a strong stem. And the blooms had a long vase life.

"Just add a few drops o' Clorox," he echoed, laughing at that simple trick—a hearty laugh with a bit of a scraping sound—and she couldn't help but laugh along with him. The ice had broken. Shattered. They spent the next two hours talking flowers. He was easy to talk to, laughed often, and had a way of repeating things she said, which made her feel as if he was truly listening to her.

Though Liam McMillan wasn't old (somewhere in his midthirties, Jaime guessed), there was something kind of old-fashioned about him. A bit of a Southern gentleman. Mama would swoon.

Liam explained that he was looking to expand Epic Events services and bring flower designing in-house. He wasn't always proud of what a vendor delivered. "To protect the integrity of our business," he said, "I want t' wrap our brand around everything. Every detail. Bringin' the flowers in-house is the next step."

Jaime could hardly breathe. She felt as if she had just stepped into a fairy tale. She had never, ever imagined she'd be having coffee with Liam McMillan one day, much less that he'd be offering her a job. Before he finished saying there'd be a dedicated space for a floral workshop, she'd said yes to his job offer without waiting for him to offer it.

Looking back, Jaime might could have asked more questions. Like, would she have the freedom to create her own floral arrangements? (The answer would've been no. Liam, she quickly discovered, was a control freak.) And did this to-be-designed dedicated workspace have a generous budget? (Nope. More like a string-bean budget. It shocked her to discover how small the margins were for event planners. Razor thin.)

But she still would've accepted the job. All because of Liam McMillan. The man had *style*. He combined Old World flair, known for its mass of flowers, into New World chic—with a focus on lines, simplicity, and symbolism—and he did it seamlessly. He'd been named a top wedding vendor by *Martha Stewart Weddings*, *Vogue*, *Harper's Bazaar*, and *Brides* magazines. His skills ran from floral design to cake artist to event planning. He was a living wonder.

Not a day went by when Jaime didn't feel grateful for this job. When she first moved to New York City, she thought she knew just about everything there was to know about flowers. She might have had a knack for arranging flowers, but she knew *nothing* about the business of flowers. Nothing.

She had learned so much from Liam. About planning, about creating recipes for floral arrangements for all kinds of events, especially large-scale weddings. She'd learned about scheduling and execution, billing (recognizing that her time was as valuable as the flowers), about building a brand and cultivating good long-term relationships with vendors. And working with brides! Lord have mercy. Brides came to Epic full of ideas (hugely impractical ones), and Liam would gently persuade them to hand the creative controls over to him. His style was always better, classier, more chic. Brides would end up thanking him profusely.

Jaime's salary had doubled—still not grandiose but at least she could pay her rent on her dinky apartment without having to resort to a diet of ramen noodles at the end of every month.

But best of all was just being near Liam. If she'd started at Epic Events with a from-afar crush, her feelings had sailed past dangerously smitten and landed on hopelessly in love. As much as she admired him as an employer—he was kind and affirming, accessible as a leader, instructive, willing to share all he'd learned—she just liked him so much. Enjoyed his personality, his optimism, his humor. And that Scottish brogue! It never failed to make her knees turn to cornmeal mush.

Jaime and Liam spent quite a bit of time together. At first, to teach her the floral designs and styles he preferred. She caught on quickly, but he kept popping into the workshop. To deliver recipes or pick up shears to help whatever arrangement she was working on. They talked and talked as they worked, about Epic, about upcoming events, about Jaime. He liked hearing about her life in a one-stoplight town. She tried to find out more about his childhood, but he seemed uncomfortable, deflected questions, so she stopped asking.

She often wondered how Liam felt about her. If thoughts of her ever consumed him all day long like thoughts of him consumed her. If everything he did and everywhere he went, he wished he were sharing it with her.

Probably not.

Really, her life would be perfect, a complete dream job . . . were it not for the type of customers who sought out Epic Events. They weren't like the customers who had ordered Apology Bouquets from Instagram posts. They weren't like the locals in North Carolina. Most of them were ridiculously high maintenance, like Mrs. Zimmerman. They reminded Jaime of the children she'd nannied. Spoiled, overindulged, entitled. The bigger the wedding budget, the more demanding the clients.

Coming from a modest upbringing—she was raised by a single mom who worked in a Dollar General store—Jaime was very comfortable with deal-scrounging. In fact, she enjoyed the hunt. She'd found a great bargain on a huge, gently used walk-in cooler—the very one with the door that stuck tight for Mrs. Zimmerman's mock-up meeting. It had a large steel door and a dim automatic light and was big enough for two to stand inside.

She'd built shelving from scrap wood to hold every supply or tool a florist could imagine needing. She'd scoured tag sales to find vases and urns and other vessels. She'd bought used drop cloths, tool bags, clippers, knives, flat irons, glue guns, drills and bits, ribbons, frogs, chicken wires, cable ties. You name it, Epic's workshop had it. In the center were long folding tables. A row of cheap LED lighting above. Bright enough to work but without giving off any heat that might trick the flowers into thinking sunshine was overhead. She'd done the whole thing. The only thing she didn't skimp on was getting a sink installed with running water, cold *and* hot. Very important. Cutting stems under hot water, especially roses, prolonged a flower's life.

The workshop became Jaime's happy place—which was good because she worked long, long hours. Epic Events was housed in an old brick warehouse in Brooklyn. It had started as a one-man show (Liam!); he would hire hourly workers to handle the burden of weekends. As Epic's reputation quickly expanded, so did the company. By the time he had brought Jaime in as the floral designer, the staff had grown to five. Six, if you included the unpaid intern, Todd.

This morning, Jaime had worked on two table arrangements for a corporate lunch. She'd just put the last vase in the walk-in cooler. These corporate events brought an injection of cash, necessary with the seasonal work of weddings. But weddings were the bread and butter. Or as Liam would say, "They put th' butter on th' bread."

Weddings were his passion. At his heart, Jaime soon realized, Liam was a romantic. He remembered everybody's birthday, he surprised the team with "just because" treats from upscale bakeries, he sent everyone home for Christmas with personalized, thoughtful gifts. (He'd given Jaime a generous gift certificate to a laundromat in Brooklyn that picked up and delivered clothes, ironed and folded. He'd overheard her complain about schlepping laundry in the snow. Touching! He was *such* a good listener.)

Liam's long-term business plan was to book only high-end weddings, especially destination weddings that covered two to three days of back-to-back events. He wanted to be involved from setup to teardown, every detail—from the choice of stationery font on the wedding invitation to the ribbon tied around the guest favor. He wrapped his hands around every single logistical detail of the wedding. Each wedding was unique to him. Every bride had her own customized Liam flower recipes. He even provided a listening ear to the bridal couple, to provide mediation to manage tricky family dynamics. He wanted the total wedding, start to finish.

At first, Jaime assumed Liam was pursuing destination weddings for the income. While it was true that high-end weddings provided the best profit margins, he wasn't about living in high cotton. He wanted to have more time, fewer distractions, so that he could get to know the clients. He liked to make each bride and groom feel as if they were Epic's only client. When he did, "beautiful stories come out." He would find ways to incorporate the stories into the wedding, bringing a remarkable personalization to each one. After all, "a weddin' *is* a story," he would say. "The best one." Hence, the Liam magic.

Every Monday morning, Liam held team meetings to review the weekend's events and look ahead at what the new week held. Jaime considered them to be more like motivational talks. He'd start with high praise for the weekend events, specific compliments for each team member. Then he'd shift seamlessly, subtly, into his main message: "Remember, these big and well-deserved wins rack up consistently when we continue t' perform under pressure easily, effortlessly, and efficiently. So, regardless of the client praise we just earned o'er the weekend, as well deserved as 'tis, as swaggery a feeling as it might bring, we have another hill t' climb this week." He would look around the table at his team, each one transfixed by Liam's charisma, by his rolling Scottish *r*'s, and they would feel renewed, recharged, ready to climb Mount Everest with him. Jaime was first in line.

And each Monday morning, Jaime would leave the meeting with the same thought: Had Liam's eyes lingered a bit longer on her than on other team members? Had he asked her to sit next to him for a reason? Split and shared his donut with her because he knew it was her favorite?

Probably not. Probably just a figment of her imagination.

ℓ·ℓ·ℓ

Sometime in the night, a text message came in from Liam. It was the first thing she saw in the morning.

> Did you enter the Zimmerman bridal bouquet in a contest?

She bolted out of bed. Why would he ask that? Hands shaking, she scrolled through her email until she came to one from Blooms to Bouquet. The subject head read "Congratulations! Your floral design is a finalist!"

Whaaaat? Her design finaled? No way. But there it was, in print! She let out a squeal of joy.

And then she gasped. Liam! She should have asked him first. She should have found out when the finalists would be announced. She knew not to post anything ahead of a wedding—brides deserved the first look, the big reveal. The privacy. It was a cardinal rule at Epic Events. The bride came first.

But she never dreamed she'd actually be a finalist.

How had Liam found out that her entry had become a finalist?

She scrolled through her Instagram feed, there it was, plain as day. The Zimmerman bridal bouquet, with a tag to Epic Events. It already had thousands of likes, hundreds of comments.

So that's how he knew.

> I can explain.

> Just come to the office as quickly as you can. Mrs. Z is on her way.

If Mrs. Zimmerman had already caught wind of it and was arriving at a Brooklyn warehouse at the crack of dawn, this was bad. Really, really bad. She wasn't sure all that it meant, but Jaime knew one thing: Mrs. Zimmerman would throw a hissy fit.

ℓ·ℓ·ℓ

By the time Jaime arrived at Liam's office, Mrs. Zimmerman was already there, gasping like a fish that had just been thrown from the lake. Facing Liam, she shook her smartphone in the air. "This . . . this is an outrage!"

Jaime inhaled for fortification. This woman was madder than a wet hen. All color had drained from Liam's face. He looked like he hadn't slept a wink—his hair wasn't combed, his face was unshaved, his clothes were rumpled. This was really, really bad.

Timidly, she tapped on the door. "I take full responsibility."

Mrs. Zimmerman swirled around. "You! You did this heinous thing!"

"I'm truly sorry."

"You're *sorry*?" Mrs. Zimmerman turned back to Liam. "Sorry doesn't cut it for a wedding of this magnitude. A private element of my daughter's wedding has been *leaked*. Liam, according to my lawyers, you have broken our contract."

Leaked? Lawyers? Broken contract? Jaime felt as if she might throw up.

Liam nodded slowly. Jaime knew that nod. It gave the illusion that he was thinking things over, but she could tell his mind was completely blank.

"Perhaps I should let you both finish the conversation in private." Jaime backed out of the room and headed down the hall to the workshop. The walk of shame.

What did Mrs. Zimmerman mean when she said Liam had broken the contract? What kind of a threat was that? Would she pull the wedding from Epic Events and give it to another company? Could she do that? The wedding was this weekend, just days away!

She hadn't felt this responsible for something gone bad as all get-out since that last day in Rose's Flower Shop. That, too, happened because one thing led to another, which ended in a catastrophe. She'd never, ever wanted to feel that sickening shame again.

She flicked on the lights to the workshop and set her purse down. Tying the apron strings around her, she tried to focus on today's floral pieces. Four table centerpieces for a retirement dinner at Goldman Sachs. She looked through the paperwork for Liam's recipe but couldn't find it. She let out a breath. On a normal day, she arrived at work to find recipes waiting for her. On a normal day, Liam would have the recipe waiting and Jaime would order flowers from a wholesaler to be delivered by midmorning. That's how things rolled for these small corporate events.

She looked through the paperwork again. No recipe to be found.

If this were a normal day, she would walk back to his office and ask him what he had in mind for the recipe.

But this wasn't a normal day. No way was she going back to that office and facing the wrath of Mrs. Zimmerman. She was blowing up a storm down there.

What to do? What to do? The clock was ticking. This was a high-value account for Epic Events. She opened the door to peek down the hall. Liam's office door was still closed. She closed the door, crossed her arms, and paced. What to do? What to do?

If Mrs. Zimmerman pulled the wedding, it could bankrupt Epic Events. Liam could be left holding the bill for everything that had been done, everything that had been ordered. She squeezed her eyes shut. Jaime's flower order alone came to tens of thousands of dollars.

She shook her head, hoping to promote the flow of blood and oxygen to her brain. She had to do something.

Cooler.

She crossed the room to see what kind of inventory she had to work with today. Not much. She'd been trying to clear it out to create room for the Zimmerman flowers later this week. She glanced at the clock. Then she grabbed her keys and quietly slipped out the back door.

five

Love is the flower you've got to let grow.
—John Lennon

Moments like this made up for the costly nuisance of keeping a truck in the city. And it was a nuisance. Every other day, she had to get up at the crack of dawn to move her truck to the other side of the street so the street cleaners could sweep. Bridge tolls alone equaled a week's groceries.

Still worth it. She loved her truck. Anyone from the South would understand that. Cars and trucks were almost a family member where she came from, as dear as a hunting dog. Tin Lizzie, an old Ford pickup, had once been her grandpa's. It brought plenty of guffawing, but no thief bothered to break into it. It was obvious there was nothing inside of value. Even the seat cover was worn through, with springs attempting to pop out through the duct tape.

Sloane said Jaime would never be a real New Yorker until she conquered her fear of the subway. All those people stuffed like sardines into a can, hurling through the earth at the speed of light?

And you never knew about the stations, from what she'd heard. Everything could be fine one day, dangerous the next. No thank you, ma'am.

She drove Tin Lizzie as quickly as she could to the flower district. Normally, she only drove into Manhattan at five o'clock in the morning to get to the flower market when it opened. Nine o'clock in the morning? It was a whole different city. Crowded streets, crowded sidewalks. Obnoxiously aggressive drivers who honked at her without mercy. No parking spot left, so she ended up paying a fortune in a parking garage.

And then, another disappointing discovery. The flowers she had in mind—ones she knew Liam preferred—were gone, picked over by the professionals.

She walked down one side of the street and back the other, still coming up empty of ideas. Distracted, too, by the shop owners who shouted out congratulations to her for being a finalist in the Blooms to Bouquet competition. The New York City Flower Market was a small community—everyone knew each other. She could barely go from one stall to the other without someone wanting details: Where had she sourced that Café Latte rose? How many mini-orchid stems? And the most repeated question: How'd she come up with the idea of using black flowers? Two wholesalers asked for the recipe.

A recipe. *Me. Me?* It astonished her to think she was being asked for her recipe by these people. They had decades more experience with flowers than she did. And her brief career was on the brink of ending. She fully expected Liam to fire her today.

Once again Jaime's work needed her full attention, and once again she struggled to keep her thoughts off Liam to make that happen. Flowers, flowers, flowers. She had to return to the office with flowers. Beautiful, *sumptuous* flowers.

What did Liam have in mind for the retirement party?

Find your own style.

She stopped short, so abruptly that a man bumped into her

from behind. "Oh, I'm so sorry, sir!" but he just sidestepped her, dismissing her apology with a huff, and went on his way.

Find my own style. A Rose-ism. Thoughts of Rose kept popping unbidden into her mind. This time, she couldn't blame it on the registered letter. As nice as it was to have the congratulations of the wholesalers and vendors, the person she really wanted to know about the Blooms to Bouquet competition was Rose. But she couldn't. She couldn't just call Rose, out of the blue, after all that had happened, despite her recent letter.

Find my own style.

Jaime stepped out of the stream of people near some rhododendron bushes in full bloom. Lovely, but nothing like the size of blooms found in the North Carolina woods. She squeezed her eyes shut. *Get your head back in the game, Jaime!* What would *she* choose for a retirement party? A corporate event, held in a restaurant, not a cozy home setting. A retirement of a career was an end . . . but it was also a beginning.

New beginnings.

Yes! Flowers that symbolized a new beginning. Daffodils. Daisies. Calla lilies.

Eyes still shut, she crossed off daffodils. They'd been picked over in the stalls. She'd seen a lot of daisies, but they seemed too pedestrian for Goldman Sachs. And there was a stall with buckets full of ivory calla lilies. She opened her eyes. *Perfect.*

In her mind, she imagined whitewashed wooden boxes filled with single-stem ivory calla lilies. Nothing else. She spun around and hurried back to the wholesaler who had buckets of calla lilies. "I'll take them all," she shouted. Then she ran to the vendor who sold vessels and searched the shelves until she found just the box that matched the one she had imagined. She bought five, just to be safe. Then she hurried back to the wholesaler, who had wrapped up all her calla lilies. After she paid him, he called his son to help her get everything to her truck.

She drove down Manhattan in heavy traffic, then slipped slowly onto the Brooklyn Bridge. No matter what time of day or night, there was always a traffic jam on this bridge. For all that was frustrating, she still loved driving in New York.

During the pandemic, when streets were eerily empty, she would go out for long drives, covering every nook and cranny of the city, from Queens to Harlem. It was her way to get to know New York. Not just the five boroughs, but the neighborhoods within. They had their own architectural style, their own restaurants, their own vibes.

Ten minutes later, she was in the workshop, setting bundles of calla lilies in buckets of fresh, cold water. She set the wooden boxes she'd bought on the bench and took out a ruler. She tried a few different stem heights of calla lilies, then settled on one that suited the box and started to cut stems. Happily, calla lilies required no preparation. Roses, as one example, required stripping of foliage and thorns before a florist could begin the arrangement.

When she finished the first box, she took a few steps back to see how it looked from a distance. She smiled, pleased. It looked very sophisticated, very elegant. Very Goldman Sachs-ish.

"Goin' rogue?"

Jaime whirled. Liam was leaning against the doorjamb, arms folded. "I . . . I didn't see a recipe for today's event, and I knew . . . well . . ." Her words drizzled to a stop. She expected him to seem upset, but there was relief on his face.

He pushed off from the doorjamb and crossed the room to examine the arrangement up close.

She stepped away so he could get a better look. Her heart was pounding. "Calla lilies mean—"

"New beginnings." He cast a glance at her. "Aye, an apt choice."

"If you don't like it, I'll start again with your recipe."

"Nay. 'Tis bonny. Perhaps add an ivory ribbon 'round the box to glam it up. No bow, o' course."

Oh, thank goodness. He liked what she'd done. "Liam, you don't have to fire me. I'll resign. I know I've caused damage."

He held up a hand to stop her. "All is smoothed o'er."

Jaime's eyes widened. "Mrs. Zimmerman didn't yank the wedding from Epic?"

"Nay. In fact, she left happy. It helped when Sloane interrupted with an opportune phone call from the *New York Times*."

She lifted her eyebrows, curious. Hopeful.

"The weddings editor happened upon the post o' the bouquet and called t' feature the wedding in the Sunday Styles section. Turns out they'd been hankerin' t' have a piece at the New York Botanical Garden." He lifted his hands. "So yer bouquet combined with the NYBG was like strikin' gold, she said."

That, Jaime knew, was a gift from above. Normally, wedding planners steadily submitted information to woo the interest of the *New York Times* weddings editor and hoped, hoped, hoped for a bite. A nibble. But a feature? *That* was a miracle. "I take it Mrs. Zimmerman was pleased with the turn of events?"

"Indeed she was. 'Twas a timely boon. It considerably changed the direction o' the wind in m' office."

"Bless that editor. Bless Sloane for daring to interrupt your meeting." Jaime wasn't sure she would have had the guts to do it. Actually, she was sure. She couldn't have done it. "Did you say . . . hankerin'?"

"Did I?" He scratched his forehead. "Nay. Perhaps that's how y' heard it."

Maybe so. It was something she would say.

The morning had turned upside down . . . or right side up. So why wasn't Liam back to his cheery self? There was a look on his face that was hard to read. "Liam, I'm very sorry that I didn't tell you I had entered the competition. I made a number of mistakes."

Leaning against the sink, he had his hands in his trouser pockets. "Why did y' enter the contest without tellin' me?"

Why? There were so many reasons she didn't know where to start. The clincher, no doubt, was Rose's unsettling letter that included a challenge to enter a contest to test her talent. Jaime had always longed for validation. She wanted some concrete evidence that she should be in this business.

And then there was Liam. She yearned for him to see her and value her as a floral designer, with ideas of her own. She'd been working for him for over a year, and he had yet to let her try out a single original design. She longed for more creative freedom, but she wished she didn't have to ask for it. She shouldn't *have* to ask for it. It offended her that he didn't think to offer it. And then she realized how passive-aggressive that sounded. A Southern female tradition.

The truth was that Mrs. Zimmerman's enthusiastic reaction to her spin on a cascading bridal bouquet gave her the burst of confidence she needed to fill out the entry form.

She wanted to tell Liam that becoming a finalist was frightening and thrilling at the same time. She wanted to ask if he was proud of her. Yet all the things she could think of to say were things she was afraid would drive them apart.

She had to give him something, though. He was waiting for an answer as to why she had entered the contest without telling him. "On a whim," she settled on. "I did it on a whim."

"A whim," he echoed, unconvinced. "Jaime, it made m' wonder if—"

His voice sounded so tentative that she knew whatever he was about to say was the real question at stake. "It made m' wonder if y' might be thinkin' o' leavin' . . . Epic."

"Leaving Epic Events? What would make you think that?" She couldn't imagine leaving Liam.

He locked eyes on her. "Y'll be getting a lot o' attention now. Offers t' work elsewhere."

He wasn't wrong. At the flower market this very morning, a wholesaler offered her a job. "I didn't enter the competition because I wanted to leave Epic. I don't want to leave."

He pushed off from the sink and walked closer to her. "I'm glad t' hear that." He took one step closer, locking eyes with her, studying her from just a few inches of distance. The air between them grew charged. "We . . . make a good team, y' and I." The sentence slowed as his focus dropped to her lips.

Time spun out. Jaime's heart was drumming so loud she wondered if he could hear it. Slowly, Liam's head bent down, his lips grazing hers with a gentle, tentative kiss. Her head was swimming, her body was floating. She lifted her arms to wrap around his neck.

And suddenly he drew back.

Don't pull away!

But he did. He stepped back and gave a slight shake of his head. "M' apologies. I dinna think that through." He raked a hand through his hair. "'Tis been an eventful day." He pointed to the calla lilies. "Those will do nicely. Perhaps . . . just . . ."

"Subtract."

"Aye. Subtract." His face softened in a grin. He left the workshop, closing the door quietly behind him.

She plopped down on a stool, slightly winded, completely confused. Hands down, that was the best kiss she had ever experienced in her entire life. No one compared to Liam McMillan. No one.

Her gaze turned to the calla lilies. Subtract? She turned the arrangement around and around. It was balanced, symmetrical, eye-catching. The sleek blooms didn't expand like other flowers. She really didn't think she needed to subtract a single stem. But today didn't seem like the day to push it.

Jaime's thoughts tugged her back to that kiss with Liam. She wondered if he thought about it, if he wanted to repeat it. Or if it was just one of those things that happen between two people who work together a lot. Just a response of relief to the drama of the day. After all, it had been quite a dramatic day. Jaime's bouquet was a finalist in the Blooms to Bouquet contest, Epic Events teetered on the brink of a lawsuit, then her job was in jeopardy . . . and suddenly, it all turned out just fine. Better than fine.

She sighed. Relief was most likely the reason Liam let down his guard and kissed Jaime. And then he instantly regretted it.

But it was worth everything, that moment.

six

A flower does not think of competing
with the flower next to it. It just blooms.
—Zen Shin

Starting Wednesday, Jaime knew she would hardly sleep until Saturday night, when the Zimmerman-Blau wedding was over. Flower shipments started arriving on Wednesday and she wasted no time. Hundreds of Café Latte roses had been flown in from Kenya and needed foliage and thorns stripped, stems trimmed, before drinking up water in their buckets in the cooler. Parrot tulips and Hot Chocolate calla lilies came in from Holland. She stayed late in the night at the workshop to prep the flowers and woke up early the next morning to head to the flower market to purchase fillers and foliage. All day Thursday, she worked on some of the heartier foliage displays—vines that would drape over the windows and mirrors. On Friday, hourly help would arrive to get started on all the other floral arrangements.

After one more trip to the flower market early Friday for more foliage, she hurried back to the workshop to provide recipes for the helpers. She set them up to work on different elements while she started on the bridal bouquet.

Mercy, it was warm in here. Whenever a bead of sweat trickled down Jaime's back, she felt her worry spike up a few notches. Still April, but the air was so thick with heat, you'd have thought it was summer.

The weather shouldn't be this warm. It shouldn't be this humid.

Heat could devastate most flower arrangements. Imagine setting a vase of long-stemmed roses in the hot sun. Wilting, drooping, sagging. Devastating.

She took a break, hands on her hips, stretching her back. Her gaze went up and down the long table, assessing each helper's progress. Mentally, she went down the checklist of pieces that were getting worked on: bridal and bridesmaids' bouquets, flower girls' nosegays, dais decorations, corsages for the mothers and grandmothers, groom and groomsmen boutonnieres, large triangular reception arrangements, table centerpieces, chair flowers, escort card table arrangement. Still to go: the chuppah. She'd saved the large floral arch for last, for Saturday morning, because it would be too large to keep in the cooler. As big as it was, the cooler was stuffed to the rafters with flowers. They were up on shelves, down in buckets, pushed in the back; they occupied every square inch. She glanced at the large clock on the wall. It was nearly midnight.

The door opened and in came Liam. His eyes searched the workshop until they landed on Jaime, then he strode toward her, a big smile on his handsome face, and she felt her insides turn to mush. It was getting to where she couldn't keep a thought in her head when Liam was around.

"Just came from the Botanical Garden, lass, and we are on track for another epic event." His *r*'s rolled with a dramatic flourish when he was especially enthusiastic.

"What about the weather?"

"What 'bout it?"

What about it? Was he serious? "The heat. The Botanical Garden's air-conditioning is working, right?"

"O' course! 'Tis not so very hot. Fret not y'self, Jaime."

She frowned. Indeed it *was* so very hot for flowers! How could she not worry about these lavish displays, expected to hold up for hours and hours in such unexpectedly warm weather? Liam knew that. She had to hand it to him for keeping an upbeat attitude. Once he had told her, "You ought not t' be in this line of work if yer not an optimist."

Slowly, he walked up one side of the table and down the other, complimenting the helpers on their work while giving them advice. Then he went inside the walk-in cooler and assessed the finished pieces. She knew he was mentally checking off every recipe he'd made for this wedding—other than the bridal bouquet. When he reemerged from the cooler, he found Jaime at the sink, clipping rose stems at an angle. "Everything looks wonderful. But, ah, where is the chuppah?"

"I thought I'd try to get a few hours of sleep tonight, then come back early to do it. It won't fit in the cooler and I want to keep the flowers as chilled as possible."

"But y' canna do it alone, lass."

But she could. "I'll manage." She liked working alone. In fact, she much preferred it.

But Liam wasn't having it. She could tell he didn't like the idea of leaving the arch until morning. He turned around to face the helpers, many of whom were packing up to head home. "Who might b' willin' t' stay late t' help Jaime build up the arch?"

Two guys in the back stuck up their hands.

"Excellent. Problem solved."

But she hadn't seen the arch as a problem. The only problem she could foresee had to do with tomorrow's heat wave.

"Todd," Liam said, "will bring the truck for the flowers at—"

"Seven o'clock in the morning. We've gone over this."

He nodded. "And let's not forget that the Zimmerman wedding

is Epic's grandest event." He gave the *r* in "grandest" a distinctive roll.

"Yes, I know, Liam. How could I not know?" She sounded snappish, but she was tired, with hours of work ahead of her, and he wasn't really helping matters by reminding her of the pressure.

"I'll be off, then. Back to the Botanical Garden to oversee a few things." He grinned and gave her a slight salute.

She felt bad after he left. If she felt pressure, imagine how much more pressure he was under. Mrs. Zimmerman was one of those clients who drained the life out of others. But Jaime still planned to leave the arch until morning, when she was rested and the flowers were chilled. She told the two guys who'd volunteered to stay to go on home, and they were out the door in a flash. A wave of exhaustion hit her. She needed to get some sleep to be ready for tomorrow. As the workshop emptied out, she made sure the cooler door was closed tight, and she drove Tin Lizzie back to her dinky apartment.

e·l·e

Jaime slept deeply, then woke to the pinging sound of a text on her phone.

Liam

> I stopped by the workshop in the wee hours and saw you'd left. Decided it would save time to arrange the chuppah at the venue. I had Todd bring over buckets of flowers and your toolbox, so go straight to the NYBG.

Squeezing her eyes shut, she covered her face with her hands. Argh! Why couldn't Liam trust her to get the job done? He had just made this arch so much more difficult. The workshop had such a variety of tools, so many mechanics, resources, tricks of the trade . . . right at her disposal.

She blew out a puff of air, pushed back her covers, and made herself get out of bed. After a quick shower (cold! the hot water was on the fritz again), she stared at the mirror and groaned. She looked as tired as she felt. Since Wednesday, when the first flowers arrived for the Zimmerman-Blau wedding, she'd hardly had more than a couple of hours of sleep.

Just a few more hours and this wedding would be history—for her, anyway. As soon as the flower arrangements were safely delivered and set up at the venue, her work would be done. Everything else in the wedding and reception would be handled by Liam and the team. She could come back to her dinky, noisy apartment, put on her three sound machines to drown out the molar-rattling street noise, and catch up on her sleep.

After arriving at the NYBG, she parked and took a small red child's wagon out of the back seat of Tin Lizzie. In it, she placed her toolbox from home—drill and bits, hammer, some weights, along with floral tools like gloves and clippers. She hurried carefully, as it was still dark, but she knew this place well. The 250-acre grounds was a National Historical Landmark in the Bronx, established in the late 1800s by botanist Nathaniel Lord Britton. If Jaime remembered correctly, he'd visited London's Royal Botanic Garden and returned inspired to replicate something similar in New York City.

When Jaime first moved to the city, she spent many afternoons wandering through the gardens and conservatory. All kinds of varieties of plants and trees were spread out over the grounds, even an old-growth forest split by the Bronx River—the only freshwater river in the entire city. An enormous library sat on the north side. Somewhere on the grounds was a laboratory for scientific botanical research projects. Her favorite wandering place was the stunning Haupt Conservatory on the west end. But today she was headed to the Garden Terrace Room.

It didn't completely surprise Jaime that Mrs. Zimmerman had chosen a site like the New York Botanical Garden for her only daughter's wedding—it was, to quote Sloane, an absolute stunner. But the Garden Terrace Room did strike her as odd for the venue.

Jaime would have held the wedding ceremony right in the middle of the Old Growth Forest, so you could look up and see the majesty of the ancient trees. Or near the Old Stone Mill, with the sound of rushing water to drown out any city noise. Or on the steps of the Haupt Conservatory, with the large glasshouse behind them.

Not that there was anything wrong with the Garden Terrace Room. It was a lovely ballroom with arched windows and doors, and it flowed out into a tent for cocktail hour. But once you were inside, you could have been anywhere. Even the catering company, as good as it was, came with the NYBG.

Maybe Mrs. Zimmerman didn't care so much about the food, or the outdoors, but she did care about the flowers. She wanted the interior of the Garden Terrace to be covered in foliage. Over the tall mirrors, Jaime planned to drape garlands with Italian Ruscus, a versatile, hardy vine that could hold up for hours without water. The vines had been assembled and tied together yesterday and were ready to be draped this morning. She hoped Liam had thought to bring them over with the flowers for the arch. It still irked her that he had interfered with her plans for the morning. She wondered if there was some residual lack of trust in her over the Blooms to Bouquet misstep. Or could it be that he regretted kissing her that day? Maybe he was trying to recalibrate their relationship by reminding her that he was the boss.

She sighed. Probably. He'd certainly acted entirely professional and disappointingly distant toward her since that kiss.

By the time she reached the wooden WELCOME TO THE WEDDING sign to the Garden Terrace Room, dawn was breaking. She paused for a moment to switch hands on the wagon pull and noticed for the first time how warm the day already was. Too warm. Worrisome warm. She wiped some sweat off her forehead. It felt like a morning in July. This was terrible for the black tulips. Terrible! Other flowers could handle the heat, some loved the humidity, as long as they'd been properly prepared and had plenty of water in their vessels or mechanics. But tulips drooped at the slightest provocation. As Rose used to say, flowers need water like we need air.

Another Rose-ism. They were coming back to her on a daily basis. She couldn't stop thinking about Rose, about Claire and Tessa, about life back in the North Carolina flower shop. How happy they'd once been.

Was it like this for Rose? Dealing with difficult customers, with impossible demands? If so, Jaime didn't remember stress in the flower shop. There were certainly times when they were under pressure to get arrangements done in time—Valentine's Day, Mother's Day, weddings, and funerals. Maybe Jaime was revising history, but she remembered customers who appreciated the flowers, who came by the shop to thank Rose and let her know how those flowers touched them.

Jaime couldn't remember a single customer returning to Epic to thank her for her efforts.

New Yorkers were different. Thanks came in different ways. Recommendations to others, for example.

But each client felt an almost desperate need to be the next best thing, to have the display that no one else had thought of. The most eccentric flowers, the most unusual arrangements. As much as Jaime longed for more creative freedom, it was the flowers she wanted to celebrate. They deserved their own glory.

Mercy, she was really going down a rabbit hole of negativity this morning. She shook off those thoughts as she reached the arched door to the Garden Terrace ballroom, and when she opened it, she gasped out loud. Liam had transformed this ballroom venue into a botanical paradise. Diaphanous drapes covered in fairy lights hung from the corners of the ceiling to the chandelier in the center of the room. She found him on a ladder, hanging her Italian Ruscus vines over the tops of the mirrors, trailing down the sides. She looked up at him. "You remembered the Ruscus."

He gazed down at her with a fond smile. "O' course, mo leannan. We're a team." He looked so tired. Jaime was pretty sure he hadn't slept all night. "Everything for the arch is set in the cocktail tent. Todd and I already did the basic construction."

She went into the tent room where the ceremony was going to be held. Another odd request of Mrs. Zimmerman. Why not have the wedding outdoors in one of the gardens? Too many pests, she said. Jaime wasn't sure if she was referring to mosquitos or gawkers.

Jaime dragged her little wagon to the cocktail tent and unpacked her tools. Liam had brought half of her workshop. She shouldn't have doubted him. He was more detail minded than she was. She set to work wiring olive branches over the arch to act as the foundation for flowers. They had a lovely silvery undertone that showed in photographs. Next, she started to attach the flowers, stem by stem, running down the arch like a waterfall. The sun rose, warming the tent, causing her to worry about the flowers holding up until tonight. She misted them each time she stopped to reach into a new bucket of flowers. When the arch was about halfway done, she had to take a break. She stretched, yawned, and checked her phone, wondering if Todd had brought the rest of the flowers yet. By now, the finished arrangements from the workshop should be in the ballroom. She should have thought to bring a banana or a bottle of water. Something. She bent down to go through her purse to see if she could find a forgotten granola bar when a horrible caterwaul came from the direction of the ballroom. The baleful yowl of a mother elephant who has just watched her calf get shot down by a poacher. It went on and on and on.

seven

Flowers whisper "Beauty!" to the world,
even as they fade, wilt, fall.
—Dr. SunWolf

Jaime bolted over to the door to the Garden Terrace room, but it was locked. She ran from door to door and finally rushed around the back of the tent where there was an opening to let the breeze in, then around the tent to the front of the building to find a way in. By the time she reached the main ballroom, it was empty. Of people . . . not of flowers. Todd must have arrived with the flower arrangements while she was in the tent. The vessels were all over the dance floor.

But . . . something seemed off. Confused, she walked closer to inspect them and gasped. They were all wilted. Every single arrangement, every flower—from the tulips to the roses to the mini-orchids—looked like it had been left out in the sun all day long. What in the world had happened? She knelt by the bridal bouquet, the *beautiful* bridal bouquet, and pressed her hand under the stems. No water. She reached into each vase. Hardly *any* water. In this heat! She'd forgotten to check them last night before she left the workshop. How could she have made such a rookie mistake? For this wedding, of all weddings?

She walked through the dance floor, examining each vessel. If there was any chance to revive these flowers, she needed to fill these vessels immediately. She looked around for an empty bucket, a pitcher, something, anything, and then the door opened and Todd came running in, looking rode hard and put up wet. "Jaime, I've been looking for you!" He stopped in front of her.

She grabbed his arm. "I need water!"

He gave her a confused look. "You need water?"

"Yes! For the flowers. Go bring pitchers full of water. As many as you can carry. Hurry!" She scrambled to separate the most desperate-looking bouquets from the ones that looked salvageable.

"Jaime, it doesn't matter."

She gave him a *look.* "We've got to try. This wedding's too important. Please, go and get water."

"Jaime, stop for a second. It doesn't matter because the wedding's been canceled." He looked around at the sad, wilted flowers. "There wasn't any water in the vases this morning. I wasn't sure what to do . . . and then Sloane told me the news."

She stared at him, not understanding. "The wedding is canceled?"

"Yeah. Canceled." He drew a line across his neck. "Not happening."

"But . . . this can get fixed." She shot up. "I need to go find Liam."

"He just left with the mother of the bride, bawling on his shoulder."

Jaime froze. "She . . . Mrs. Zimmerman? That wailing sound was from her?"

He nodded. "Something set her off." He cast a glance at the wilted-flower vases all over the dance floor.

And in that look, she knew why the wedding had been called

off. Mrs. Zimmerman had seen these ruined flowers. Jaime had singlehandedly ruined the wedding.

ℓ·ℓ·ℓ

Jaime wasn't ready to give up. She sent Todd back to the kitchen for more water and pulled out her phone to call Liam. There *had* to be a way to salvage this wedding. Flowers could be surprisingly resilient. And for those that didn't revive, she could call in some favors from vendors to get more flowers delivered. Just as she unlocked her phone, a group text arrived from Liam to the team.

Zimmerman-Blau wedding is definitely off. Heading to the hospital with Mrs. Z. Send all questions to Sloane. She'll explain and coordinate details.

Not twenty seconds later, another text came in from Liam, directly to Jaime:

We'll talk later about the flowers.

She hung her head in shame. As group texts from the startled team started pouring in to Sloane, Jaime completely turned off her phone. She couldn't handle it. She couldn't bear another minute of facing this colossal failure. The team had worked so hard to make this wedding everything Mrs. Zimmerman had wanted it to be. Had paid handsomely for it to be.

She thought of the indifferent bride, whom she assumed was in the suite provided by the NYBG, getting dressed with her bridesmaids. Or maybe she was sobbing as she changed back into street clothes? She thought of the groom and the groomsmen. Of three hundred guests who were preparing to come to this wedding today. Many, no doubt, had traveled long distances. She thought of the caterer, with three hundred covers that would go to waste. The baker, who was probably putting the finishing touches on the cake right now.

Poor Sloane. Bless her heart. She had to untangle the mess while Liam did what he could to placate Mrs. Zimmerman. And then there was the *New York Times* feature . . . what story would be told about this wedding for all to know? Jaime could see the eye-popping headline: *Florist Ruins the Wedding of the Year.*

She cringed. Would Epic go under because of this? Liam had told her stories of times when clients went bankrupt and he was left with unpaid bills.

And Mrs. Zimmerman had to be carted off to the hospital? Heart attack? Panic attack? She didn't think she'd ever forget the sound of that mournful caterwaul.

Slowly, she packed her tools in the toolbox, cussing at herself for being so lamebrained. Why hadn't she double-checked the water in the vessels before she'd left for the night? Granted, she was tired and irritated with Liam, but there was no excuse to forget such a basic task. Such a simple thing to do, and she'd been worried about the heat. She knew better.

She slipped out of the tent opening and ran all the way to her truck, pulling her wagon of tools behind her. As soon as she got inside Tin Lizzie, the tears started, one right after the other, until she could barely see out the windshield. She wished she could have the last twenty-four hours all over again. She wished she would've remembered to check the water levels. She wished she were braver, stronger, emotionally sturdier, so that she could help Todd return all the flowers to the workshop, but she just couldn't face anyone.

If wishes were horses, Rose often told the girls, beggars would ride.

And Claire, with her sassy streak, would say, "Well, that never kept a beggar from wishing."

She drove to Brooklyn, to her dinky apartment, and fell right on her unmade bed. She cried, and slept some, and woke up only to remember what she'd done, so she cried some more, slept some more, and woke up around three o'clock in the afternoon. She sat up, gasping, cold, panicked.

Had she learned nothing from that terrible incident with Rose? Running away didn't erase the guilt. Time didn't lessen it.

She had to face this. She had to go to the Epic Events warehouse and accept the consequences for the disaster she'd created. And hand in her resignation. An Apology Bouquet couldn't fix this one.

ℓ·ℓ·ℓ

Jaime thought the team would be at the warehouse, licking their failed-flower-inflicted wounds, but the parking lot was empty. As she walked in, she heard laughter in Liam's office and knew it was him. She loved his laugh, low and hoarse, and despite everything, she found her skin warming at the sound of it.

She peeked in his partially opened door. There was Liam, feet up on his desk, relaxed, chatting with someone on the speaker-phone. Quickly, she stepped back from the door to lean against the wall. Thankfully, he must not have seen her because he kept on talking and laughing, not a care in the world. For a long moment, she stood with her back up against the wall, listening to his conversation, baffled. At first, it was his jovialness that confused her—after all, Epic Events had just experienced a colossal disaster thanks to Jaime's negligence and he sounded as happy as a hog in rain—but then she realized exactly what was confusing her. His Scottish accent. It had gone missing.

Not only missing, but replaced with a pronounced thick-as-molasses drawl. One Jaime recognized from her own upbringing in the mountains of North Carolina. *Is he making fun of me? Laughing at me?*

"And then, Meemaw," he said, laughing, "you jist won't b'lieve it. Them flow-ahs was all si-goggling. Droopin' and wiltin' like snow cones at the state fair in high August."

Meemaw? Who was Meemaw? That was Southern-speak for Granny.

Laughing along with him, Meemaw said, "Tell it agin, Billy Bob."

Billy Bob? Jaime's brain was thoroughly discombobulated, then she felt a knife to her heart. It was like watching heavy gray clouds roll through, and then a flash-crack of lightning lit the sky.

She rocked back on her heels. Floating puzzle pieces started locking into place. So many moments ran through her mind, ones that had left her with questions. The look on Liam's face when she caught him listening to Southern gospel. Certain words that slipped out now and then, like *hankerin'* or *down yonder*. His favorite food was biscuits and gravy. His favorite beverage was sweet tea. How uncomfortable he always seemed when she asked him about his childhood. How he would deflect personal questions. No wonder! Liam McMillan hadn't been raised in Scotland at all. He was from Appalachia.

Jaime's hands were shaking. She hurried down to the workshop and sat in the dark on a stool at her desk, shaken to the core. She took several calming breaths, trying to get her racing heart to settle down. She felt like she'd been looking at a circus mirror of distorted images. She thought she knew Liam McMillan, thought she had loved him. She didn't know him at all!

She had truly believed Liam was a Scottish lord who had brought the old culture he had known as a child and used it as an inspiration to create a new style of flower design that evoked his roots. It was the main reason she had first noticed his work, had followed him on social media for years. He was the reason she had moved to New York City. He was the reason she stayed. Falling in love with him had been inevitable.

The foundation of her life had turned out to be a lie.

It was like finding out that astronauts walking on the moon had been a complete farce. That they'd actually been tucked away in a Hollywood movie studio, walking in front of a green screen, while some wily producer created special effects.

Liam isn't Scottish.

Her bewildered heart hurt so bad she wished she'd never laid eyes on him.

In the corner of her desk was Rose Reid's registered letter. She reached for it. Going home again wouldn't be easy. It would mean reconciling with the past, with Rose, with finding Claire and Tessa. It would mean facing the consequences from that awful day at the flower shop when everything changed.

But Jaime couldn't stay here. She didn't belong in this world.

She felt terrible about failing the flowers for the Zimmerman-Blau wedding, she truly did. But right on its heels was a boiling fury for being duped by Liam's Scottish aristocrat facade. How dare he pull the wool over so many people's eyes! How lame-brained could she be to fall for a . . . a . . . an imposter! A complete fraud! Her white-hot anger helped crystallize her decision.

She pulled out a stack of Post-it notes from her desk drawer and wrote, *Subtract me.*

Then she tore off another one to add, *And subtract the phony Scottish accent, Billy Bob.* She stood up to leave, then sat down again to write one more note: *But I am sorry I ruined the wedding. I truly am.*

At the door to the workshop, she turned and looked around. She had crafted this room, had spent hours in it. She'd never had a space like this to work in, and probably never would again. She loved this place. She would sorely miss it.

Quietly and carefully, she stuck all three notes on Liam's office door and kept on going, right out the door to her truck. She was going home. All the way to North Carolina.

eight

Every flower blooms in its own time.
—Ken Petti

*J*aime made a lot of stops on her one-way road trip to North Carolina. First, she stopped at her apartment and packed up her belongings, the whole nine yards, which didn't take very long. Subletting a furnished apartment had its drawbacks, but at this moment, it was a bonus. Harrison helped carry her suitcases to the truck. "I wish you weren't leaving," he said, still sad from her news. "What am I going to do the next time my mother's mad at me?"

Jaime heaved her suitcase into the back of Tin Lizzie. "Harrison, there was a wall plaque hanging on the first flower shop I ever worked in. It said, 'The opposite of caring is forgetfulness.'"

His saucer eyes drooped a little more.

"In other words, stop forgetting about your mother and you won't need another Apology Bouquet."

He nodded. "Say, would you like one of my paintings as a going-away gift?"

Lord have mercy, no! No, no, no. "Tin Lizzie's as full as a

70

tick. But thank you for the generous offer. It means a lot to me, Harrison. And I'll keep following you on Instagram. We'll stay in touch." But she wasn't really sure they would. He was a good neighbor to her, but she wasn't always sure his roof was nailed on tight.

It didn't take long to weave her way out of the city and into New Jersey, heading due south. She'd purposefully kept her phone shut off—she didn't want to talk to anyone or to hear from anyone. Her resolve didn't waver, not one little bit. Her love affair with New York City and its inhabitants (Liam McMillan!) was officially over.

She drove through Pennsylvania and Maryland before she knew she needed to stop and rest. She spent the night in an inexpensive motel chain and fell sound asleep as soon as she got settled in her room. She woke with a startle, realizing the sun was streaming around the curtains. She sat straight up in a panic, disoriented, and reached for her phone—but it was turned off and then she remembered where she was, and why. She plopped back on the pillow. She didn't have to hurry anymore. Or, at least not right now.

After stopping at Starbucks for coffee and a muffin, then getting gas for Tin Lizzie, Jaime set out on the road again. Another full day of driving lay ahead of her, but at least it was daytime and she could see the beauty of the land around her. She kept driving south—passing through West Virginia, Virginia, a corner of Tennessee. She was better rested today, and her thoughts seemed less like scattered buckshot. She still felt all tangled up inside, like a snarled ball of yarn after a kitten had finished its play. But the hours alone in the car with her phone turned off gave her time to pray, the kind of praying she saved for "when things get real." Long and lingering and soulful. There were times in your life when you felt a shift deep down in your soul. And today, Jaime felt that bone-deep shift.

For most of her life, she had dreamed of a new life. She'd been desperate for it. Rose used to warn her about her tendency to romanticize. "All that glitters is not gold," she would remind Jaime.

But of course, Jaime didn't listen. She'd gone after her dream—putting herself through college, moving to New York. She found the life she'd been chasing after, only to discover it wasn't what she dreamed it would be. Not at all.

When Jaime was a little girl, there was a beautiful old oak tree in front of the mobile home where she and her mama lived. During one winter storm, that tree crashed down, shaking the earth around it, as frightening as an earthquake. Turned out the beautiful oak tree was rotted on the inside.

That's how Jaime felt about herself. Rotted on the inside. Chasing all the wrong things. The wrong person.

It was time to get herself back to church. Regularly. Ironically, that was just what Mama had feared for her when she'd moved to New York City. Mama didn't think there was a church to be found in that unholy city, but she was wrong about that. There were churches, vibrant ones. Big ones. But Jaime had to admit that it took considerable intention to get yourself out of bed and off to church on a Sunday morning. Church wasn't part of the tradition in the North like it was in the South. No one she knew went to church, or if they did, they didn't talk about it. She thought of Liam's comment about letting faith grow dormant, that it can come back to life.

Around six o'clock in the evening, she crossed the state line into North Carolina. Mama, she knew, would be at church for the next few hours. Every Sunday morning, Sunday evening, and Wednesday evening, that's where Mama would be. They had a standing phone call each Sunday night at nine o'clock, when she got home from church. Tonight would be a surprise for Mama. A happy surprise. First time she'd seen her mother in two years. Mama had been after Jaime to come home for a visit. Better still, to stay and work locally.

Jaime wasn't entirely sure where she'd be working, or even where she'd be living—most likely in her mother's double-wide for the short term—but she had made one decision. If she ever needed a new dream, it was now. If she ever needed to wake up her faith, it was now. With that thought, an unusual feeling came over her. Rose used to talk about such things, and Jaime and Claire and Tessa used to scoff. Now that Jaime had experienced it for herself, she'd never scoff again. It was the peace that passed all understanding.

ℓ·ℓ·ℓ

By the time Jaime rolled into Sunrise, it was after seven o'clock. The sun had set behind the mountains, but there was still light, something she was grateful for because the winding road through the mountains was full of shadows and she'd forgotten how narrow the shoulder of the road was. Slip one tire off the road and you were in a ditch. She'd forgotten how tall and looming the trees were—hemlock, Frasier firs—all skirted with rhododendrons, their blooms as big as dinner plates. And quiet. She'd forgotten how quiet it was.

She drove through the tiny one-stoplight downtown and took a deep breath as she went down the road that led to Rose's Flower Shop. Her truck slowed and gave one last bone-jangling bounce before the engine died. She had run out of gas. She coasted over to park and breathed out a little thank-you. She'd made it all this way without any problems. This, she could handle.

She got out of the car and stretched, breathing deeply of the fresh mountain air, tinged with the scent of smoke from woodstoves. She closed her eyes. Home. She didn't even know how much she missed it, how much a part of her it was.

"Leannan."

Jaime whirled around. Liam was standing in front of Rose's Flower Shop, one hand behind his back, the other in his jeans pocket. He looked tired—dark circles under his eyes and a five o'clock shadow on his chin.

"How the Sam Hill did you find me?"

"Your neighbor. He said you'd left for home. I took the first flight I could get to Asheville this morning and drove to Sunrise."

"You've been waiting here all day?"

"I have. You weren't answering your phone, so I drove all over the town, hoping to catch sight of your Tin Lizzie." His gaze swept the road. "Sunrise is a lovely town. A lot of potential."

His Scottish brogue. It was gone. She heard a Southern accent, but not nearly as pronounced as when he was talking to his meemaw. He spoke carefully, as if paying attention to how he sounded. As if it felt rusty from lack of use.

"Then I stopped at Rose's Flower Shop to get flowers."

"She's open on Sundays?" If so, that was new. Nothing was open on Sunday in Sunrise.

"Not open. I caught her as she was coming in to get a few things done and I begged her to make this." From behind his back came a bouquet. There was an allium in the center. "I showed her a picture and tried to explain the concept behind the Apology Bouquet, but it seemed she already knew of it. We had a nice chat. She's quite a wise woman. I ended up telling her everything."

"You . . . told Rose about . . . ?" Your phony-baloney aristocrat facade? The Zimmerman-Blau wedding disaster? The failed flowers?

"Everything." His voice a gruff whisper now.

Jaime's eyes darted to the flower shop. He had told Rose *everything*? She wondered how Rose would have responded to him. She abided no chicanery . . . though she did have a blind eye for her nephew, the one who had started all the trouble between the girls in the first place.

Liam held out the flowers to her and cleared his throat. "Jaime, I owe you quite a few apologies."

He did. He really, really did. But she owed him one too. She took the bouquet from him and breathed in its fragrance. It might've looked like Jaime's style, but it smelled of Rose's Flower Shop. Maybe it had to do with Jaime first getting introduced to florals through Rose, but there seemed to be something unique, special, about flowers arranged by Rose.

"Look, Liam . . ." She paused. "Is that even your name?"

"William is my name. William Robert McMillan." He rolled his eyes sheepishly. "My granny is the only one allowed to call me Billy Bob."

She nearly smiled. "So you're not a Scottish aristocrat."

She saw him swallow hard, like the truth was stuck in his craw. "Not even close. I was raised over yonder in Kentucky." He pointed a thumb behind him. "My heritage is Scotch Irish, but I highly doubt there's a drop of noble blood in me. More likely my kin were running from the law." He took in a deep breath. "I transferred from a community college to Morehead State University. I didn't know a soul and was given an exchange student from Scotland for a roommate. We got along famously. I mimicked his accent, just for fun. But I was good at it, and then I noticed how differently strangers reacted to me when they thought I was Scottish. For the first time in my life, people took me seriously. My roommate left, but my accent stayed."

He crossed his arms against his chest and kicked a toe at a crack in the sidewalk. "Jaime, I have always suffered from a crippling insecurity about my roots." He scraped a hand across his jaw. "I came up with the idea of reinventing myself. Of moving to a new city, where no one knew me as Billy McMillan. Instead, I was Liam McMillan, Scotsman. I have to say, that Scottish accent opened doors that would've remained shut." He dropped his head, then lifted it. "I've never told that story to anyone. It must sound crazy to you. I doubt you could ever understand the need to reinvent yourself."

Actually, she understood the desire to reinvent yourself quite well. "Liam . . ." Should she call him Liam? Why not? That's how she thought of him. "My turn. I owe you an apology. I'm so sorry about ruining the Zimmerman wedding."

He looked at her, confused. "What do you mean?"

"The flowers. I didn't check the water levels on Friday night. It was a terrible mistake on my part. I'll pay for everything. It might take me a few years, but I will pay you back every cent."

His eyes snapped right to her, his expression somersaulting through confusion to something like surprise. "Jaime, hold up. Mrs. Zimmerman never even saw the wilted flowers."

"But—"

"The wedding wasn't called off because of the flowers. And it wasn't your fault they wilted. If it was anybody's fault, it was Todd's. He was the last one out of the workshop with flowers for the arch in the middle of the night and he left the cooler door open. Wide open. He knew he'd done it. He told me all about it when he arrived at the Botanical Garden."

Jaime's mind started spinning. "But . . . I heard her. Mrs. Zimmerman let out a wail. A horrible bone-crushing howl. I thought she saw the flowers and . . . I thought that was why you had to whisk her off to the hospital."

"The howl, the hospital, that's all true. But it wasn't because of the flowers. Her daughter had just called to tell her that she and her fiancé had eloped and were off to the Virgin Islands."

Jaime stole a sideways look at him. "That's why the wedding was called off?"

"That's the reason. There was no bride and groom. I mean, we all knew the bride wasn't terribly into the wedding, but it turns out she really, really wasn't." He put his hands on his hips. "Have you been thinking your flowers were the reason?"

She nodded.

"Your flowers for the Zimmerman-Blau wedding were . . . inspired. Brilliant." He inhaled a deep breath. "There's something else I need to confess to you."

She braced herself. What else?

"The reason I was, well, flustered when I found out you were a finalist for the Blooms to Bouquet competition was because . . . I had entered the contest myself. My arrangement didn't even make it to the final rounds. It was the best display I've ever done, and it didn't hold a candle to yours. Somehow, your bouquet had a kind of . . . wildness under control. I never would have thought to add black tulips or black calla lilies in with those big bronze Café Latte roses. I've been working with flowers for as long as I can remember, and I have yet to see anything so breathtaking. Jaime, you have a gift. You shouldn't doubt yourself anymore. I'm confident you'll win that contest."

Win it? She had been thrilled to be a finalist. She hadn't dared to allow herself to think of winning it.

But if he really thought she was so talented, why didn't he ever let her try her own recipes? Why such micromanagement? Well, she had nothing to lose by asking him. So she did.

A surprise lit his eyes. "Why haven't I given you more freedom? To be honest . . . because your lack of confidence concerned me. You seemed so relieved when I handed you recipes. Like you couldn't trust your own instincts." He took a step closer. "You can have all the artistic freedom you want at Epic. Anything you want, you can have. More helpers, more money, more time off. You name it. Just say the word. Just say you'll come back."

She shook her head. "I can't."

His eyes were pleading. "I can change, Jaime."

"I'm not asking you to change. Not your accent or your name. You always encourage the team to take time to reflect, to examine mistakes, to anticipate challenges. So that's just what I did on the long ride home. I don't belong in New York. I tried and tried, but city living is just not for me. I still have never taken the subway anywhere. Not once. I like going places in my own truck. I have to sleep with three sound machines on to drown out the sirens or the car doors slamming or the blare of a radio. I can't move as fast as New Yorkers move. I can't even *think* as fast as New Yorkers think. People snap at me in the grocery line to stop chattin' up the clerk and keep things moving. Tin Lizzie gets honked at by every New Jersey driver in the city."

"Well, you know what they say about New Jersey drivers . . ." Liam said, a smile tugging at his lips.

But she wasn't done. "And to be perfectly honest, since that's what we're doing here, I just can't handle the Mrs. Zimmermans anymore." She cringed. "There are so many of them in New York. You handle those kinds of people so well. You attract the right clients for Epic. But those uppity types make my stomach hurt. I can't go back. New York and I have parted ways."

Before he could respond, she added a few more thoughts gleaned from her long drive. "I am sorry to leave you without a flower designer just as the wedding season is gearing up. So I have a solution."

A slight smile lit his eyes. "Will you return for the season?"

"Not me." She shook her head. "Sloane."

His smile dimmed.

"You could teach her. She's interested in flower design and she's a quick learner. Someday she wants to own her own event company."

"Jaime—"

She lifted a hand in the air to stop him. "I know what you're going to say. Who can step in as project manager? I gave that some thought. Todd, with a little training, could be a crackerjack project manager. He's super detailed, superefficient. Just keep him away from the walk-in cooler. And as for replacing him, well, you can always find another intern."

"Jaime, hold your horses. Stop fretting about Epic." His eyes were locked on hers. "Look, I understand you're giving up on New York, but I hope that doesn't mean you're giving up on me." He spoke so softly it was hardly his voice at all. He took one step closer to her. "My facade was working until you came along, Jaime. I knew I was in trouble the moment I met you. The more time we spent together, the more I regretted the act I'd created for myself. I even found myself thinking of how to tell you . . ."

"Why didn't you?" She would have understood. She hoped she would've.

"I was afraid of what you'd think of me. Of shattering the myth."

It wasn't a myth. To Jaime, it was a fairy tale. A dream come true. Then not true.

He took another step toward her, setting his hands on her shoulders, his touch light and gentle. "It matters to me, what you think of me. You matter to me. Jaime, I'm in love with you."

She hated that her first thought was how much she'd been longing to hear those very words from him. But in the last twenty-four hours, everything had changed. "Liam, I don't even know you. Not really."

His hands were still on her shoulders, and he let them drop to her upper arms and gave them a gentle squeeze. "You do, Jaime. Liam/Billy, we're one and the same. I'm still me. I never lied to you. I admit I didn't answer your questions about my upbringing, but I didn't lie. I let the accent play a role, but it never changed the man I am. You do know me, Jaime. Flowers brought us together. Flowers can keep us together."

Well, it was a little more complicated than that. She didn't even know why he loved flowers in the first place. "Liam McMillan belongs in New York City." Her gaze swept the quiet streets, then it landed on Rose, standing in her shop by the window, a curious look on her face. A patient look. "And I belong right here." Jaime had work to do . . . some repair work.

Liam was quiet for a long moment, as if pondering how serious she was. She could see the contemplation in his eyes. And then his eyes grew shiny, and his face softened in that tender look he had for her, the one that really was just for her. She knew that now.

She nearly buckled. Nearly caved in. But she didn't let herself. She knew herself better now, and she wasn't going to let her feelings run the show.

He rested his forehead against hers. "Jaime Harper, somehow, someway, I'm going to be worthy of you. I'm going to win you back. You wait and see." He kissed her softly on both cheeks, then stepped around her and walked down the sidewalk to his rental car.

She watched him drive away, asking God to bless him. When his taillights disappeared around the corner, she turned and went into Rose's Flower Shop, bearing Liam's Apology Bouquet. This one, she realized, was meant for Rose.

a BOUQUET of DREAMS

Cast of Characters

Claire Murphy—(age 25) floral stylist for Same Day Delivery in Savannah, Georgia

MaryBeth Cooper—(late 60s) co-owner of Same Day Delivery flower shop; often mistaken for Betty White

Arthur Cooper—(early 70s) co-owner of Same Day Delivery flower shop but prefers to spend his time on the golf course

Ivan the Illusionist—(seems to be very, very old) Christian magician

Sophie—(20-something) rather well-endowed flower shop worker in Savannah, Georgia

Jim Turner—(middle-aged) third-generation owner of Turner Flowers in Savannah, Georgia

Christopher Reid—(age 24) nephew of Rose Reid (owner of Rose's Flower Shop in Sunrise, North Carolina). An important person to Claire until a hot August night, seven years ago. Since then, they've been estranged.

Floral Glossary

fillers—material used to fill gaps or empty spaces

floriography—(aka the language of flowers) a symbolic form of communication using specific flower meanings; it has been used for centuries across cultures as a poetic means of expressing emotions and conveying hidden messages, particularly during the Victorian era

focal point—the area of dominance or emphasis where the eye naturally travels

foliage—greenery, such as plant leaves

forage—harvesting free material, such as blooming forsythia branches, taken from public or private properties (only with permission, please!)

mechanics—the hidden foundation that holds flowers in place (such as flower frog or chicken wire)

negative space—a planned open space within a design that contains no flowers or foliage

recipe—a set of instructions to prepare a specific arrangement

reflex—open petals of a flower

vendors—sources for flowers (local growers, farmers' market, a wholesaler, or international)

vessels—containers to hold arrangements (such as vases, urns, compote bowls); all kinds of objects can become vessels to hold flowers—mason jars, bottles, crocks

It's not what you look at that matters, it's what you see.
—*Henry David Thoreau*

one

Even the tiniest of flowers can have the toughest roots.
—Shannon Mullen

On Sunday nights, Claire Murphy often thought of that old adage about knowing whether you'd chosen the right career by how you felt as you faced the coming week. For her, there was nothing more exciting than the prospect of walking into the flower shop on Monday morning, breathing in that beautiful clean air, putting on her apron, and getting to work with her beloved clippers. Flowers were more than a career choice for Claire—they were her passion.

And that was the very reason she didn't understand why her employer at Same Day Delivery had insisted that she attend a conference on customer service training. On her twenty-fifth birthday, of all days! MaryBeth did apologize to her for the unfortunate timing. "Sweet pea," she'd said, "you'll have plenty of other birthdays."

True, hopefully true. But Claire's twenty-fifth birthday was a day she'd looked forward to all her life. It was a target, a bull's-eye for her big life plans to land on.

Instead of celebrating the way Claire had planned, the way she should have, the way most twenty-five-year-olds would have, she would be indoors in a lame hotel at that mind-numbingly boring conference. And all because MaryBeth thought she didn't have what she called "the magic touch."

Claire didn't even know what that meant. She was direct. She was straightforward. She was candid. She looked for every opportunity to share her love and knowledge of flowers. And she was always willing to go that extra mile to help a customer. Take last Saturday as an example.

Claire had been in the workshop, putting the finishing touches on a pavé bouquet. She leaned back to look at it. Perfect. How could it not be? She'd made hundreds of these little bouquets—a crowded, contrived arrangement of stick-straight stem flowers, all in a uniform color, devoid of any personality. As dull as packed fruit. How many times had she begged MaryBeth to let her experiment with different shapes and sizes, unusual florals and faunas, to give customers a wide choice of options? Too many to count. Innovation was not part of Same Day Delivery.

Anyhoo, as she put the bouquet into the cooler, Mr. Wilson came in and asked Claire to make something really special. All that remained in the cooler were the day's remainder flowers, but he said he didn't mind at all. Then he told Claire that it was his fiftieth wedding anniversary and he wanted to bring flowers home to his wife.

"Did you know," Claire said as she pulled buckets from the cooler, "that only six percent of married couples make it to their fiftieth anniversary?"

Mr. Wilson looked at his watch. "How long is this going to take?"

That should've tipped Claire off, added to the fact that he had come to the shop five minutes before closing time. Alas, at that moment her mind was completely focused on the flowers, and the occasion. "During the Victorian age," she said, as she opened the cooler doors to find the right flowers, "when people began to marry for love rather than other reasons, a tradition grew of recognizing anniversaries with specific flowers. Year one was carnations, year ten was daffodils, asters for year twenty, and so on and so on. The fiftieth anniversary was so rare that it was given the special status of two flowers—violets and yellow roses." In the back of the cooler, she found buckets of both flowers and pulled them out to show Mr. Wilson. He seemed unimpressed.

While he waited, Claire created a bouquet of lavish beauty. She staggered the bloom height for a loose, lush look. She used an ingredient from this morning's foraging on her way to work—long stems of scented geraniums. The finished arrangement had an airy, natural appearance, as if it seemed to be growing right out of the vase. Stunning. She set it in a floral box and presented it to him, expecting a thank-you for creating an on-the-spot, after-hours gorgeous bouquet.

So did Mr. Wilson thank Claire? Nope. He had the gall to ask for a discount! He said the flowers were like day-old bread and should be sold half price. Vexed, she charged him double. Plus, she told him to go home and thank his wife for putting up with him for fifty years.

Unfortunately, MaryBeth had come into the store through the back entrance and must have overheard Claire's parting remark. She walked toward the front retail area with her hands tucked into her apron pockets. "Sweet pea, have you noticed you've been acting a little squirrelly lately?"

"Squirrelly?"

"Restless. Short-fused. Unpredictable." MaryBeth said it in her gentle Southern lady way, but still it found its way to push Claire's button.

Well, of course she'd been acting squirrelly! By now she'd thought she'd be the owner of the Same Day Delivery business. Maybe have started a chain, sold a few franchises. Several years back, Arthur and MaryBeth Cooper had said that she could buy the company from them when they retired. Claire recalled it as a solid-gold promise. Their memory over that conversation had grown fuzzy.

A few months ago, Claire had boldly asked about retirement plans. When, exactly, were they going to retire?

"Lately," MaryBeth had said, "we've been rethinking a few things." She didn't elaborate.

So Claire went to Arthur. "What exactly did MaryBeth mean by rethinking a few things?" And he hedged. Changed the topic.

What in the world was taking those two so long to hang up their clippers? They complained constantly about feeling exhausted from the shop's daily demands. Flower work required long hours, mostly weekends. They wanted more free time. MaryBeth's heart was at church. Arthur's was on the golf course. They needed the Same Day Delivery business to pay the bills, but they didn't have a passion for flowers anymore.

Claire worried about them. She adored Arthur and MaryBeth. They were a combination of grandparents and employers. She had a soft spot for older people, which came from spending her high school years living with grandparents while her dad was stationed overseas with the army. She liked being the one who could help, liked having them depend on her. If she were being honest, she liked belonging to them. Belonging wasn't merely a desire for Claire, it was essential. A necessity.

Arthur and MaryBeth didn't dote on Claire quite like her grandparents had done, but she did feel beholden to them. Seven years ago, they'd taken a chance on Claire, only eighteen years old, brand new to Savannah, with limited floral experience. They'd given her a job and helped her find a place to live.

Over the years, they had encouraged Claire to learn all aspects of the business and sent her to community college to take some business classes in accounting. To her utter surprise, when it mattered, she could actually figure out math. She had created systems to keep Same Day Delivery in fine working order. She'd added value with some steady-income-producing ideas, like her idea of creating light, decorative headpieces for the church lady hats. *Brilliant.*

MaryBeth, a true church lady, wore a different hat to church nearly every week. Claire had been helping MaryBeth make carnation boutonnieres for an upcoming wedding. Not Claire's choice for a boutonniere. While it was true that carnations got a bad rap—they were, after all, sturdy and reliable flowers—they were soooo trite. She had begged MaryBeth to show the bride something unusual, like pairing lavender and olive leaves. So perfect for a summer wedding. But no, MaryBeth stayed in her groove of what she called "tried and true."

Anyhoo, out of those remainder flowers from that wedding, Claire had made MaryBeth a little fascinator of carnations to pin onto her church hat. That Sunday morning, her friends oohed and aahed, and suddenly Saturday afternoons were the busiest times in the shop. All orders for the church ladies. Genius.

And then came Covid. Disastrous for small businesses like Same Day Delivery.

Until Claire came up with a magnificent idea. Even MaryBeth had admitted that Claire had kept Same Day Delivery alive during the global pandemic.

After the first few weeks of lockdown, Claire happened to be listening to a podcast about how people were desperate for connection. A light bulb went off in her head. Flowers were messengers! So why not encourage customers to send flowers that conveyed a message? *I miss you* (pink and red carnations, Stargazer lilies), *I love you* (red roses, red chrysanthemums), *I'm thinking of you* (daisies, lilies, tulips), on and on. Claire's favorite: *Have patience* (aster). MaryBeth had given Claire's idea a rare thumbs-up—probably because sales had dwindled so dramatically and she was scared. Claire proposed a subscription service for Same Day Delivery, where customers would spend a fixed amount each month to send two bouquets to whomever they wanted. What a difference it made! Same Day Delivery weathered the pandemic and Claire had proved her worth.

So why were MaryBeth and Arthur waiting to retire? Claire was more than ready. And she was turning twenty-five—her target age to start her empire. No wonder she was acting squirrelly lately.

But she didn't say any of that out loud. As petite and coiffed and manicured as MaryBeth was, something about her scared Claire.

Out of her apron pocket, MaryBeth pulled a brochure. She handed it to Claire. "Plan on attending this."

The Georgia drawl in Mary Beth's voice had thickened like clotted cream. There was a tone to it that meant *end of conversation*. If that wasn't clear enough, she turned and went through the swinging door into the workshop.

Claire looked at the brochure's cover. *Blooming with Excellence: Elevating Customer Service Skills for Florist Shop Workers.* Tidy, prim little flower arrangements covered every spare inch of the brochure. *Ick.* And that's when Claire realized she was going to have to give up her birthday to sit in a room and listen to speakers teach her things that she already knew. Unbelievable! This was not how turning twenty-five was supposed to roll out.

two

Every flower must grow through dirt.
—Laurie Jean Sennott

Early the next day, Claire woke to the buzz of an incoming happy birthday text on her cell phone. She picked it up, blinked, yawned. It was her dad, texting from Germany. She smiled. He always remembered.

Dad
Happy birthday!

Claire
Thanks!

A package should arrive soon. It's Nana's Bible.

It came! Thank you! I love it. I remember how often she read it at the kitchen table. I'll take good care of it.

Maybe read it now and then too.

Haha.

Have you given any more thought about moving to Germany? They need florists here too.

Nope. Can't. My plans here are in liftoff mode!

Sort of in liftoff mode. More like . . . sputtering-to-start-the-engines mode. But there was no way on God's green earth that Claire would move to wherever Dad was stationed. She knew the drill. As soon as she arrived, he'd get transferred somewhere else.

She set her phone down, slipping into a vortex of memories. She'd spent her entire childhood as a military brat. Her mother had gone AWOL (Dad's euphemistic term) after a few years as a military wife, when Claire was a toddler. "One too many moves" was all Claire knew of her mother, or why she'd left them. Years later, she thought she might understand it. By high school, she'd been to seven schools and Dad had new orders for another move—this one was somewhere in the Middle East. Enough, she'd decided, and told Dad she wanted to live with his parents in Sunrise, North Carolina. Happily, he didn't object. It was a good decision. She had loved high school, other than the school part. And she had adored her grandparents.

So what was she doing in Savannah, Georgia?

Well, first and foremost, the South was the only place to live. Claire had seen enough of the world as an army brat to know that much for herself.

By Claire's senior year in high school, life at home was rapidly changing. Her grandfather had passed away suddenly. Dad was given compassionate leave to fly in from overseas. While Nana was napping, Claire and her dad had sat in the big room near the woodstove, sipping tea. She'd been telling Dad that Nana seemed to be getting forgetful in the worst way.

Dad was listening carefully before he dropped a bombshell. "Claire, I'm moving Nana to a nursing facility. That's one of the things I came back to do while I'm on leave."

Claire's stomach rose and fell. Hold the phone! She wanted her dad to say he was coming home to stay . . . not to put Nana in a home. She tried to object, insisting that she could take care of Nana, but she knew she couldn't. A tiny part of her was relieved when her dad wouldn't hear of it. Nana liked to wander, especially during the night. Right after Grandpa had died, Claire had woken and couldn't find her. She'd finally called the police, and they had found Nana walking in her nightie along the dark, winding mountain road that led to Asheville. Speeding cars, wild animals, slippery ditches. Terrifying.

"The thing is," Dad said, "Grandpa had compensated for her in more ways than we realized. With him gone, Nana's dementia is not only more obvious but far worse."

And then came another blow. To pay for Nana's nursing home costs, Dad needed to sell the house. "You can stay in the house until it sells, which ought to happen right around graduation time," he told Claire. "Then . . ."

Then *what*? She would turn eighteen in July. She had a pretty good idea what came next in his mind. "I'm not joining the military."

His brow wrinkled. "I thought we'd agreed you planned to join up."

"Nope." Claire shook her head firmly. "I never agreed to that. You've just always hoped I'd follow in your military footsteps."

He frowned. "It's a good life."

"Sure, if you choose it. You did. I don't."

His frown deepened. "So what *do* you want to do after you graduate?"

College wasn't an option. School had never been easy for Claire, and she was happy to leave academics behind. Dad had never pushed her to excel, which she had appreciated. "Just get your diploma," he would tell her. "That's all the army needs." Joining the military was his constant drumbeat. Learn a trade, travel the world, enjoy excellent job security. And don't forget duty to your country. That was probably his top reason to join the military. He was a patriot through and through.

"I want to have my own flower shop."

His eyebrows shot up. His voice rose an octave. "Flowers?" No career choice could be farther from his. Her dad was an army mechanic. He worked on diesel engines. He could fix anything. It was why he was wanted at army bases all over the world. His face scrunched up. "Flowers? You want a lifetime of sticking flowers in a vase?"

Put that way, it sounded silly. But it wasn't silly. It was so much more than arranging flowers in a vase. Flowers touched a person's life in a deep and personal way. They marked life's important milestones—from births to weddings to funerals, and everything in between. They could transform an environment like magic. Flowers *were* magical. "Rose said that anyone who works with flowers is in the business of happiness."

"Rose. You really think a lot of her, don't you?"

"She's fabulous. She's taught us so much. She lets us help make arrangements. Not the whole thing, but she lets us start it. Jaime and Tessa and I are planning to have a shop together. Just yesterday, we told Rose that someday we want to buy the flower shop from her."

"What did she have to say to that?"

"Rose said . . ." Claire paused and looked up at the ceiling. "Actually, she didn't have an answer. She just told us to get back to work."

He laughed. "Well, let's get you to the finish line for high school." He held up her report card, which wasn't her best. "Then we'll figure out what comes next."

"Don't you worry, Dad. I can handle what comes next."

But what came next turned out to be a *disaster*.

Nana's house sold quickly, and three months later, Nana died in her sleep. Claire had been staying at Rose's—an arrangement her dad had cooked up before he left for Germany. He didn't want her to be alone. On that hot August night when everything changed—and she meant *everything*—she had hopped on the first bus that passed through.

Nine hours later, the only reason Claire got off the bus in Savannah, Georgia, was because the bus driver said it was the end of his route. Something about the reluctant way she left her seat must have tipped him off, because he swore under his breath. "You a runaway, ain't ya?"

"Nope," Claire said, clutching her backpack. "I'm not. I'm not running away." She was running *to* something. A new life. A fresh start. "And I'm over eighteen." Just barely.

He gave her a suspicious look. "But you got no place to go?"

"Well, you see—"

The driver pointed to a tall steeple down the road. "You go to that church and ask for a lady named MaryBeth. That lady's an angel. Tell her Hiram sent you. She'll make sure you're looked after."

Claire did *not* need looking after. She just needed . . . a little immediate help. Some food and a place to sleep. Just for tonight. She'd been in such a panic to leave that she didn't even bring the wad of cash she kept hidden under the bed at Rose's house. "Thanks," she told him and started down the road to the church. At some point, she knew she would have to process the tumultuous events of the past twenty-four hours, to try and figure out how everything went so badly. Someday, but not today. For now, she wanted to live in the world of possibilities.

But she was hungry and tired after spending the night on the bus. The front door to the church was locked, so she walked around to the church office. A small, dour woman sat in front of a computer at a desk and looked up when Claire opened the door to her office.

"I'm looking for MaryBeth."

The woman pointed to the door. "She's in the kitchen. Down the hall to your left."

Claire went down the hall to her left, following a scent of baking bread that could've led her to the right place without directions. In the kitchen, she saw a handful of women at different spots at the counter. It looked like they'd baked bread for communion, because now they were cutting the bread into tiny little squares, the way Claire's nana used to do at the church in Sunrise. The women chatted companionably as they sliced and diced. Claire felt a sweep of longing for Rose's Flower Shop. This was what it had been like for them—for her, Jaime, and Tessa. How could it all be over? All because of Rose's charming yet deceptive nephew, Chris Reid.

Struggling to tamp down emotions, Claire's eyes started swimming with tears, and she hunted through her backpack for a tissue.

A thickly accented Southern voice interrupted her moment of self-pity. "Sweet pea, can I help you?"

Claire's head snapped up. Standing just a few feet away from her was a Betty White look-alike. A petite older woman who dressed with care: a crisp, bright pink blouse over ironed white pants. Her face was pretty, with fine features and carefully applied makeup, sprayed hair, and big pearl earrings. Something about the kind, maternal look in her warm eyes made Claire know she'd found the right person. "If your name happens to be MaryBeth, then you sure can."

And so she was.

Anyhoo, that was then and this was now. She squeezed her eyes shut. Only the good memories, she reminded herself. It was her mantra. Only remember the good memories. She threw off the covers to start the day. Today was her twenty-fifth birthday!

three

Where flowers bloom, so does hope.
—Lady Bird Johnson

MaryBeth turned out to be an angel and here was why: When runaways turned up in Savannah, they were often lured by unsavory characters into the world of the supernatural and paranormal. Savannah, a beautiful historical place, enjoyed the reputation of being the most haunted city in America. It was said that someone was buried below every square inch of the city. Interior ceilings in houses were painted "haint blue" or haunt blue to trick the ghosts into thinking it was water or the sky, and not a home to settle into.

Ghost tours were big business in Savannah. Old modified open-topped hearses were unique to Savannah. In the evenings, they'd drive people around the historic district, telling ghostly stories. Besides ghost tours, Savannah was home to psychics and tarot card readers, spiritualists, mediums, and fortune tellers. All the work of the devil, MaryBeth explained to Claire, in great detail. Her church had started a ministry to provide shelter to runaways and give them job skills, with the hopes of keeping them far, far away from the devil's work.

Frankly, Claire did not consider herself to be the kind of person who would be vulnerable to apparitions. Hardly that. But she did need a little bit of help—she was so hungry her stomach was rumbling—and this looked like a good chance to get it. So she did her best to look vulnerable and a little scared, like easy prey. Not a simple thing, especially as she thought of how the boy whom she had once loved desperately had described her as warrior looking. But she shook off that worry, the way she shook off thoughts of that boy. She had left Chris behind in Sunrise to face his due comeuppance.

Her vulnerable act must have worked. MaryBeth swept her under her wings and fed her breakfast—scrambled eggs and toast made right in that church kitchen. After Claire had eaten, the woman held out her cell phone. "Sugar, I'm sure someone, somewhere, is worried sick about you. Would you do me a favor and let that someone know you're safe?"

Was there anyone worried sick about Claire? She didn't think so. "The only person left in my family is my dad, and he's in Germany, stationed with the army."

When she heard the word "Germany," MaryBeth slipped her phone back in her apron pocket. "An email, then?" she said. "It's only fair to let him know you're safe."

Well, Dad knew Claire would be all right. He'd raised her to take care of herself. But MaryBeth didn't know that, and Claire appreciated her concern. "I will. I promise. First, though, I need to find a flower shop that's looking for a skilled floral stylist." She was being modest. She wasn't just a skilled floral stylist. She was a gifted one. All she lacked was years of experience. Even Rose had said so.

Then came the part that really put the shine on MaryBeth's halo: Turned out that she and her husband owned a flower shop. Owned it! And they just happened to be looking for a new flower girl. (Claire held her tongue from correcting MaryBeth. She *wasn't* a flower girl. She was a floral *stylist*.)

She'd been in Savannah for less than an hour, and she had a full stomach and a new job. Not bad, Claire Murphy! She had to give props to that weary bus driver who had sent her to the church to find MaryBeth. It made a body think that Somebody Up There was looking after her.

MaryBeth and Arthur were kind and caring employers. They knew of church interns who needed a housemate. They included her in their family holiday gatherings. Really, they were wonderful people. Claire's only complaint was how stifled she felt as a floral stylist. Within the first week, she realized that MaryBeth had certain ideas about flowers and *that* was *that*.

In the industry, there were basic shapes to all flower arranging—some professionals said six, some said nine, some said even more. Whatever the number, every arrangement had recognizable shapes. Shapes like the arc, the circle, the oval, the curve, the right angle, the S curve, the triangle. Once you started to notice them, you couldn't *not* see them.

But MaryBeth believed all floral arranging should take three basic shapes: the circle (her beloved pavé), the triangle (a shape she called the Father, Son, and Holy Ghost), and the oval (a big egg). She had a formula of colors and availability of flowers for each season, and those lists never wavered. Never. She was known for her single-stem arrangements, stuck in a block of green oasis. (No earth-loving florist used oasis anymore! Except for Mary-Beth.) Master the fundamentals—that was MaryBeth's mantra. Fundamental. It suited her in so many ways!

Sometimes Claire felt like she was working in an ice cream shop that only served one flavor: vanilla. A favorite for many, but not new, not exciting.

MaryBeth resisted all change. As hard as Claire pushed, Mary-Beth did not budge. Not on flower selection, not on marketing tools. Same Day Delivery had no website. No social media. Mary-Beth was a firm believer in word-of-mouth advertising. A recommendation from a trusted source, she insisted, was the best marketing of all.

Maybe so. But most of those customers were as old as Methuselah. Who was going to order flowers from Same Day Delivery when all those loyal but ancient customers had gone to meet their Maker?

It didn't take long for Claire to see she wasn't going to make much of a dent in MaryBeth's thinking. After she'd been working at Same Day Delivery for a few weeks, she'd brought in some long stems of cherry tomatoes to add an unexpected pop in a bouquet. The most horrified look came over MaryBeth's face. Like Claire had just added trash to an arrangement.

Anyhoo . . . bottom line, MaryBeth was the boss. So Claire focused on learning other things. In fact, she decided she was going to learn as much as she possibly could about running a flower shop. As soon as Arthur gained confidence in her abilities, he let her do the ordering and manage the books.

The one freedom MaryBeth gave to Claire was permission to do whatever she wanted with remainder flowers each week from church orders for altars, weddings, anniversaries, baby showers, holidays, and funerals. Mostly funerals. Same Day Delivery was known in Savannah for being the go-to florist for funerals. The remainders, MaryBeth said, were hers to "fiddle with"—a description that made Claire wince. Floral stylists did not "fiddle." They were artists. They created ephemeral art.

l·l·l

As the weeks turned into months turned into years, Claire's own style emerged. She had always been more inspired by texture than color, with movement and air over tightness. Foliage became her trademark, the more uncommon, the better. She became a shameless forager. She never went anywhere without her clippers. Savannah's natural beauty had taught her that.

The many urban parks in Savannah were boons for unusual foliage. This city might be known as the most haunted city in America, but it was also famous for its gardens and parks. It was the first planned city in America, the oldest in Georgia, and city parks lined the historical district. Forsyth Park was the most famous of the urban parks, with a beautiful fountain in the center. Lovely, but it was in the little pocket parks that she found the best foliage for arrangements. Sometimes, from even the private gardens that could be spotted from the sidewalks. Window boxes overflowing with luscious greenery. She had learned, after being caught red-handed, to always ask the homeowner *before* foraging. Homeowners weren't always understanding about that. The thing about foraging was that you needed to clip long stems. You could always edit later, but you needed plenty of stem to start with.

Spring and summer dressed Savannah in her full glory. Early mornings and early evenings, Claire scoured the city to take advantage of all she had to offer, nature-wise. Some of her favorites were feathery pampas grass, buttonweed with seed pods, lacy Amaranthus, fuzzy lamb's ears, statice, brunnera, and stems of rosemary or eucalyptus. Actually, seed pods of any kind might be her favorite foliage: Scabiosa, echinacea, chestnut, poppy, Craspedia, and fern curl. They added unexpected touches of texture and variation.

Away from work, she spent time studying Pinterest and Instagram photos of floral stylists, eager to learn the latest trends. She thought of them as her floral heroes. Whenever there were remainder flowers, she'd stay late in the shop after closing hours to create her own recipes, happily shrugging off MaryBeth's predictable arrangements. During those evenings, she found and fine-tuned her own style. Claire discovered she liked air in an arrangement. Negative spaces. Movement. Asymmetrical instead of symmetrical. Less was more. Completely the opposite style of the Same Day Delivery shop's fondness for tight, dense bouquets.

Claire would put her arrangements in the cooler to show Mary-Beth in the morning. Surely, she thought, MaryBeth would see the magic that came with variety and innovation. She hoped she might let her sell her creations in the shop, but that hope quickly fizzled. After getting a less-than-lukewarm reaction ("But, sweet pea, aren't those weeds?" or "Sweet pea, why would you reflex the tulip petals? Tulips are just fine the way God made them." Or she'd tilt her head to match the asymmetrical design line. "But, sweet pea, everything is cattywampus. Just a little bit off, wouldn't you say?"), she stopped showing her work to MaryBeth and just took the arrangements home with her. Sadly, her housemates weren't flower savvy. "Pretty," one would say. Or "Cool."

Seriously? That was no way to express the wonder of flowers.

In a notebook, Claire recorded her recipes, tweaked them, added photographs to document the arrangements. It was all part of her preparation to become the owner of Same Day Delivery. The name would be the first thing to go. She hadn't decided what would replace it, though she did keep a running list of possibilities in her notebook.

She had so many ideas for her future flower shop! Workshops, for one. She'd seen other floral shops host workshops in the evenings. Customers would pay a basic fee; the shop owner would provide the flowers, food, and drink, and demonstrate a basic recipe. That, she had learned through many trial-and-error moments as she honed her design skills, was the key to mastering floral design—following a process. Then, in her mind's eye, the customers would create their own arrangements, and Claire would act as a roving teacher, helping them improve their bouquets. To point out beginner's mistakes (*Don't choke the flowers!*). To gain confidence in their own style (*Give it a try!*). To not be afraid to follow their gut (*If you love it, go for it!*). Recipes were meant to guide, not to stifle, innovation. There was plenty of room for experimentation with flower arranging.

Now and then, Claire practiced teaching the workshop as she imagined herself with the attendees in the class—reminding novices to always cut stems at an angle, to start with foliage because it gave structure to an arrangement. Then add the focal flowers, the larger blooms. Next came the fillers. She promised herself that she would never criticize anyone's creation. She would suggest ways to enhance their work, but it was their work of art. And all art should be respected.

That's what Rose Reid had taught her, and she'd never forgotten.

Two years ago, working late on a warm June night, Claire finished an arrangement—assorted dahlias, snapdragons, astilbe, yarrow, and red gaillardia for a pop of texture, all arranged in a bright orange ceramic vessel. She took a picture, studied it, stood back to look at the bouquet, and felt a spiral of pleasure deep into her bones. Stunning. So beautiful, so appealing. Someone, besides her housemates who really didn't appreciate flowers at all, should see this.

So she entered the photograph into a local floral contest . . . and she won! It was something she'd never thought she'd do. Truth be told, she used to make fun of Rose for entering so many contests. Rose would tack her awards on her front window display, and now Claire wished she could take back all those snarky comments about what she called Rose's trophy shelf. After Claire's first win, she got hooked. Competition fired her up. She entered another and another, increasingly competitive contests, and she kept placing, if not winning. And now she was a finalist in the Savannah Blooms contest—the best and biggest one in all of Georgia.

four

The flower that follows the sun does so even in cloudy days.
—Robert Leighton

Claire was dreading the next two days. Torture. Sitting in a low-budget hotel conference room with marginal air-conditioning, punctuated by tedious breakout circles to practice skills. And it was all done by a Christian company, of course, because MaryBeth only trusted and supported Christian businesses. Even the wholesalers she ordered flowers from were all Christians. Claire was a churchgoer, but sometimes MaryBeth made church out of everything.

Claire looked through the notebook she'd been given. First lecture: "Why Customer Service Is Important."

Ridiculous. That topic did not need a full hour lecture. Claire could stand at the podium and deliver the answer in less than one minute. Customer service is important because flowers wouldn't get ordered without it. Check. ☑

Breakout circles were planned after each lecture to role-play customer service strategies. Attendees' name tags had a color code to show which circle they belonged to, each one led by a professional in the industry.

Okay, Claire thought. That sounded more promising. She liked the idea of gleaning good ideas to handle customers from other attendees. After all, they were in the trenches, like she was. Customers weren't easy! Essential but not easy.

She flipped the page to the second lecture: "How to Improve Customer Service."

A defeated sigh escaped her lips. *This* was why MaryBeth had sent Claire to this conference—to work on improving her customer skills. She'd have to pay attention to this lecture. MaryBeth would want a full report on the topic.

Claire turned the page and realized that the entire rest of the day would be spent answering that question. Each lecture took a different piece of the topic:

"Strengthen Customer Service Skills" (*Right*. That's why she was here.)

"Adaptability" (So maybe . . . she could use a little flexibility polishing.)

"Clear Communication" (She did communicate clearly! Too clearly. It was the very reason MaryBeth was often annoyed with her.)

"Work Ethic" (Claire had a sterling work ethic. ☑)

"Knowledge" (Who knew more about flowers than her? ☑☑)

"Thick Skin" (A particular strength of Claire's. ☑☑☑)

Then she spotted something in the conference notebook that made her nearly laugh out loud. Tonight, after dinner, a Christian magician was going to perform for the attendees, with an emphasis on flowers.

If MaryBeth knew of this, she would have a conniption. She would say that a Christian magician was a self-canceling phrase and all magic belonged to the devil. Claire would try to tell her that magicians used tricks of illusions, that everything they did could be explained, but MaryBeth wouldn't buy it. Claire was *not* a fan of magicians, not after knowing one rather well. She'd skip the show tonight. She'd rather go foraging.

A high-pitched squealing noise from the microphone onstage made everyone cringe. A nervous-looking woman stood behind the podium with a stack of notes, waited until the audio feedback was fixed, and then started the conference with a timid welcome. After five minutes of listening, Claire decided that nothing was new to her, so she started doodling ideas for a dramatic flower arrangement that had been rumbling around in her mind. She was an avid student of the Victorian era and its emphasis on symbolism in flowers. She kept a notebook of flowers that were common in Victorian prints. On her notepad, she sketched tall, dark fritillaria persica, black hellebores, and parrot tulips with their bulbs and roots still attached—the unexpected touch. It was a technique that Rose liked to use. Surprise the eye.

As Claire finished the sketch, she squinted her eyes to assess it. Stunning. This bouquet would be so perfect for a wedding—if Same Day Delivery might ever have a client who had a desire to astonish.

"Why keep the bulb and roots?"

Claire looked up. Unbeknownst to her, a woman seated next to her had been watching as she sketched. "This is for a wedding reception. The bulb means new life, the roots symbolize the growth of life."

"I like it," the woman said. She seemed young, like Claire, with fuzzy brown hair that framed a wide, innocent-looking face. She gazed at Claire with admiration in her eyes. "It's unexpected."

Yes. Yes it was. That was the thing about working with flowers—they surprised Claire every single time. Claire smiled at her and read her name tag: *Sophie.* "Thank you, Sophie. I'm Claire."

She smiled. "I knew I'd make some new friends at this rehab conference."

Claire laughed. Maybe the conference wasn't a total loss. Her birthday might be looking up.

Sophie stuck to Claire like sticky floral tape. She even followed her to the bathroom during a short break. It didn't take long for Claire to learn that Sophie seemed somewhat unaware of how others perceived her, and for that, she felt a sense of camaraderie. On the walk back to the conference room, Sophie asked how long Claire had been "tinkerin'" with flowers.

Claire did not tinker with flowers. She styled them. Since Sophie was a new acquaintance and probably not a lasting one, Claire held back from correcting her. "Since I was sixteen," Claire said. "And I plan to be working with flowers till the day I die."

Sophie's eyes went wide. "Get *out*! How do you know that?"

How did she know? Claire had known what she wanted to do with her life since she was sixteen years old and first walked into Rose's Flower Shop to ask for a job. Rose Reid went to the same church as Claire's grandparents, but even if she hadn't, Sunrise was one of those small towns where everyone knew each other. It made the teenagers nervous.

Rose had been watering some indoor plants and set the watering can on the counter to give Claire her full attention. "You want to work here?"

"I saw the Help Wanted sign on the window, and I thought I'd just come on in and apply."

"Do you have any floral experience?"

"Some. I'm, uh, self-taught." Claire loved flowers dearly, but her floral experience consisted of picking wildflowers near the creek and arranging them in an empty peanut butter jar. She knew nothing about styling flowers other than what she'd studied on Pinterest; she'd never even made an official bouquet with flowers of this quality. She didn't know their names. She'd never used floral tape or cage frogs or paddle wire or any of the mechanics she'd learned about. She'd never even seen them in real life.

Rose led her to the workshop in the corner of the shop, handed her an apron and clippers, and said, "You've got fifteen minutes. Use whatever you want from the cooler. Let's see what you can do." Then the bell chimed on the door, and she left Claire alone while she went to tend to the customer.

Was Rose serious? Claire stood there for a full minute, shocked. She thought she'd be working a cash register, not creating flower arrangements.

Out of the corner of her eye, she saw some brightly colored ranunculi in a white bucket. Above the workbench was a shelf full of an assortment of vessels. Something clicked and she snapped out of her stupor. She chose a small glass vase with a long neck. Then she took a few ranunculi and trimmed their stems and leaves (at least she knew *that* much) before placing them in the vessel. She found some floral wire and cut several long pieces, placing a wire carefully into each blossom so that it traveled down the stem. The wire allowed her to bend and shape the stem so that the blossoms almost seemed to float in the air.

"Where'd you learn that trick?"

She looked up to see Rose at the edge of the workbench, arms crossed, watching Claire. "Instagram."

Rose's eyebrows shot up. "You know much about social media?"

"I'm a whiz." That was the gospel truth.

Rose walked over and studied the small arrangement. "Bless your heart."

With that, Claire stiffened. "Bless your heart" was Southern code for many things: *You poor thing. You're an idiot.* Or *What on God's green earth made you think that was a good idea?*

But it could also mean someone was struck speechless and didn't really know what to say. "Absolutely lovely," Rose finally said. "Simple but elegant." Then she looked at Claire. "I do believe God has given you a special gift." Then she smiled. "There's only one thing that's missing."

Claire studied the arrangement for a very long moment before cringing. "Water."

Rose laughed. "Honey, you're hired." She wrapped her arms around Claire and gave her a true Southern-style hug. Practically knocked the wind right out of Claire. Rose gave great hugs.

"I do believe God has given you a special gift." Those ten words changed Claire's life. That, and *"You're hired."*

Teen years were fragile for everyone, but especially for Claire. It might have had something to do with being a little bit overweight, or maybe it was a result of growing up with a mom who went missing, or maybe she'd just moved too many times as an army brat. No one would think it, but she had very low self-confidence. She had never in her life felt like she was naturally gifted at anything. And now here she was, managing with little discernible effort to do something that was, Rose said, absolutely lovely.

The joy of it. The pleasure, the satisfaction. Flowers were astounding to her.

She wanted to stay at Rose's Flower Shop forever.

But that was *before.*

Everything changed after that hot August night. That was the hardest day to remember, so Claire did her best to forget it.

But she didn't want to share all that mental rumbling with Sophie. Honestly, she didn't talk about her former life in Sunrise to anyone. She might mention Rose in passing once in a while, but Claire never expressed what she really meant to her. She wasn't sure why. That was then and this was now. They didn't mix. She didn't want them to.

Wide-eyed, Sophie waited for an answer. How did Claire know she wanted to spend her entire life working with flowers?

"I just know," she said.

five

Don't let the tall weeds cast a shadow
on the beautiful flowers in your garden.
—Steve Maraboli

s Claire sat in the first breakout circle, the leader, Jim Something-or-other, pointed to her. "You're Claire Murphy, right?" he asked, startling her out of her brooding over her birthday.

She was so surprised he knew her name that all she could do was nod.

Jim Something told Claire to play the role of a flower worker while he played the customer. Disappointing. Claire could do an excellent job if she played the role of the customer, because she'd had a great deal of experience with them. Crazy stories!

People sent flowers for all kinds of reasons. Like the one where old Mr. Miller got drunk late one night, wandered into his neighbor's house, and fell asleep on the couch. He startled awake to the sound of a rifle cocking. He had landed on Widow Dosker's couch, a woman who believed in shooting first and asking questions later. Fortunately, Widow Dosker was renowned for being a poor shot,

114

and she ended up hitting a large potted plant. Mr. Miller jumped off the sofa and ran out the door. He felt he should send flowers to apologize for his accidental break-in. Claire listened to his whole story and said, "Well, there's no better way to apologize than with flowers. For this situation, I'd recommend blue hyacinths. They express sincere remorse."

"I was thinking red roses."

"Well," Claire said, "that would send a sincere message. Red roses convey romantic love."

Mr. Miller's bloodshot eyes went wide. "I have no romantic feelings for Widow Dosker."

"Exactly. That's why I'd go with hyacinths."

As Claire wrapped a bow around the hyacinths, she noticed a fiddle-leaf fig pot in the corner of the store that hadn't sold. "May I suggest you send a new potted plant too?"

Mr. Miller happily agreed. He would've sent anything to appease Widow Dosker. She was a prickly neighbor.

That reminded Claire of another customer who had sent flowers to his ex-wife on the day their divorce was finalized. He had asked for a spiky cactus to represent his ex-wife's personality. Claire talked him out of that grim notion (she knew his ex-wife! knew everybody's business in Sunrise, North Carolina) and into an arrangement that expressed his emotions *today*. A new, hopefully wonderful chapter of life was about to start for him. After all, this was not only a day of endings but of new beginnings. She suggested blazing hot orange blooms of birds-of-paradise, large yellow cymbidium orchids, and long stems of Safari Sunset Leucadendron. She arranged them carefully in a large glass cube vase lined with a ti leaf. Astonishing. The delighted customer thanked her profusely. He left the shop with a lightness in his step.

That might have been one of her all-time favorite customer moments. It wasn't often that flowers were meant to convey a negative message. Those were just some of her unusual customer stories. She had more. "Couldn't I play the customer?"

Frowning, Jim Something shook his head. He told Claire to respond to him as a customer the way she normally would. "Just the way you do at your shop."

"Right," Claire said. "Shoot."

Jim Something leaned forward in his folding chair. "I'd like to order a dozen yellow carnations."

"That's it? That's the best you've got?"

A puzzled look came over Jim Something's stern face. "What do you mean?"

"Well," Claire said, "if you're trying to create a realistic role-play, then my customers like to explain why they're ordering flowers."

"That's true," Sophie said. "Mine do too."

"Yeah," another woman agreed. "Customers think they need to tell you everything."

"Right?" Claire said. It was nice to hear from other floral stylists.

Jim Something seemed slightly exasperated. "Fine, fine. It's my girlfriend's birthday. She said she wants yellow carnations."

Claire's eyebrows shot up, her eyes wide. "Your girlfriend asked for yellow carnations?"

"Yes."

"Does she know much about flowers?"

He coughed a laugh. "She knows everything about flowers. She's a wealth of information."

"Oh boy."

"What's wrong now?" Jim Something's annoyance was growing. "Don't tell me your shop is out of yellow carnations."

"We have yellow carnations. The thing is . . . if your girlfriend knows flowers—"

"She does."

"—then she is sending you a very clear message."

"She's *what*?"

"Flowers convey meanings," Claire said. "Yellow carnations

represent disappointment or rejection. Most likely, a breakup is imminent."

Jim Something paused, considering her remark before rejecting it. "That is rubbish."

Claire shook her head. "It's not rubbish. It's historical. It comes from the Victorian age." She tipped her head. "Are you not in the flower industry?" If not, why was he here?

"Yes, of course I am. Perhaps you've heard of us. Turner Flowers."

Sophie looked at him, awestruck. "You're part of Turner Flowers?" The entire circle gasped, all together, as if they suddenly discovered they were in the presence of royalty.

Grinning, he puffed out his chest, nearly bursting his shirt buttons. "I sure am. Jim Turner. Third-generation florist."

Sophie broke out in song. "'Turn her day around with Turner Flowers.'"

Ick. That annoying song. Claire couldn't stand it. It was the kind of tune that got stuck in your head. "I never understood that ditty."

"I composed it." He gave Claire a *look.* "What's wrong with it?"

Well, he asked. "Your commercial makes the assumption that only women would want to receive flowers."

He scoffed. "Because most of our customers are women." He looked around the circle, making eye contact with each attendee.

Claire got the impression that it was a strategy, a way to get everyone on his side. When did this turn into a battle? "Men like flowers too."

Jim Turner didn't seem to agree. "Turner Flowers knows who our customers are. Three generations of success."

Claire tipped her head. "And you don't know the language of flowers?"

"Flowers do not speak. I've heard about that language of flowers hullabaloo. Old-fashioned nonsense. You're just creating an illusion for your customers with all that mumbo jumbo about flowers and messages. Flowers are just flowers."

Claire's eyes went wide in disbelief. "Flowers are *not* just flowers!"

Jim Turner narrowed his eyes. "Is this how you work with your customers?"

Oh, so now he was back to the role-playing exercise. Fine. Back they'd go. "I might suggest sending two-toned carnations. They're a symbol of parting."

Jim Turner's face was starting to turn red. "Look, I came into your shop to send flowers to my girlfriend for her birthday. Something you're making very difficult. And you are making me—your customer—extremely uncomfortable."

"I'm trying to help. I don't want you to be surprised when your girlfriend dumps you."

"Flowers *are* just flowers! People like them because they like them. They're pretty. They smell good. End of story." At this point, Jim Turner rose, pushed his chair back, and glowered at Claire. "It's very clear to me why you have been sent to customer service rehab." With that, he left the circle.

Why did everyone keep referring to this conference as customer service rehab? This was supposed to be a conference designed to help flower stylists round out their skills. To prepare them so they could eventually own a shop one day. "He's kidding, right?"

"He's not kidding," Sophie said. "My boss told me that I had one more chance to improve or I'd be let go." She looked around the circle. "What about y'all?"

"Same." A man nodded. "I've been put on probation."

Customer service rehab. Well, didn't that just beat all.

six

Don't wait for someone to bring you flowers.
Plant your own garden and decorate your own soul.
—Luther Burbank

Sophie leaned over to whisper to Claire. "You sure got Jim Turner riled up. I'll bet you ten bucks that he's leaving to call his girlfriend and ask if she's dumping him."

Claire watched Jim Turner march toward the back of the room to the exit. The thing was, she wasn't trying to get him riled up. This *was* how she acted with customers. It hadn't been an unfamiliar customer interaction for Claire, maybe more so in the last few months since she'd gotten "squirrelly." She never started out with the intention to deliberately upset a customer. It wasn't a habit. She just couldn't seem to hold back on sharing her opinion, especially when it came to the possibilities of flowers.

Take yesterday. A customer had called in to say he needed a lavish flower arrangement that would convince his girlfriend to take him back. Still stinging after being chastised by MaryBeth for telling Mr. Wilson more than he wanted to hear about fiftieth wedding anniversaries, Claire knew not to ask any leading questions.

Stick to the facts. Her job, MaryBeth reminded her, was to take down the flower order, get it done, and get it delivered. So she asked the customer how much he wanted to spend on the arrangement.

"How much *should* I spend?" he asked.

"If you really messed up, then I'd suggest a budget of one hundred dollars."

The man cleared his throat. "What if I really, really, really messed up?"

Three *really*s. She took in a deep breath and kept her voice as businesslike and nonjudgmental as possible. "Then I would suggest you triple your budget."

"Okay." Long pause. "And could you send an identical bouquet to my other girlfriend?"

Ick. Claire lost it. Her voice dripping with distaste, she gave this man a piece of her mind for cheating until he hung up on her.

MaryBeth came out of the workshop, shaking her head. "Sweet pea, how much of a sale did you just lose?"

Claire cleared her throat. "How much?"

"Dollars. How much?"

"Two sales, actually." She swallowed. "Three hundred each."

MaryBeth didn't say anything, which was worse. She seemed more tired than angry. She just returned to the workshop, shaking her head.

So maybe Claire did have a habit of riling people up. For the first time, she got a glimmer of understanding for MaryBeth's complaints, like she had peered into her own house from an outside window and discovered a new perspective on a familiar scene.

Even while Claire was back in high school, working at Rose's Flower Shop, Rose would chide her now and then, reminding her that not every thought needed to be expressed. "Consider what a great forest is set on fire with a spark," she would quote. "The tongue also is a fire."

A man in the breakout circle cleared his throat, and Claire realized they were all waiting for someone to take charge. This she could do. "Surely you know about the meaning of flowers?" Her gaze swept the circle. Blank faces looked back at her. "I'll tell you what. I'm going to give y'all a crash course, so don't just listen up. Take notes." She pointed to them. "This is how to take your flower skills to the next level."

Nine eager faces leaned forward in chairs, hands poised with notepads and pens.

Claire enjoyed sharing her knowledge of flowers. "It all goes back to the Victorian era, when so much was forbidden. The culture put taboos on just about everything you could imagine. A woman's exposed ankle could create a scandal. Any part of the human body could not be mentioned. It was considered improper. Why, even piano legs were covered in homes. So flowers ended up becoming a secret language to express emotions that couldn't be said aloud. A fancy word for it is *floriography*."

Sophie lifted her hand in the air, like an obedient child in a classroom. "Can you give us an example?"

"Yes, ma'am. Let's think about a Victorian man who was interested in developing a friendship with a woman. He might send her a bouquet of periwinkles. If she replied with an iris, it meant she reciprocated his feelings. Let's say things started to advance between these two. If he sent her a red rose, it was a way to tell her that he loved her. If she responded with a bouquet of red tulips, it meant she loved him too."

"What happened next?"

"Between our two lovers? Well, let's see." Claire was on a roll. "There came a day when he saw her chatting with another man, so he sent her pink larkspurs, which represent fickleness. And that made her mad."

"So what then?"

"So she sent back a geranium, which means stupidity. Turned out, she'd been talking to her brother. With that information, her lover felt terrible. So he sent her a purple hyacinth to let her know how sorry he felt." She wagged her finger in the air. "But our girl wasn't having it."

"No!" Sophie clapped her hands on her cheeks. "She wouldn't forgive him?"

Claire shook her head. "She was offended that he didn't trust her, and a purple hyacinth wasn't enough to soften her heart. So he sent her pink roses to beg her to believe him. Then primroses to say he couldn't live without her. And finally, he sent her Cleome." Claire's voice dropped to a whisper. "He was asking her to elope with him."

Sophie grabbed Claire's arm. "Tell us! Did she say yes?"

"It took her a very long time to decide how she was going to respond. She wanted him to suffer. But at long last, she sent him a bundle of narcissus. It was her way of telling him that he was the only one she would ever love."

Sophie sighed with happiness. A skeptic in the circle squinted at Claire. "And how is that supposed to take our business to the next level?"

Claire clapped her hands on her knees and leaned forward. "Flowers are not merely tokens of beauty. They have meaning and purpose. Start sharing your knowledge of the language of flowers with your customers. Trust me, your business will blossom."

That, in a nutshell, was the bedrock for Claire's future flower shop empire.

seven

In joy and in sadness, flowers are our constant friends.
—Kakuzō Okakura

*L*unch. *Awful*. A buffet of beige food. Even the sweet tea was beige. No vegetables, no fruit. Claire was going to give feedback after this conference ended and let them know that beige was an offensive color to florists, unless it happened to be a rare cappuccino rose, just flown in from Kenya.

She liked to follow wedding planners and see what the latest trends in flowers were. Her favorite wedding planner was Liam McMillan, a Scottish event planner who lived in New York City and did all kinds of "wow" weddings. Her high school friend Jaime Harper landed a job with his Epic Events, which was how Claire first found out about him. Even though she hadn't talked to Jaime since that August day, she did follow her on social media. Claire wasn't really into "wow" weddings, not like Jaime had always been, but she did love to follow the latest, greatest trends in flowers. It helped to balance out the limitations on her daily work at the shop.

"So how come you got sent to customer service rehab?" Sophie asked.

Got sent? Sophie was funny, in her own way. "I'm here because I plan to have my own florist shop soon, and I want to be as ready as a person can possibly be."

Sophie stared at her with wide, admiring eyes. "Then you could do arrangements the way you've always wanted to."

"YES!" Claire could have hugged her. Someone understood! "Yes, yes, yes. Exactly that. I can't wait to have the freedom to do my own arrangements."

"My boss won't even let me touch the flowers."

"Why not?"

"I have no formal training. He just wants me to ring up customers and take orders and sweep the shop."

"So then," Claire said, "why were you sent to customer service rehab?"

"I've been told I flirt too much with the male customers. I don't even realize I do it. But I must say I get asked for my phone number a lot."

That explained so much. Sophie was cute, in a wide-eyed, naive way. And very, very well endowed. Her outfit revealed a lot of cleavage. Quite a lot.

Midafternoon, the conference took a decided upturn for Claire. The floral stylists were given time to create an arrangement. Cut flowers in buckets were brought in, and while they weren't Claire's taste (so many carnations!), there was definitely more variety than she usually had. They said they were going to have a prize for the best arrangement.

Now the conference was cooking with gas. Claire loved competition. She thrived on it.

Sophie trailed Claire as she examined each option, choosing the stems that fit in the arrangement in her head. Whatever flower Claire picked out, Sophie chose as well, right down to the number of stems she'd taken. Sedum, yarrow, smoke bush. All textures.

To Claire, textures added structure and interest. But she needed a focal flower, a star—something to make your eyes pop. She walked up and down the table of buckets, and then, in the back, she saw what she wanted: protea. She picked out sprays of it and one king protea. Gorgeous.

As Sophie reached for the proteas, Claire let out an exasperated breath. "Don't you want to show off your own style?"

Sophie squinted. "I never really thought about it. Do I need one?"

Claire nearly dropped her king protea. No wonder Sophie's boss didn't let her touch the flowers. Every flower shop had a distinctiveness. Even MaryBeth's old-fashioned style was her own. "You can't argue with a classic" was her mantra. Everyone in Savannah knew that if they wanted a traditional flower arrangement, go to Same Day Delivery.

Claire had to set aside concern for Sophie's future so she could focus on her own composition. "Well," she said, "you can learn a lot by looking around." She certainly had. Most of Claire's spare time was spent studying other florists, or botanical information, or walking around Savannah to get inspired with new ideas. And, of course, to forage.

She chose an oval white ceramic vase—ordinary, common. Ideal for what she had in mind. She didn't need a personality piece for this arrangement; the flowers would provide the drama. Oftentimes, a vessel could add to an arrangement by providing an exciting backdrop, but a king protea needed no help. It could speak for itself.

Claire cut off some chicken wire from a big roll to create a "pillow" in the vase. It was going to be a dense arrangement, so it would need the support. She went off to a table in the corner where she could work with minimal distractions. Sophie followed. Claire started with the king protea, resting the bloom on the rim to one side of the vase. Next, she trimmed the sprays of smoke bush. She tucked them into the chicken wire on the opposite side of the king protea. She trimmed the sprays of small protea and stood back to appraise it with a critical eye. She wanted a nearly horizontal line of protea sprays from one side to the other, so she cut the stems to sit slightly above the rim of the vessel. Next came the yarrow stems. She trimmed them and placed them in tight, low clusters at the front of the vase, filling the space under the proteas. She finished by adding in the stems of sedum, trimming one to pop out through the yarrow at the front of the vase and others at the back. A cardinal rule: Never forget about the back of an arrangement.

She stepped a few feet away to peer at what she had created. Knowing when to stop was tricky. A smile came over her face. Yes. She was happy with this.

Claire realized that someone was nearby and looked up to see a guy she didn't know staring at her with odd intensity.

"Are you Claire Murphy?"

"Sorry?" she said, blinking.

"Are you the same Claire Murphy who won the Blooms Proclaim contest?"

"That's me." She wondered how he knew. This guy was in his late teens, she guessed. He wore bland clothes—blue shirt, black pants. Terrible acne, which made her feel a little sad for him. But that didn't mean she wanted him to hit on her. It was nice of him to try, but he was way too young for her.

"Will you sign this?" He held out a paper napkin to her.

"You've got to be kidding." He wanted her autograph? She could not have been more mystified. "You like flowers?"

He shrugged. "Eh, they're okay. I don't not like them. But this is for my mom. She loved your bouquet. She tacked up the newspaper picture on the bulletin board in our garage."

Claire would have liked to say something, but no words came to mind. She just stood there, gaping like a hooked fish. This had never happened to her before. Even when she won the contest, there was little fanfare. A picture of her arrangement, plus the recipe, had gone into the local newspaper. Her housemates didn't notice and used it to line the cat's litter box.

Sophie stepped in to help Claire. "So, sweetie, is your mama a florist?"

The guy did a double take when he turned to Sophie and caught sight of her cleavage. "No. She wants to be, but for now she's just doing flowers for friends out of the garage. I work here at the hotel. I was sweeping up leaves and flowers that you people drop everywhere—"

True. The floor in the conference room was littered with discards. Typical of florists.

"—and overheard that guy"—he pointed to Jim Turner— "complain about you. When he said Claire Murphy, I started looking around. Then I saw your flower bouquet. I figured it must be you."

He again held out the napkin to Claire and a pen, and something about that jerked her into action. "What's your mother's name?"

"Lisa."

Claire wrote: *To Lisa. Keep arranging! Claire Murphy*

Claire's birthday had taken a turn for the better. She couldn't keep from smiling.

ℓⁱℓⁱℓ

Then came the afternoon breakout circle. Like the morning circle, it did not go well. Claire wondered about Jim Turner's phone call with his girlfriend—he seemed to be in a particularly foul mood.

Jim Turner read from his notes in a monotone voice. "Business-woman Mary Kay Ash always said that you should imagine every person who comes into your store is wearing a big sign that says, 'Make me feel important.' If you keep that in mind every day, your business will flourish. So will your life." He dropped his notes in his lap. "That's bogus. I tried, every day, to make my girlfriend feel important, and now she's breaking up with me."

See? *Just* what Claire had thought. Those yellow carnations had been a clear message.

"Bless your heart," Sophie said, placing a hand on his shoulder as the rest of the circle nodded sympathetically.

Claire had no sympathy for him. "How did you try to make your girlfriend feel important?"

"She loves flowers," he said. "That's how we met. She came into my shop to get flowers just for herself. That doesn't happen very often. So I sent her a bouquet of flowers and asked her for a date."

"What kinds of flowers did you send her?" Claire said.

"Just whatever we had too much of."

"Remainders," Claire said, pinching her eyes shut, squeezing her hands together. This was painful. "There's the problem, right there."

"What?"

"Well, if she knows flowers like I think she does, she would be aware that you're sending her a careless bouquet. No theme. No message."

He rolled his eyes. "I sent flowers to her every day until she agreed to go out with me. And every day since then. There's a theme in that."

"Every day?" Claire said. "You might be overwhelming her. Some women wouldn't like that."

"But some would," Sophie said. "I would love it if a man treated me like that." She cast a side-glance at Jim Turner just as he looked at her. Their eyes met.

What was happening here? "Um, should we role-play how to make customers feel important?" Claire asked.

Eyes still on Sophie, Jim gave a slow nod, then his phone buzzed and he answered it. Seconds ticked by as the group sat watching him until he pulled the phone away long enough to say, "Do the role-play. I've got to take this call," and left.

All eyes turned to Claire as she pointed to a woman whose bottle-blond hair was scooped up like an ice cream swirl. "Here's an example from my shop. Let's say the store is full of customers and you're working alone. A customer has called in to order flowers, but she keeps changing her mind about what to say on the card. Now a line is forming at the register and the customers are glaring at you while you're on the phone. How would you handle the customer on the phone?"

The woman crossed her ankles and put her hands in her lap. "She is my top priority. I would tell that customer that I had all the time in the world."

"Really?" Claire didn't expect that.

"That's exactly what we're supposed to do, aren't we? Make each customer feel like they're the reason we're in business." The ice-cream-swirl woman looked to Jim Turner for confirmation as he rejoined the circle.

"Exactly right," he said. He turned to Claire, eyebrows raised. "So how did you handle it?"

Claire cleared her throat. "I told the customer to call back when she knew what she wanted to say on the card."

The woman across the circle looked horrified. Jim Turner let out a loud scoff. "Yet another reason why MaryBeth sent you to customer service rehab."

Hold on a minute. Just hold on. Claire narrowed her eyes. "How do you know MaryBeth?"

"MaryBeth? Our families are old friends." His lips lifted in the corners, like he was attempting a smile. "She asked me to get to know you during this conference."

"Why?"

More of that odd smile. "You know MaryBeth. She wants everyone to be friends."

That, Claire knew, was true. But there was something else in his eyes, like he knew something she didn't. Something was afoot.

eight

Minds are like flowers; they open only when the time is right.
—*Stephen Richards*

fter a dinner of rubber chicken, dried-out rice, and a limp, overdressed salad, Claire was even more determined to skip the Christian magician act tonight. She'd had enough magic nonsense to last her a lifetime. Instead, she thought about going for a run to get some exercise. But Sophie wouldn't hear of it.

"Everyone says that Ivan the Illusionist is supposed to be fabulous," Sophie said, which Claire highly doubted. "Please, please, please? I don't want to go alone."

Reluctantly, Claire buckled. They returned to the conference room where they'd spent the entire day, settled into the same uncomfortable metal folding chairs, and waited for the show to begin. The lecturer's podium had been moved, and in its place was a large black box.

Did all magicians use a black box? She only knew one magician, and she tried not to think about him. But in the lull before the performance, Claire's mind traveled to the last time she'd been onstage with Chris Reid, acting as his assistant—the senior class put on a talent show during the last week of high school. It had been a big deal for Chris to be allowed to participate. He had been in so much trouble over the year that the principal wanted to ban him from all public gatherings. His aunt Rose intervened, like she usually did.

Chris surprised everyone, including Claire, with a daring new trick using a ring of fire. She knew it was his way of tweaking the principal. Bravely, Claire walked right through it. It had gone so well that the audience rose to give them a standing ovation. Chris took Claire's hand for a bow, but then he whirled her into his arms and bent her backward for a dramatic kiss. Best kiss ever. She floated on a cloud for days, weeks. It was the start of the best summer of her life.

With a sigh, she dropped her chin. *And then Chris had to go and ruin everything.*

Loud, dramatic music signaled the start of the show. A big puff of smoke appeared, and Ivan the Illusionist slowly emerged out of the large black box, wearing a black eye mask like the Lone Ranger and a big red flashy cape. Sophie gasped so loudly that Claire almost burst out in a laugh. So cheesy!

Ivan the Illusionist moved like an old man, climbing out of the box with great effort, nearly falling a few times before both feet made it onto the stage, then he shuffled slowly around the stage to peer at the audience. He spoke in a thick Eastern European accent, so overdone that it only added to the cheesiness. Why had she let Sophie talk her into coming?

Sophie jabbed her with her elbow. "Look! Look what he's doing now!"

Ivan the Illusionist had levitated himself a few inches off the ground. Seriously? Such a kid's birthday party trick. Positioned diagonally, he stood on the ball of one foot that was farthest from the audience. The Balducci levitation trick. Sophie loved it.

Then Ivan reached into the box to lift an empty vase and set it on a small table. He filled the vase with water, also found in the box. He faced the audience and pulled a flower bouquet out of his sleeve, first the right one, then the left. Claire knew that flower ring trick. He set the flowers in the vase. From where she was sitting, they actually looked real.

Next, Ivan asked for an audience member to come up, and a woman jumped at the chance. Ivan took one of the flowers out of the vase and held it out to her, but the bud fell off. "It broke off on me!" he said in his thick accent.

Claire's head jerked up. He had just used flower shop jargon. *Broke off* was a common phrase.

"Does this ever happen to you?" he asked, and the audience murmured, nodding. "Wouldn't it be wonderful if you could just . . ." Ivan reached down to pick it up off the stage and plop it back on the stem. He waved the flower in the air. "If you could just magically put that bud right back where it belonged."

The audience clapped. Claire's opinion of the cheesy magician had lifted ever so slightly. He handed the woman the flower, but as she reached out to take it, she knocked the bud off again. "Not to worry," Ivan said, which sounded more like "Not to vorry." He reached down and replaced it again. The woman was astounded, the audience entertained. But Claire knew that trick too. There was a lever on the stem so the magician could make the flower disconnect and connect again with a silent click. Ivan turned to the vase and took a flower out to hand to her. "For you, madam." She left the stage, sniffing the flower.

Clever. Old Ivan must have fresh flowers in the vase along with those fake ones. Claire knew enough about magic acts to know that Ivan had diverted everyone's attention to watch one thing while he quietly did something else.

Hmm. Ivan the Illusionist's mystique was growing on her.

Then Ivan took the entire bouquet out of the vase, gathered the flower stems in his hand, and let them go. They levitated. Right in the air! He waved his hand over the bouquet, under the bouquet, to show the audience there were no strings attached.

Claire leaned forward in her chair. There were all kinds of

132

ways to create the illusion of levitation, but it was just that—an illusion. She knew most of the basic tricks. She knew how cards and phones could be levitated—all through thread, tape, and the infamous sleight of the hand. All these tricks took a little practice, but anyone could do them.

But how was Ivan the Illusionist able to levitate a heavy bouquet of flowers?

Out of the black box, Ivan lifted up a birdcage with a dove. He covered it with his cape, and then it disappeared. Sophie squealed with delight, but Claire knew the wire birdcage was designed to collapse. The dove might've seemed lifelike, even moving its wings, but it wasn't real. The loud music masked sounds, and the magician never stood still—techniques to divert the audience's attention to later confound them. The human brain was constantly filling in gaps, so in the time that the magician forced spectators to look at one thing, he had created an illusion.

Ivan's next acts were just as predictable—engaging audience members with card tricks, bending pencils, pulling a rabbit out of his hat. Looking around, Claire could see that the audience was totally into Ivan the Illusionist. Attention was riveted to the stage, looking for his secrets. She yawned, determined not to be drawn in. Not anymore.

Instead, Claire took out her sketch pad and started to draw the fine petals of a dahlia blossom, half listening to the magician's spiel. She noticed the hotel employee, the boy with acne who had asked for her autograph, push a cart full of coffee pitchers and platters of what she hoped was a dessert. She was hungry. She looked at her menu—*beignets*, according to the card. *Call them what you will*, she thought. *Those are donut holes.*

Now and then, she would look at Ivan to see what he was up to now. He had pulled a long rectangular Pyrex tray with sides out of his black box and set it on the ground.

"How in the world did he fit so much into that box?" Sophie said, awed.

Claire had to smile. There was an entire industry that created products for magicians to use. Most likely, the tray was collapsible. Ivan the Illusionist shuffled back to the black box, reached in, and pulled out another large glass pitcher of water. A frail old man, he had trouble lifting the heavy pitcher, but once he had a secure grip, he shuffled back to the Pyrex tray and poured the water into it. Twice more, he went back to his black box to get another pitcherful of water. He filled the tray to the top with the water. Satisfied, he said, "And now, I am going to walk on water." *Valk on vater.* Everyone, even Claire, leaned forward in their seats. She hadn't seen this trick before.

Slowly, because Ivan seemed to do everything slowly, he lifted a leg and placed one wobbly foot on the tray. He lifted his other leg and nearly fell. Hands waving, he recovered his balance and took another step on the water. Again, nearly falling, he caught himself just in time. Little by little, he made his way across the long tray. The audience cheered.

Not bad for an old guy, Claire thought.

Ivan the Illusionist went to the front of the stage. "But all of you know that was a trick. There is only one who truly defied gravity and walked on water. His name is Jesus."

Out of his cape, he pulled a large light bulb. "*Abracadabra* is the most universally understood word in the world. It's actually Aramaic, and it means, 'As I speak, I now create.' In the book of Genesis, God's first words were, 'Let there be light.' And that is what God continues to do, when he sent his Son to be the Light of the World." He released the light bulb, and like the flower bouquet, it levitated.

Watching him, an odd uneasiness filled Claire, a sense of familiarity. Of déjà vu.

And then Ivan dropped his phony accent. "You come to a magic show to be entertained by illusions. Each of these tricks is done by fooling your perception of reality. That's all these magic tricks are. Tonight, I want you to leave knowing there *is* an alternate reality—but this one can be trusted. No trickery involved. The

Light of the World is the only one you can trust." The light bulb turned on, and the audience gasped. They started to clap and cheer for the magician, and he took off his hat to bow.

Suddenly, Claire felt a head-to-toe shaft of hot surprise sizzle through her body. As vivid as a shock of electricity, though it took her a moment to identify why. And then she got it.

She *knew* him! She knew Ivan the Illusionist! He might have worn a disguise, spoken in a fake accent, acted like a frail old man, but she had no doubt Ivan was Christopher Reid.

Boiling anger rose up inside Claire. Her heart started pounding, her hands started shaking. Chris was the one who had caused so much trouble for Rose and Jaime and Tessa, and for her. He was the reason the girls had all fled from Sunrise, never to return. He had ruined everything. *Everything!*

Claire lost it. She strode over to the long table of refreshments that had been set out for the attendees to enjoy after the show ended. That big platter of donut holes was just calling to her. She picked up a handful and hurled it at the magician. Then another, and another. They kept falling short.

Ivan stopped bowing to look out at the audience to try and find who was throwing things at the stage.

Claire grabbed a tray, moved closer to throw more handfuls, and finally nailed him in the stomach. "Don't clap for him! He's a cheat! A fake!"

The room grew silent as the crowd stopped clapping. Ivan ducked as donut holes pelted him.

"You! You of all people! You are my worst nightmare! I never wanted to see you again. Not ever!" Claire had emptied the platter of donut holes, so she went back for another. She turned and threw a donut hole that nailed Ivan right in the forehead.

Jim Turner rose to his feet and shook his fist at Claire. "Stop that woman! Stop her! She's here to make trouble!"

It was as if Jim Turner had yelled "Fire!" Suddenly, pandemonium broke loose. Chairs toppled over as attendees made a run for the exits. Claire kept throwing donut holes at Ivan the Illusionist until a security guard arrived and grabbed the platter and her arm to make her stop. He escorted her to the hotel manager's office, where she was told to settle down, sit down, and wait for the police to arrive.

nine

Flowers grow back, even after they are stepped on. So will I.
—Unknown

Claire tried to explain to the hotel manager that she had a good reason to disrupt the magician's act, but before she could say much, Jim Turner burst into the office, Sophie trailing behind him.

He pointed at Claire. "That woman should be banned from the conference. She's done nothing but stir up trouble, all day long."

"Banned? Me?!" Claire tried to stand up, but the security guard had a hand on her shoulder and pressed her back down onto the chair.

"And no matter what MaryBeth said about your *amazing* flower skills, I will not hire you."

MaryBeth said that? Even in the chaos, it was a nice compliment to hear. Claire scoffed. "I would never consider working for Turner Flowers."

"Then you'd better start looking for a job."

Hold on. "What does that mean?"

Jim Turner flashed her that odd smile again. "Because Mary-Beth is selling Same Day Delivery to Turner Flowers. She hoped I'd get to know you during this conference so you could keep your job, but there's no way I would ever let you set foot in any of my shops." He took a few steps to the door, then stopped and turned around, snapping his fingers in the air. "After I spread your name around Savannah, no one will hire you. How's that for a magic trick?"

He disappeared down the hall, but Sophie remained at the door-jamb. "Don't you worry, sugar. I'll go tell him that you were only having a little hissy fit."

"But I wasn't!" Claire's voice rose an octave. Didn't matter. Sophie was gone.

The hotel manager turned wearily to Claire with long-suffering in his voice. "Now, what exactly happened?"

Before Claire could get started, the desk phone rang and the hotel manager answered it. He listened, sighed deeply, and said, "I'll be right there." He left his office without another word.

Claire gave a sideways look at the security guard, a stout man with extravagant gray eyebrows. "I think I'll just be off then."

Unfortunately, he took his work far too seriously. "Not a chance. Police are on their way."

"Seriously?" She was just about to list her objections when she saw Ivan the Illusionist standing at the open door in full magician's garb.

He took a step inside the office and put a hand on the security guard's shoulder. "Would you mind if I speak to this woman alone?"

The security guard shook his head. "I need to stay. She's exhibited dangerous behavior."

"Dangerous?" Claire's jaw dropped. "I threw donut holes at him!"

The security guard lifted his bushy eyebrows. "Scuffles always start small. They escalate from there."

"To what?" Claire said. "Cream puffs?"

Ivan lifted a hand. "I'll take full responsibility. You can stay right outside the door if you like. I'd just like to speak to her before the police arrive."

The security guard gave that some serious thought, helped along after Ivan slipped him a twenty-dollar bill. "I reckon it'd be okay." But he walked over to the hotel manager's desk and made a show of confiscating scissors, a stapler, and sharpened pencils, as if Claire had already staked out her next weapon. Holding everything against his round belly, he narrowed his eyes at her. "I'll be right outside that door."

As the door closed, there was a heavy quiet that filled the room. Ivan took off his hat, his mask, then his beard, and set them on the desk.

Yep. It was him. Christopher Reid.

ℓ·ℓ·ℓ

Chris sat in the hotel manager's chair, facing her. Appraising her. "Wow. You look great, Claire. Really, really good."

In spite of herself, a spiral of pleasure started in her. She didn't look her best tonight, but she was definitely better looking than she had been in high school. Over the years, she'd lost weight as she gained a daily habit of exercising, and she'd finally found a hairstylist who knew what to do with wild, curly hair. "And you . . . you look like an old man."

"Yeah. My agent suggested it."

He had an *agent*? Claire had to swallow a smile as this thought ran through her head: *He has an agent who booked him gigs like this one? Sad!*

Reading her mind (something he'd always been good at), he said, "My agent's brother-in-law runs these customer service conferences. He customizes them for specific industries. Tonight's was flowers. Tomorrow night, I'll be in Charleston at a grocery clerk rehab conference." He shrugged. "Steady work.

Attentive audiences. Interesting travel. Good money. Can't complain."

"And better than jail." That was snarky.

Chris ignored her. He leaned his elbows on the desk, clasping his hands together. "So have you been in Savannah for the last seven years?"

She nodded.

"I've looked everywhere for you. I even contacted your dad."

Did he? Her dad had never told her. "He knew not to let you know where I was."

"He told me you were safe and you were happy."

Good for Dad.

"*Are* you happy, Claire?"

She took in a sharp breath. She hadn't expected *that*. Not from Chris. And she wasn't sure she wanted to answer him. What business was it of his, anyway? He'd lost the right to know anything years ago. "Why should it matter?" she said, tapping her fingers on her knees in a poor facsimile of nonchalance.

His eyes, beneath his fake gray eyebrows, grew soft and tender. "It matters to me if you're happy. It's always mattered."

Oh no. No, no, no. Not again. He had certainly fooled her once, but she wasn't nearly as trusting or naive as she'd been when she was seventeen. Not anymore. She crossed her arms and tapped her foot, growing impatient. "If that's what you came to say, then you said it. Feel free to leave and let Barney Fife back in."

Chris leaned back, as if to convey that he was doing the questioning here. "I can press charges, you know. Assault and battery. Disturbing the peace. Disorderly conduct."

She slapped her hands on her knees. "Donut holes!"

"*Beignets*. And they were stale. They hurt! And I have plenty of witnesses out there to corroborate the facts."

"Then just go ahead and press charges. Let someone else take the blame, like you always do."

He gave her a sharp look. A long moment passed before he said in a quiet voice, "Things aren't always the way they seem."

She coughed a laugh. "Says the magician."

"I can say it because I *am* a magician. That's what I love best about magic. It can shock people into realizing there's more going on than they know."

"Unless you know the magician's tricks. Then you're only disappointed."

"So the end of my show disappointed you?"

"What? The come-to-Jesus moment? Was that the spiel you used to buy a 'get out of jail free' card?"

"It's not a spiel." He spoke firmly. "I use my performances to share my faith."

Right. She wasn't buying it. She'd always known him to be the kind of guy who could talk the spots right off a leopard. "I'll bet you change each show to suit your audience." He probably had magic tricks for every belief system. He was *that* clever. *That* shrewd. *That* much of a chameleon.

He took in a deep breath and let it out. "Claire, you think the only view is your view. But there are other ways of seeing things. Maybe what you see isn't the whole story."

"I know what I saw seven years ago at Rose's."

He lifted his chin and looked her straight in the eyes. "You *think* you know."

She stared back at him.

He exhaled, like he could see he wasn't convincing her of anything. "You should go to Sunrise. Go see Rose. Talk to her."

"I will never go back. Neither will Jaime or Tessa. You ruined it for us. You burned the whole town down."

"The fire burned Rose's shop and damaged the two buildings on either side. I didn't burn the whole town down." He held her gaze with a stubbornness that surprised her. "And I didn't have a 'get out of jail free' card. I spent a year in a state prison. That time changed me."

Did it? She wondered.

He sensed her skepticism. "God picked me up and set me on solid ground. And I thank him for it every day." He crossed his arms against his chest. "Jaime's come back. She's working at Rose's."

"No she is *not*."

"*Yes* she is so." A slight smile tugged at his lips. "You don't know everything, Claire Murphy."

"I know what I know."

"Do you? Because I think you just know what you think you know."

For one brief moment, they were bantering the way they used to.

He lifted one eyebrow. "So how did I walk on water?"

She shrugged. "Every magic trick has an explanation. You taught me that."

"Yep. You were a quick study. Best assistant I've ever had."

Do not look at him, she told herself. *Don't do it*. She kept her eyes on the top of the desk. She refused to get sucked back into his charms. She'd been down that road before, and it took a long, long time before she felt like herself again. He was the reason she had a habit of dating guys a few times, then ghosting them. Trust issues. She didn't trust *herself*. Clearly, she had terrible judgment about men.

"So what's the explanation?"

She wasn't entirely sure. "Your shoes. Clear heels?"

He lifted his foot in the air so she could see his shoe for herself. "Nope."

"Was there a top to the tray?"

He shook his head.

No, she hadn't thought so. Water sloshed as he nearly tumped over.

"Sometimes, the simplest explanation is the correct one."

Right. He had taught her that too. But she couldn't quite figure out this trick.

"See? You don't know everything." He was enjoying this . . . too much.

"I know that you chose Tessa over me." That seemed to put the damper on him.

His eyes sobered. "I suppose it might have seemed like I chose Tessa over you."

"It was my birthday. You were holding her in your arms on *my* birthday. I saw you! Don't deny it." Claire had always felt a twinge of jealousy over Tessa's God-given looks. Every guy in high school drooled over her. Truly drooled. Faces went slack, mouths hung open. Jaime and Claire called Tessa a male magnet. They said it in a teasing way, but there was truth behind it. And envy.

He let out a sigh. "I'm not denying anything. Whatever you saw, it didn't mean I didn't care for you. I did. I still do." He picked up his hat and beard and mask and went to the door. "You know, Claire, it's not such a bad thing to get to a point where you realize life isn't working out very well on your own. To know you need Christ."

As his hand reached the doorknob, she said, "Do *not* tell Rose or Jaime how to find me. Promise me."

He turned to face her. He was silent while he mulled this over. "Can I ask why?"

"No, you can't." She wasn't a teenager anymore. She'd learned a lot about life in the last seven years. And she didn't want Chris to be the one who set things in motion for her. If she ever did go back to Sunrise to face Rose, she wanted to be the one to do it. "The least you can do is to honor my request."

Such a sad look came over him that she had to look away. Her resolve to remain aloof and detached was melting faster than ice cream in a Savannah heat wave.

"Claire, I am sorry I hurt you. I am truly, truly sorry."

She had to look away.

"You should go home to Sunrise. Go home or . . ."

She jerked her hand up and narrowed her eyes. "Or what?"

143

"Or I'll reconsider pressing charges for battery and assault."
He lifted a finger in the air. "Maybe . . . aggravated assault." He
bent slightly, like he was almost bowing goodbye to her. "One
more thing. Happy birthday, Claire."

If she had more donut holes, she would've pelted him.

ten

There are always flowers for those who want to see them.
—Henri Matisse

The police never did show up. Apparently, Chris told the hotel manager Claire was part of the act but the audience misunderstood and things got out of control. The hotel manager didn't seem entirely fobbed off by that explanation, but he did seem happy to call off the police. Bad publicity for the hotel, he said.

However, he told Claire she had to leave the hotel and forgo the second day of the conference. So she packed up her little overnight bag to head home.

She had mixed feelings about leaving. Sorry to leave Sophie, whom she kind of enjoyed. Not sorry to leave the rest of the conference. Sorry to have to tell MaryBeth that she'd been kicked out. Not sorry to tell MaryBeth that Jim Turner was spreading lies about purchasing Same Day Delivery.

Later, at home, when Claire was trying to fall asleep, she couldn't stop thinking of Chris. A little spark of happiness kept trying to flare up while they were alone in the hotel manager's office. Frustrating. Seven years had passed and she still struggled to tamp down her feelings for him.

When she had first arrived in Savannah, that very first Sunday, she'd gone to church with MaryBeth and heard the pastor preach, "Block the pain and you block everything."

Not a bad strategy when you felt a deep ache in your heart. She wasn't sure that's what the pastor had in mind, but she took the advice and did her best to block all thoughts and feelings of Chris.

For the first time in seven years, she let herself picture Chris as she remembered him. His face came to her in little bursts, like a jigsaw puzzle taking shape. The way his eyebrows shot up in surprise. The cleft in his chin. The mischievous sparkle in those blue, blue eyes when he knew he had pulled off a trick. Seeing Chris had released all kinds of buried emotions. Anger, sadness, grief, loss . . . and love. He'd been her first love. Her first everything.

They'd met in English class during senior year. She sat in a corner in the back row—the best spot to avoid getting called on by the teacher. It was her seat. By senior year in a small high school, everyone had their seats. One day Claire had come into the classroom, and there was a guy who looked a lot like Prince Harry, sitting in her chair. Chris. She told him to move and he wouldn't budge. He patted his lap and gave her a flirty wink. "You can sit right here, darlin'."

And so she did! She sat down on him.

That moment set the stage for their "spirited" relationship, which took off from there. All senior year, they were inseparable. They'd go roaring around town in his noisy old Ford Mustang. He helped her search for Nana on those frightening nights when she went missing. His friendship, his lightness and laughter, his daring ways—he'd been a great comfort to her over the year as she lost her grandparents and then their home. Chris helped Claire to not take life too seriously—something she was prone to do.

Chris had been recently released from a stint in juvenile hall and was staying with his aunt. Rose Reid, for all her practical, no-

nonsense ways, had a blind side when it came to her nephew. Chris was the son she'd never had. In her eyes, he could do no wrong.

But Chris did plenty of wrong. Rose just didn't see it. Or maybe she didn't want to see it.

Maybe, Claire admitted to herself in the wee hours of her sleepless night, maybe she didn't want to see it either. Neither did Jaime, or Tessa. Especially beautiful, male-magnet Tessa.

As Claire tossed and turned in the night, she thought about returning to Sunrise, like Chris had suggested. Mainly thought about why she would not do it.

ℓ·ℓ·ℓ

The next morning, Claire arrived early at Same Day Delivery. One step inside the door and she closed her eyes to take in a deep breath, inhaling the clean, sweet perfume of the flower shop. Her favorite scent in all the world.

And then her pleasure evaporated. She heard K-Love blasting on the radio in the workshop, and the sound of the cooler door opening and shutting. MaryBeth was already in the shop.

Claire set her purse under the counter. Before she went to the workshop to face MaryBeth, she mentally rehearsed her explanation as to why she wasn't at the conference.

The radio turned off in the workshop. "Sweet pea, is that you?"

Claire braced herself. She had never told MaryBeth about why she left Sunrise, but maybe the time had come. She went back to the workshop to find MaryBeth processing Zinderella zinnias—large, spherical blooms that were both gorgeous and lush. Perfect focal flowers.

She glanced over at Claire. "Hold on just one minute till I finish up with these darlin's."

All zinnias were MaryBeth's darlin's. Her go-to sturdy summer flower. She had specific flowers for every season. Her summer list included standard hothouse roses, hydrangeas, calla lilies, zinnias. And carnations, of course. After all these years, Claire still became sad when she saw the selection. Summer offered such bounty of beauty. The possibilities were endless! Anemone, black-eyed Susan, foxglove, Amaranthus, ranunculi. MaryBeth finally agreed to add sunflowers to her summer list, but only because Claire had verified to her that they could hold up for long periods of time without wilting. A flower had to prove its worth—in both dependability and affordability—for MaryBeth to even consider ordering it. Mostly, the latter.

Claire waited patiently until MaryBeth put the processed zinnias into a bucket of water. She set the bucket in the cooler and turned to Claire.

The time to tell all had come.

Unfortunately, there wasn't time to tell.

MaryBeth folded her arms across her chest. "Last night I got a call from Jim Turner. Sweet pea, what on earth has gotten into you?"

Claire lifted a finger in the air. "I can explain!"

MaryBeth held her hands in the air like a stop sign. "Don't even bother. It doesn't matter anymore. As soon as Arthur arrives, there's something important we have to discuss."

A sick feeling started in Claire's stomach and spread throughout her entire body. She hadn't felt this way since the night her dad told her he was moving her grandmother to a facility. Change was coming, and it wasn't going to be good.

eleven

All the flowers of all the tomorrows are in the seeds of today.
—Native American proverb

As soon as Arthur arrived, MaryBeth closed the workshop door and sat on a stool, ready for that chat. Apparently, Claire learned, MaryBeth and Arthur had been in negotiations to sell Same Day Delivery to Turner Flowers for quite some time. "Now, I know you had a hope to buy Same Day Delivery," MaryBeth said, "but the truth is, you don't have the money to buy it. This shop has been our livelihood. It's our retirement package. The whole kit and caboodle. If we sold it to you, we'd have to be your bank, and you'd be paying us in installments. That's assuming that you make a success of the shop. What if things took a downturn? Flowers rise and fall with the economy. They're a luxury, not a necessity. If things go bad, Arthur and me, we don't have years and years to recover. We're getting older. We need the money now."

"But I would make it a success." Claire knew she would. She just needed the chance.

"Sweet pea, you just got kicked out of a conference designed to improve customer service skills. If that doesn't tell you something about yourself, I don't know what will."

Claire opened her mouth to defend herself, but MaryBeth wagged a finger in the air.

"I had such high hopes for you, sweet pea. I told Jim Turner to keep a lookout for you. I was hoping he would hire you on, so you could stay right here. And what happened? You got yourself ejected because you lost your temper."

"It wasn't my fault! You see, I recognized—"

"Jim Turner told me you were belligerent in the breakout circles."

"Belligerent?!"

"That's what he said. According to Jim Turner, you sounded like you knew better than the customer about what flowers they should send. I had no words to defend you, Claire. I've seen you do the same thing with customers at the shop. Always suggesting something else." She let out a deep sigh. "I'm sorry. I really am. I know you're disappointed, but Arthur and me, we've done all we can for you. You're twenty-five years old. It's high time to figure things out on your own."

Claire felt her stomach rise and fall like lead. Her vision grew distorted, and she blinked to get it back into focus. She tried to keep her game face on, tried to remain calm. Later. She could fall apart later. "But you promised. You promised to sell the store to me."

"No, sweet pea. *We* never promised. Did we, Arthur?"

As if on cue, both Claire and MaryBeth turned to look at Arthur. He swiveled, suddenly terribly interested in straightening the tools on the peg wallboard.

Arthur was the one who had told Claire that she'd be a good choice to take over Same Day Delivery one day. She had counted on his words as a promise. But MaryBeth had never been a part of that conversation. She'd never said a word about selling the store to Claire. Only Arthur had. And MaryBeth ran the show. Big mistake.

ℓ·ℓ·ℓ

A numb feeling settled over Claire, which turned out to be a blessing. She made it through work all day without any unpleasant emotions rising to the surface, she handled customers very politely, and she processed a large order of carnations for an upcoming wedding. She kept as busy as possible to crowd out troubling thoughts of the future, or unbidden ones from the past. *Later*, she reminded herself. *Later, you can fall apart.*

At the end of the day, she arrived home to an empty house. Another blessing. Her housemates had some church event tonight and wouldn't be back until late. She tossed her purse on the little table by the door, kicked off her shoes, and flopped onto the couch. In just two days, she had lost everything and everyone that mattered to her. She still had her dad, of course, but he was thousands of miles away. She had thought, mistakenly, that she belonged to MaryBeth and Arthur. But she didn't. She didn't belong to anyone. She didn't belong anywhere.

Now, she could fall apart.

Claire wasn't sure how many tissues she'd gone through when an incoming text buzzed. Dabbing her eyes, she lifted her phone to read it.

Sophie
CONGRATULATIONS!!!!

Claire
For what?

The Savannah Blooms contest! YOU WON!!!

Claire bolted upright.

How do you know?

Just announced on Facebook. Aren't you watching?

No.

For goodness' sakes, girl. Why not?

Because she forgot all about it.

Got some bad news today at work. My employers are selling their shop to Turner Flowers. I'll be out of a job soon.

Well, don't you worry. After winning Savannah Blooms, you'll be getting more job offers than a dog has fleas!

Hope you're right! Doubt it, but I hope you're right.

ℓ·ℓ·ℓ

Sophie's optimistic prediction was wrong, just like Claire had thought it would be. That week, she did receive some local media attention for winning the coveted award, lots of pats on the back, but not a single job offer. All because of Jim Turner. He spread the story about Claire's outburst all over town, and it grew bigger with every telling. Sophie said she heard the words "domestic terrorist" linked to Claire's name. Ridiculous! But effective.

Since the conference, Claire had become a flower shop pariah. She thought of striking out on her own and arranging flowers from her kitchen, but when she looked into it, she found out that Jim Turner's influence reached to local suppliers. No one would give her a line of credit. There was no way she could buy flowers for clients' events without that.

Less than one week to go before the Same Day Delivery business became Turner Flowers. That stupid ditty "Turn her day around with Turner Flowers" was stuck in Claire's head, like a song on repeat. Well, Jim Turner sure did turn her day around. Her life had turned upside down.

One morning, MaryBeth put a hand on Claire's shoulder.

"Sweet pea, why don't you go get yourself a new hairdo? That always makes me feel better. I'll treat you to my gal. She's a whiz."

Noooo thank you. MaryBeth's hairdo was something straight out of the 1970s. It never, ever changed. Very Betty White–ish. "Thanks, but my hair stylist is quite territorial. She'd be furious with me if I went elsewhere." That was partly true.

Later that day, MaryBeth said she had to cut back on Claire's hours.

"Cut back?" Claire was an hourly employee. How could she manage to pay her bills if her hours were cut back?

"With the shop going to Turner Flowers soon, I just don't want Same Day Delivery to take on any new orders and run up a tab to get more flowers. I think it's best to use up the inventory we have with walk-ins. And I can handle those, sweet pea."

When Claire said she'd like to stay and help, MaryBeth hemmed and hawed, and then gave her the truth. "Sweet pea, customers are a little put off by how woebegone you've been lately. I think that maybe you need a little time to yourself."

"But I don't," Claire said. She had way too much time to herself. Her thoughts were not good ones. Talking to customers, even annoying ones, was better than thinking. "I'll try to act less woebegone." Whatever *that* meant. It was true that the famous Claire temper had disappeared. She didn't feel like eating, she didn't feel like sleeping. There was nothing to look forward to, nothing to feel happy about, and nothing she could bring herself to do. Was that what being woebegone meant?

Claire set aside her woebegone feelings and tried to be clearheaded and rational. At one point, when the store was empty, she took out a pad of paper to brainstorm, to examine her options.

Where should she go? What else could she do?

The problem was that she didn't want to do anything else with her life but work with flowers. They were all she knew. All she loved. All she counted on. Unlike people, flowers did not disappoint.

But if she wanted to work with flowers, it meant she'd have to move somewhere else far, far away. Those Turners were related to just about everybody in the state of Georgia. Her rent was paid to the end of the month, but she didn't have enough saved to coast along for another month or so. Saving money had never been easy for Claire. She didn't make much at the flower shop, and when she did have a little extra cash, she spent it on flowers. She was under the curse of living paycheck to paycheck. It worked so long as nothing broke.

She thought about emailing her dad, taking him up on his offer to move to Germany. But then what? He never remained long at any base. That scenario had happened all through her childhood. She'd barely have time to make a friend and *boom!* Dad would be sent elsewhere.

It was a recurring cycle in her life, this loneliness. She couldn't seem to outrun it.

MaryBeth came in from the workshop. "Arthur just called. He's coming over to help me do inventory. You can head on home. We'll take everything from here." When she saw the disappointed look on Claire's face, she added, "Sweet pea, I know things haven't worked out the way you wanted, but when the Lord—"

Oh no. Claire braced herself. Here came a platitude.

"—shuts one door, he opens another."

MaryBeth loved those little sayings. She thought of them as cherries on top of ice cream sundaes. Claire thought of them as wimpy Band-Aids over a gaping wound.

twelve

To plant a garden is to believe in tomorrow.
—Audrey Hepburn

As Claire left Same Day Delivery for the last time, MaryBeth reassured her that they'd stay in touch, that they'd see her each week at church, that they'd always be there for her. Claire thanked MaryBeth for everything she'd done for her, meaning it sincerely, all the while knowing that something had ended.

Outside the shop, she looked up. Despite the implosion of her life, the sun had carried on its business of heating the earth. She had a free afternoon, a blue sky, yet nowhere to go where worry wouldn't find her. She felt a familiar looming pessimism settle in, like a houseguest who overstayed.

She started walking toward the Savannah River. It was ninety-five degrees out and who knew what the humidity was. She took a hair elastic out of her purse and twisted it around her curly hair, making a topknot that probably looked silly. But she couldn't stand having it down in this heat.

Down by the riverfront, Claire walked past restaurants, souvenir shops, and T-shirt stores. The Savannah River cast a heavy, humid scent in the summertime. She stopped by the Olympic Torch and watched the slow-rolling river wind its way to the Atlantic. The Savannah River marked the border between Georgia and South Carolina.

Claire walked past a sleeping homeless man and then stopped. She dug into her purse and found a couple of dollars, then returned to tuck them into a cup he had left out for donations. She watched him for a while, wondering about him. When had things gone off the rails for this guy? Had he been young, like she was, when his hopes and dreams were yanked out from under him? Could this be her story one day? She felt as though something inside her had gotten turned in the wrong direction.

She tucked her chin and walked on.

Claire ended up back at her house, sweaty and tired from her walk to nowhere. She kicked off her shoes, changed out of her work clothes, then plopped on the couch to scroll her phone for job openings. Seeing that homeless guy scared her enough that she decided to look outside of flowers for other jobs. She found plenty of fast-food and dog-grooming jobs. *Ick.* Scrolling made her eyes tired, and she closed them for just a moment.

The doorbell rang, startling Claire out of a deep sleep. A moment had turned into an hour. Groggy and disoriented, she stumbled to the door to open it. There stood a sandy-haired young man on the doorstep. He looked like Prince Harry, but he couldn't be. She blinked, rubbed her eyes. Man o' man, this guy was cute.

"It's me," the man said, as if he sensed Claire's dreamlike confusion. "Chris. Chris Reid."

She slammed the door and dove back onto the couch, headfirst. The doorbell rang again. Paused. Rang again. Paused. Rang again.

He wasn't going away.

She sat up, redid her topknot, grabbed some lipstick from her purse and put it on between ring five and ring seven, and opened the door, one hand on a hip. "How did you find me?"

"Abracadabra." Chris waved his hand. "A little internet magic. While I was driving here today, I got to wondering if abracadabra was the very word God used in Genesis 1. You know . . ." He formed a fist with his hand and spread it suddenly, like an explosion. "*Boom.* To start everything going."

What was happening? Who was this Bible-thumping Chris Reid? And why was he here? *That's* the question she needed an answer to. "What are you doing here?"

He held out an envelope to her. "Rose wanted you to have something."

Claire's eyes went wide. Another betrayal! "You *promised* you wouldn't tell her where I was."

"Actually, I didn't promise. You just told me to promise not to tell her. But I did honor your request. I didn't let her know where you are. But I did let her know that I saw you."

Claire took the envelope from him. There was her name written in Rose's neat handwriting. She'd always loved Rose's distinctive cursive. She looked up and noticed an old Ford Mustang parked in front of her house. Seriously? He still drove that thing? She'd forgotten all about it. He had straight piped the exhaust so everyone in town could hear him coming from two blocks away. "You drove all the way from Sunrise to bring me this envelope?"

"I did. Whatever its contents, it's supposed to be important. Rose said so, anyway. She's had it for a while, but she didn't know where to send it. When I told her I'd seen you, she asked me to deliver it."

Slowly, Claire opened the envelope and pulled out the handwritten note to read. In it, Rose asked Claire to consider returning to Sunrise because she was planning to retire soon and wanted her to take over the flower shop. She said she was making the same offer to Jaime and Tessa. However, she said, each of the girls would have to enter a flower contest *and* win it. She wrote that she wanted to make sure each girl still had the fire in her belly for running a flower shop.

Fire in her belly? Claire? She'd always had a flaming inferno in her belly. Until this week.

The last line in Rose's letter gave Claire goose bumps. *All is forgiven*, Rose wrote. *It's time to come home.*

Sure. Right. As if forgiveness was that simple. Snap your fingers and it's done. Twenty-five years may not be a lifetime, but Claire had already learned that lesson. Forgiveness wasn't like a switch to turn on and off. Innocence was not something you could get back.

Claire folded the letter and put it back in the envelope. Chris had been patiently waiting for her to read it. She glanced at him. He looked really hot. The sun was beating down. She should probably invite him in. Offer him a glass of sweet tea.

He tipped his head. "Claire, you look . . ."

She narrowed her eyes, wondering what he was about to say. She didn't look great, she knew that. She was wearing a floppy old T-shirt and cutoff shorts, and her hair was springing out of its topknot. But if he said anything rude, she would slam the door in his face.

The expression on his face didn't say rude. It was soft, his eyes kind. Even his voice sounded tender. "You look . . . like someone who could use a friend."

Sympathy from Chris Reid, of all people, completely took her off guard. She felt tears start rising in her throat. *Do not cry, do not cry.* She hated to cry in front of people! And Chris Reid was top of her list.

He reached out to touch her arm. "So, what's really going on?"

Chris's softness touched Claire in a way that sharpness never could. "I don't know." Claire framed her cheeks with her hands. "I just don't know anything anymore."

thirteen

A rose can never be a sunflower, and a sunflower can never be a rose. All flowers are beautiful in their own way, and that's like women too.
—*Miranda Kerr*

*I*n the little kitchen, while Claire poured Chris a glass of sweet iced tea, she recovered her composure, reminding herself of the damage he had done. She handed him the glass, and he downed it like he was parched. She refilled it and they went into the small living area.

She wondered what he was thinking of her living conditions. This dumpy little house had a garage-sale vibe. She cast glances at him as he walked around the room. He looked a little rumpled from the car ride, but his clothing looked pricey, like he had moved up in the world. Could his magic show be doing that well?

Sitting on the couch, Claire tucked her hands under her. "You shouldn't have bothered to come. I can't go back to Sunrise."

Chris sat across from her on a bean bag, downing the sweet tea refill. He was thirsty. After polishing off the tea, he set the glass on the floor beside him and shifted to get comfortable in the bean bag. One of Claire's housemates had found it on the street and dragged it home. Claire wouldn't go near it. "Why not? Why can't you go back to Sunrise?"

Because it was just too, too hard. But she couldn't admit that to him. Instead, she decided to switch the interviewer roles. "So are you ready to tell your tale?"

His eyebrows lifted. "The 'walking on water' trick? There were Pyrex platforms inside the tray."

Huh. She hadn't thought of that. "I didn't see them."

"Just because you don't see it doesn't mean it's not there."

She gave that some thought. It was just the kind of response she had enjoyed so much in knowing Chris. He had a different way of thinking than most people did. It's why he could trick people so easily. Good magicians could tell who was vulnerable, and Chris was a very good magician.

Don't forget, she reminded herself (though she didn't need the reminding), *that you were one of those vulnerable people.* "Actually, I was referring to the tale of that August night, seven years ago."

"I can tell you part of it. But I think the part you're looking for will have to be told by Rose. And she wants to tell it in person." He crossed one ankle over his knee. "So. Here goes what I can tell you about my tale. After the fire, I pled guilty to a Class D felony and was sentenced to thirty-eight months in a state prison. Got out early for good behavior. It helped that I was a minor when the fire occurred."

She knew most of that by following the story online. Because he had pled guilty, Jaime, Tessa, and Claire didn't need to return to Sunrise to testify in a trial.

"Prison wasn't easy, but I wouldn't trade it. Turned out to be the best thing that ever happened to me."

"Because you had a come-to-Jesus moment?"

He tilted his head. "Now, that's the second time you used that phrase. What does that really mean?"

160

"Your eyes were opened." She sang a high-pitched "ahh" note to emphasize a religious conversion. She knew she was being sarcastic . . . but this *was* Chris Reid. Aka Ivan the Illusionist. He could convince anybody of anything.

He kept his eyes on her. "If it means that I got to a point in my life when I had nowhere else to go, no one else to turn to, when I realized my indescribable need for a Lord and Savior . . . then yeah, you could say I had a come-to-Jesus moment. But it didn't end in that moment. I'm a different person, Claire. My whole purpose in life has changed."

"Uh, you're still a magician. You're still deceiving people."

"I love magic the way you love flowers. But my purpose has changed. What I want to do with my magic shows has changed. I'm not trying to deceive people, not anymore. I want to open their minds to an unseen reality. I want them to know that Jesus saved me. He healed me. He can do it for them." He sat up in the bean bag and rested his elbows on his knees. "And he can do it for you."

She wondered at the meaning of all this. Was he for real? Could he have changed that much? Maybe she was still dreaming. She pinched her bottom to find out and swallowed a yelp. Nope. Definitely not dreaming.

He was thoughtful as he looked at her. "Claire, can't you see how much God loves you? Do you even see how God is at work in your life?"

A scoff burst out of her. "Right. Look at me. Jobless. Soon to be homeless." She lifted up a hand to stop his preaching. "And I do believe in God."

"There's a difference between believing in God and trusting in God. Can you honestly tell me that God wasn't watching out for you when you landed alone in a new city? When you found a job in a flower shop? When you started winning contest after contest for your arrangements?" He leaned forward. "Culminating in winning Savannah Blooms, the most prestigious award in Georgia?"

How did he know *that*?

He read her mind. "Google."

"Well, that and a dollar might buy you a cup of coffee. It doesn't bring any job offers. I can attest to that."

"Claire." His eyes went soft and sweet on her again. "Those contests are recognition of your incredible talent. Something Rose had spotted in you from the day she met you."

The thought struck her heavily, as hard as a kick to the gut. Chris was hitting in her most vulnerable places. But he wasn't doing it to hurt her. He was speaking so tenderly, so kind and caring. She looked out the window at Chris's Ford Mustang. She looked down at the cheap rug on the floor. She did whatever she could to contain herself. She felt as if she was holding back a closet door that was jam-packed. If she dared open it another inch, everything would come tumbling out.

"Look, about Rose. She wants you, Jaime, and Tessa to come to Sunrise. Jaime is back. I've found you. We're trying to find Tessa. Time is of the essence."

"Why? What's the hurry?"

He shrugged, but he didn't hold her gaze. "Rose says she wants to retire."

"Since Jaime is back and wants the store, maybe Rose should just let her have it." Claire tried her best to sound nonchalant, unconcerned, but she didn't mean a word of it. That flower shop was part of her DNA.

"It's not just about the shop. Rose has something important to tell all of you, and she wants to do it in person."

"Why don't you save everybody the trouble and just tell me?"

"Because this part of the story belongs to Rose."

"Well, there's really nothing more I need to know about that August night."

From the look on his face, he didn't believe her. "I think you do."

"I was there too. I saw the fire start."

"We all experience life a little differently. Our brains are different, our world experiences are different."

"It's hard to cast doubt on an eyewitness."

"Oh yeah?" He leaned back and said, "Let me tell you about The Dress Debate of 2015."

She squinted. "What are you talking about?"

"A Scottish mother took a picture of a dress she was considering for her daughter's upcoming wedding. She sent the picture to her daughter, and the two of them disagreed about the colors of the dress. So the daughter posted it on Facebook to get feedback from her friends, and it went viral. Crazytown viral. Some people saw it as white and gold, though it was actually blue and black. Finally, scientists figured out that the difference in perception had to do with how the brain perceives color, based on experience. It's caused a huge stir in the scientific community, lots of studies trying to figure it out. I don't think they've figured it out yet. It's a perfect illustration of how our experiences shape how we perceive things. That's the whole point, Claire. Things aren't always the way they seem to be."

He waited awhile for her to respond, but she didn't know what to say or how to say it. She felt as stuck as molasses on a January morning.

Chris shifted on the bean bag and pulled a folded envelope from his back pocket. He tossed it to her. "Your wad of savings. Money you left behind at Rose's house. She's been wanting you to have it." He rose to his feet. He was thoughtful as he looked at her. "Go home to Sunrise, okay?"

"I can't go back," she said.

"No, you can't go back. But you can go forward." He cleared his throat as he walked to the door, almost as if he wanted to say more but choked the words down. He opened the door, then turned around to say, "It's good to talk to God, Claire."

She remained on the couch, but as soon as she heard the Mustang roar to life, she felt that old wound start festering. What was wrong with her? What was she trying to prove? She had nothing left. Nothing. No one. She looked around the dumpy little house.

Is this how she was going to live the rest of her life? Lonely and alone.

Why couldn't she swallow her pride and go back to Sunrise? Why not? She had nothing to lose that she hadn't already lost.

She jumped off the couch and bolted to the door, opening it just as the Mustang drove off. She ran down the steps to try and catch Chris's attention, but the muffler was too loud. He didn't hear her calling or see her waving to him. The Mustang turned the corner and disappeared, the sound of a way back to Sunrise fading in the distance.

Slowly, she turned and went back into the house. She felt a shaky chill in her middle that spread throughout her body, despite the Savannah heat. She had just stood at a pivotal fork in the road, a right path and a wrong one, clear as a bell. And with her pride keeping her glued to the couch, she'd chosen the wrong one.

fourteen

Love is the flower you've got to let grow.
—John Lennon

Inside the house, Claire flopped on the couch, facedown. Something pinched her stomach and she rolled over to find Rose's letter. Sitting up, she read it again. Tears stung her eyes when she got to that line, *All is forgiven. It's time to come home.* It dawned on Claire that Rose knew the fire wasn't all Chris's fault. It was easy to blame him because . . . he messed up so much. But it wasn't all his fault.

She thought of Chris's parting shot: *"It's good to talk to God."* She lifted her eyes to the ceiling. She'd always believed in God . . . but trusted in herself. And look where that had gotten her. Nowhere else to turn, no one else to turn to.

It's good to talk to God.

She lifted her eyes to the ceiling. "I could use a little help down here, God. Because I have run out of options."

One tear after the other started down her cheeks until she was sobbing, heaving, weeping uncontrollably. She never cried like this . . . not even when her grandparents had died. Not even when her dad left for Germany.

She was wailing so loudly that she nearly missed it—the loud, rumbling, roaring sound of an engine without a muffler. It was only because she was inhaling a deep breath right before another sob that she heard it at all. She jumped off the couch and ran to open the door. There, coming down the street, was the ear-splitting, deafening sound of Chris's Ford Mustang. As the car came to a stop, silence filled the air.

Chris got out of the car and waved. He reached into the back seat and brought out a flower arrangement. "I nearly got to the highway before I realized I'd forgotten to give these to you. They're from Rose. She said you'd know what they meant."

In his arms was an enormous arrangement of yellow roses, the traditional flower meant to convey a longing for the familiar. A floral way to say *Come home.*

She covered her cheeks with her hands as tears started all over again, flooding down her cheeks.

He set the wilted roses on the ground. "Claire," he said, holding the car door wide open, waiting for her to make a move. "Let's go forward."

Claire looked at the wilted flowers, then at Chris, back at her house, and back at Chris. Something hard dissolved inside her. It was like tossing a bath bomb into the tub and watching it disintegrate. Watching it turn into something soft and soothing.

Without a word, she spun around and bolted toward the house. Leaving the front door wide open, she ran into her room and pulled her suitcase from under her bed. She grabbed handfuls of hangers from her closet and threw them into the suitcase, then emptied her small dresser drawers on top. Tossed some important papers and her grandmother's Bible in and sat down on it to make it close. Then tugged the zipper around it and dragged it to the door. There was a chalkboard on the wall for the housemates to leave messages. With a piece of chalk, she wrote, *Heading home*

for good. Rent paid to end of month. Come visit me in Sunrise!
XOXO

Grabbing her purse, she hurried to the door. There was Chris, still standing in the hot sun, waiting for her. He looked happy when he saw her, but not surprised. He walked toward her and took the suitcase from her, a smile on his adorable face that went from ear to ear. "Ready to go home?"

"Almost," she said. She bent down to pick up the wilted yellow roses. She sat in the passenger seat and buckled in, the flowers snug on her lap. Now she was ready. Chris closed her door, then walked around the car, slipped into the driver's seat, and buckled his seat belt.

She shifted in the bucket seat, trying to get comfortable. She'd forgotten how scratchy they were. "On the drive, you can tell me how you levitated that light bulb."

"Nope. You'll just have to guess."

"A wire?"

"Nope."

"A hidden switch?"

"Maybe." Grinning, he gave her a side-glance, then turned the key, and the Mustang roared to life.

a FIELD of BEAUTY

Cast of Characters

Tessa Anderson—(age 25) new owner of a field in Asheville, North Carolina, with plans to turn it into a flower farm

Dawson Greene—(somewhere in his twenties—he's suspicious of personal questions) soil expert, instructor of the Sustainability Certificate program, and soon to be the farm manager for Tessa's flower farm

Tyler Thompson the Third—(late twenties/early thirties) Tessa's boyfriend who is running for Asheville's city council

Lovey Mitchell—(she won't say her age) hair salon stylist and part-time jewelry maker

The neighbor—(late thirties) wildly successful mystery writer who lived next door to the Andersons' summer home in Sunrise

Rose Reid—(late sixties) owner of Rose's Flower Shop in Sunrise, North Carolina

Floral Glossary

annual—a flower that completes its life cycle in one growing season, such as a zinnia

biennial—a plant that completes its life cycle in two years or seasons, such as foxglove

compost—decayed organic material used to fertilize plants or condition soil

cover crop—a crop grown to cover the soil and prevent erosion, such as clover; often incorporated into the soil later for enrichment

cut flowers—flowers grown to be cut

fish emulsion—fertilizer produced from the fluid remains of processed fish

hoop house—a small, high tunnel made of plastic, used to shelter or cultivate plants

perennial—a plant that persists for more than two years, such as a rose

tuber—a thickened underground stem for certain plants, such as dahlias

wholesale house—suppliers of fresh flowers, plants, and floral supplies to a wide range of professionals

Just like a flower, your true beauty shines from within.
It's the authenticity and kindness in your heart
that make you truly beautiful.
—Debasish Mridha

one

Minds are like flowers; they open only when the time is right.
—Stephen Lee

When Tessa Anderson looked in the mirror, she didn't see a beautiful woman. She didn't understand whatever it was that drew men to her like bees to a blossom. In fact, she thought of it as her "whatever." Whatever it was, she sure didn't trust it. She knew better than to trust it. So when Dawson Greene, a woolly haired, long-bearded, back-to-nature kind of guy, came into her life and didn't seem at all dazzled by Tessa—*not at all*—she knew he was just the one to help her turn a recently purchased acre of worn-out, beat-up land into a flourishing flower farm.

She still hadn't told her parents or older sisters about this big idea to own a flower farm. Two reasons. First of all, the Anderson family did not farm. They didn't even mow their own lawns. They hired people who did that sort of thing. Second of all, her family had never understood how deeply Tessa loved flowers. As a teenager, she had worked in a floral shop in Sunrise, North Carolina, where her family had a summer home. While there, she'd developed a keen appreciation for how flowers filled the senses—sight, scent, touch, memory. Senses mattered. She'd learned that from Rose, the owner of the flower shop.

But Tessa had forgotten about the importance of flowers until just before her last quarter in college. Her advisor had reminded her that she was short on science credits and recommended an off-campus Sustainability Certificate program. It would suffice for needed credits in both biology and chemistry. Tessa *had* to graduate this spring—after dabbling for five years, her dad said the college funding tap would shut off in May—so she agreed to the program. That's where she met Dawson Greene, an instructor on sustainability. And that's where her idea to have a flower farm first came into focus. Then into reality.

On a cool spring day, Dawson had been teaching students the finer skill of composting. They had gathered around a steamy compost pile, and just as Dawson was about to stab a hayfork into the pile to turn it, Tessa let out a shout. On one side of the pile was a delicate narcissus flower in full bloom. Such delicate beauty had survived in the midst of old leaves, grass clippings, and who knew what else! It took her breath away. That little white flower represented the miracle of something beautiful out of something ugly, a shriveled bulb in a compost pile. And suddenly, she knew she wanted to be reminded of that miracle every single day. She needed to be around flowers. But not in a shop. At a flower farm. Hers.

Tessa cashed in some stocks left to her by grandparents and looked for a plot of affordable land. Through an unexpected tip, she ended up buying Mountain Farm, a small tomato farm in Asheville. Really small, as in one acre. It had once been part of a large farm, but over the years, section by section had been sold off, including the acreage with the big house. There was a little carriage house left where she planned to live. The land had potential—a flat acre, full sunshine, no trees or stumps, a well for irrigation, and close to town to sell the produce—but the soil was miserable. Gray, cloddy, tired, and weary.

Immediately, Tessa thought of Dawson Greene. She needed his help.

Dawson might look like a hippie with a furry beard and a bandanna tied around his shaggy hair, but he knew soil. He'd received consulting job offers from companies that sought his skills. She'd overheard him tell another instructor that he was considering a change from teaching the program and had some good opportunities.

If he could just see the land, she thought she'd stand a better chance to persuade him to help her transform Mountain Farm. So, on the pretense of asking his advice about the condition of the soil, she remained after class one day to invite him to come to see land that needed his expertise. What a weird connection to have with someone. *Soil.*

He looked at her as if she might have spoken in a foreign language. "What was your name again?"

So much for a connection. She'd been a student under Dawson's instruction for months while doing the certificate program, and he'd never really noticed her. Most girls would be insulted. Not Tessa. She was pleased. He may not have noticed her, but she had noticed him. He had an understanding of nature like nobody's business, not even Rose Reid, the owner of the flower shop where Tessa had worked.

"Tessa Anderson," she said.

"Tessa Anderson," he repeated, with a little nod.

"So will you come to the farm to give an analysis of the soil? Nothing official. Just a general opinion of its condition."

"And this is for the owner?"

She hesitated, just for a moment, before saying, "Yes. For the owner."

He looked up at the sky to check the time. She remembered him saying in class that he didn't wear a watch because the sun told the time. "I suppose I could go now."

Now? "Then . . . let's go."

He drove his old Ford pickup truck behind her brand-spanking-new Audi sedan, a gift from her parents after (finally!) graduating from college.

After arriving at Mountain Farm, they walked out to the field, and Tessa swept her arm in a wide arc. "What do you think?"

Dawson bent down and picked up a clod of soil, crushed it in his palm. He rubbed the soil between his fingers, sniffed it, then tasted it. Wordlessly, he left her to walk up and down the fields, crouching down here and there to study the dirt. He was not the type to be quick to react, she reminded herself, though he did seem to be taking an extraordinarily long time. When he finally returned to Tessa, he said he would need to run some tests to determine the soil's mineral content. "It'll take a couple of days to get back the results."

"Dawson, you *tasted* the soil. I have no doubt you know exactly what this dirt needs."

He shielded his eyes from the sun to scan the field. "Well, the soil is severely depleted. Desperately impoverished. A perfect environment to host foliage-devastating insects."

She had expected that kind of report. "But it's not beyond repair, right?"

"Soil is never beyond repair. That's the great mystery of it. Nature is constantly at work to heal the mess humans make of this earth."

A mantra he repeated often throughout the program. As critical as Dawson was of people's stewardship of the planet, he was an admirer of how the earth could repair itself. It was a new thought to Tessa, full of hope.

"So," she said, "what do you suggest?"

"Tell the farmer to stop whatever he's been doing and grow cover crops that can be tilled back into the soil to replenish the lacking nutrients."

Yes. That was exactly what she had thought too.

He turned to look at the tired-looking little carriage house. "Is the owner in that shed?"

"Not a shed. It's a house."

"Huh. Really? Want me to be the bearer of bad news and give the owner the diagnosis?"

Tessa inhaled a deep breath. "You just did. I bought it. The full acre."

His head jerked and his eyes went wide. "You bought *this* land?"

"Yes, sir, I sure did." She gazed at the field. Was it really so bad? Had she made another impulsive decision that she would regret? She had no faith in her gut instinct. It took her down terrible paths. Had she done it again? "I want to convert the entire acre to flowers."

He squinted in disbelief. "Flowers?"

"Yes. Cut flowers."

"Cut flowers?" He sounded like he'd never heard of such a thing.

"Flowers that are grown to be cut. Like, a supplier for flower shops. I'm going to change its name to Mountain Blooms Farm."

"Flowers? The entire acre?" He sounded completely baffled.

"Yes, sir. That's the plan. I'm convinced there's a market out there for flowers. And if all goes according to plan, I'll start buying up more acreage." The road Mountain Farm was on was full of dumpy little houses on overgrown, neglected acres. Ripe for the picking.

"You have data? You can support this market demand?"

She was ready for that question. She knew, from the Sustainability Certificate program, that Dawson Greene relied heavily on scientific data. "According to a recent article in the *New York Times*, there's a global upward trend for fresh-cut flowers. Everybody, all the world over, loves flowers." Except maybe for Dawson Greene. "Did you know that blooms from suppliers are usually two weeks old by the time they arrive at the wholesale house? Think about it! There's such a huge opportunity for local flower growers."

Hands on his hips, he turned in a half circle. "And that's your business plan? Flowers?"

Business plan? She had no idea. She had never heard of such a thing. This venture was all based on a hunch. She could just sense a growing demand for fresh-cut flowers in Asheville. The small city had a hip, trendy vibe, with restaurants and art galleries and upscale boutiques. Of course they would all want cut flowers. Of course!

"But, Terry—"

"Tessa."

"Do you have any experience as a flower farmer?"

She looked down at her feet. "Noooo, not exactly. But I do have some experience working with cut flowers. And I love them, I know that."

The look on his woolly face! He thought she was crazy. Maybe she was. Well, if she was, she was going whole-hog crazy.

"You mentioned a cover crop," she said. "I've got the perfect one. Sunflowers." She'd done research on cover crops. Sunflowers had deep, large taproots that could penetrate compacted soil, breaking up the soil and improving the structure so nutrients and water were able to infiltrate. The blossoms attracted bees too.

He considered that.

"And here's the best part of all. While the sunflower roots are doing their work, I can sell the flowers." She snapped her fingers. "Instant cash crop."

His brows furrowed. "You really think it's as easy as that?"

Maybe. She hoped so. "So what do you think of my plan?"

"I think you don't have a plan. You have an idea. But I am in favor of using sunflowers as a cover crop."

She took in a deep breath. *Whole hog.* "I'd like you to come work for me as farm manager." When his dark, fuzzy eyebrows shot up, she quickly added, "For one year, just to help me get the flower farm up and running. It's an incredible opportunity for a man with your knowledge. Dawson, this is what you do! You're all about transforming soil."

She had him there. And he wasn't saying no yet. She had braced herself for a flat-out decline. *No thank you, ma'am.*

So she continued her sales pitch. "Think about it! It's a dream come true. Imagine taking this tired old acre and transforming it into a lush garden of flowers. It's a golden opportunity." She was banking on a hope that Dawson Greene understood what it was to devote yourself to a cause.

"Tina—"

"Tessa."

"It's an interesting idea . . . but I don't think you can afford me."

She couldn't *not* afford him, that much she knew. She was willing to do anything to bring him on board, even if it meant selling her new car to pay his salary. "I'm prepared to offer you a base salary plus thirty percent of the profits."

He scoffed. "Turning a profit could take years. If ever."

Nope. She was determined to make a profit in this calendar year. Absolutely determined. She cleared her throat. "Forty percent."

"Think you'll even last a year?" His gaze slid down her outfit to her feet.

She was wearing a white tee tucked into a short blue-jean skirt, and sandals. Red nail polish on her manicured fingers and toes. Maybe she should've thought through what to wear when hiring a farm manager. "I guarantee it."

"And you're offering me this golden *opportunity*"—he added air quotes—"for one year?"

"That's right. Just one year." That was how she had explained the purchase of the land, after escrow closed and it was a done deal, to her parents. Just a one-year venture. "Flowers," she said with a smile, "can work miracles."

He remained quiet for a long, long moment, and she wondered what was running through his mind. Finally, he turned to her and looked her straight in the eye. "Base plus fifty-fifty."

She could've hugged him! But she was pretty sure that Dawson Greene would run for the hills if she did. He was the kind of guy who radiated an invisible sign around his neck: *Do not touch.* So instead she stuck out her hand. "You, sir, have got yourself a deal."

two

Happiness held is the seed; happiness shared is the flower.
—*John Harrigan*

And so they set to work. Despite the heat and humidity of a North Carolina summer, Dawson tilled the field with a rented hand rototiller. It was a laborious task, but he was convinced it was the only way to keep the land from getting compacted like it would've with a tractor. Tessa followed him to break up large clods of dirt with a pitchfork. More than a few times, he would stop, stretch, turn around, and say, "Do you see how bad this soil is, Tessa? Not a single worm."

Worms, to Dawson, were evidence of healthy, well-nourished soil. He was right about Mountain Blooms Farm. Tessa had yet to see a single worm in the tilled gray soil. No worms, but at least he finally got her name right.

Tessa had found some rusty tools and a wheelbarrow with a flat tire behind the house. Dawson repaired the wheelbarrow and oiled the tools. He knew the owner of a horse farm and brought truckloads of manure to Mountain Blooms Farm. Then he and Tessa took turns pushing load after load out to the field. When they were working side by side, that was when some tension would begin between them. Tension . . . because of constant interruptions.

Tessa's boyfriend, Tyler Thompson the Third, was blessed with the gift of communicating. He called and texted Tessa frequently, interrupting whatever she was doing. The frequency of Tyler's communiqués exasperated Dawson, who texted only if absolutely necessary and probably did not have a girlfriend. Tessa finally started ignoring Tyler's calls and texts, and tried to remember to keep her phone on silent when she was working closely with Dawson. He felt she should just leave the phone in the house, but she liked having it with her to listen to music.

Tyler had come into Tessa's life through her father's introduction. A few months ago, her dad had been nearby for business and made a quick stop in Asheville to check on Tessa. While there, he met a friend for coffee—Tyler's father, whom he'd known from college days. The two dads schemed together to introduce Tessa and Tyler. It was a successful matchmaking endeavor, at least from Tyler's point of view. As cute as he was—and he really was!—she wasn't quite so enamored, especially with the way he homed in on her like a bee to honey. That kind of behavior from a male always made her uncomfortable. She had learned *that* lesson in Sunrise.

And she was even less interested in Tyler after he told her he was running for a seat on Asheville's city council in a special election, replacing a councilman who had passed on to glory. Tyler was a big fan of using social media, big into publicity of any kind. Not Tessa. She liked her phone, but she had avoided social media addiction. Since Sunrise, she had avoided getting involved with anyone too.

Partly, she hadn't met anyone who interested her. Mostly, she had a deep-down fear that where men were concerned, her judgment might be off-kilter, like she was a bad picker. Flowers were easier. So much less complicated.

But her dad had kept encouraging her to go out with Tyler, and so, after he had lost the election, she finally accepted a date with him. Just coffee. She happened to mention that she was looking for nearby acreage to turn into a flower farm. "I don't want to be too far out of the city."

The strangest expression came over his face, and then he smiled. He had just the place for her, he said, and drove her out to meet the owner of Mountain Farm. She was impressed, more so as Tyler helped her with all the tedious paperwork—both making an offer and then closing the deal. Tessa felt appreciative of Tyler, truly grateful because she had no understanding of contracts. But she still wasn't enamored with him. Nothing like the feelings Tyler expressed for her. "Struck by a lightning bolt," he told her more than once. "That's how I felt when I first laid eyes on you. Destiny. You're the girl who's meant for me." Sweet.

But then she turned him down for another date. Her reluctance only fueled his determination. He wouldn't take no for an answer. Not for his campaign—he had immediately started work on the next one—and not from Tessa. He was relentless. She went out with him for dinner, and another time to a country music concert. In due course, she found herself growing fond of him. His optimism and confidence were refreshing to be around after spending so much time with Dawson, who was on a mission to find what mineral was missing in the dirt (metaphorically and practically!). The two men couldn't be any more opposite. And they did not like each other. No ma'am, not at all.

Tessa paid no attention to Tyler's digs about Dawson as an ignorant field hand, or Dawson's disdain for Tyler's enthusiasm for "intrusive" government. Her mind was on her farm.

The drab gray field of Mountain Blooms Farm was starting to take on hues of brown. By August, Tessa was anxious to start planting before the growing season officially ended. She was eager to see something green in her acre of earth—sunflowers or fava beans or clover. But Dawson wasn't satisfied with the amounts of amendments that had been dumped on the field. "Still not good enough," he would say. He'd heard about free compost offered from the county and hauled in more truckloads. He wasn't the kind of guy who showed much emotion, but he couldn't stop grinning over the county's free compost. On many levels, it suited his dire skepticism about government.

In mid-August, Dawson rented the rototiller again to till the compost deeply into the soil. Not only was it much easier than the first and second time of rototilling, but it actually looked like soil that could support life.

"Now?" Tessa asked after he finished. "Good enough?"

He wiped sweat off his brow and shook his head. "Not quite."

The next morning, Dawson arrived at the farm and stood outside her screen door to ask for help to carry worms to the field. She didn't believe him.

"Worms?" she said, studying his eyes to see if he was kidding. It was hard to tell with all the fur on his face, but she had learned to read his eyes. When there was a fan of crinkles on the edges of his eyes, she knew he was teasing her.

"See for yourself," he said. "Thousands and thousands of worms. Maybe millions. They're very successful reproducers."

She winced, suddenly aware of a crawling sensation up her legs, inside her overalls.

"Worms are miracle workers. They eat through anything, then their castings enrich the soil."

"Worms."

"Don't look so horrified. Worms are very underappreciated. Kinda like goats."

"Where in the world did you find millions of worms?"

"Along the riverbed. Free for the taking. The government hasn't figured out how to tax digging for worms yet."

"Dawson! You went digging for worms? You hauled them to the farm in your truck?"

"In buckets. Not loose." He shrugged, like it was no big deal.

It was a big deal. A very big deal. So sweet! She could have hugged him. He had done all this just to help her dirt be at its optimum. She was incredibly grateful to have his help. Dawson Greene was the difference between Mountain Blooms Farm surviving or thriving. Not a day went by when she didn't thank her lucky stars for him.

Forcing her squeamishness aside, she put on gloves and boots and helped Dawson sprinkle wiggly worms all over the acre.

Finally, he was satisfied. "Now it's ready to plant a cover crop."

That was late August. Too late for sunflowers but just right for red clover, a type of legume. Dawson and Tessa spent a couple of days forming rows in the field for planting. Now and then she would stop and look over the tidy rows, delighted at how the field was finally starting to look like a farm that could support life.

Tessa had agreed to spend Labor Day weekend with Tyler's family at their lake house, but when she saw Dawson arrive Saturday morning with bags of red clover seed in the bed of his truck, she couldn't go. She hadn't expected Dawson to work over the holiday weekend, though she should've known better. Farmers worked every day. At the last minute, she called Tyler to cancel, and quite frankly, she felt a little relieved to have a bona fide excuse. Spending an entire weekend with his family seemed premature for their relationship. After all, they'd only been dating a few months. And they hadn't had a lot of dates—maybe once a week or so. Mostly, they just texted or called.

"What do you mean you're not coming?" Tyler sounded nonplussed. "I was just walking out the door to head over and pick you up."

"I'm sorry. I need to stay here and help sow seed."

"But, Tessa, that's why you hired the field hand. He's getting paid to sow your seeds."

"Farm manager, not field hand. And this is important, Tyler. We've worked hard to get the field ready to this point. The timing for planting is critical."

"Honey, it's important to me that we spend time together. Between my schedule and yours, we hardly see each other."

"As soon as the field is planted, I'll have more spare time. I promise."

Tyler kept pressing. And pressing.

"Here's an idea. You could stay and help Dawson and me sow the field."

He coughed a laugh. "Ohhhh no. I'm no farmer. Besides, this whole weekend was about introducing you to my family. I know they'll adore you like I do." He wanted to show her his family's lake house, to go canoeing and swimming and lounge on the dock, sipping iced tea. To sit around the kitchen table in the evenings and play cards and board games.

Tempting. She started to wobble. The temperature in Asheville this weekend was going to be in the midnineties, with unseasonable humidity that made it feel even hotter. The window air-conditioning unit in her carriage house had stopped working, and a weekend at a mountain lake did sound delightful. When he told her that his mother had planned a special dinner just for her, she opened her mouth to say yes.

But before the word left her mouth, in that brief pause, she happened to glance out her kitchen window. Dawson was pushing a wheelbarrow full of heavy seed bags from his truck to the field. She snapped her mouth shut. Nope. She couldn't go. She wanted to be right here this weekend and nowhere else. "Please give your mother my apologies. I'm sorry to disappoint you, Tyler. I really am." She braced herself, expecting him to keep up the pressure. Persistence was his middle name! It's why she had no doubt he would have a successful life in politics.

To her surprise, Tyler backed down. "Well, darlin', I guess this is the price a man has to pay when he's fallen head over heels in love with a flower farmer. I'll sure miss you. When I get back to town, we'll go out for a nice dinner."

She looked down at her cell phone. What just happened? Did Tyler tell her he loved her? He'd waxed poetic about destiny and lightning strikes, but he'd never mentioned love.

Sweet! But . . . discomforting.

They'd hardly had more than a handful of dates! He was right about their schedules—neither of them had a surfeit of spare time. She wasn't sure what her feelings were for Tyler . . . other than feeling consistently overwhelmed by his enthusiasm. But maybe that quality wasn't so bad in a man. Maybe she needed someone like Tyler, who was so convinced she was *the one*. After the Sunrise experience, she didn't think she'd ever trust her instincts again. Maybe she should be more open-minded to Tyler's plans for a future together. He was articulate, well groomed, successful, and an all-around catch. A man her parents would heartily approve of. She wasn't in love with Tyler, not yet, but what did she know about love? Not much.

Switching mental gears, she changed out of her dress and into her overalls, grabbed her hat and gloves, and hurried out to help Dawson. He was on his way back to the field with another load in the wheelbarrow and stopped as she approached him. "I thought you were going away with 3T's."

Dawson referred to Tyler as 3T's because his name was Tyler Thompson the Third. Tyler always introduced himself with his full name . . . which could sound a bit pretentious. But the Thompson family had a long history in Asheville, and Tyler was campaigning for city council. The first political office of many, he hoped. He had big aspirations.

Dawson didn't care much for Tyler's politics, or for Tyler's silver-spoon upbringing, or for Tyler. Then again, Dawson didn't really like most people. He was a loner. Sometimes Tessa wondered what his living conditions might be like. She imagined him in a neglected Airstream tucked somewhere off in the deep woods. She glanced at him. Underneath that hippie hair might be an attractive guy, she thought, though she couldn't be sure. Other than a pair of blue eyes and a Roman nose, his fuzzy beard covered his face. He was certainly physically fit, strong, hardworking. Maybe she should try and find a girlfriend for him. Someone who had low social needs, who didn't require conversation. A librarian, perhaps. An undertaker.

She shrugged. "It got canceled."

Dawson's bushy eyebrows lifted, and she wondered what was running through his mind. Did he suspect she had done the canceling? Was he pleased she would be sticking around for the weekend? But he revealed nothing more than surprise. "Well, then, better go get your hoe. We've got seeds to sow."

Tessa took the lead as the sower, scattering red clover seeds over each row. Dawson worked a few feet behind her, turning soil over the seeds and tamping it down. Come winter, he would till the rows of clover into the earth to decompose, adding vital nutrients. Green manure, Dawson called it. Full of nitrogen.

Tessa had expected and needed Dawson's help to improve the soil, but to her delight, he plunged headfirst into the science of growing flowers. She'd had a grandiose plan to divide the acre into three sections, to grow different varieties of flowers that could be sold at market for spring, summer, and fall. Pretty good idea, she thought. Sweet peas and peonies in the spring, durable zinnias in the summer, dahlias in the fall. "This way," she said, "we can be a steady supplier of fresh-cut flowers. Nearly all year long."

But Dawson nixed her plan. Too many varieties grown too soon, he said, would be distracting. Different plant needs, different problems, different harvests. "From everything I've researched, fall flowers are in high demand with a shortage of supply. That's our window of opportunity."

Research. He had done *research* on the supply of cut flowers! She had to hold back a smile.

He proposed growing one rare variety of a popular cut flower and to grow them well. "What do you think of chrysanthemums? Easy to grow. Always in demand."

"No!" Tessa might have replied louder than intended, because his eyebrows shot up. She couldn't grow chrysanthemums as her first crop. They took her right back to the flower shop in Sunrise.

The scent of them, the sight of them. Rose used all kinds of chrysanthemums in arrangements. "Definitely not chrysanthemums." She cleared her throat. "What about dahlias? They grow from tubers and can be a little difficult, but they're considered the peonies of autumn." She knew that from working in Rose's Flower Shop.

He nodded. "That was my second choice."

"No other varieties?" She had such a vibrant image in her head! The field was full of colorful blooms.

"Adding varietals can come later," he said. "This first year, we need to start slow, start strong, and establish the name of Mountain Blooms Farm in Asheville."

Such a thought made Tessa's heart sing. Someone believed in her dream!

three

The very best relationship has a gardener and a flower.
The gardener nurtures and the flower blooms.
—Carole Radziwill

A few weeks later, Tessa was starting her daily early-morning stroll through the field when she saw tiny green clover leaves poking through the soil at Mountain Blooms Farm. Dawson had been watching for this moment. He had plans to spread rolls of plastic mulch over the rows, cutting holes for the clover plants to grow, to protect young plants from frost damage over the winter. A lot of backbreaking work! Tessa thought he might be going overboard, considering the clover would be tilled right back into the soil in a few months. Considering not a single bug was on this field without his permission.

He shook his head. "We're not just doing this for clover. We'll be doing this for the main crop plants too. Mulch is better than sliced bread. Better than salad in a bag. Better than—"

"Gotcha," Tessa said. But that didn't stop him from explaining how mulch helped to keep the weeds down, lengthened the growing season, and protected plants from insects. By the end of his mulch lecture, she was a believer. Mulch was a miracle worker.

Early one morning, Tessa was hosing out an old horse trailer she'd bought for a song at a tag sale over the weekend. She'd always been drawn to unusual things that most people overlooked. When Dawson drove up, she saw rolls of plastic mulch in the truck bed and knew what they'd be doing this week. All week long.

"Morning, Dawson. What do you think of this?"

He turned around from hoisting a roll of mulch out of the truck bed and gave her a certain look, as if to say, *What now?* It was their shtick. She'd pose a new idea and he'd react in a long-suffering way. "I think it's an old horse trailer."

"It *was*," Tessa said. "But I'm converting it into a flower trailer so that we can take it to farmers' markets."

"The WNC?"

The Western North Carolina farmers' market. "No. That's way too big for us. I was thinking of small farmers' markets. The ones that pop up all over Asheville in the summers. You know, once a week for a few hours in the morning." She turned off the hose to set it down, then walked over to him. "Can't you just imagine it cleaned up, filled with buckets of flowers inside, and our new logo painted on its side?" In the evenings, she'd been doodling ideas for logos.

"It's a trailer. How're you planning to haul it to farmers' markets?"

Hmm. He had her there. Tessa hadn't thought about how to get it from place to place. She should've, and probably would've, but the guy she'd bought it from had volunteered to deliver it to the farm, and she had happily accepted. She scratched her head. "I haven't ironed out all the details yet."

This was a common complaint of Dawson's. Tessa had big ideas, but he was the one who had to figure out how to make them happen.

"How'd you get it here?"

"I, uh, well, you see . . ."

He lifted a hand. "Don't tell me. Another rescue."

"What?"

"Some hapless, eager guy offered to bring it to the farm. Once it was parked here, then you shattered his hopes."

Tessa frowned. She didn't *mean* to take advantage of the guy. But she had to admit that after he delivered the trailer, he asked Tessa out on a date and seemed miffed when she declined. Dawson had noticed similar scenarios a couple of other times, like when Tessa had first rented the rototiller and the clerk shared his employee discount with her. When Dawson rented it, he had to pay full price.

So maybe there had been a pattern in Tessa's life: getting rescued at just the right moment. And, she had to admit, usually by an eager guy.

Her cell phone went off and she reached into her pocket to see caller ID. She was expecting a call from her mom—living seven hours away in Saudi Arabia meant they had to schedule calls. But it was Tyler checking in, something he did each morning around this time while driving to his campaign headquarters. She looked up to catch Dawson rolling his eyes.

"Maybe 3T's can loan you his golf cart to schlep it around." He lifted a hand in a dismissive wave. "I gotta get to work."

She answered the call, half listening as Tyler told her about his day. He was a talker. He might be a little self-absorbed, maybe a lot, but he was a glass-half-full kind of guy. Nothing was impossible. Nothing was out of reach.

She glanced over at Dawson as he dropped rolls of plastic mulch at the end of the field.

No, Tessa didn't have a pickup truck . . . but Dawson did.

ℓ·ℓ·ℓ

One week later, the field was covered with plastic mulch as small clover plants peeked through cut holes. Tessa's hands had blisters from making all those repetitive cuts with the shears. Farming was such hard work.

On Monday morning, Dawson arrived at Tessa's screen door with tubers held in his outstretched palms. "Look at these beauties," he said. "Incredibly valuable."

She looked down at the small, ugly, swollen roots. "Dahlias?"

"Not just any dahlias. These are one of the oldest and rarest varieties of dahlias—the Yellow Gem of 1914."

"Where'd you get your hands on them?"

He wiggled his dark eyebrows. "The soil world is full of sources."

"So what's your plan for them?"

"These are going to be the debut flower of Mountain Blooms Farm."

She stared at him. "Five? Our debut flower consists of five little dahlias?"

"Five dahlia *tubers*. Over the next few months, we are going to turn these five tubers into hundreds of dahlias."

She stared at him. Was he kidding? No. He was entirely serious. "Dawson, how in the world—?"

"Ever heard of the parable of the mustard seed?"

"You mean . . . from the Bible?" She vaguely remembered something from Sunday school about Jesus and a mustard seed and faith.

"Watch and see what will happen with these tubers." He looked past her into her house. "First, I need a dedicated growing area that's completely sheltered."

"Let's buy a greenhouse!" She'd been wanting to buy one from the start.

He frowned. "Unless you're a trust-fund baby like 3T's, we're not buying anything like that until the farm turns a profit." Dawson was extremely frugal with costs—he found a way to fix, barter, or borrow almost everything they needed.

Tessa was trying to adopt his strategy, but it was a complete mind shift from how she was raised. Her family wasn't fabulously wealthy, but they were well-to-do. She'd never had to pay back any school debts like Dawson did. She had never worried about making ends meet. Until now. "I'm not a trust-fund baby."

"Didn't think so."

Dawson had figured that out after she started driving a used Vespa. She'd sold the Audi plus the rest of her inherited stock certificates to provide for the year—property tax, his salary, and everything in between. "So if we can't afford a greenhouse, how can we create one?"

He looked past her into the house. "Do you have a spare room?"

Not hardly. This old carriage house was a tiny box. One bedroom, one airplane-sized bathroom, a small kitchen, and a sitting area. She lifted a finger in the air. "I could empty out my closet. Give me thirty minutes and it's yours."

First, she moved the clothes that were hanging in the closet onto her bed. As she folded up her dresses to fit into a chest of drawers, it surprised her to realize that just a few months ago, she had worn a dress every single day. Appearing feminine was part of being Southern. She caught sight of herself in a small mirror on the wall. Most days, she wore overalls and a T-shirt. Imagine if her mother could see her! Hair was gathered into a messy bun, usually hidden under a big straw hat. Nails were clipped short, polish-free, and always had dirt under them. She couldn't even remember when she'd last had a manicure. Her mother would faint at the sight of Tessa's tanned, muscular arms!

And yet, for the first time since Tessa was twelve or thirteen and became conscious of her looks, she *felt* beautiful. It dawned on her that she had always felt the opposite of beautiful, no matter what others said or how they treated her because of her looks. It was the strangest moment of self-discovery, one she would never forget. *Feeling* beautiful was better than *looking* beautiful.

Tessa wasn't sure if she felt beautiful because of the work that she loved, or the connection she felt to her field of flowers, or if it might even have something to do with being around Dawson, who seemed oblivious to her looks. It was like he saw her on the inside, not the outside. Maybe it had something to do with sheer happiness. Whatever it was, she had discovered that *feeling* beautiful really had nothing to do with one's appearance.

Her reflections were interrupted by Dawson's knock on the door. She opened the screen door for him to enter, but he hesitated. In the time they'd been working together, he'd never come into her little house. He stood there awkwardly, and then she felt awkward. She was used to being with him, but outside. Not inside.

That initial discomfiture got shrugged off, though, as Dawson went to work. He rigged up a growing space in her closet by adding shelving and wiring grow lights. Then he potted the tubers in soil that he called his "special sauce." Peat moss, bonemeal, crushed eggshells, coffee grounds, and who knew what else. All this preparation was to trick the tubers into "waking up," he said. To make them think spring had arrived.

He checked on the planted tubers every day, several times. More than once, Tessa had come into the house to get something and caught him singing to the plants in a gentle, rumbling, deep voice. Sweet! She had no idea he could sing, much less *would* sing. Singing seemed so . . . cheerful. So unlike him. In those moments, she would tiptoe back out of the house. For such a gruff, wild-looking guy, he had a charmingly tender underbelly.

And sure enough, seven days later, signs of green started to poke out of the soil. By fourteen days, all five tubers had sprouted. When they had fully leaved out, Dawson taught Tessa how to take cuttings to root. Carefully, he would trim a stem with some leaves, dip it in rooting hormone, and set it in a tray of potting soil. Her tiny kitchen was now turned into a temporary greenhouse. Dawson rigged up grow lights above the counters and insisted that Tessa keep the windows closed and the heat turned up to seventy-five degrees.

Each morning, while Tessa waited for the coffee to brew, she would check on the "babies." She'd mist their little leaves and make sure the soil was damp but not soggy. All details that Dawson taught her to watch for.

One morning, she woke to see evidence that the cuttings were rooting—new leaves appeared on several plants. When Dawson arrived at the farm, she opened the door and called to him. "Come and see!"

He slammed his truck shut and bolted past her, into the house to examine the dahlias. He was as pleased as she'd ever seen him. So was she! "Dawson Greene, in just a few months, you have turned five dahlia tubers into hundreds of plants."

He was bending over a tray to examine the leaves and didn't even look up. "Not me. Growing is in the Almighty's department."

In February, Dawson rented the rototiller again to till under the clover crop. Watching him work, listening to the steady whir of the rototiller, Tessa felt a little sad to see the clover disappear into the dirt. These last few weeks, the verdant green of the clover field had filled her senses, taken her breath away. She knew, though, that its best work was happening now, as it decomposed and added much-needed nutrients to the soil.

In March, for three overcast and cool days, Dawson and Tessa planted the young dahlia plants in long rows in the field. Over the winter months, Dawson had fashioned hundreds of hoops made out of bamboo. As soon as a row was entirely planted, he would stake the hoops in the ground. Together, working on opposite sides of the row, Dawson and Tessa covered up the plants with a lightweight diaphanous material to protect them from frost and sun damage until they'd had time to harden off. It was slow, tedious work, and she was exhausted at the end of each day, yet Tessa had never felt so satisfied. She loved this work. Loved it.

A few months later, in late June, a miracle unfolded right before Tessa's eyes. Small yellow pompon dahlias started to blossom in the field of Mountain Blooms Farm. She would go out in the early morning with a cup of coffee, right before dawn, just to watch the sun start to touch the field for the day. If she squinted her eyes, it almost seemed as if the field was ablaze with yellow flames. The sight took her breath away.

Dawson had chosen an ideal variety to debut the flower farm—sturdy and long-lasting, with multiple blooms. They held up beautifully in bouquets. He never failed to amaze her. How would a soil guy have known to choose the best qualities for flower arrangements!

As blossoms ripened for harvest, Tessa took bundles of them into Asheville floral shops as gifts, just to introduce Mountain Blooms Farm and to leave her business card. Word must have spread, because a day or two after the first harvest, a wholesale floral supplier called Tessa. He'd heard about the Yellow Gem dahlias and wanted to buy a large quantity for an upcoming wedding.

After Tessa hung up with the supplier, she ran out to the field, screaming Dawson's name.

He was harvesting blossoms at the far end of the field and dropped what he was doing to bolt toward her at full speed. "What's wrong? Did you hurt yourself?"

She hadn't meant to cause alarm! Relief poured into his eyes when she told him why she'd screamed. Sweet! Normally, he was all business. But in that one moment, when she caused him concern, when she saw the worry in his eyes, she realized that while she might technically be his boss (though you'd never know it because he was the one who told her what to do each day), he was also her friend.

Dawson Greene was the first male with whom Tessa felt as if she could be entirely herself—no makeup, baggy overalls, hair pulled back in a ponytail. It was like he was blind to her . . . *whatever*. Whatever it was that drew most males to Tessa. Whatever it was that made it difficult for her to have girlfriends, because girls were jealous of her and thought she might steal their boyfriends. (She would *never*!) Tessa hadn't had a friend like Dawson since working in the Sunrise flower shop alongside Claire and Jaime. They were blind to her *whatever* too. At least, they were until the night that changed everything.

A night that Tessa did her best not to remember.

four

One person's weed is another person's wildflower.
—Susan Wittig Albert

The best time to harvest flowers was early in the morning, when temperatures were low and plant water content was high. Tessa and Dawson were out in the fields at dawn, cutting stems of every dahlia bloom that was ready for harvest, filling buckets to the brim. They were heading to Asheville's City Market today. Or . . . as close as they could get to it.

There'd been such a long waiting list for vendors at City Market that Tessa nearly gave up, but then she realized the horse trailer could solve that problem. They could park it along the road near the entrance of the farmers' market and skip the waiting list. Skip the whole process of fitting into a market's stiff requirements. Skip the costs too. And every penny mattered at Mountain Blooms Farm.

So on the way into town in Dawson's pickup truck, with the converted horse trailer behind them, Tessa said, "I have an idea. Turn the horse trailer into an actual flower shop. Like, find a spot in town to set up a shop."

"Maybe next year."

Her insides smiled when he talked about next year's plantings. There was always a hitch in her gut that he would leave, go find a job that paid well. She counted on him heavily, far more than she had expected and more than she wanted to admit. If or when he left Mountain Blooms Farm, she'd be in trouble. "Speaking of next year," she said, "what do you think about adding wild-flowers?"

One eyebrow arched in that wry Dawson way. "I think wild-flowers are weeds."

"Not at all! Do you know the difference between a weed and a wildflower?"

He didn't answer.

"It's whether someone wants it or not. Flowers are very subjec-tive, you know."

He scoffed.

"Here's another idea. What do you think about starting a sub-scription service? To local residences?"

"And who would be delivering those boxes?"

Hmm. Tessa hadn't thought about the delivery part. Maybe she could hire a part-time delivery guy. "And I've been thinking of moving up our timeline to buy a greenhouse."

"The one we have works well enough."

Yes and no. It was Tessa's kitchen.

"But think of the benefits a real greenhouse could offer us. Early starts, more varieties. Overwintering. Endless possibilities."

He didn't respond. Dawson liked to act as if he wasn't affected by flowers, that his only interest had to do with what nutrients they brought to the soil or took from it, but Tessa knew there must be something about flowers that touched his soul. Flowers had the ability to soften the hardest of hearts. Why else would he stay?

He glanced at her. "The plan was to turn a profit for three full months. We agreed. Nothing new until we stop running in the red."

She pinched her thumb and index finger together. "We're getting soooo close."

"We're not anywhere close to getting out of it."

Please. Maybe the farm wasn't exactly lucrative, but it wasn't teetering on the brink of disaster. Closer to break-even. And there were some tax benefits to that, she had discovered. Like a big fat refund that she hadn't expected to receive. Then, during a week in July, more money came in to Mountain Blooms Farm than went out. Ten whole dollars. She'd been doing the books and realized the profit, so she went straight out to the field to hand Dawson a crisp new five-dollar bill.

He'd been adding some fish emulsion to a few dahlias that had yellowing leaves, and it smelled to high heaven. He pulled off his gloves to take the bill from her. "What's this for?"

"That, sir, is half of Mountain Blooms Farm's first bona fide profit."

To Tessa's delight, Dawson let out a whoop! As he did, he stood up and knocked over the bucket of disgusting fish emulsion, splattering it all over the five-dollar bill . . . and Tessa.

He froze. "Uh-oh."

Fish emulsion looked and smelled disgusting, even more pungent because Dawson made it himself and it was fresh. He pulled off his bandanna to wipe drops of it from her face and looked so worried that she had to laugh. The last thirty seconds were the biggest display of emotion she'd ever seen in him!

She pushed his hand away. "I'm going in to take a shower and think of how I'm going to spend my five dollars."

"Tessa."

She turned.

"Congratulations."

She smiled. "You too."

"But maybe you shouldn't spend it."

Until they turned consistent profits, Dawson discouraged all spending, unless it was something that could directly benefit the field and the flowers. He was a self-made man, remaining staunchly in the camp of what he called frugality. She called it scarcity. He thought she was spoiled. She thought he was a miser. They came from very different worlds, though she didn't know much about his world because, unlike her, he wasn't much of a talker. But she didn't have enormous college debt like he did. She didn't lose sleep at night about keeping the farm afloat. And she knew she could always turn to her parents if she really needed financial help. But she did work hard.

They passed a billboard that had Tyler's face plastered on it, along with a *Vote for Me* caption.

"County dogcatcher, right?"

She swallowed a smile. "Now *that* was an unnecessary remark." Based on a costly mistake by an intern in Tyler's election office who'd been given the task of proofreading the ads. The billboards neglected to say what office Tyler was running for, and it had become a standing joke around Asheville to fill in the gap. County Coroner, Trustee for the Cemeteries, Port Commissioner for the French Broad River (there was no such thing). "Tyler said it's going to get fixed soon."

"So you've said. Why doesn't he fire the intern? Oh, that's right. He's a cousin."

"Another unnecessary remark." True, though. "Tyler knows that mistakes happen. I'll bet you've even made a mistake or two."

"Oh yeah. I've made plenty of mistakes."

She wondered, though. As far as she could tell, Dawson was squeaky clean.

"What about you?"

"Me?"

"Surely you must have done something you regretted."

That silenced her.

"Well, what matters is you clean things up. Right?" He glanced at her.

Had she cleaned up things she regretted? No. No, she hadn't. She'd left a mess behind her.

ℓℓℓ

Not a minute later, they arrived near the City Market and thoughts of regretful moments were set aside as they focused on finding a spot to park. Tessa hopped out of the cab to help Dawson guide the trailer. When satisfied, he climbed out of the truck to unhook the trailer, and Tessa opened the back to start pulling out buckets of flowers. A loud voice startled them.

"Y'all! Dawson!"

Dawson and Tessa looked up at the same time as a woman with bright pink hair came flying over, arms wide open, to envelop him in a hug. He looked as if he might die of mortification. She released him to turn her attention to Tessa, reaching out a hand with long fingernails painted a shiny bright blue. "I'm Lovey Mitchell." She shook Tessa's hand vigorously and handed her a business card. "I work in the best hair salon in Asheville." She mussed the top of Dawson's hair so that it stuck up out of his bandanna. He looked even more mortified. "You two look like you could use a little spit and polish." She saw the horse trailer and let out a gasp. "Are y'all setting up right next to me? Don't that just beat all? If we can't get the farmers' market to let us in, then we'll just move the farmers' market to us."

Lovey Mitchell never stopped talking as Dawson and Tessa set up the buckets full of beautiful dahlias, in and around the horse trailer. Next to them, Lovey had a card table set up beneath a white canopy. On the card table was jewelry—earrings and necklaces, all made with long, fluffy bird feathers. It wasn't until customers started to arrive at the horse trailer that Lovey returned to her table.

Mountain Blooms Farm had a good morning. In fact, the trailer was a smashing success—it caught the attention of customers as they headed from the market to their cars. Nearly every flower bucket was empty. Even Dawson seemed impressed. He told Tessa they should plan to double the cut blooms next week.

As they were putting things away, Dawson carried buckets over to the street sewer to empty water. Lovey came over to the trailer and watched him walk off in the distance. "Wouldn't you just love to see what's underneath all that?"

Tessa had been bent over the buckets, gathering leftovers together. "Huh?" She looked up to see Lovey staring at Dawson as he tipped buckets over. "Underneath . . . Dawson?"

"Mmm-mmm. Imagine ripping off that bandanna and getting your hands into that mop." She made it sound a little R-rated.

Tessa turned to look at Dawson as he headed back toward the trailer.

"What?" He eyed them suspiciously. "What are you both staring at?"

"Just wondering," Lovey said, "how much handsome is under that shaggy carpet."

"Keep dreaming," he said, tucking the empty buckets into the horse trailer. He took the leftover dahlias from Tessa and handed them to Lovey, who giggled like a schoolgirl.

Was Dawson *flirting*? With Lovey Mitchell? Tessa felt a trickle of . . . what? Annoyance. Lovey Mitchell wasn't at all the kind of woman Tessa would've picked out for him. She hadn't actually found the right girl for him, but she definitely wouldn't have been a pink-haired hairstylist.

Later that afternoon, when Tessa was back at Mountain Blooms Farm, walking through the dahlia fields to see how the blooms were doing, Dawson's earlier question returned to nag her, like a buzzing mosquito. Had she ever made a mistake she regretted?

Of course. Plenty. But the worst mistake she'd made was compounded by another mistake. It meant the end of her time at Rose's Flower Shop. It meant a fire at the shop that caused considerable damage and lots of blame. It meant that Tessa, Jaime, and Claire, now jobless, all left Sunrise because none of them had a reason to stay. But they didn't leave together. It also meant that their friendship went up in the fire.

That was seven years ago, and yet there were times when Tessa felt like it was yesterday. She hadn't been in contact with Jaime and Claire since she left Sunrise, and certainly not with Rose. How could she? Shame craved secrecy.

five

Chase your wildflower dreams, because even the
smallest buds can become something beautiful.
—C. V. *Sutherland*

The following Saturday, Tessa and Dawson packed the horse trailer with double the amount of last week's blooms. As Dawson drove into town, a funny look came over him, like he was trying hard not to swallow. All of a sudden, Dawson chuckled.

Tessa looked at him, shocked. "What's got you grinnin' like a possum?"

He slowed the car and pointed to a Tyler Thompson the Third billboard.

"Oh no. No!" Tessa said. Tyler had told her that the intern had solved the billboard "lack of clarification problem" of what office he was running for. A giant sticker had been overlaid on the right corner of the billboard to announce it. A good solution, but unfortunately, *Council* was spelled *Counsel*.

Dawson's chuckling developed into a full belly laugh, tears

running down his face. "He's running to be Asheville's first elected therapist."

"It was the intern's fault," she said quietly, trying very hard to stay somber, but it didn't last long. A snicker, a chuckle, then full laughter.

Dawson wiped tears away with his shirtsleeve. "Are you sure this intern isn't a planted saboteur?"

Tessa's cell phone rang, and she glanced at caller ID to see Tyler's name. She had to let it ring a couple of times, taking in deep breaths to stop laughing, before she could answer. "Morning."

"What's that noise?"

"Hello to you too. The noise is the truck. I'm heading to the farmers' market."

"Why can't the field hand take care of the market today?"

Tessa cringed. "Because I need Dawson's help." Tyler had all kinds of snarky terms for Dawson: field hand, handyman, plow guy, tiller. In his mind, there was no way a guy would work at Mountain Blooms Farm unless he had the hots for Tessa. He just didn't understand the working partnership between Dawson and Tessa.

"How late does it go? I need to be there by six o'clock."

"Where?"

"Very funny, Tessa. Tonight's the night that's going to change everything for me."

She sobered instantly. *Oh boy.* She had completely forgotten about a big fundraising event to be held at the Biltmore Estate. The governor of North Carolina was the keynote speaker, and Tyler was hoping to get his endorsement for councilman.

"I'm having a dress sent over for you to wear."

"You're *what*?"

"No overalls tonight, Tessa. And I made an appointment for your hair at that blow-dry bar you like. Get an updo, okay?"

She glanced at Dawson, pretty sure he must have overheard Tyler because he had stopped laughing.

Tyler carried on. "This is huge for me, Tessa."

"Right. I'll be ready."

"I have two extra tickets if you'd like to bring some friends."

She reached over to jab Dawson in the arm and gave him a thumbs-up, as if to say, *Want to come?* He shook his head vigorously. She smiled. They passed another *Vote Tyler Thompson the III for City Counsel* billboard.

"Um, Tyler, have you seen the billboards?"

"No. Why?"

"You might want to see them before the governor arrives in Asheville."

"Why?" His voice went flat. "What's wrong with them?"

She exchanged a glance with Dawson, who was now grinning broadly. "Well, there seems to be a typo."

She heard Tyler groan. "I'll check it out. Plan to be ready at six."

Slipping her phone into her purse, she said, "Would you consider coming to the dinner?"

He scoffed. "Us field-hand types don't know what to do with all them utensils."

"Sorry about that. I've explained that you're the manager of Mountain Blooms Farm. Tyler doesn't understand the farming life."

"So now you're letting him pick out your clothes?"

Actually, the thought of Tyler sending over a dress did irk her. The request for an updo hairstyle annoyed her. She could make her own styling decisions, thank you very much. "Dawson, come tonight. It's a fun chance to go to the Biltmore. And a gourmet dinner. All free."

"It's not at all free. The cost is to have to listen to politicians. That's a steep toll on my sense of well-being."

"But you do love good food. And we can walk through the gardens of the Biltmore without having to pay a hefty entrance fee. You've never been."

"I'll get there someday."

"This could be your chance. Imagine the fall colors that are starting in those historical gardens. You're the one who told me the landscape architect designed it for four seasons of color." She shifted on the truck's seat to look at him. "Come on, Dawson. Say you'll come." Simply because he wasn't adamantly refusing the offer made her think he was considering it. "I'll even find you a date."

He scowled at her. "I do not need your help to find a date."

Oh, *really*?! This was news. She wondered if he'd been seeing someone. If so, who? She was intensely curious but knew better than to ask. "Great! Then plan to be at the farm at six o'clock."

He sighed, as if cornered.

"And maybe, um, you know . . . time for a little . . ." She pantomimed scissors trimming.

He frowned and didn't bother to respond.

ℓ·ℓ·ℓ

As soon as Tessa returned home, she canceled her appointment at the blow-dry bar. Nor did she bother even trying on the dress Tyler had sent for her to wear. She wore one of her own and washed her hair but wore it down in loose curls. A little before six, she heard Dawson's truck arrive and went out to meet him, but someone else stepped out of the truck—a man she didn't recognize. Not at first.

Then she realized this man was none other than Dawson Greene wearing a roguish smile. His shaggy hair and beard were gone. He had a very stylish cut, short on the sides, longer on top, and his shaven face revealed strong cheekbones, a square jaw. She stared at him. He looked like an updated James Dean.

"What? You said to get a trim."

"Everything? You cut off everything?" He looked like a freshly shorn lamb.

He ran a hand over his head, like he wasn't quite used to it himself. "The barber gave me a two-for-one deal."

She couldn't stop herself from staring at him. Maybe it was the low angle of the sun, but minus the bushy beard and long hair, he was rather good-looking. Like, knockout handsome. She found herself a little fixated on what seemed to be double dimples in his cheeks. Why had he been hiding *those*? He wore a dark suit, a white collared button-down shirt, and a striped tie. She didn't even know he owned a suit.

He was looking at her with an equally curious expression.

"What?" She looked down at herself and tugged at her hem a little, making sure she was entirely covered. "Do I have a stain? Did I miss a button?"

"Um, no. You look, um, just fine."

Then a funny little moment happened when he looked into her eyes and she looked right back into his . . . and then they both looked away, embarrassed.

Dawson cleared his throat. "Where's 3T's? I figured he'd hire a limo."

"He called to say that he had a chance to go early to the Biltmore to talk to the governor. I can drive us."

"Nope. Your Vespa is too small for three. I'll drive us in the truck."

"Three?"

At that moment, the passenger door of the truck opened. Tessa hadn't realized someone else was waiting in the truck. She pulled her eyes off Dawson to meet his date.

six

To plant a garden is to believe in tomorrow.
—Audrey Hepburn

The Biltmore Estate was a national treasure. It was the largest home in America, built over a century ago by George and Edith Vanderbilt. Or, as Dawson described it, built in the days before federal income tax. The four-story house was an architectural masterpiece, surpassed only by the landscaping of over eight thousand acres. Designed by landscape architect Frederick Law Olmsted, the gardens were, in a word, magnificent.

And Tessa hardly noticed them. She was too busy wondering about Dawson's date—Lovey Mitchell, who had dressed up in a low-cut gold sequined dress that showed every line of her Spanx underwear. Her hair, tonight, had been dyed a deep purple.

On the drive to the Biltmore, Lovey sat between Dawson and Tessa in the front seat, all three squeezed in. Lovey's perfume was so strong that Tessa inhaled fresh air from the window, which rolled with a crank, and held her breath until she needed to exhale. Lovey chattered away during the entire drive, just like at the

214

farmers' market. Tessa hardly listened until Lovey started talking about Tessa.

"So Dawson says you're a real hard worker."

Did he? Well, he's right. She had never worked so hard in her life, but she didn't know that Dawson had noticed. "He's the one who makes those flowers grow."

"Don't sell yourself short, honey. Dawson says that fixing soil is easy. Creating the vision is the hard part."

He said *that*?

"He says you've made something beautiful out of nothing with that farm of yours. Isn't that just so sweet?" Lovey gave Dawson a jab with her elbow.

Tessa leaned around Lovey to look at Dawson, but his focus stayed on the road. His ears seemed to be turning a little pink. They were nice ears. She hadn't seen them before.

She settled back against the truck seat. Wow. Something beautiful out of nothing. That might be one of the best compliments she'd ever received.

Maybe Lovey wasn't so bad.

No sooner had Tessa thought it than Lovey flew off to talking about a new hair mousse she'd discovered that could make your hair stick straight up like you'd stuck your finger in an electric socket. Even in a hurricane wind, she said. "Y'all may think it's crazy, but it's the best thing for gals with short hair. That's the latest trend, y'know."

Hair. Trendy hair.

Could Dawson and Lovey really be dating? Tessa would never have thought a woman like Lovey would be his type, but what did she really know about Dawson's personal life? He showed up at her screen door each morning and mumbled what he'd be doing that day and told her what she needed to be doing. Ninety percent of their conversation was about growing flowers, and the remaining ten percent was entirely her doing. She did most all the talking, though he didn't seem to mind.

Still, Lovey Mitchell and Dawson? Mind boggling. She couldn't stop thinking about why Dawson was attracted to Lovey. Frankly, it was disturbing that she had no idea he had a girlfriend. She spent hours every single day with Dawson. How could she not have known that he was dating someone? And Lovey Mitchell, of all people!

Then a startling thought struck her. Was she jealous?

Oh my goodness. She might be.

Right on the heels of that realization came another one: Tessa didn't want Dawson to have a girlfriend. Especially not Lovey Mitchell.

Somewhere along the way, Tessa had started to have territorial feelings for Dawson Greene, who had never shown any romantic interest in her at all. None.

Maybe just that one time.

It was in late June, on a sunny morning, and the first dahlia had bloomed, literally unfolding before their eyes, like it was taking its first breath. They were crouched down in the field, close together, and without even realizing it, they held hands as if they were parents watching their baby take his first steps. Afterward, they realized what they were doing at the exact same moment, and both let go like dropping a hot potato. For the next few minutes, Tessa had felt a tingling in the hand he'd been holding.

She squeezed her eyes shut. Those thoughts felt disloyal to Tyler. He had been waiting for them near the front door. As Tessa stepped out of the truck, he stared at her as if a princess had arrived. Sweet . . . until he snapped out of it and turned back into Tyler the aspiring politician.

He was acting very amped-up tonight. Very weird. During the walk through the gardens led by the governor, the mayor of Asheville, and lots of eager journalists and photographers, he kept trying to muscle into conversations with the governor, to jump in on photos. He held a tight grip on Tessa's hand, pulling her along with him, though she was far more interested in trying to observe Dawson and Lovey's interaction.

At one point during the walk through the conservatory, the governor stopped and sniffed the air. "Is someone making cotton candy?"

Tessa answered without thinking. "It's the scent from that Japanese katsura tree over there." It was a beautiful tree with heart-shaped, buttery-yellow leaves.

The governor turned, searching for who had responded. His eyes lingered on Tessa like she was the only female in the room. He motioned for her to come stand by him. "Tell me again the name of that tree." Then a photographer told them to look over at him, and the governor put his arm around Tessa's waist, squeezing her close to him, and a picture was taken.

Afterward, Tyler whispered crossly, "The least you could've done was to include me."

Include him . . . in what? The whole thing lasted fifteen seconds. Too fast for her to even think about it. Tyler wanted that moment with the governor. She couldn't have cared less.

She shrugged with a sigh. As she turned away, she saw that Dawson had been watching the interaction between her and Tyler. His gaze fluttered toward hers. Their eyes met and then flicked away.

During dinner, Tyler barely sat down. Networking, he said. Dawson sat between Lovey and Tessa, eating the meal with gusto while Lovey talked and talked and talked. When Lovey got up to go to the bathroom, Dawson rose, partially, a sign of good manners. He looked up when he felt Tessa's gaze.

"Since when did you turn into a Southern gentleman?" Tessa asked.

"I've always been one," he said, eyeing her dessert. "Are you going to eat that?"

She pushed it toward him. "So how long have you been seeing Lovey Mitchell?"

Between bites of key lime pie, he mumbled, "Long enough."

"Long enough for what? Are you serious about her?" As he

217

thoughtfully chewed, she kept at him. "The two of you are opposites. How is it even possible that you're together?"

He swallowed. "People can surprise you."

"Dawson—your favorite topic is compost. Hers is the latest hairstyle."

"Speaking of, did you know that human hair can deter deer from eating plants? I brought back my shorn-off beard to try it on the dahlias." He polished off the last bite of her dessert.

Tessa's eyes went wide. "Don't tell me that Lovey is the barber who gave you the two-for-one haircut."

Before Dawson could finish chewing to respond, Tyler returned to the table and sat down with a satisfied look. "I'm getting close. The governor's assistant promised me a moment with him before he had to leave. If I can get his endorsement, my city council position is as good as gold."

"Got your beauty shots?" Dawson said.

"Not yet. Working on it." Tyler didn't realize Dawson was mocking him. Or maybe he did. "So, Dawson, what are your plans?"

"Plans?"

"You'll probably need to get a real job at some point."

Tessa twisted in her chair to look straight at Tyler. "He has a real job."

Dawson pointed his fork at Tyler. "It's good to be prepared for the future. You never know what could be coming right around the corner."

Tessa whipped around to Dawson. What did he mean by *that*?

Dawson reached out to hold the plate of Tyler's untouched dessert. "Mind if I eat it?" Before Tyler could respond, Dawson had his fork in the pie.

Suddenly, Lovey plopped down in her seat. "Y'all! Guess who I just had a little chat with! The mayor of Asheville! He was coming right out of the little boy's room just as I was leaving the little girl's room. I gave him my business card and told him I could fix

that awful haircut for him, and he said he'd give it some thought."
She sparkled with excitement. "I'll tell you *what*. He is a charmer,
that is *for sure*." She motioned to a waiter to fill her coffee cup.
"Tyler, honey, what's all this fuss about rezoning property? Sounds
like my beauty shop could be in jeopardy. The whole block. Good
thing I'm only renting my chair in the salon. I'd be furious if I
owned the shop."

Tyler shot out of his chair. "There's the governor's assistant.
He's waving me over. Wish me luck."

Lovey looked at Tessa. "The mayor told me all about it when he
saw the address on my business card. Something about four sites
in Asheville that were . . . what was them big words he used?" She
scrunched up her face. "Identified for high-density living." The
waiter came by to refill her cup of coffee. "I can't remember where
those other sites were, but, Tessa, honey, he said something about
a site down your way."

Dawson and Tessa locked eyes.

And not ten seconds later, Tessa felt someone draw close to her.
She startled and turned to find Tyler down on one knee, holding
an engagement ring out to her. "Darling?" he said. "Say yes."

Before she could string a thought together in her mind, a photographer's flash went off. First one, then another and another,
as Tyler slid the ring on her finger.

seven

Even the tiniest of flowers can have the toughest roots.
—*Shannon Mullen*

S ame kitchen, different view. The next morning, Tessa stood at her sink, filling her coffeepot with water, noticing the light play off the ridiculously large diamond ring. It should bring her delight, but it only brought annoyance. She couldn't get it off! The whole proposal moment was so public, so staged. Why would Tyler think she would want something like that? For that matter, why would he give her a ring like this one? The diamond looked just plain silly on her small hand. She was a flower farmer! She had working hands. She hardly wore jewelry anymore. Even more importantly, what made him think she was ready to make a commitment?

She heard a familiar rumble and leaned forward over the sink to crane her neck. Dawson was here! He never came to the farm on Sundays, so she went outside to see why he'd come. As he walked toward her, she noticed a five-o'clock shadow covering his chin and wondered if the return-to-full-beard had already started. She kind of hoped so. This GQ Dawson felt disorienting to her.

He gave her a toe-to-head look. "Glad to see you're back in your overalls."

"Why wouldn't I be?"

He held up a copy of the *Asheville Citizen-Times*. On the front page was the story of the governor's dinner at the Biltmore, including a large photograph of Tessa, looking surprised as Tyler knelt on one knee to propose. "Now that you're famous, I hope you don't turn into a diva. You run a worm farm, after all."

She snatched the paper from him. In the picture, she looked more than a little shocked at Tyler's proposal, and not in a good way. Frankly, she looked horrified. She read the caption under the picture:

> *The governor couldn't resist adding his endorsement to this council candidate's "proposal" and hopes he'll be invited to the wedding. Pictured: Tyler Thompson the Third and his fiancée, Tessa Anderson of Mountain Blooms Farm.*

She sighed. At least Tyler got his coveted endorsement. And Mountain Blooms Farm got a mention. "This could be good for the farm, right? A little publicity never hurts."

"Unless it's linked to politics. Then it's tainted."

She ignored him. "Do you think more people or fewer people read the newspaper on Sunday?"

"More."

She folded the paper. "I'm glad you're here this morning. There's something we have to talk about."

"Right. I've been thinking about that too." He looked at her left hand, at the lavish, impractical, too-small ring with the too-large diamond.

It felt uncomfortable to her, foreign to her hand, so not her taste, and wedged on her finger. Tyler hadn't even given her a chance to respond to his proposal—he, along with everyone else, just assumed that she had said yes. She stuffed her hands in her overall pockets. "Not this. Other stuff."

"Like what?"

"New ideas for the farm. Ways to open the farm up to the public."

"Open it up? Tessa . . . do you realize what happened last night?"

Of course she did! But she didn't want to think about Tyler right now. "Hear me out. And hold your judgment too. I've been thinking that we should open the farm up to the public. Like a U-pick farm for flowers. Or maybe . . . have events, like teaching people about how to arrange flowers. How to grow flowers. I was talking to a woman last night at the Biltmore, and she said she'd like to bring a group of friends to the farm for a flower event for her fiftieth birthday. She asked me if we hosted events . . . and of course I said yes! Imagine it, Dawson. I could have champagne and appetizers and teach them how to arrange flowers and—" She stopped when she saw the mocking look on his face. Since his facial hair was gone, she could definitely see his expression of ridicule. "What?"

"Do you even know how to arrange flowers?"

"I do, actually. I used to work in a flower shop. I'm a little rusty, but I think I could teach the women a few things."

"You used to work in a flower shop?" He looked at her curiously, as if to say, *Why haven't you mentioned that before?*

She hadn't mentioned it because she tried to block it out. Too painful. The end, that was. "I did. I loved it." That part was true. Working in the flower shop had been a wonderful experience. When the woman had asked about celebrating her fiftieth birthday with a flower event at the farm, it caught Tessa's imagination, and she came home to pull out her old flower books. Techniques and tricks that Rose had taught her kept bubbling up in her mind. Moments in the shop alongside Claire and Jaime.

Tessa was never as naturally good at flower arranging as Claire and Jaime were. They seemed to have an intuitive sense of what was lacking, or what was needed, or how to keep the eye traveling over an arrangement. Rose had to teach fundamentals to Tessa; she'd been so patient with her. She'd even given Tessa all her flower-arranging books to study—the very books she'd flipped through last night. Tessa remembered feeling so exasperated with herself for missing the little things in a bouquet—the focus flower, or fillers. Rose would put a hand on her shoulder and say, "Tessa, those little details can be taught. You have something that can't be taught. I call it the Flyover Effect. You can imagine the big picture. Most people get stuck in the details. Watch and see. I have no doubt that you're going to create something remarkable one day."

Tessa had never forgotten Rose's words, but she hadn't really understood what they meant. Not until a late summer morning when the field of Yellow Gem dahlias was in full bloom. This had been her vision, all along. She needed help (Dawson! his genius and hard work) to turn it into reality, but it had started with her. That's what Rose had seen in her. And maybe Dawson saw it in her too. She kept thinking about that secondhand compliment—that Tessa had turned "nothing" into something beautiful. Those remarks, from Rose and from Dawson, two people whom she thought of so highly, were words she would always treasure.

"If you loved the flower shop so much, why'd you leave?"

This was too much. Too many memories, too many emotions. Going through Rose's flower books last night had made her so maudlin and teary and sentimental that she finally put them away and went to bed . . . and then she tossed and turned. Dawson kept his eyes on her, waiting for the answer. She wasn't ready to give it to him. "Let's stay focused on the flower event concept. What do you think about it?"

"Sounds like a lot of work."

That was his typical response to her ideas. "Yes, but good work. The kind that improves our profit. The kind that makes people happy. Did you know that cut flowers raise people's feelings of compassion?"

"Where'd you read that?"

He always questioned her sources. "A Harvard University Medical School study done by a psychologist. She found that having fresh-cut flowers in the home for even a few days had a positive effect on people. They said they felt less anxious and worried." Tessa lifted her hands in the air. "See? Flowers work miracles. Say . . . maybe we should call the events 'Flower Power.'" She grinned. "So what do you think?"

"I think this is all sounding like work and it's Sunday and I have to go or I'll be late."

"Late to what?"

"Church."

"*You* go to church?"

"Yes, ma'am. Every Sunday."

That was completely new information to her. Or had she just not noticed? She knew he didn't cuss, she had never seen him drink alcohol or talk about it, and he'd never mentioned women the way guys her age did. She knew he was honest as the day was long. She thought of the subtle comments he would make, like after they'd make an order for flower tubers or bulbs or seeds, and Tessa would say, "This time next spring, think of all those flowers!" Only to have Dawson quickly add, "Lord willin' and the creek don't rise."

She'd thought he was just being Southern. Maybe he wasn't. Maybe it's what he really believed. How many times had Dawson looked over the blooms in the flower fields, his hands on his hips, a satisfied look on his face. And then he would say, "And why do you worry? See how the flowers of the field grow. Not even King Solomon in all his splendor was dressed like one of these."

Too many times to count.

She looked at him as if seeing him for the first time. How had she missed the signals? Dawson Greene was religious. As she stared at him, she could feel by the weight of the air between them that something had changed.

"Church is where I first met Lovey."

You what?! Lovey went to church? To Dawson's church? Tessa had to check this out.

He lifted his hand in a wave and started toward his truck.

"Hold on! Dawson, wait. Wait for me. I'm coming too!"

eight

A *flower cannot blossom without sunshine,*
and a man cannot live without love.
—Max Müller

Dawson's church was nothing like the traditional church Tessa had grown up in. His church met in a junior high gym, people *drank coffee* as they sat on the metal folding chairs, and there was a *band* warming up on the stage, with a *drummer*.

Tessa couldn't remember the last time she'd gone to church. It struck her that it might have been when her family had still lived in Atlanta. They'd been fairly regular churchgoers, like most good Southerners, but when it was convenient. Never in the summers in Sunrise. And when they did go to church, it stayed in its Sunday compartment.

Tessa's mother would flip out at a drummer in church. Probably walk straight out. There are just times when things go too far, she would say. Tessa thought her dad might enjoy it. He was a little more open to new ideas than her mom.

And more surprises came. Everyone knew Dawson, young and

SUZANNE WOODS FISHER

old, and they oohed and aahed over his freshly shaven look, and he seemed to enjoy the attention. Yes, ma'am. Dawson Greene, laughing and smiling and joking. Wonders never ceased.

Lovey was serving coffee in the back, standing next to a large vase full of purple chrysanthemum flowers that looked a little weary, as if they were bought last night from a grocery store. Tessa noticed because Lovey's hair color matched the blooms. When Lovey spotted Tessa, she gave her a little wave, and blew a kiss at Dawson. "Do you want coffee, honey? You look like you could use it."

Apparently, she meant Tessa. "I'd better not," she said. She'd already had a cup or two before Dawson had shown up at the farm. Her emotions were already overly wired this morning. She turned to Dawson. "But don't let me stop you."

"I never drink the stuff. Poison to your nervous system."

"Right. That's why most everyone in the world loves coffee."

"They don't realize they're addicted to it."

Please! Dawson. So negative.

And then suddenly Dawson's attention turned to the stage, and he left her with Lovey while he went to join the musicians.

"Isn't he just the sweetest man alive?" Lovey whispered.

Dawson? Sweet? Super mellow, yes. Super smart. Yes. But sweet? That's not a word Tessa would use to describe him. But maybe he was sweet. He certainly did a lot to help Tessa, even things she knew he'd rather not do, like spend hours at the farmers' market. But there seemed to be more layers to Dawson Greene than she had noticed. She certainly didn't expect to discover he was a regular churchgoer, much less part of the worship team. She glanced at Lovey, wondering again how serious things were between her and Dawson.

Onstage, Dawson grabbed a guitar and stood in front of a microphone, welcoming everyone, while tuning his guitar, then nodded to the drummer and started to sing in a baritone voice. That same deep rumbly voice she'd heard him sing over the baby

227

dahlia plants! People joined in, waving hands in the air, and soon it seemed the entire gym was rocking out. Tessa wasn't familiar with most of the songs, but she tried to follow the words on a display screen.

Lovey slipped into the seat next to her and handed Tessa a flower from the little vase on the coffee table. "He cleans up mighty fine, if you want my opinion."

Tessa's gaze shifted to Dawson. She barely recognized him as the same man who liked to talk about compost and worms. She was astounded at the changes she'd seen in him in the last twenty-four hours. Or had she just never noticed?

She was pondering that very thing as he started a new song that Tessa did recognize. Rose used to play it at the flower shop, nearly every day. Without thinking, she lifted the chrysanthemum bloom to her nose . . . and suddenly she was eighteen years old, working in the shop, arranging flowers. It was the scent—flower memories held such power! Strong emotions started rolling over her, ones she had tamped down for years. One tear started, then another and another. Soon, a flood of tears washed down her cheeks.

Lovey, seated next to her, reached over to put her arm around her and whisper, "I know, honey. I know. The Lord uses music to talk to our hearts."

That remark set off another river of tears in Tessa. She wiggled past Lovey and hurried to the door. She went straight to Dawson's truck, mad at herself for not driving her Vespa, but thankful the truck was so old that the lock on the door didn't work. Sitting inside, she searched through her purse for tissues to wipe her face, because the tears wouldn't stop coming. And right behind the tears came a flood of upsetting memories.

ele

Tessa's home situation had been different from Jaime's and Claire's. Sunrise was her family's vacation home; Atlanta was their main home. Jaime and Claire needed to work, but Tessa didn't have to. She wanted to. She liked work and always preferred to be busy. So during the summers of high school, she had worked part-time at Rose's Flower Shop, and that was where she met Jaime and Claire, her besties.

Tessa's dad worked for an international oil corporation, and after her junior year of high school, he announced to the family that he was being transferred to Saudi Arabia.

No. Way.

There was no way Tessa was going to spend her senior year of high school stuck on an expat compound in a very restrictive Arabian country.

She relentlessly pressured her parents into letting her stay in Sunrise. With an autumn birthday, she was on the older side of her classmates, turning eighteen in October. No longer a minor, she pointed out. Repeatedly. She had two older sisters—one in Chicago, one in New York, both married. If she needed help, she could go to them.

A couple had moved into a fixer-upper next door to Tessa's home in Sunrise. The wife had a demanding job and traveled a lot, but the husband worked remotely. He was a wildly famous suspense author whose books her father voraciously read. He convinced Tessa's dad to let her stay in Sunrise and promised that he and his wife would keep an eye on her. The neighbor said he had moved a lot as a teen and understood how hard it was.

Finally, Tessa's dad relented. She was so grateful!

The neighbor made good on his promise. He would drop by now and then to see how Tessa was doing, fix something in the house that needed fixing, make sure her car was working. Tessa felt somewhat indifferent to the neighbor's drop-ins. It wasn't that she was immune to his appeal—he was a lithe, handsome man somewhere in his late thirties with a fabulously charismatic smile—but she didn't really need someone looking after her.

In October, she grew more comfortable with the neighbor. He remembered her birthday with a funny card and a cake he'd baked himself. It was nice to be treated this way, and soon the age difference between them started to melt away. He was funny, easy to talk to, had a way with words, and was so much more interesting than high school guys. Boys her age were, well, idiots. The neighbor made her feel special, like the times when he would read his work-in-progress to her and ask her opinion. He took Tessa seriously. He would notice little details about her, like calling her long blond hair a lion's mane. Living alone had been harder than she'd expected it to be. Lonelier.

Over Christmas break, Tessa went to Saudi Arabia to be with her parents and missed the neighbor far more than she'd expected. She wondered how he might phrase the sight of the ridiculous-looking camels at the camel market. Or how he'd describe the wail from the minarets as muezzins called faithful Muslims to prayers. Or what he would have to say about everything in the city shutting down—everything, even hospital services—during those calls to prayers. Five times a day!

By February, she found herself eagerly preparing for visits with the neighbor—planning her clothing, her hairstyle. He noticed everything about Tessa. They spent their time over at his house. It was a fixer-upper that wasn't getting any fix-up. His wife was gone more than she was home, and it didn't sound like she was the kind of woman who made a house a home. Super focused on her career, he said. Now and then, he confided to Tessa about how unhappy he was in his marriage. How lonely.

Looking back, Tessa thought Rose might have suspected something didn't seem quite right about the neighbor. Once, after he dropped by the flower shop to say hello to Tessa, Rose made an odd remark after he left. "That's the kind of man who forgets he's someone's husband."

Looking back, Rose's warning should've acted like a waving red flag. *Caution, caution!* Did Tessa heed it? No, ma'am. Did she ever think to confide in Rose? In her best friends? No, ma'am.

By March, Tessa was spending nearly every evening with her

neighbor. They'd make dinner together, play Scrabble or cards, maybe watch a movie. One night, as the movie ended (and it was a romantic comedy), he reached over to grab the remote and his face ended up close to hers, and time stood still as he leaned in to kiss her.

And oh my goodness, *what* a kiss. The kind that left a girl breathless, weak in the knees, the whole kit and caboodle. So *this* was what it felt like to be in love!

A few days later, things between them did venture on to the whole kit and caboodle.

On some level, Tessa knew this situation wasn't exactly . . . well, right. She knew her parents would be mortified. Knew that if she told Jaime and Claire, they would tell her to stop. They would say that she was being taken advantage of. They would remind her that this was another woman's husband.

So of course she didn't tell anyone.

Because whatever anyone might think, it wasn't like that between Tessa and the neighbor. Their story was different. Their love was different. He'd never felt about any woman the way he felt about Tessa. He said so, again and again.

By April, nearly every waking thought Tessa had was consumed with the neighbor. She was crazy-obsessed. When he left for a few days on a business trip, she missed him so much that she overrode his rule and texted him. He didn't text back, so she texted again, and again. And then she called him. He didn't pick up.

When he returned to Sunrise, he came right over to her house. She'd been watching for him to return, so she opened the door eagerly, expecting a very different reaction from him.

To her surprise, he closed the door behind him and turned to her with a dark look in his eyes that she'd never seen. He was *furious*. "How dare you text me! Or call me! Are you trying to destroy me?"

"No! No, I just was thinking of you and—"

"You were thinking of me? So you just thought you'd text me like we were in high school?" He practically spit the words. "Look, this isn't a game. Do you have any idea how it could damage my reputation with my agent or publisher, with my readers, if they knew about us? You could ruin me!"

"I just . . . I missed you."

"You *missed* me," he scoffed. "I don't have time for this. I thought you were mature for your age."

"I am!"

"You can't act like a kid and expect to have an adult relationship. Maybe . . . we should just call it quits now." He reached for the door handle and opened the door.

"Wait!"

He stopped and turned to her. "What?"

"I shouldn't have called you. I won't do it again."

He put his hands on his hips and let out a deep sigh. "Look, either you follow my rules or we're through."

"I get it," she said. "I do." She was practically begging, and a part of her felt disgusted with the desperate sound in her voice. But she hadn't thought of how she could have hurt his career when she texted and called him. She should have realized! His work was so important.

She couldn't bear the thought of losing him. Her whole life revolved around him. Being with him was all that mattered to her. She had let the deadline to enroll in the University of North Carolina roll on by—she didn't want to leave Sunrise.

He closed the door, came to Tessa, and put his arms around her, holding her close against him. "You're so young, Tessa," he said. "You're so beautiful that I keep forgetting just how young. I'm sorry too."

And things were good again. That moment was forgotten.

As senior year came to an end, Tessa spent less and less time with Jaime and Claire. Her neighbor discouraged her from spending time with them—he thought they were immature. She wasn't even sure if her friends realized how isolated she'd become—Jaime was working overtime to help Rose with some summer weddings, and Claire's full attention was riveted on Chris Reid, her magician boyfriend. She was even acting as his assistant.

Normally, the girls told each other everything. Dreams, hopes, crushes. They planned to have a flower shop together, but they couldn't agree where it should be. Jaime wanted it to be in New York City, near her "Instagram-crush" wedding planner, Liam Mc-Millan. Claire wanted everyone to stay in Sunrise, so she could be near Chris. He was Rose's nephew, which, Tessa thought, was half the reason Claire was in love with him. Claire wasn't raised with a mother, and Rose filled that hole in her heart.

The girls were still close. Tessa would confide some of her hopes and dreams with Claire and Jaime, but she didn't talk about her neighbor's visits. They felt too private, too special. Jaime, with her single-minded focus on New York City, and Claire, who was so crazy about Chris, would never understand how Tessa got herself tangled up with a married man. She couldn't believe it herself, but then, she stupidly thought she wasn't a cliché.

And then, in August, her period was late. She was never, ever late. When she told the neighbor she thought she might be pregnant, he went stone-cold. He accused her of trapping him, of setting him up, of trying to ruin his career, his marriage. He told her he would deny her, deny this baby, deny everything. He called her a terrible name, then opened the door of his house and shoved her over the threshold, then slammed the door behind her.

Overwhelmed, distraught, Tessa went straight to Rose's Flower Shop, hoping Rose or Jaime or Claire would be there. But the only one manning the shop that afternoon was Chris Reid. Somehow, he was just the right one. He ended up saving her life.

nine

Flowers grow out of dark moments.
—Corita Kent

Dawson opened the driver's side door to the truck and peered at Tessa. When he saw her tears, he climbed in and closed the door. "Look, maybe we can fight this. Gather signatures, have a sit-in at city hall. It's a David and Goliath story."

She wiped her eyes with a tissue. "What are you talking about?"

"The same thing you're crying about."

"I'm crying because of the chrysanthemum Lovey gave me. It just . . . took me back to a time in my life that I try very hard not to remember."

He shifted on the bench to look at her. "Why?"

"Because it was a time when I made one mistake after the other and ended up hurting a lot of people who had been very good to me."

Dawson took this all in. His face got serious. "And that's why you're crying?"

234

Obviously. "Yes," she said. "Why do you think I'm crying?"

"Because Lovey told you what she found out."

"What did she find out?"

"That the city council has marked the farm for urban density housing."

Wait. What? "The farm . . . as in Mountain Blooms Farm? My farm?"

He nodded. "A developer has been lined up. Apparently, this week you're going to be receiving an offer of"—he made air quotes—"fair market value."

"But I can say no, right?"

"Apparently, you've already said yes. According to . . ." He held up three fingers.

He didn't need to say it. She knew. Tyler.

ℓℓℓ

On Monday morning, Tessa walked into Tyler's campaign office and slapped the original contract she had signed to purchase Mountain Farm on his desk. It had taken her all Sunday afternoon and evening to find it, then to read it thoroughly. Afterward, she was furious. With Tyler, but even more so with herself. "How could you?"

Tyler looked up, surprised. "What's wrong?"

"*That's* what's wrong." She pointed to a small detail buried in a long paragraph of text in the contract. "The land had been identified for urban density. You knew it had. And right underneath that sentence comes one that says that the developer will get first rights of refusal when I sell." She could see from his expression that he wasn't surprised.

He leaned back in his chair. "I thought you knew. It was right there. You signed the papers, Tessa."

She flipped back through her memories. He kept rushing her through the escrow signing because he had some kind of campaign speech to give or babies to kiss or something like that. Now the pieces fit together. "You hid it from me! You intentionally skipped over that *significant* piece of information."

"I did not hide anything from you. It's never been a secret that the city has identified those sites. You could've checked into it. Frankly, you should've. You shouldn't have signed your name without reading the fine print."

"How could you have done such a thing? You've seen how hard we've worked this property. We have worked our butts off."

"You don't have to sell the land. This isn't eminent domain."

"Every other property that surrounds mine will be turned into high-rises. I spoke to the developer, Tyler. I saw the plans. My field won't get more than a few hours of sunlight each day, if that!"

He shrugged. "You still don't have to sell. However . . ." He seesawed his hand in the air. "However, you'll be getting a fair market price from the developer. There's a pretty good chance that the longer you hold out, the lower in value that land will be."

"So if I don't accept what the developer offers me now, I'm going to lose money."

"Probably. Historically."

"What I can't figure out is what you were hiding. Unless . . ." Ah. Of course. "The developer promised you a huge donation to your campaign." She covered her cheeks with her hands. "So let me guess. The tomato farmer wouldn't sell out. You needed a new contract that said the developer could get the first crack at it."

He didn't deny it. "Tessa, you're looking at this in the wrong way."

"Look me in the eye and tell me that this sale wouldn't benefit you immensely."

He glanced up at her, but he didn't hold her gaze. "It's a win-win, Tessa. We'll find you another little plot of land. Your field hand can work his soil magic."

"His name is Dawson Greene, Tyler. And he's much more than a field hand."

His head jerked up. "I knew it," he said, his eyes narrowed. "I knew there was something between the two of you."

"What are you talking about?" Tessa squeezed her fists in the air. "Stop twisting things! You lied to me, Tyler. You virtually stole this land from me."

"I did no such thing!" He slapped a palm against his chest, then dropped it with a sigh. "I was helping you with something you knew nothing about. You're young, Tessa. You're so beautiful that sometimes I forget how young you really are."

A chill went down her spine. She thought Tyler was so different from the neighbor, and in many ways they were. But at their core, they were the same man. They both took advantage of her. "You don't get it, do you?" From her pocket, she took out the engagement ring that she'd finally gotten off last night with the help of Vaseline and smacked it on his desk.

At the door, she turned back. "And by the way, three billboards along Highway 74 have been slathered with graffiti."

Tyler looked like a fish out of water, with his mouth opening and shutting in a panic.

ten

Don't let the tall weeds cast a shadow
on the beautiful flowers in your garden.
—Steve Maraboli

Tuesday morning, Tessa was out in the field, walking up and down through rows of dahlias almost as tall as she was. Many were starting to fade from their late summer glory, though blooms would keep appearing until the first killing frost. Just a few days ago, she and Dawson had talked about whether they should try and overwinter the dahlias by covering them with straw, or dig up the tubers and store them in her little house.

Thinking about selling the land gutted her. Overwhelmed her with wrenching sadness.

As she walked down a row, it seemed as if she was practically standing on a sponge. What a difference Dawson had made in the soil! Butterflies danced over the dahlias. Bees hummed. Birds sailed past Tessa and into the boxes he'd had built for them. The man was a genius when it came to soil biology. He had turned gray cloddy dirt into something beneficial, nurturing, able to support all kinds of life.

Tessa didn't know what she'd have done without him. Or would do without him. Tyler was right about one thing. Dawson should move on to a real job. And Dawson was right too. You never knew what was coming around the corner.

She turned in a circle, sweeping the fields with her gaze. All their work was for naught. This time next year, condos at some stage of building would be covering this beautiful field. Even if she didn't sell her field to the developer, she would be surrounded by construction in progress. And in the end, she'd have very little sunlight for her flowers.

She heard a familiar whistle and spun around to find Dawson heading toward her, waving a large white envelope. "This just got delivered. Overnight mail. I figured you'd want it right away."

Ugh. The developer's offer. She walked a few paces to meet him. "I'm not sure I want to open it. Once that offer comes in, everything starts to change."

"I've been doing some research on this. You can refuse the offer."

She gave him a half smile. *Dawson and his research.* "What about the rest of the street? This field will be hemmed in by sky-scrapers."

He rocked his hand in the air. "Not exactly skyscrapers, but I get what you mean. I talked to a lawyer friend at church and found out you can try to block the urban density tag on this area, but it'll mean you'll be spending a lot of money in legal fees."

Money that she didn't have.

"And . . . he also said that if you look at current trends in urban development, you'll probably end up losing the battle." He handed her the envelope.

When Tessa saw the return address, she felt a shock sizzle through her entire body. So surprised she couldn't speak for a moment. Couldn't open it. Trembling, she held it in her hands. "It's . . . not from the developer."

He hesitated. "Maybe I should go."

"No. Don't go." It was from Rose Reid, the owner of the flower shop in Sunrise. She didn't want to be alone for this, whatever its contents held. She opened it up and unfolded a letter, handwritten in Rose's lovely cursive. Tessa would know that handwriting anywhere. She read through the letter, then looked up at Dawson, who was patiently waiting, watching. "Rose, the flower shop owner in Sunrise, saw my picture in Sunday's newspaper and realized where I'd been living." She skimmed the letter again. "She wants me to return to Sunrise. She said she wants to retire and hopes that I might consider running the flower shop. She's offering it to Jaime and Claire too. Those are the two girls I used to work with."

"Where are they now?"

"In Sunrise, Rose wrote. They've come back." That surprised her, especially Jaime, who was working for Liam McMillan, the hotshot wedding planner. Tessa knew that from Instagram. Knowing Jaime and Claire had felt comfortable to return to Sunrise only magnified the sense of guilt she felt. That fire was her fault.

"Maybe you should go. Check it out."

"Go *back* to Sunrise? Why would I do that? I don't want to run a flower shop."

"They must need flower growers there. Go find some cheap land that needs worms and compost and tilling."

She looked at him like he was crazy. "You have got to be kidding. Start all over again?"

"Yeah. Or consider what Rose is offering you."

"Dawson, you don't understand. I can't go back. I can't."

"Why not?"

"Because I just can't!" She turned and headed down the row.

He followed her. "This woman is asking you to consider something. She's offering you an opportunity. You should at least go see what she's got on her mind."

"I know what she's got on her mind." Even though Rose said all was forgiven, that it was time to come home, Tessa didn't believe her. How could Rose forgive when she didn't know the whole story?

240

"What?"

"She wants to blame me for . . . what happened!"

"So what happened?"

Tessa whirled around. "Just some mistakes I made, okay?"

He seemed unfazed. "What teenager hasn't made some mistakes?"

Tessa opened her mouth, then shut it. "Dawson, this wasn't something you can just brush off like typical stupid teenager stuff. It's bigger than that. I just can't go back. I won't go back." She spun around and started marching off again.

"Y'know," he said, following her, "when you can't talk about something, it doesn't go away. It just gets stuffed down."

She threw her hands in the air. "Advice from a man who doesn't talk about anything other than soil!"

"I can talk about other things!"

She stopped. Slowly, she turned around. "Like what? Like . . . the fact that you're involved with a purple-haired woman? Like . . . the fact that you're a churchgoer and never once mentioned it?"

He frowned. "More like . . . I've done stupid stuff in high school."

"Not as stupid as me."

He walked up toward her. "Okay, I'll go first. I hung around with a bad crowd. We used to siphon gas out of cars to fill up my truck."

She looked over at his old truck. "That same one?"

"Yep."

"Well, that might've been stupid but—"

"Hold on. Once, I tried to siphon gas out of an RV and ended up mistakenly siphoning from the sewage tank. The fumes made me so sick that I passed out. When I came to, cops were standing around me."

Despite the foul mood she was in, Tessa couldn't hold back a smile. "So, I guess that's where your interest in composting began."

The fans around his eyes started to crinkle. "Your turn." He took a step closer to her. "Take some advice from Fred Rogers."

"Mr. Rogers?"

He nodded. "He was my hero. He said that if you can talk about something, you can manage it."

She stared at him. She had never told anyone the whole story. Not a single soul. And look where that had gotten her—stuck in the same pattern. She inhaled a deep breath and slowly let it out. "When I was a senior in high school, I got involved with a married man."

She expected Dawson to look shocked, to show some kind of horrified reaction, but he just listened calmly as she talked, as she explained how this neighbor convinced her to keep quiet, how their relationship isolated her from her friends. And then, almost surprising herself, she told him about telling the neighbor she might be pregnant.

Again, he just listened.

"He pushed me out the door so hard I nearly fell. I was desperate and scared and went to the flower shop to get help." She turned away from him and folded her arms against her abdomen. "From there, things went from bad to worse. There was a fire at the shop . . . and I'm sure something I did was the cause of it . . . but I let someone else take the blame for it. I left Sunrise like a coward, and I never looked back. I hurt people I loved, who loved me." She turned back to face him.

"So, were you?"

"Was I what?"

"Pregnant?"

"No. Just late." She folded her arms against her chest. "So, I think I win the stupid teenager award." He didn't react to her attempt at a joke; he just kept looking at her with a concerned expression.

She expected to see shame in his eyes, disgust. She didn't expect kindness. Overwhelmed, she had to look away. She started heading

242

down the field again, though she really wasn't going anywhere in particular. She just had to keep moving.

"Hey!" He hurried to catch up with her. "Where are you going?"

"Nowhere. I am going nowhere. Absolutely nowhere." She slipped through a row of dahlias and started striding down the other side.

"Hey, stop. Tessa, stop!"

She turned to see him take a large step through the dahlias to reach her. He took a step closer, then another, and then another.

He came close, so close she could smell his soap, and he put his hands on her shoulders to make her look at him. "You know what I love most about . . ." Their eyes met as he paused.

For a long moment, it seemed as if everything went quiet. Even the birds stopped singing. His hesitation didn't last long, but there was enough time for Tessa to realize that her confession had done the opposite of what she'd expected. Instead of pushing them apart, they were closer. She held her breath. What was he reluctant to say?

"—composting?"

Composting. She squinted. "What are you talking about?"

"A compost heap is full of mistakes. Full of leftovers and discards. And look what it ends up turning into. Something good. Something nourishing for the earth. Something useful. Maybe even something beautiful. Remember that narcissus bloom you found?" He swept his hands out in an arc, leaving them palms up to indicate the fields around them. "That's what God can do with our mess. But you can't fix what you don't face." He wiggled his eyebrows. "Give that a little thought." And he left her in the field, puzzling over that bit of wisdom. About halfway down the row he turned and walked backward. "And I *did* tell you I went to church. You just weren't paying attention." He lifted a finger in the air. "Might be a good time to have a long talk with the Almighty."

Yeah? she thought. *What about purple-haired Lovey? I would have paid attention to* that.

eleven

Flowers grow back, even after they are stepped on. So will I.
—*Unknown*

The next day's mail brought an offer for Mountain Blooms Farm from the developer. A fair market value offer, Tessa had to admit. But she just couldn't sign the papers. Couldn't even look at them.

Instead, she hopped on her Vespa and drove in circles around Asheville, wandering aimlessly, just like her life felt. How had something like this happened to her? She loved Mountain Blooms Farm so much. She'd poured a year of hard work into it, relishing every minute. She'd even grown fond of worms. And it was all about to disappear.

She felt a text come in on her phone and wondered if Dawson was texting her about something. He should be out job hunting, but instead he was in the field, starting the long process of digging up dahlia tubers. This morning, he told her that until she signed the papers, the farm was still in operation. She should go home and help him. She pulled into a parking lot to turn around and stopped to check her cell phone. It was from Tyler, pleading with her to please forgive him. Eight texts in three days. Six phone calls.

She blocked his number.

Why had she blindly trusted Tyler? She seemed to have terrible judgment about men. Terrible. Was she just a bad picker? Stupidly naive? Doomed to be taken advantage of?

She looked up to see the Cathedral of All Souls right in front of her. She'd driven past it but had never been inside. She got off her Vespa and walked over to read a small plaque. Built in 1896 by George Vanderbilt, it was a parish church for the Biltmore Village. Meant for everyone, it said. All souls.

Even battered and bruised souls?

Maybe Dawson was right. Maybe it was time she had a word or two with the Almighty.

She went inside and slid into a pew toward the middle of the church. She sat down on a needlepoint cushion that she suspected had been made by local parishioners and tucked her chin reverently. She tried to quiet her mind, but it was full of wishes—a wish that this mess would go away, a wish that she could break this terrible pattern of trusting the wrong men, a wish that Mountain Blooms Farm could be protected, a wish that Dawson wouldn't leave to find a "real" job now, though she knew he probably would and should. On and on her wishes went, one after the other.

She had always leaned on someone to rescue her in a time of need. This time, the cavalry wasn't coming.

Compost. Dawson's remark swirled around her head like a butterfly. Could something good actually come out of the terrible mistakes she'd made in high school? Of all the damage she had caused others? She'd never forget that look on Claire's face when she found Tessa crying in Chris's arms. Claire was always quick to jump to conclusions. Too quick. She'd shouted that she would never forgive them, not Chris, not Tessa. From the workshop, Jaime overheard and burst into the room to see what was going on. Everything went south from there. In a brief span of ten to fifteen minutes, life changed completely. Tessa, Jaime, and Claire fled from Sunrise, and Chris, poor Chris, went to jail.

In Rose's letter, she wrote that all was forgiven. But how could that be? Rose didn't know the whole story. The very thought of facing Rose made Tessa shudder. Of all people, she had disappointed Rose the most.

The sun broke through the clouds, sending rays of color down on Tessa. She lifted her head to see the apse, to the stained-glass window behind the altar. And then she noticed a small glass vase of flowers on the altar, like an offering—a cluster of narcissus blooms. Hold on—they were out of season. They shouldn't be blooming right now! A shiver went down her spine.

In her mind's eye, she saw the narcissus bloom on that heap of compost in the sustainability class, when she first met Dawson. The vision wouldn't let her go.

Tessa took in a deep breath. She needed to go to Sunrise and face her past mistakes. Right now.

She looked straight up at the ceiling. "If you can help me fix this mess I made," she whispered, "then I'm all yours."

twelve

*Love is like wildflowers; it's often found
in the most unlikely places.*
—Ralph Waldo Emerson

Tessa got back on her Vespa and started to drive south on 26, a route she'd intentionally avoided for over seven years. It hadn't changed much—still two-laned and tree-lined with a few areas to pass when you got stuck behind a slow tourist who wasn't used to the curves. Without even thinking, she slowed as she drove into Brevard. Sure enough, there was a police officer in a car, waiting to pounce. It made her smile. Some things, like speed traps, never changed.

She stopped at the Sunrise Café, her favorite local restaurant, wishing it were open so she could buy a bagel, but it closed in the early afternoon. That, too, hadn't changed.

She checked the time on her phone. Nearly five o'clock. Sunsets came early in these mountains, so she got back on the road. She didn't want to be driving a Vespa on Route 26 after dark. She drove on to Sapphire. From there the road began its twisty descent. She slowed as she approached the turnoff to Sunrise and headed into town.

As she stopped at the one red light in Sunrise, her heart started pounding, her palms started sweating. She felt as if she was going through a scrapbook in her mind and not all the pictures were good. What if the neighbor still lived there? What if she were to see him?

If the neighbor did still live here, she would leave Sunrise, right away. She couldn't stay here, not even for five minutes. Not a chance. Too hard. Too full of regrets. Stupid choices.

Then she thought of Dawson's remark. What teenager doesn't make mistakes?

Was forgiveness really that easy? Especially forgiving yourself?

She drove along Main Street, past Rose's Flower Shop, slowing to notice that it had been entirely rebuilt from the fire, though it looked pretty close to the original version. Then she drove out toward her parents' old home, arriving at the driveway minutes later. Clearly, a young family lived there now, with bicycles and toys strewn all over the front yard. Slowly, she drove past her old home to the neighbor's house, heart pounding. She had to see if the neighbor was still there. She cut the engine as she drew close to the last stand of trees and coasted for a few yards.

The neighbor's fixer-upper looked the same, still in need of a fix-up. But it looked empty, deserted. No lights. No signs of life. And then in the gloaming, she saw a For Sale sign out front.

She sat there for a long while, looking at the house, thinking about how narrowly she'd escaped from consequences that might've altered her life forever. The path in the bushes that she had made going between the two houses that year was now grown over. The property looked completely neglected. She noticed a box attached to the For Sale sign and went over to see if there were any flyers inside. One was left, so she pulled it out. It was curled on the edges and faded, but she could make out the information: *Foreclosure! Selling as-is. Three full acres!*

The name and phone number on the bottom line belonged to a county foreclosure center.

Tessa walked around the entire house, twice. While she was no contractor, it was obvious that this house had been vacant for a long, long time. She peered in the windows and saw leaks from the roof, puddles on the floor. A disaster.

And then Dawson's word circled around her again. *Compost.* Compost. Compost.

An idea started to blossom.

She gazed around the yard. A level lot, few trees to block sunshine. She bent down and scratched up a handful of dirt, sniffing it, squeezing it. Not bad. Not good, but much better than the soil had been at her Mountain Blooms Farm before Dawson arrived, that much she knew was for sure.

She let the dirt drop from her hand. What if she bulldozed this house that held so many dark memories? What if she turned this acreage into a new flower farm? She'd done it once. She could do it again. Something good could come out of the mess she'd left behind. The one she had run from.

If she accepted the developer's offer, which was a decent amount, she could afford to buy the property and turn it into a farm, just like she'd done at Mountain Blooms Farm. She could rent a mobile home and haul it here to live. Mobile homes were everywhere in Sunrise.

A breeze moved the trees along the property line, and she shivered, rubbing her arms. She should've thought to bring a coat. It would be a cold drive back over the mountain.

Could she really do this? Buy this property?

It would mean that she'd be returning to Sunrise. Returning to Jaime and Claire. To Chris. She would need to face Rose, to tell her everything that had happened that August night. To take responsibility for it. To clean up her mess.

What would her parents say? Probably that she was lucky she

A Field of Beauty

had pocket change from her year as a farmer. Her sisters would say it was time to start a real career.

But growing flowers *was* Tessa's career. She knew that now more than ever. She wasn't going to give flowers up.

She took in a deep breath. Could she do this, all alone?

She wondered if Dawson would consider joining her in this venture. It would be asking a lot of him—a move from Asheville to a tiny town.

And then there was Lovey Mitchell. She winced. Lovey was so wrong for Dawson. How could he not see that? He needed someone more like . . . Tessa.

She knew she depended on Dawson heavily, but she hadn't realized how much her feelings had been changing for him until . . . it was too late.

But what if she asked him to come? Join her for just one year, like he'd done at Mountain Blooms Farm. After all, he was a man who understood a good cause.

Then again, Dawson had often accused Tessa of playing the damsel in distress. She didn't even realize she did it, but once he'd said it, she recognized it. She didn't want to play that card anymore.

Maybe it was time to not ask or expect anyone to rescue her. Not even Dawson.

But she did need a little help. She looked up at the sky and spotted the first star. "What do you think, Almighty God? Should I do this?"

She waited, as if listening for an answer. None came, not audibly, anyway. But inside, she felt a sweep of peace warm her from head to toe.

She smiled. *Okay. Decision made.*

Good or bad, she was returning to Sunrise to stay, despite everything she'd done to run from it. She felt her phone buzz from a text and reached into her pocket to read it.

Dawson
You OK?

> Better than OK. I'm going to accept the developer's offer. And then . . .

She paused. Once this was declared, it would be real. No turning back.

> Then what?

> Then I'm going to buy a 3-acre plot in Sunrise and start another flower farm. I'm looking at the property right now.

Pause. A long, long pause.

> I know.

> What do you mean?

> Turn around.

She spun around to see Dawson standing by his truck, parked across the road. He must have followed her all afternoon, quietly keeping an eye on her but never interfering. So like Dawson. She started toward him, slowly. She felt a wash of shyness come over her. He pushed off from his truck and walked toward her. They met in the middle of the road.

"Were you following me?"

"Maybe." He tried to sound super casual, as if he hadn't been trailing her for the last few hours. He took a few more steps to close the gap between them. He was so close that she caught his unique Dawson scent—soap and earth and fresh air. "Looks like the house has been deserted for quite some time."

"It sure does." She turned slightly from the waist to lift a palm in the direction of the property. "What do you think? Can you see the possibilities?"

He lifted his chin to look over at it. The sun was starting to set behind the trees. "You've done it before. Ready to do it again?" He looked at her as if her answer was extremely important.

"I am. First thing I want to do is to knock down the house and start again."

"You'll need a good farm manager."

She tipped her head. "Do you have anyone to suggest?" He was pretty well connected in the farming world. "I know it's asking a lot of someone. Moving to Sunrise is a big deal. It's a very small town. And I couldn't even pay a base salary. I was thinking I could offer a sixty-forty split of the profits."

To her surprise, hands on his hips, his gaze swept the property. It was a familiar stance that she'd seen him do hundreds of times at Mountain Blooms Farm. "I can think of someone. For a fifty-fifty split, I think he'd do it."

"Who?"

He pointed his thumbs at his chest.

She almost couldn't breathe. "You'd come to Sunrise? You'd help me farm this land?"

He lifted a shoulder in a shrug, like it was no big deal. "Look what we did with an acre in just a year. Might be interesting to see what we could do with three acres."

"But . . . what about Lovey?" She had to ask. She had to know.

His eyebrows lifted. "Lovey is . . . she's just a friend." A slow grin came over his face. "She offered to pinch hit for the Biltmore dinner."

Just a friend? *That* would have been nice to know. Tessa regretted all the mean thoughts she'd had about Lovey. Suddenly shy, she kept her eyes down. "Why would you do this?"

"Hard to resist a chance to fix a patch of soil."

But Tessa knew it was more than that. He could have plenty of opportunities to work on large-scale farms, where there'd be low risk and deep pockets. "Dawson," she whispered. "Why would you do this *for me*?" She hated to ask, but she needed to. "Are you rescuing me?"

"No, I'm not rescuing you. I know you could figure this out on your own." He looked down, kicking the ground with the toe of his boot. "I just thought, y'know, that we make a good team." He lifted his head. "So do we have a deal?" He put a hand out to shake. "Partners?"

Tessa looked at his outstretched hand, then up into his blue eyes. She thought his ears were turning a little pink and wondered if it was the only outer evidence of his carefully hidden emotions. If so, she wasn't going to let him grow his hair long again.

So maybe her picker wasn't as bad as she thought it was. She might have made mistakes with other men, but with Dawson, she had chosen well. The weight of her past mistakes seemed to diminish around him. Her hand slowly reached out and gently clasped his. "Partners," she said with a smile, knowing he only wanted the best for her, something she had sensed from the start.

No wonder she felt beautiful around him.

a FUTURE
in BLOSSOM

Cast of Characters

Rose Reid—(late sixties) owner of Rose's Flower Shop in Sunrise, North Carolina

Jaime Harper—(age 25) floral artist and event planner at Rose's Flower Shop

Liam McMillan—(age 30-something) owner of Epic Events in New York City

Claire Murphy—(age 25) floral stylist and shop manager of Rose's Flower Shop

Chris Reid—(age 24) nephew of Rose Reid, self-employed as a magician

Tessa Anderson—(age 26) new owner of three acres in Sunrise, North Carolina, with plans to turn it into a flower farm

Dawson Greene—(somewhere in his late twenties—he's suspicious of personal questions) soil expert, the farm manager for Tessa's new flower farm in Sunrise, North Carolina

Floral Glossary

annual—a flower that completes its life cycle in one growing season, such as a zinnia

biennial—a plant that completes its life cycle in two years or seasons, such as foxglove

compost—decayed organic material used to fertilize plants or condition soil

cover crop—a crop grown to cover the soil and prevent erosion, such as clover; often incorporated into the soil later for enrichment

cut flowers—flowers grown to be cut

fillers—material used to fill gaps or empty spaces

fish emulsion—fertilizer produced from the fluid remains of processed fish

floriography—(aka the language of flowers) a symbolic form of communication using specific flower meanings; it has been used for centuries across cultures as a poetic means of expressing emotions and conveying hidden messages, particularly during the Victorian era

focal point—the area of dominance or emphasis where the eye naturally travels

foliage—greenery, such as plant leaves

forage—harvesting free material, such as blooming forsythia branches, taken from public or private properties (only with permission, please!)

hoop house—a small, high tunnel made of plastic, used to shelter or cultivate plants

mechanics—the hidden foundation that holds flowers in place (such as a flower frog or chicken wire)

negative space—a planned open space within a design that contains no flowers or foliage

perennial—a plant that persists for more than two years, such as a rose

recipe—a set of instructions to prepare a specific arrangement

reflex—open petals of a flower

tuber—a thickened underground stem for certain plants, such as dahlias

vendors—sources for flowers (local growers, farmers' markets, wholesalers, or international)

vessels—containers to hold arrangements (such as vases, urns, compote bowls). All kinds of objects can become vessels to hold flowers—mason jars, bottles, crocks

wholesale house—suppliers of fresh flowers, plants, and floral supplies to a wide range of professionals

The flower that blooms in adversity
is the rarest and most beautiful of all.
— *Mulan*

one

I am in awe of flowers. Not because of their colors,
but because even though they have dirt in their roots,
they still grow. They still bloom.
—D. Antoinette Foy

TESSA ANDERSON

*I*f only memories could get sent to the dumpster as easily as debris could. Tessa watched the bulldozer remove the last remains of the foreclosed-on house she'd bought in Sunrise, North Carolina, and wished it could carry away all the reckless moments stuck in her mind too. Those were harder to get rid of.

Dawson Greene, her soil expert guy, liked to remind her of the concept of composting. "It takes garbage and transforms it into something valuable and enriching to the earth." He said it often, with confidence, and he was right. About soil, about life. Tessa took a deep breath and smiled as the bucket of the bulldozer emptied the last debris from the house into the dumpster. Gone. Gone at last. Finally, she could move forward.

In just two months, Tessa had done the impossible. She'd sold

Mountain Blooms Farm, her flower farm in Asheville, to a developer who planned to build high-density housing on it. She'd purchased this foreclosed property, rented an old Airstream trailer so she could live on the land, filed permits, and hired a demolition team to tear down and remove the old structure.

A lot had been happening in the last few months, but some things had yet to happen. Important things, like paying a visit to Rose Reid, the owner of the flower shop in Sunrise where Tessa had worked during high school. Seeking out her friends Jaime Harper and Claire Murphy. Or facing Chris Reid, to whom she owed so much.

Tessa dreaded those important things.

Dreaded them . . . but she was also in Sunrise because of them. Rose had sent her a letter to ask her if she would consider running the flower shop, but that's not why Tessa returned. No thank you, ma'am. She had zero interest in running a retail shop. She wanted to be outdoors, in the fields growing flowers, all the time.

In the letter, Rose had said all was forgiven. That was what Tessa couldn't ignore. That was what brought her back. There was no way that Rose could forgive her without knowing the whole story. Seven years ago, Tessa had left Sunrise full of shame, holding tightly to it, because shame craved secrecy.

But it was time to clean up her mess. She'd run out of excuses.

She heard Dawson call her name and turned to see him approaching.

"I'm not happy about this." Dawson had been walking the property, bothered about the compacted soil created by the demolition team.

She had to smile. Dawson took his work very seriously. She watched him for a while, noticing how his hair and beard were growing back after his annual trim. He was looking scruffy again, which was just the way she liked him. "We knew there'd be some fallout damage, Dawson. There's no way a whole house could be removed without help from large equipment." Everything except the foundation, which would require a separate team to jackhammer and haul away the broken-up concrete.

Hands on his hips, he turned in a circle, frowning. She knew what he was thinking. Was the ground too hard for plowing? Was there time to plant a cover crop? "Tessa, instead of digging up this concrete slab, what would you think of putting a greenhouse on it?"

What? That came out of the blue. "A greenhouse?" It would be a huge greenhouse. The remaining foundation was a rectangle.

"You've been talking about it from the start. And this way we could grow more varieties. The greenhouse would make that possible."

She walked out to where he was standing. "You mean, you want us to grow a variety of flowers? The idea I first had for Mountain Blooms Farm before you shot it down?"

"That was one acre of land. This is three acres. I think this land could support varieties." He scratched his forehead. "Even if we had a clean slate, I think this is where you'd want a greenhouse to be. Full sun, east-to-west orientation, level, good drainage, close to a water source. And it creates a wind block for the south acre."

"You're actually trying to convince *me* of buying a greenhouse?" It was true that Tessa had always wanted one. Longed for it, the way some people longed for a luxury car. The benefits would be enormous. But she'd had a small shed-sized one in mind. He was talking about a commercial greenhouse. Huge. Expensive.

"I got a call from a grass-supplier buddy over in Asheville. He ordered the wrong size greenhouse and can't return it. Still flat packed. It's a steal of a deal. He even said he'd deliver it here."

"How much?"

He looked away. "Still negotiating that."

"Any chance you've done a favor for this grass-supplier buddy?"

A sheepish look came into Dawson's eyes. "He's a really good guy."

Tessa smiled. Dawson's life was all about favors. Mostly, he gave them. Now and then, he received them. It was his preferred approach to life—barters and favors rather than consumerism and taxes.

"I think we should get it." He clapped his hands and rubbed them together. "I'll give him a call and get the ball rolling."

"But, Dawson . . . aren't we getting ahead of ourselves? We don't even have a name for the flower farm yet."

"You're the one with the imagination." He pointed to the far corner of the lot. "Think about it. Acid lovers over there, near the pines."

In Tessa's mind, she envisioned rows of blue hydrangeas and creamy white gardenias and rhododendrons with blossoms the size of dinner plates.

He turned a quarter circle. "Spring blooms over there."

Sweet peas, peonies . . . oh, and bulbs! Tulips and daffodils. Imagine how lovely they'd look in the full glory of spring.

"Over there, where the sun hits first, will be the summer annuals."

She turned to the right, her mind spinning. Snapdragons, zinnias, cosmos, asters, ranunculi. She could see it all! Daffodils in the spring, ending with dahlias in the fall. Loveliness all year long. A year of flowers.

She turned in a circle, imagining all those flowers on what was now a mess of brown dirt. Without Dawson, it would stay a mess. But with him, by next summer, these three acres would be transformed into a lush garden. She imagined hosting flower events and teaching people how to grow flowers and selling flowers to suppliers or at farmers' markets.

"You'll be able to see the flowers bloom from your lavish digs."

She turned to the used Airstream she'd bought, tucked against the edge of the property. Dawson had rented a small house in town and thought she was crazy to live in a trailer, but she wanted to live right here, watching over her land.

"Here's something else to think about. A fellow in town told me that the woods next to these three acres might be going up for sale soon. Six more acres. I walked through it this morning, and it wouldn't take much to clear the land. If we bought it, that could mean nine acres. More than enough for the kind of year-round flower farm you have in mind."

Buy it? Six more acres? Tessa loved the idea of it, loved it so much . . . but . . . six more acres would require . . . a lot of cash. A *lot*.

"And if we use only solar power, we might be able to get a grant from the energy company."

She grinned. "You? You're willing to accept financial assistance from the public utility grid?"

He lifted his chin. "I am willing to be rewarded for using the sun in the way the Almighty intended it to be used."

She laughed. Dawson had a deep distrust of government and an abhorrence for politics. And then a nagging worry spilled out. "Dawson, what if people think we just have a hippie farm?"

He spun around, a curious look on his face. "A hippie farm," he repeated in a flat voice. "Since when did farming become a hippie thing?" He took a few steps closer. "What's up? Why are you freaking out?"

"I don't know. I just . . . Last night I lay awake in the trailer wondering if I might have made a huge mistake. And then I dragged you into it." When he should be getting a real job. Real as in a consistent salary, and medical benefits, and a retirement plan. Not a high-risk flower farm.

His dark eyebrows lifted. "You couldn't have dragged me into something I didn't want to do."

True. Dawson was no pushover. She looked up at him. "But are you sure we can make it a success?"

"I'm sure we can give it our best efforts. Mountain Blooms Farm was a success. This soil is in much better shape than that clay dirt was."

"It's just that Sunrise is such a small town. Do you think we'll be able to find a market for flowers? We're going to have to take flowers to Highlands or to Asheville. We'll be on the road constantly."

"Not constantly. Only when the flowers are in full bloom." He took a step closer to her. "So, what's really up?"

"What do you mean?"

"You're the one who's never doubted there's a market just waiting for fresh-cut flowers." He folded his arms against his chest. "So what's really bothering you?"

"Um, well, I . . ." She looked down at her green Wellies. "I seem to . . . have run out of reasons to postpone seeing Rose." She blew out a puff of cold air. She'd tried to avoid this encounter for seven years.

Dawson knew what this meeting meant to her. How hard it was for her. "You can do this, Tessa Anderson. You're stronger than you think."

"Right." Absolutely. She was stronger than she thought.

No, she wasn't.

two

Gardens and flowers have a way of bringing people together,
drawing them from their homes.
—Clare Ansberry

JAIME HARPER

Five months ago, when Jaime left New York City behind to return to Sunrise, she would've bet money that she'd never see Liam McMillan again. He told her otherwise, but she didn't believe him. Why should she? There'd been so much about Liam that turned out to be smoke and mirrors, not unlike Chris Reid's magician tricks. Liam had eschewed his humble Southern roots and taken on a Scottish persona.

Totally fake. Totally successful.

Liam McMillan was considered one of the fastest-rising stars in the wedding world. Just this past year, *Martha Stewart Weddings*, *Vogue*, and *Brides* magazines had named Liam's company, Epic Events, as a top wedding vendor in the entire country.

Jaime had bought into Liam's facade like the rest of the world. She'd even fallen head over heels for him—her boss and mentor!

Until it all shattered on that day when she overheard him on the phone with his Kentucky grandmother. There was no mistaking his origins after that moment. Liam McMillan was a big fat lie.

And yet Jaime, knowing all of this, thought of almost nothing but Liam. She couldn't stop herself from replaying memories of him or tracking him on social media. Couldn't stop checking her phone ten times a day, hoping he would text or call or email. No sir, not a single peep in five months.

She was thankful for the heavy workload she'd stepped into at Rose's Flower Shop because it kept her busy and distracted. It helped to keep a lid on her annoying preoccupation with Liam.

Last night, Jaime had worked late into the night to prepare table arrangements for a favorite customer's meet-the-boyfriend tea party. It was a Southern tradition. When a young woman's gentleman caller came to town to meet the parents, her mama would host an innocuous tea party for friends and family to check the young man out. Those poor fellas had no idea what they were getting themselves into.

Jaime had already delivered the arrangements, stopped for a cup of coffee, and was heading to the flower shop to clean up her mess before it opened this morning. The last thing she'd expected was to find Liam McMillan waiting in front of the locked door. About ten feet away from the shop, she froze. She couldn't think, couldn't breathe.

"Hello, Jaime."

Her mind was spinning fast, but words were stuck in her throat. Liam looked as gorgeous as ever. Heart-stopping handsome. Freshly shaved, he'd had a recent haircut and was dressed in his typical casual-but-expensive clothing. She fought back an impulsive desire to launch herself into his arms and kiss him right on the lips. *No ma'am*, she told herself. *You will not.*

"Yer lookin' bonnie."

So . . . he was still playing the Scottish Liam. And no, no, she really wasn't looking bonnie. Certainly not at this moment, anyway. She hadn't planned to see anyone this morning. Claire was scheduled to open the shop at ten, so Jaime had dressed in yoga pants and an oversized sweatshirt. No makeup. Hair pulled in a high side pony. She was nowhere near bonnie looking! These were the thoughts that were flying through her head.

He tipped his head. "Have you nothing t' say? Or"—he paused—"maybe 'tis the accent?" His expression softened, imploring. "I won't be two-faced with you. It truly comes naturally now, even with Meemaw."

Imagining his granny's reaction, Jaime couldn't help but smile. But that faded quickly as her thoughts bunched up in her mind like a traffic jam. *Why haven't you bothered to get in touch with me? Didn't you miss me? Don't I matter to you at all?* She let out a breath. "I . . . certainly didn't expect to see you."

"This morning? Or ever?"

"Not ever." She cleared her throat. "I've never heard from . . . anyone at Epic."

"Ah, I suppose it's the New York City way. Everyone's totally consumed with what's right in front of 'em. Putting out fires, all the time."

In other words, "out of sight, out of mind." Jaime tried to pretend his casual dismissal didn't bother her . . . but it did. It really, really did.

"This year's wedding season was a marathon. 'Twas Epic Events' biggest year."

If he was telling her that to make her feel guilty, she already did. She had left Epic without giving two weeks' notice just as peak season began, and she still felt the sting of guilt. She just couldn't stay in New York City after the disastrous Zimmerman wedding. Rose's letter, asking her to come back to Sunrise, tipped the scales for her.

A cool breeze swirled around them, shaking her out of her daze. "Why don't you come in? I'll make some fresh coffee."

"I'd like that." He smiled. "To tell the truth, I'd prefer tea."

Right, right. She'd forgotten that he wasn't a coffee drinker, being Scottish and all. She tried not to roll her eyes.

He followed her to the workshop, which had been left in such a state. "I had to work late last night. I was just coming in to clean up."

As she flipped on the lights and turned on the heat, he poked around the workshop. "I see you've employed the same organization that we had at Epic."

In the middle of filling the electric kettle with water for tea, she stopped to look up. He was right. She had learned so much during her time in New York City, especially from working with him. He had helped her create the Epic workshop to maximize efficiency and minimize waste, and she'd brought those design concepts back to Rose's. Happily, Rose had given her a free hand—a significant change from when Jaime was working here in high school. Back then, Rose had a strict protocol for the workshop—keep everything where she, and she alone, had put it. The organization made sense to Rose but no one else. The improved workshop was now ready for anyone to step in and find what they needed. "I suppose my time at Epic is now part of me."

He gazed at her with a look she couldn't quite discern. "Aye. I understand how that can happen."

The kettle clicked off, so Jaime poured hot water into a cup with a teabag and handed it to him. "So what brings you here?"

He sat down on a stool to drink his tea. "A destination weddin'."

So then, not me. She tried to hide her mounting disappointment by busying herself with cleaning off the workbench. "Where?"

"Here."

She spun around to face him. "Here . . . as in Sunrise?"

"Aye. Jaime, I came to see if y' might be willin' t' help me pull this wedding off."

"When is it?"

"As soon as humanly possible."

Her eyes went wide. Weddings with Epic Events were booked a year in advance. Sometimes . . . years ahead.

"I see the look of shock on yer face. 'Tis a long story, but this client's . . . well, she's got some history with us. With you as well."

Jaime's mind flipped through a Rolodex as she recalled the Epic weddings she had worked on. A terrible thought bubbled up. *Oh no. Please not . . .*

"Aye." He read her mind. "'Tis Mrs. Zimmerman. More specifically, her daughter. The very same one who eloped. Apparently, she didn't elope after all. She just didn't want her mother's version of a wedding."

Jaime had to sit down on the other stool. Mrs. Zimmerman's daughter eloped (allegedly!) on the day of the planned wedding, leaving her mother's dream of her daughter's big day in tatters. "Why in the world would she want a wedding in Sunrise?"

"The daughter said she wanted a wedding to be the opposite of what her mother had planned for her. The place, the setting, even the date. Somehow"—he paused and looked away—"Sunrise came up in a conversation and she seemed to latch on to it."

Confused, Jaime tried to put the pieces together. Why would Sunrise come up in a conversation with a New Yorker? It was a tiny mountain town that people flocked to in the summer to escape the city heat. Hardly anyone up north even knew of its existence.

"I know what yer thinkin'. The daughter, y' see, knew about the Blooms to Bouquet contest, about you winning it and all, and she wanted you t' do her flowers. I told her that wouldn't be possible, seein' as how y' lived in Sunrise. She asked me some questions about Sunrise, and next thing I knew, she decided it sounded like just the place she had in mind for her wedding."

"Here." Jaime still couldn't get her head around everything. Liam McMillan was here, in Rose's Flower Shop, bringing in a client for a wedding. "Where is the venue for this wedding?" Summer was one thing, early fall was even better, but she couldn't think of many options for a late fall/early winter wedding.

"That's another reason I'm here. I need to find a venue. She's got very specific ideas, this bride. A bit like her mother, though

273

opposite from her mother in most every way. You've met her, I believe."

"Yes, but only once. What I do remember was that she was extremely disinterested in her wedding."

"Exactly. Because her mother was callin' all the shots. This time, the daughter wants to call the shots."

"Is the daughter as difficult as the mother?"

"Aye." Spoken definitively.

"Liam, did it occur to you that you could say no? Decline the client?"

He blinked. "It did not."

Jaime had to smile at that. Liam was so kind. It was one of the many reasons that he was so successful in a competitive industry, full of unkind people. It was also one of the reasons Jaime couldn't get over him. She hung the tools she'd been collecting on the pegboard, swept discards off the workbench and into a trash bin, and picked up a pad of paper and a pen. She sat on a stool, pen poised, just like she was meeting with a new client. Trying very hard to keep her mind focused on the task at hand and not on Liam. After all, she told herself, he wasn't here for her. He was here for a client. "So, then, let's start a list. What kind of flowers does this difficult bride want? Actually, let's back up a little. What kind of venue does she want?"

Liam leaned his back against the workbench and folded his arms against his chest. "Outdoors."

"Outdoors," Jaime repeated in a flat voice. "For a winter wedding."

"Aye. Y' see my dilemma. She wants it to be very . . . hmm, how did she describe it? Earth mother–like. Nature nurturer, I believe, were her exact words. And yet lovely and refined. Elegant."

"For an outdoor *winter* wedding."

"Aye, and that's why she chose Sunrise. She thinks the South has no winter." He scratched his forehead. "I suppose it's easier to pull off than skydiving while saying vows. That's a recent request

I handed off to Sloane." He pointed a finger at her. "By the way, increasing Sloane's responsibilities was a fine suggestion. She's more than capable."

So . . . he *had* listened to Jaime. She'd felt so bad stepping out of Epic without notice that she gave him office staff recommendations. Sloane was the project manager who longed to plan events. Good for Sloane.

But it might have been nice to know that. Might have been nice to have heard from Liam now and then. Might have—*No ma'am. Don't go there.* She pulled her thoughts back to the task at hand. Once she started down that personal path with Liam, of the romantic relationship that had barely lifted off the ground before it crashed and burned . . . she would lose her focus. And right now, she needed to stay focused. She kept her eyes lowered to her pad of paper. "So let me get this straight. This bride wants a wedding opposite of everything her mama wanted. And she wants it to happen as soon as possible. That's an opposite too. Her mama had been planning that wedding for two years." She scrunched up her face. "*What* is the big hurry, anyway?"

His beautiful eyes brimmed with humor as he waved his hand over his abdomen in a large arc. "A bairn is due soon."

A *bairn*. A baby? "Oh my goodness. This truly is an opposite wedding."

"That's it! That's what we'll call it. The Opposite Wedding." Liam chuckled, then slid into full laughter, tears streaming down his cheeks. "Y' nailed it, lass."

Oh, how she had missed his laugh. It was contagious. He'd always had a knack for making light of difficult situations, just the way he was doing now, and somehow things became manageable.

Slowly, he sobered up. "So will y' help me, Jaime? You're just the one I need. You know this area. You know the bride's mother. If you just keep in mind that it's an opposite wedding, we'll have a happy bride." He couldn't have looked any more pleased.

And Jaime couldn't be any more crushed. She could've cried.

Liam hadn't come to Sunrise for her. He was here to give another bride her perfect wedding day. It's what he did, what he was known for.

"There's one aspect to this wedding that isn't the opposite. No budget. Truly. The bride's father is o'er the moon that his daughter will be made an honest woman before the bairn arrives. He's gone around his wife to let me know that we're to do whatever the bride wants to do and send the bills to him."

Jaime heard Claire arrive for the day and abruptly rose from the stool. "I'll see what I can come up with and get back to you soon." She tried to sound utterly professional as she concluded a client meeting. Calm, cool, and collected. The truth was, she wanted Liam to leave the store before she lost the composure she was barely clinging to. Despite her best efforts, she could feel a hot flush creeping up her chest. Soon it would reach her face, turning it a telltale, double-crossing bright red.

A look of confusion flicked over his face, but then he heard the sounds of Claire in the front of the shop. He rose from the stool and paused, as if he had more to say, but then changed his mind. "Sounds like your workday has started. I'll be off, then." He stopped at the door that led to the front of the shop and turned to Jaime. "Thank you."

Without even looking him in the eye, she said, "Don't thank me yet. I really have no idea what kind of venue would work to satisfy an earth mama."

"I have confidence in you, lass. I'm heading to Atlanta to meet a client, but I'll be back in a few days."

See? Her feelings dipped even lower. If she needed any more evidence that he hadn't come to Sunrise for Jaime's sake, hadn't missed her or thought about her, he'd just handed it to her on a silver platter. Liam was just passing through on his way to Atlanta. She picked up a broom to start cleaning up the floor of discarded, wilted blooms and stems. Staying busy was the only way she could avoid blurting out what was on the tip of her tongue: *"Go! Be gone! Go back to New York City and take your phony-baloney Scottish accent with you."*

An accent she adored hearing. And right behind that was the realization that she wasn't sure she could ever make herself stop loving him.

three

A tulip doesn't strive to impress anyone. It doesn't struggle to be different than a rose. It doesn't have to.
—*Marianne Williamson*

CLAIRE MURPHY

After three months, any normal person would've sat her best friend down and had a heart-to-heart talk about the fact that they hadn't spoken in over seven years. Any normal person would've tried to clear the air and patch things up.

Did Claire? Nope. She just walked into Rose's Flower Shop like she'd never left, tied an apron on, and got to work.

Jaime Harper, the best friend in question, had looked at Claire like she was seeing a ghost. Jaime, gentle Jaime, wouldn't try to bridge the gap between them if Claire didn't make the first effort. And Claire wasn't going to touch it with a ten-foot pole. She was afraid that if she said a single word, she'd say too much, or the wrong way, or in a harsher tone than she meant, and just make everything worse. She had a habit of doing that kind of thing.

To be fair, when Claire first arrived in Sunrise a few months ago, after getting settled in an Airbnb room-for-rent that Chris had found for her, she had gone straight to Rose's house, prepared to get things out in the open. She'd found Rose out back in the garden. It was a familiar sight to Claire—Rose wearing a big hat and thick gloves, kneeling on the grass, digging or pruning or some such garden task. Foraging, mostly, to add to the shop's stock. Seven years ago, Claire had lived with Rose after her own grandparents' home had been sold. If Rose wasn't at the flower shop, she knew to look for her in her backyard garden.

On that summer day when Claire returned to Sunrise and went to find Rose, she paused at the garden gate. Chris had suggested that she say a prayer before talking to Rose. He pointed out that prayer was meant to be two ways. Talking *and* listening. He felt she had a tendency to overtalk and she didn't disagree. If she was nervous, Claire's yakyakyak switch flipped on. This was going to be an important talk, perhaps the most important talk in Claire's life, so she took his advice and whispered a prayer: "Lord, remind me to shut up."

Then she opened the garden gate and walked over to Rose. As she did, the tears started streaming. Rose seemed to sense Claire's presence before she saw her. She set down her trowel and took off her gloves and sat back on her heels. She looked at Claire with that tender but firm look that only Rose could have, lifted a hand in the air, and said, "Wait. Let's wait until Tessa comes back. Then we'll have a good long talk about everything."

End of discussion before it even began. Rose had a way of putting a period on things.

"Do you understand me, Claire, honey? Not a word."

"Yes, ma'am, I understand."

Carefully, gingerly, Rose got to her feet and wrapped her arms around Claire the way she used to—that amazing, engulfing Rose-hug. And in that hug, Claire knew she'd made the right decision to come back. Maybe things weren't entirely resolved, but Rose had forgiven her. That's all that mattered.

Well, that, plus knowing Rose had a plan to bring everything into the light. As Claire left Rose's, with instructions to take a huge bucket of just-cut scented geranium stems to the shop for Jaime to use, it occurred to her that God had answered her prayer. She'd hardly said a word.

So Claire decided to leave the big ugly mess from the night of the fire in Rose's hands and she would focus on her flower work. After Jaime's shock at seeing her, they picked up where they left off, working side by side, ignoring the gigantic chasm of unspoken thoughts and feelings that lay between them.

And boy o' boy did they work.

ℓℓℓ

In the seven years that Claire and Jaime (and the still-MIA Tessa) had been away, the one competing flower shop near the town of Sunrise had shuttered their doors during the pandemic. Rose's Flower Shop was the only game serving this mountain area, and business had exploded. No wonder Rose wanted her best workers back. No wonder Rose looked so tired. The poor woman needed a good long rest.

Claire and Jaime worked their tails off. Jaime managed all the weddings, which suited Claire just fine. She preferred taking care of the shop, ordering flowers and supplies, and creating single arrangements. She didn't know how Jaime could stand making one matching bouquet after the other. Last weekend's wedding in Sapphire had thirteen bridesmaids.

Thirteen! Back in Savannah, thirteen was just asking for trouble.

The whole notion of thinking that a number had the power to bring bad luck was a leftover from living in Savannah. It was supposed to be the most haunted city in America, but Claire had lived there seven years and never met a single ghost.

Anyhoo, somehow Jaime had the patience for weddings and

brides and brides' mothers, and Claire did not. She'd always thought Jaime had a bit of a saint in her. Claire was famous for her temper, Tessa for her looks, and Jaime for her sweetness. That's how Claire saw things, at least.

Here was something new after seven years: Claire had known that Jaime spent time in New York City after college, had worked for Epic Events, and had always had a special touch with flowers, but she was shocked by the advanced skill of Jaime's floral artistry. Again, any normal person would've asked her to share her secrets. To teach her what she'd learned in New York City. Did Claire? Nope. Instead, she carefully watched everything Jaime created, and whenever the shop was empty or quiet, she practiced what she'd observed. Jaime was *that* good. Claire, entirely self-taught, was far behind. She had a lot of catching up to do.

And something else that was different in the flower shop: Claire and Jaime didn't talk to each other, really talk, the way they used to. They communicated like two coworkers—clear and polite. Nothing more.

It was the same way with Chris. He traveled a lot with his magician gigs, so Claire didn't see him often. Maybe once every two weeks, he'd drive back into Sunrise in his old Ford Mustang at the crack of dawn on a Sunday morning, check in on his aunt Rose, and do his laundry and spend time with Claire. They'd go to church together and take a long hike in the woods in the afternoon. She'd talk about the week's flowers—what arrangements she felt good about, what she wished she'd done differently. He'd talk about his magic acts and how to tweak things and what worked and what didn't. Sometimes it felt as if they were testing the edges of their friendship, but they avoided talking about the things that lay between them—finding Tessa snuggled in Chris's arms on the night of Claire's eighteenth birthday. The fire that burned down the shop and destroyed friendships with it. The year Chris spent in prison for it.

Once or twice, Claire had tried to bring it up, but Chris wouldn't take the bait. After the third try, he said, "Look, Claire. I'm far more interested in what's ahead than what's behind."

What did that mean? Did he think there was something ahead for them? Because Claire wasn't at all sure about that. It's not that she didn't have feelings for Chris—she had plenty of them, so much she could hardly hold them in. She did hold back, though. After all, she wasn't seventeen anymore. She knew to keep her feelings for Chris in check and under wraps. But whenever she heard that Ford Mustang roar into town, her heart leapt.

Today, Claire had gone to open the shop but found Jaime had already arrived and was in the back of the store, talking to someone. Jaime often scheduled appointments with new clients before the shop opened, so Claire knew the drill. She stayed in the front of the shop to get started on the day's to-do list. She needed to clean out the walk-in cooler of leftover flowers from the weekend. She took a deep breath and turned in a circle. This was one of those moments when Claire knew she had outgrown Same Day Delivery in Savannah. Regardless of the circumstances of her departure, it was definitely the right time to go.

There was such a variety from yesterday's wedding in this cooler! Dahlias and calendulas, sprays of Christmas boxwood, even a bucket full of bay leaf. Those cuttings made her smile. Bay wreaths on the front door of the house were a common sight in Savannah during the winter. Apparently, they kept bad witches away. In seven years, Claire had never met a witch, either.

She grabbed an empty bucket and started to collect all the stems that were past their prime. They could be tossed, but the salvageable ones would be separated into a bucket of fresh water. Later, she'd arrange those into casual bouquets, tied with a pretty ribbon and wrapped in wax paper, to be set in a floral display rack of galvanized buckets out in front of the shop. The outside display rack had been Claire's idea, and Rose had loved it. It was something Claire had created during the pandemic for the Same Day

Delivery shop in Savannah. It was a great way to boost walk-in sales and use up excess flowers. No flower should ever be wasted.

As Claire stepped out of the walk-in cooler with a bucket of old blossoms to toss, she felt all the blood leave her head. In the middle of the shop stood a man she would know anywhere—he was *that* famous in the world of flowers. Liam McMillan, the Scottish wedding-event wunderkind. It was like being in the presence of royalty. Claire thought she might faint dead away.

four

Don't compare her to sunshine and roses when she's clearly
orchids and moonlight.
—Melody Lee

TESSA

Tessa was flat-out broke. After the sale of Mountain Blooms
Farm in Asheville was completed, she'd ended up with far
less than she'd hoped. Fees, mostly, plus taxes. She thought
about asking Dawson to double-check the math, but she knew his
response would've been outrage at the sticky fingers of government. Instead, she spoke to an accountant friend and discovered
the figures were correct—she just hadn't thought there'd be so
many bites chomping away at the final sales figure.

She'd been left with enough to purchase the foreclosed property
in Sunrise, and just enough for demolition. That was a huge relief,
because if that old house couldn't have been knocked down right
away, she wasn't sure she could live in Sunrise. Happily, that part
all worked out. And now the field was empty. Waiting for its next
chapter.

An expensive next chapter. It would require steep costs to get the field prepared to become a flourishing flower farm. Renting equipment to plow the fields, purchasing amendments, poly hoop houses to protect the young plants this winter, plus seed, bulbs, tubers . . . and then there was Dawson's salary. She needed him here, she wanted him here, she couldn't do this flower farm without him. But that meant a boatload of money.

She nearly forgot the greenhouse! Dawson wouldn't consider a greenhouse if he didn't think it was the right time for it. Maybe the amount saved from not digging up the concrete slab foundation might equal the amount of the greenhouse.

Which . . . really didn't matter because she didn't have the money for either. She was nearing the limit on her credit card, and her bank account teetered on being overdrawn. Tucked in the back of her mind was the knowledge that she could probably ask her parents for a short-term loan, but she didn't want to. They didn't understand her dedication to flower farming. They spoke of Tessa's passion as if it was something she'd grow out of, or worse, get bored with. She wanted to make this farm work without depending on a rescue from Mom and Dad, or anyone else. She'd done too much of that in her life. This field had been redeemed from a dark period in her life, one full of regrets, and she wanted to see it all the way through. Maybe it was her redemption too.

She parked her Vespa in front of Rose's house and cut the engine, took off her helmet, and hung it on the seat. A door closed and she turned to see Chris Reid holding two suitcases. Behind him was Rose. Chris stopped short when he saw her, a shocked look on his face.

"Looks like you're going somewhere," Tessa said.

Still surprised, Chris tipped his head toward Rose. "She is. I'm taking her to the airport now." He came down the porch steps. "You're looking well, Tessa. It's good to see you." He turned to his aunt. "We have a few minutes to spare. I'll put these in the car and wait for you."

Tessa moved out of his way and whispered a thank-you as he passed around her with the bulky suitcases. She owed him more than that, but it was a start. Rose waited for her on the porch steps. She was dressed for travel, not in the work apron Tessa was accustomed to seeing on her. And something else Tessa noticed— Rose wasn't at all surprised to see her.

"So I hear that you bought a field," Rose said.

Tessa gave her a weak smile. What made her think that anything in Sunrise could be kept quiet? "I should've come sooner. I just needed to get rid of that house before I could do anything else."

Rose nodded as if she knew. Did she? Was the relationship Tessa had had with that neighbor something that everyone knew? Shame covered her like a lead blanket. "Rose . . . I . . ."

Rose lifted a hand. "Not now, honey. When I return, we'll all have a good long talk. For now, Tessa, keep your focus on the future."

Holding on to the porch rail, she came down the steps to wrap her arms around Tessa, the way she used to. No one hugged like Rose. It triggered something deep down in Tessa and sobs welled up. Big, huge, gasping sobs. Rose just kept holding her, patting her back until Chris started the engine to his obnoxious Mustang.

Rose released her but held on to her shoulders. "My chariot awaits."

Tessa watched Chris help Rose into the car, treating her like she was spun sugar so tenderly that she batted his hands away. The familiar interaction between them made Tessa smile, then laugh. She felt so lighthearted! Rose had forgiven her.

She waved as the obnoxious Mustang pulled out of the driveway and roared down the street. It occurred to her that she had no idea where Rose was going, but she hoped it was a lovely vacation on a warm beach. Rose deserved it. "Lord," Tessa prayed as the car disappeared around the corner, "watch over her." Short, to the point, because praying was new for Tessa. Dawson said not to overthink it, just to do it, especially in those moments when things were beyond her pay grade. She hopped on her Vespa and plopped her helmet on her head.

A flower farm was waiting for her.

five

One person's weed is another person's wildflower.
—Susan Wittig Albert

JAIME

*L*iam McMillan was right about a lot of things—Jaime knew the bride's mother well enough to know what she would like. Lavish, extravagant, gaudy, over-the-top. Jaime sat in a coffee shop with a pad of paper, trying to think of a venue site for the Opposite Wedding.

So what would an opposite wedding in winter look like? If it were any other season, she would look for some suitable place outdoors. A park. A lakefront. A mountain summit. But in winter? Weather was unpredictable. The guests might freeze or get sunburned.

"I'll tell you *what*," Jaime said, talking to herself. "One trait this daughter shares with her mother is a desire to make a wedding as difficult and complicated as it can possibly be."

She had tried calling Rose to see if she had any ideas, but it went straight to voicemail, which meant her phone was turned off. So frustrating and so frequent. Jaime had had such little interaction with Rose since she'd been back in Sunrise; it was like Rose had already handed off the business. The shop was twice the size that it was before the fire, space was nicely designed and equipment had been updated, and the business had grown right along with the square footage. Claire's arrival had been a huge help. She had a tremendous work ethic—she arrived early, stayed late, and managed the day-to-day operations of the shop like a pro.

Hanging over Jaime and Claire was the question of who would take over the shop. Rose wasn't ready to discuss it. Frankly, to discuss much of anything. She'd made it clear that she didn't want anyone talking about the fire and that August night until Tessa returned and all three girls were together. So Jaime and Claire avoided the topic and ran the flower shop . . . waiting for Rose's next step.

Jaime often wondered if coming back had been the right thing. Was she going backward in life? Other than being in love with her boss and pining away for him, and other than a pandemic that shut New York City down, she had been happy. Fairly happy. Maybe a little lonely. A little socially disconnected from just about every other New Yorker.

Apart from fearing she had slipped backward in her floral artistry career, Jaime was enjoying Sunrise and the parts of small-town living that she had missed. Spending time with her sweet mama, feeling safe and cared for in this town where everybody knew each other's business. She was glad she could help Rose—she owed her more than she could ever give back to her. And while it might not look like it on a résumé, she had taken on more responsibility for weddings and special events in the last five months than she ever could've at Epic. Liam was a bit of a micromanager. Rose used to hover like Liam, but no longer. She had been hands off from the day Jaime set foot in the shop. Frankly, she was just off, in general. Jaime hardly saw her. Most of the time, she didn't even know where Rose was. Like now.

"Jaime."

She was sipping her coffee and looked up when she heard her name, then nearly choked at the sight of Tessa Anderson, standing in front of her. As soon as she stopped coughing, she said, "You've come back." She rose to her feet, not really knowing what to do or say, until Tessa reached out to give her an awkward hug. "Sit down. Please."

Tessa pulled out the chair across from Jaime. "You've done so well for yourself, Jaime. I, um, I've followed you on Instagram. Epic Events, I mean."

Jaime smiled, still uncomfortable. She couldn't believe she was sitting down with Tessa after seven years. She looked just as beautiful as she did in high school, though different somehow. Maybe a little thinner. No, not thinner. Leaner, like she worked out a lot.

Jaime never worked out.

She couldn't shake her nervousness. It was the same way she'd felt the day Claire walked into the flower shop and grabbed an apron and started to work. Like she felt as if she had traveled back in time. Like she wanted to shout, *What is happening here?*

Rose. That's what was happening. "Rose did what she set out to do. She got us all back in Sunrise to run the shop. Claire's there now." Jaime could tell by the look on Tessa's face that she already knew about Claire's return.

"I'm not here to run the flower shop, Jaime. That's for you and Claire to work out."

"You have just as much right to it as we do."

"I don't, actually. Because I don't want it. That's not why I'm back in Sunrise." She took in a deep breath, as if bracing herself. "I bought some land. Cleared some land, actually, and we're going to turn it into a flower farm. That's what we had done in Asheville. But we sold the farm—long story—and came to Sunrise to start another one."

Jaime tipped her head. "We?"

"My . . . farm manager, Dawson Greene. He's the brains behind the operation."

The slight softening in Tessa's voice as she mentioned Dawson's name made Jaime think he might be more than a farm manager. Tessa never had any trouble attracting the opposite sex. No ma'am, none at all. It was part of the Tessa-spell. She had an aloofness, a detachment, that drove high school boys crazy. Grown men too. Jaime squeezed her hands into fists in her lap. That was then and this was now. And speaking of now . . . "I suppose that since you're back, Rose will finally gather us together for that conversation she's been waiting to have."

Tessa lifted her shoulders in a shrug. "I think that will still be a wait. I just saw her. Chris was taking her to the airport."

"Airport? Where was she going?"

"No idea. She had big suitcases. I should've thought to ask, but I guess I was . . . well, nervous to see her for the first time."

And with that vulnerability, Jaime started to relax. Her hands loosened from a fist. "I'll tell you *what*. I felt the same way."

Tessa smiled, and then Jaime smiled, and things felt almost normal again. Almost.

A text came in on Tessa's phone and she read it, a serious look on her face.

Watching her, Jaime took another sip of her now lukewarm coffee. Tessa's fingernails. They were cut short, lacking polish. Tessa's nails had always, always been polished. Her long blond hair, still thick and lush, didn't look salon-highlighted like it always had. More like sun streaked. And she wore overalls! Jaime and Claire had always been in awe of Tessa's meticulous grooming, her stylish clothes, and the latest shoes. Her mother was a former beauty pageant contestant and took great pride in the appearance of her daughters, especially her youngest one. Yet somehow, this new and uncoiffed Tessa was even more attractive. She'd never needed all that fuss. "So where is this land you bought?"

Tessa set her phone face down on the table. "Actually, it's three acres next to my parents' former summer house."

"Wasn't that . . . ?" Jaime stopped herself from saying "the mystery author's house."

"I bought the property and tore down the house." Tessa frowned. "The slab foundation is still there. We're going to put a greenhouse on top. Dawson found one that fits the slab." She flipped over her phone and handed it to Jaime. "It's huge."

Jaime looked at a picture of an enormous greenhouse. "Yes, ma'am. That is one huge greenhouse."

"Due to arrive by week's end."

She glanced at Tessa. "You don't sound very excited."

"I think I'm just in shock. Dawson's always kept the brakes on expanding too fast. This . . . this is a departure for him." She sat back in the chair. "It's the right decision. In fact, it's brilliant. We can reuse the slab foundation instead of having to demo it and haul it away. It's just . . ." She rubbed her forehead, like she had a headache. "I'm just a little short on cash right now." She blew out a puff of air. "Maybe a lot short."

Jaime was still looking at the picture of the greenhouse on the phone. In her mind's eye, she suddenly saw it at night, lit with soft lighting—maybe even a chandelier or two, and fairy lights—with people milling around inside . . . and her heart started to pound. "Tessa, what kind of condition is that greenhouse in?"

"Condition?"

"Is it used? Beat up?"

"No ma'am. This greenhouse is brand spanking new. Dawson found it from a supplier who'd made a mistake in ordering it and couldn't return it." Tessa let out a breath. "Never used at all."

"Then, no mice yet?"

Tessa laughed. "Mice?"

"The greenhouses I've been in have mousetraps tucked all over them. Mice like warmth and they like seeds."

"Duly noted. I'll add mousetraps to our long shopping list. I'm sure every mouse in Sunrise will find us by springtime."

Jaime couldn't hold back a smile. "I'll tell you *what*!"

"What?"

"I might just have a way to kill two birds with one stone." She tucked her notepad into her purse and stood up. "Let's go have a good look at your land."

Still seated, Tessa looked hesitant, but then she rose from the chair. "Hope you're okay on the back of a Vespa."

She strode toward the door, Jaime following behind, asking, "A what?"

six

If you look the right way, you can see
that the whole world is a garden.
—Frances Hodgson Burnett

CLAIRE

Claire felt like she was working on a jigsaw puzzle with missing pieces. She was finishing the order of flowers for Jaime's client's wedding—or was it Liam McMillan's client? She had no idea. All she knew was that this Opposite Wedding was for a very wealthy, very pregnant bride, and that the wedding and reception were supposed to be held in the greenhouse on Tessa's land, which had yet to be delivered and installed.

The whole situation still felt dizzying, as if she might be caught in a dream. She couldn't get over seeing Tessa walk into the shop with Jaime like she used to. She couldn't get over the fact that the three girls were suddenly swept up together into a whirlwind of wedding planning, moving full steam ahead. Ideas and what-ifs were bursting from them, like fast-popping corn kernels . . . because the astonishing thing about what Jaime called this "Opposite Wedding" was that there was no limit to the budget. No concern about costs. None. She couldn't believe it when Jaime told her not to worry about fees for express shipping. "Shut *up*!"

"It's true. Liam loves everything we've planned. He says to go ahead and send him the bills."

"The perfect man," Claire said, her hands clasped over her heart dramatically. "Jaime, you'd better marry that man before I do."

Jaime tossed a spray of viburnum at her. "Liam and I have a strictly professional relationship."

Claire picked up the winter flowering viburnum. Such a perfect filler. Being back in Rose's Flower Shop, she felt like a kid in a candy shop. So many options! She'd never appreciated the endless varieties of flower arranging until she moved to Savannah and worked for oh-so-traditional MaryBeth at Same Day Delivery. "Liam McMillan would not be in Sunrise if his feelings for you are strictly professional."

"Well, you're just wrong about that."

Oh *really*? Claire barely held back from pointing out how Jaime's face turned bright red when she was embarrassed. She'd forgotten that telltale sign. She'd forgotten a lot of things. She'd worked so hard to erase that August night of the fire that she'd also blocked out all the sweet memories of the girls' friendship. How they seemed to be able to work in perfect harmony. How they inspired each other and made each other better. Rose was always telling them that they had something special, something people longed for all their life. Did they listen? Nope.

They were listening now, but Rose wasn't doing any talking. Chris told Claire that Rose had gone to Mexico, but he didn't say why. When she opened her mouth to ask another question, Chris shook his head. "You know the drill. No questions until Rose is ready." Of course, he didn't have any idea when she'd be back. Very mysterious, and a little annoying. On the other hand, the girls were so busy getting ready for the Opposite Wedding on top of the shop's regular demands, as well as holiday orders, that they didn't have much time to dwell on Rose's absence.

Claire was putting the finishing touches on a bouquet for a twenty-fifth wedding anniversary and stepped back to appraise it just as Tessa popped in the workshop door. "Greenhouse delivered?"

"Not yet." Tessa admired the bouquet. "Asters?"

"They're for a twenty-fifth wedding anniversary." Claire tucked one last purple aster in the back and tipped her head. Something was still missing. "Asters represent wisdom and prosperity, in that order."

"I forgot." A wistfulness came into Tessa's eyes. "I forgot how much you loved the language of flowers." She studied the arrangement with a thoughtful look on her face, then walked to the cooler, reached in, and brought out one yellow chrysanthemum. She clipped the stem and slipped the blossom into the front corner of the bouquet. And would you believe, it was just what was needed? The yellow blossom made the bright center of the asters pop. It provided the element of surprise.

Claire looked up. *So Tessa.* She was full of surprises. "You nailed it."

Tessa laughed. "It's your arrangement. I just added one flower."

"The right one. The right place for it." Claire set down her clippers.

"It's late in the season for asters. Where'd you find them?"

"I ordered them from a grower in Colombia."

"Hopefully, by next summer," Tessa said, "Rose's Flower Shop won't have to import flowers at all."

Claire wondered. "Think you'll really be able to get flowers out of that dustbowl by summer?"

"Yes I do," Tessa said, "and thank you very much for that vote of confidence. Be glad we haven't had rain. I'm crossing my fingers the rain will hold off until that greenhouse gets bolted down."

Jaime frowned. "So when is the greenhouse going to arrive?"

"Soon," Tessa said, suddenly interested in lining up tools on the workbench. "Very, very soon."

Jaime wrinkled her nose. "Tessa, everything is riding on that greenhouse."

Tessa set shears in the row of tools and took a few steps to the door. "Do not worry. That greenhouse will be installed and ready in plenty of time." Without looking back, she lifted her hand in a wave as she reached the threshold of the workshop door.

And suddenly Claire was seventeen years old again, watching Tessa make a fast exit because Jaime or Claire had asked her a question she didn't want to answer. She remembered it vividly. It happened whenever something was asked . . .

Something . . . something . . . what was it? Something about Tessa's neighbor. The mystery author. Everyone in town was fascinated by him. Obsessed with him. First off, he was supposed to be super successful, though Claire wasn't much of a reader and didn't care about books. More of interest to Jaime and Claire, he was crazy good-looking. The girls would quiz her on what she knew about him, hoping for everyday details—Did she ever see pizza boxes in his trash? Did he work out? No one ever saw his wife. What was she like?—but Tessa never wanted to talk about him. She'd suddenly make a fast exit. Like she did now.

Weird. It startled Claire how vivid memories could be lodged in your brain, waiting for a trigger.

A text came in and Claire stopped to read it.

Chris
How's everything coming along with the Opposite Wedding?

Great! Amazing how working with Jaime and Tessa feels so normal.

Good to hear. Heading back to Sunrise late this afternoon.

Claire set the aster bouquet in a floral box. "The customer should be coming for this any minute now. It's ready." She set the box to one side so she could clean up the workbench. "Jaime, whatever happened to Tessa's neighbor? That famous author?"

Jaime spun around so fast, with the strangest look on her face. "Rose said *not* to talk about that night! Not without her." Hearing the chimes on the front door, she picked up the floral box and disappeared into the front room.

Claire sat back on the stool, feeling scolded. What had she said that was so wrong? And what did the author guy have to do with that August night?

Miffed, she picked up her phone and texted Chris.

> Working together might *seem* normal, but it isn't.

> Ha! You just described the essence of being a magician. Things aren't what they appear. See you tonight. I'll take you out for tacos.

Claire felt better. He remembered how much she loved tacos. With a sigh, she remembered how much she still loved Chris.

seven

A weed is but an unloved flower.
—*Ella Wheeler Wilcox*

TESSA

Tessa and Dawson prepared the site for a wedding event by creating a pathway to what would be, hopefully, the door of the still-not-arrived greenhouse. They spread sand along the pathway—it was the only medium he would agree to because it would help benefit the soil, and frankly, it was the only one she could afford. Her stomach was in knots. What if the greenhouse didn't come in time? Jaime's Opposite Wedding plans would crumble. The tenuous relationship she had with her would disappear. With Claire too. And even Dawson would be furious with her for losing two to three weeks of time to prepare the soil. He wasn't keen on the notion of turning this site into a wedding venue, though he did like the benefits that came with it. They were just his cup of tea—bartering for goods and services instead of paying taxes on them.

Jaime had told Tessa that in exchange for the use of the venue (there was no venue! just a field that Jaime called a blank canvas), Epic Events would pay the cost of liability insurance for an entire year, plus pay for the entire electrical installation of the greenhouse. She said they'd leave all the components, like special lighting, for Tessa to keep for her own personal use. She even mentioned chandeliers! Tessa had yet to tell Dawson about that. She could just imagine the horrified look on his face.

Tessa felt overwhelmed by this good fortune. So grateful. It had all come about so unexpectedly too.

Last week, after bumping into each other at the coffee shop, Tessa had taken Jaime over to look at the field. Jaime had walked all around, examining it as intently as Dawson would, except that she was looking for other things besides the condition of the soil and worms. Jaime noticed things that never occurred to Tessa and Dawson.

For example, the end of the road was a cul-de-sac, which delighted Jaime. Ease of parking, she explained, something Tessa hadn't considered. She should have, though, because down the road, she had an inkling to host people at the flower farm. She'd thought about a pick-your-own-bouquet event, or classes for flower arranging. But all those ideas were for down the road . . . way down the road.

Jaime had walked back and forth along the slab foundation, noticing the angle of the sun. She took all kinds of pictures from every corner of the property and sent them to someone on her phone. Five minutes later, a text pinged on her phone. Jaime read it, smiling, and said, "Liam says to book it."

"Book it? Book . . . this, you mean, this field?" Then Tessa gasped. "Liam as in Liam McMillan?"

Jaime didn't miss a beat. "He said it's just the kind of setting the bride wants."

"Bride? A wedding? But . . . Jaime, there's nothing here."

"Exactly. It's a blank canvas." Jaime looked around. "Nothing, yet everything. Electricity—"

"Just a pole."

"Good enough. Water—"

"Well, there's hoses."

"We can make that work." She pointed to Tessa's Airstream. "Even that. It's perfect. Could we use that for staging?"

"Staging? You mean, use it for a bathroom? I suppose so, but it's pretty small."

Jaime burst out with a laugh. "Goodness no. We'll bring fancy porta potties for the guests. I meant staging for food."

"Oh. Yes, of course, you can use anything. But . . . it's just an empty field." Tessa still felt bewildered.

"Tessa, as long as the greenhouse arrives on time, we can turn this field into a winter wonderland. Trust me on that. You'd be amazed what can happen with the right lighting."

Two cackling crows in a nearby tree snapped Tessa out of last week's conversation with Jaime. "Dawson, what do we need to do to get that greenhouse here?"

Down on all fours, he'd been smoothing sand along the pathway and stopped to look up at her. "We need to wait for my buddy to bring it over the hill. Any day now, he said."

"He's been saying that for over a week."

He sat back on his heels. "He's been busy."

"But it's all flat packed, right?"

"Tessa . . ." It was his warning voice.

"Dawson, this greenhouse was your idea in the first place. Jaime's Opposite Wedding will give us a jump start on the flower farm. So how do we get it here? How can we make it happen?"

"I guess . . . get to Asheville and find a way to haul it here ourselves."

Tessa dropped the rake in her hands. "Then let's go get it."

eight

*Just living is not enough . . . one must have
sunshine, freedom, and a little flower.*
—*Hans Christian Andersen*

JAIME

As soon as she got the news from Tessa that the greenhouse had arrived and was in the process of getting installed, Jaime called Liam to fill him in. "They rented a huge flatbed truck to haul it from Asheville and caused an enormous traffic jam."

"Excellent news!" he said. "The sooner this wedding can happen, the better. Does Dawson know when it will be ready for the electrician? I realize he'll need a few days, but I'd like to give the bride's father a firm date."

"A few days? You're kidding, right?"

"Not kidding."

"We haven't even decided on the invitations. I've narrowed it down to three options, but the printer needs at least a week."

"There's been a change of plans. The bride wants to call the guests and invite them personally."

"But just a few days ago, she sent me the wording she wanted in the invitations."

"Apparently, the bride went to the hospital yesterday with false labor and was sent home. Her father is eager to hurry things along."

"So no invitations?"

"Nay. One less thing for the to-do list."

Disappointing! Jaime had found some beautiful paper samples from Japan.

"I'll be in Sunrise in thirty minutes."

She glanced at the wall clock in the flower shop. "Where are you?"

"Highlands. Checkin' on a few things. Gotta run. I'll pick y' up at the shop."

Thirty minutes? She leapt from her stool, almost taking flight. She peered into a wall mirror that was used for checking bouquets. A mess! She was a mess. No makeup, hair that needed a shampoo, T-shirt over jeans. She grabbed her emergency makeup bag from under the workshop bench and hunted through it for a small container of dry shampoo.

As she rummaged, Claire popped her head around the door. "I just found a supplier who can promise delphiniums for the Opposite Wedding."

Spraying dry shampoo over the crown of her head, Jaime looked at Claire's reflection in the mirror. "Claire, you are a whiz at what you do."

"Delphiniums symbolize goodwill. When I told the supplier I needed them for a pregnant bride and that her father was eager to get her to the altar before the baby arrived, he said he'd send them express. Apparently"—she wiggled her eyebrows—"he's had a similar family matter."

"Well," Jaime said, brushing her hair with a fury, "I think it's you. You have a way of getting people to want to help you."

"Really? No one's ever said that to me before. Usually, I'm told to think before I speak."

"I suppose that's good for all of us."

"Not you. You have a pretty tight filter." Claire came into the room. "What are you getting all gussied up for?" Her eyes lit up. "Hold it! I bet I know. Prince Liam is coming through town and you want to impress."

Jaime frowned into the mirror, which wasn't easy to do when you were trying to put on lipstick. "I've told you. We have a strictly professional relationship."

"Yes, ma'am," Claire said, giving her an exaggerated wink before she vanished into the front of the shop.

Annoyed, Jaime finished her makeup, ran the brush through her hair one last time, and looked at herself in the mirror. She looked all right. Could be better, but this would just have to do.

ℓ·ℓ·ℓ

Knowing Liam would be prompt, Jaime waited for him out in front of the shop. She wanted to avoid Claire's wiggling eyebrows and irritating innuendos. She'd forgotten how Claire didn't always realize when she stepped over a line. It didn't bother Jaime unless she happened to *be* that line.

You're being silly, she told herself. The only reason she was annoyed with Claire was because she'd hit a sore spot. Over and over.

So maybe Jaime's relationship with Liam wasn't strictly professional, but it certainly wasn't much more than that. Or was it? Jaime felt thoroughly confused. She assumed Liam would have flown to New York City after his Atlanta meeting, but he hadn't. He said he had clients to meet and venues to explore, but he kept circling through Sunrise. And when he did, he invited Jaime out for meals on the pretense of planning the Opposite Wedding, which they did rather intensely—every detail had been thought of, the caterer booked, the party rentals and supplies had been ordered, the checklists were edited by each other—but then they'd set it

303

aside and talk about everything else under the sun. Once, Liam put a temporary ban on talking about the Opposite Wedding and they went on a long hike in the mountains. Another time, she cooked for him at her little house. A true Southern meal—fried chicken and biscuits and coleslaw and potato salad. He said it was the best meal he'd had in ages, and she knew he meant it. Whenever he had to say goodbye to her, he lingered at her door as if he didn't want to leave. Something seemed to be happening between them, but she wasn't sure what it was. At times, it did seem as if Liam was surveying the area, trying it on for size. But that was just plain silly; it was Claire's teasing that gave Jaime a glimmer of hope. Foolish thoughts. Liam McMillan belonged in New York City to head up Epic Events.

After all, if he were thinking of living in the South, he wouldn't be Scottish Liam anymore. He'd be Kentucky Billy.

nine

> *You can cut all the flowers but you cannot*
> *keep spring from coming.*
> —Pablo Neruda

CLAIRE

Two more days. Then this Opposite Wedding would be over and Claire could get some control back over her life. For the last two weeks, the Opposite Wedding had dominated Rose's Flower Shop. The holidays were fast approaching! There were other customers to take care of than the Zimmerman bride. But you'd never know it if you walked into the shop. Boxes of lighting paraphernalia kept getting delivered and were stacked along the walls, waiting for the electrician to haul them away to install in Tessa's greenhouse. Jaime was on the phone 24/7, talking to the caterer or confirming porta potties or worse—trying to scrounge up high school boys as parking valets.

Over the last week, flowers had started to arrive from all over the world, filling up every square inch of cooler space. Claire and Jaime stayed late into the night to get every stem prepped, ready for arranging. That would be saved for today and tomorrow, the days before the Opposite Wedding. And it fell to Claire, because Jaime would be needed to set up and decorate the venue. Claire didn't mind doing the flowers herself, not when Jaime showed her the mock-ups of what she had in mind for the bride's bouquet and table arrangements.

Beautiful. Claire was in awe as she looked through the mock-ups. Jaime had such style, such originality. "I would never have thought of using protea in a bridal bouquet."

"The bride wanted things to look natural, like she'd picked it on the way to the wedding."

"But you've created this luscious bouquet for her, Jaime. I hope I do it justice."

Jaime smiled. "I have no doubt that you'll outdo anything in the mock-ups." She nudged her with her elbow. "I've seen your work."

"Mostly I just copy," Claire said.

"Everyone gets their inspiration somewhere. And you do more than copy, Claire." She tipped her head. "Feel free to take my mock-ups and improve on them."

"No ma'am. Your mock-ups are perfect."

"They're drawings, not reality. You know as well as I do what it's like to have flowers in front of you that don't look anything like the ones in your imagination. Claire, I want your input. We're better together."

Claire stared at the drawing. "You mean, I can forage?"

"Forage away," Jaime said with a laugh. "I trust you." She turned to face her. "I wish you could see yourself the way others see you. You run this whole shop like a well-oiled machine. Rose always said you had a head for business."

Claire stilled. She'd forgotten. Rose did tell her that, often. Tears started to prick her eyes.

Jaime looked around the front room. "Hard to believe that we're at the finish line for this wedding." She let out a sigh.

"What's that sad sigh for?"

"Oh, I just wonder what comes next."

Claire yawned. "What comes next for me is a long winter's nap." She flipped off the lights and held the door for Jaime. "We'd better get some sleep while we can. I have a feeling there won't be much chance for it in the next two days."

ℓ·ℓ·ℓ

Early the next morning, Claire woke to the ping of a text on her phone. Drowsy, she reached over to pick it up and read a group text from Chris to Tessa, Jaime, and Claire.

> Please come to Rose's as soon as you can. She's ready to have The Talk. Coffee's started.

Seriously? Today? Claire sat up in bed. Rose was finally ready to have this long-overdue clearing of the air on the day before the big wedding? This morning was critical prep time! Every single minute counted. She was just about to object when Tessa and Jaime texted back that they'd be right there. Fine. She let out an exasperated sigh and tossed the covers off.

Claire's rented Airbnb room was only a few blocks from Rose's house, so she dressed quickly, pulled her big curly hair into a ponytail, and walked over. Jaime and Tessa drove up just as she arrived at the house, so they went to Rose's front door together.

Chris met them with a tray of coffee mugs. "Morning. Make yourself at home."

Claire thought he looked off, like he either hadn't slept or just woke up . . . or like he'd been crying. He avoided eye contact with Claire, which hitched up her odd feelings. Why did this gathering seem so stilted and formal? Not to mention the timing. It couldn't be any worse!

Rose was in the living room, seated in her favorite armchair, wearing a big, thick sweater, sipping coffee in front of a roaring fire like there was a raging storm outside. Yet it was actually quite a pleasant sunny morning. The three girls sat across from her on the sofa. Chris settled into a chair near Rose, chin tucked to his chest.

"Girls, thank you for coming," Rose said. "I know you have a busy day ahead, so I'll get right to the point. The night of the fire. Who wants to go first?"

Whoa. Claire, Tessa, and Jaime all looked down at their coffee cups.

"Well then," Rose said, "I'll start things off. You should know that I'm the one responsible for that fire."

All three girls snapped their heads up.

"You?" Tessa said. "Not you, Rose. I'm the one to blame."

"No," Jaime said. "It was me."

"Nope," Claire said. "I'm the one who started it. I know that for a fact."

Rose smiled. "The truth was, we all had a part in it. Ironically, everyone except for Chris—"

Chris shook his head. "I had a role in it too, Rose. If it weren't for my—"

"No, dear," she interrupted, waving him off with her hand. "The truth is that you took complete blame for the fire just to keep the rest of us out of trouble."

Claire turned to look at Chris. He had done that? She stared at him, willing him to lift his head, but he seemed determined not to look at her.

Rose took in a deep breath, as if gathering strength for what she was about to say. "The shop had that old knob and tube wiring. I should have had it upgraded, but there was never time to allow for it. Especially that summer. So many weddings."

"Funerals too," Claire said. "Big summer of funerals. I did all the flowers."

After taking a sip from her mug, Rose nodded. "That summer, the motor on the cooler had started acting up. It would go out, and Chris would get it working again, only for it to go out again. Before I'd left on that August day, the cooler felt hot to the touch, even though the interior was still cool. I felt in my bones that something was wrong. An accident was waiting to happen. But I pushed that feeling aside because I had wedding flowers to deliver." She exhaled, as if this revelation had taken a toll on her. "I should never have left the shop."

Chris reached over to take Rose's hand. It struck Claire that it seemed like Rose's hands had shrunk or shriveled. They were once working hands, strong and calloused. Now they looked like an old woman's hands, swollen knuckles and blue veins. Was that what seven years of aging did to a woman?

Before she could think much more about it, Chris spoke up. "I told you to go. I told you that I'd take care of the cooler. I should've. I just . . . got distracted."

"I was his distraction," Tessa said. "I came into the shop looking for Rose, but she wasn't there. Only Chris. I was upset about something, and Chris stopped what he was doing to help me." She put a hand on her chest. "I'm responsible for the fire."

"No, Tessa. It was my fault." Jaime rubbed her face with her hands. "I had come into the workshop to get a ribbon for a bride's bouquet. The ribbon had fallen off and someone stepped on it and I needed to replace it. I was in a hurry, and the only ribbon I could find was all wrinkled, so I put the iron on as hot as it could go and started to iron it, and that was when I heard Tessa sobbing about her neighbor."

Tessa visibly stiffened. "You heard?"

Jaime nodded. "But I already knew."

Claire blinked. "What neighbor?"

Tessa, leaning around Claire, ignored her. "Jaime, how did you know?"

"One afternoon, Rose wanted me to drop off some flower books for you. You didn't answer the door. I left the books on the front porch, but as I was getting back in my car, I saw you come out of your neighbor's house. It was pretty clear something was going on."

"What neighbor?" Claire repeated. "You mean, the famous mystery writer? What was going on?"

Everyone looked at Claire. Suddenly, the light bulb switched on. Full wattage. "Oh. Oh. Oh. Oh my goodness." How had she missed *that*?

Jaime turned her attention back to Tessa. "I should've said something. I should've stopped it. I should've told Rose. I just . . . didn't know what to do."

Tessa shook her head. "You couldn't have stopped anything from happening."

Jaime lifted her head. "I could've told Rose."

Tessa coughed a laugh. "Jaime, don't you remember what it was like being a teenager? I would've just become all the more secretive. You couldn't have changed anything."

"One thing," Jaime said. "I could've done one thing. I didn't turn off the iron. I heard Claire come into the shop and shout at Chris and Tessa—"

Claire waved her hand in the air. "Hold it. I'm still back with Tessa and the neighbor. You knew, Jaime? How could you have kept that from me?" Another light bulb in her brain switched on. Why was she always the last to figure things out? "So *that's* why you came into the front room and shouted at me to leave them alone, that I didn't know what I was talking about. I thought you meant Chris and Tessa. I thought you were defending them for sneaking around behind my back. I thought you had betrayed me like they had. But you meant Tessa and the neighbor." She let out a breath. "No wonder you forgot to turn off the iron." She dropped her head in her hands. "I'm responsible for the fire. No one else."

"Claire," Rose said in a quiet voice, "why don't you tell us what went on that night from your point of view."

Claire had to take a minute to pull herself together. Did she really have to say this out loud? Apparently, she did. Slowly, she lifted her head. "I'd come into the shop and found Tessa in Chris's arms, and I just turned into a crazy woman. I thought they were together. I've always been so jealous of Tessa and—"

"Me?" Tessa said. "Why would you be jealous of me?"

Claire gave her a look. "Because of all"—she waved her hands up and down in front of Tessa—"*that.*"

Tessa frowned. "Well, then maybe you should know that I've always been a little jealous of you."

"Me? Why in the world would you be jealous of *me*?"

"You say whatever's on your mind and you don't care what others think."

"I care. Sometimes. Saying whatever's on my mind was the very reason I got fired from my job in Savannah. I might have said too much."

Chris snorted. "Think so?"

Claire frowned at him. But it was the first normal interaction between them this morning and it felt good. Still, she kept her frown on.

"Claire," Rose said, "I believe you were telling us that you had turned into a crazy woman."

"It was my birthday and Chris had promised to take me to Highlands for a special dinner, but then he didn't show up when he said he would, so I went to the shop to get him. And there he was, holding Tessa."

Chris lifted his hand. "I was *comforting* Tessa."

Claire turned to him and locked eyes. "That's *not* what it looked like."

"That's all it was, Claire," Tessa said. "I'd never try to steal your boyfriend."

"You never *had* to try. You just did it . . . just by being you." The look on Tessa's face! Claire had had it all wrong. Tessa, Chris, all the anger and disappointment Claire had held on to. Seven years of feeling hurt and betrayed. And she'd had it all wrong.

Rose pulled her back before she could head down that long road of remorse. "Claire, let's get back to that August night. What happened next?"

"I saw Chris's magic circle of fire on the register counter. That circle . . . it meant so much to me. He'd done that trick during the senior talent show and gave me that amazing kiss, right in front of everybody—"

"It *was* an amazing kiss," Chris said.

Claire froze, locking eyes with Chris. For seven years she'd assumed that incredible, passionate kiss had meant something only to her, not to him. She felt her face start flushing red.

"Please continue, Claire," Rose said.

But Claire's mind had gone blank, her thoughts went missing. Chris had stunned her voice right out of her. She had to force herself to look away from him to try and remember where she'd left off. "So . . . um . . . so I picked up the circle of fire and broke it into pieces and . . ." Her eyes filled with tears. "Suddenly sparks went flying everywhere." She splayed one hand against her chest. "Don't you see? I'm the one who started that fire."

"Hold on a minute, Claire," Chris said. "You can't claim credit for what you didn't know. I'm the one who's truly responsible for that fire. That afternoon, I should have been trying to fix the cooler's motor like I told Rose I would. Instead, I spent the afternoon practicing the circle of fire whenever there weren't any customers in the shop."

Jaime gasped. "Oh no you didn't."

Chris looked at her. "Oh yes I did."

Despite everything, this moment brought a smile to Claire's face. It conjured up echoes of similar conversations in the flower shop. Jaime was such a rule abider and Chris was such a rule ignorer.

Jaime's forehead was furrowed in a frown. "Rose told you over and over that you weren't supposed to practice your magic in the store. Too dangerous, she said."

"I know," Chris said, scratching his forehead. "I wasn't listening much to anyone back then."

A laugh burst out of Tessa. "Don't you remember the fright

you gave poor old Mrs. Smithfield when you tried to swallow the sword?"

"Yeah," Chris said. "That one didn't work so well. I punctured a tonsil."

"I'd forgotten!" Claire said. "You had to get both tonsils taken out."

"Chris," Rose said, sounding weary, "let's stay focused on that August afternoon."

"Right," Chris said. "Normally, the circle of fire has propane inside the ring. I had a performance that evening and hadn't practiced the circle of fire in a while. So I went to the gas station to get propane, but they were out, so I had to buy a substitute gas. Acetylene."

"Oh my goodness," Tessa said.

"What's that?" Claire said.

"It's a highly flammable gas," Tessa said. "I only know because Dawson uses it for welding. He's always warning me to keep away when he's using it. It's very unstable."

"Yeah. Not a good choice for a magic trick." Chris scrunched up his face. "I'd just finished refilling the circle of fire when Tessa came in, all upset and crying. Then Claire came in, all, you know"—he waved his hands in the air to indicate the state she was in—"and then she must've pulled the trigger when she picked it up."

"So, Claire," Rose said, "let's get back to that moment."

"The sparks started flying and then Chris yelled at all of us to run for our lives. So we bolted out of the shop and down the street, and sure enough, suddenly there was an explosion coming from inside the shop. I kept on running. Right to the bus station."

"So did I," Jaime said. "I hopped in Tin Lizzie and took off."

"I ran too," Tessa said. "All the way to Saudi Arabia."

"And that," Rose said, strength back in her voice, "brings up the heart of the matter. You ran." She looked at each girl. "All three of you fled Sunrise and left me to pick up the pieces alone. All of you ran but Chris. He's the one who confessed to arson, just to avoid entangling the rest of us."

"Why did you do that?" Jaime said. "The fire was an accident. We all played a part in it."

Chris rocked his hand in the air. "Yes and no. I'm the one who brought a highly flammable fuel into the shop in the first place, despite being warned, repeatedly, by Rose. The fire investigator determined the fire originated with the acetylene. When I learned that, I knew how things would roll out. I'd already been in juvey for arson. It made more sense to plead guilty to third-degree arson than risk being charged with first degree." He shrugged a shoulder in a careless way. "Prison was the best thing that could've happened to me. Turned me around."

Rose lifted a hand. "Chris went to prison on an arson charge just to protect your reputations. All of you."

Claire looked at Chris at the same moment he looked at her. He'd gone to prison to protect *her*. Shame pierced her soul, as sharp as an arrow. She'd had no faith in him. No faith in anyone.

Rose let that settle in for a long moment. "Running away bothered me, much more than the fire. The fire . . . Jaime is right. That fire was an accident and we all had a role in it. Accidents happen. Buildings can be rebuilt. But not friendships. Not the kind of friendship that you girls had together. The three of you worked in harmony in a way I've never seen before, in all my years as a flower shop owner. There were times when I watched you all at work, and it felt like it had been choreographed. You brought out the best in each other. I knew I had something special here, and I tried to teach you everything about flowers that I could."

"You did, Rose," Jaime said, tears streaming down her face. "You taught us so well that we've all chosen to make careers in flowers. All three of us."

"Separately," Rose said. "Not together. That's been the greatest disappointment to me. The first difficult moment you encountered together made you all run away, in different directions. God gave

314

you a beautiful gift and you threw it away like it was worthless. You ran away and you stayed away."

Claire cleared her throat. "Until you brought us back."

A long pause followed, until Jaime crossed the room and crouched down in front of Rose, taking her hand. "I should've asked for your forgiveness a long, long time ago. I'm so sorry. I ran because . . . I was scared."

Claire dropped to her knees and scuttled over to take Rose's other hand. "I ran because I was scared, but I was also mad."

Tessa joined them, crouching down on the other side of Rose's chair. "I think I was mad more than I was scared. Mad at the wrong person. And then I lost all the right people."

"Running away is no answer. That was the reason it took me such a long time to try and find you girls. I had to wait until I could forgive you." Rose held each girl's gaze for a long, long moment. "And I have. I truly have. I needed to set things right, for my sake as well as yours. Time is so short." Her face softened into a tired but sincere smile. "And now, there's a rather important wedding to prepare for. Perhaps the most important one in Rose's Flower Shop history. Chris, will you see the girls to the door? Time is short."

Just then, Claire realized why Rose had been so absent these last few months, why she seemed so tired, so frail. As she walked to the door, she glanced at Jaime and Tessa. She could see that they were thinking the same thing. Rose wasn't at all well.

ten

Flowers teach us that nothing is permanent: not their beauty, not even the fact that they will inevitably wilt, because they will still give new seeds. Remember this when you feel joy, pain, or sadness. Everything passes, grows old, dies, and is reborn.
—*Paulo Coelho*

TESSA

Tessa drove over to the field and went straight into the greenhouse to find Dawson. He was high up on a ladder, putting bulbs into a chandelier. He saw her coming and said, "If you're looking for Liam, you just missed him. He's on his way over to the shop to pick up fiddle-leaf fig trees." He looked at her and climbed down the ladder, coming to her at once, his expression drawn with concern. "What's happened?"

She didn't say anything. She couldn't. She just dove into him with a sob, and he wrapped his arms around her, holding her tight as she cried and cried and cried.

l·l·l

JAIME

Jaime was dusting off the leaves of some fiddle-leaf fig trees. Liam had just texted to ask how many trees the shop had because he wanted to use them in the reception. Fortunately, Rose had quite a few of them in supply because of a mistake in an order. There'd been a lot of similar mistakes Jaime had found since she'd arrived last summer. She had just assumed that Rose was overwhelmed and needed help because the store had more work than she could manage. Jaime hadn't put all the pieces together until today. Rose's frequent absence, her lack of interest in the shop's day-to-day management, the way she handed off decisions to Jaime and Claire, Chris's insistence not to trouble Rose with shop questions. And then there was the sight of Rose. Until this very morning, Jaime hadn't realized how frail Rose was. How thin her once-strong hands had become, how cold they felt.

"That leaf is gettin' its very life dusted out of it."

Jaime stopped her frantic leaf polishing. She didn't trust herself to look at Liam.

"Is somethin' botherin' y', lass?"

One giant sob overtook her, and Liam put his hands on her shoulders, turned her around, and held her close against his chest.

CLAIRE

An hour later, as soon as Claire heard the roar of Chris's Mustang come down Main Street, she rushed out of the shop to meet him. He had barely opened the car door when she said, "Why didn't you tell me? How could you not have told me? I didn't even see it coming. Not until she kept saying time is short. She said it over and over. Chris! How could you not have said anything?"

Slowly, he closed the door to the car and turned to her. "Because it wasn't my place to tell."

"She didn't go to Mexico for a beach vacation, did she?"

He shook his head sadly. "Some kind of alternative last-chance cancer treatment . . . that didn't seem to deliver on its promise of a miracle."

Last chance? "Chris . . . is she . . . is Rose dying?"

He'd been watching her, tenderness on his face. Claire's knees started buckling. Chris didn't say a word but reached out to embrace her, holding her tightly in his arms.

eleven

Flowers are the Romeos and Juliets of the nature.
—Mehmet Murat ildan

TESSA

The bride and groom were late. As soon as they arrived, the Opposite Wedding at Tessa's nascent flower farm would begin. Tessa had been so absorbed in the greenhouse— first, the process of getting it installed onto the slab foundation, wired for electricity, plumbed for water, and then transformed into a winter wonderland—that she hadn't given much thought about the actual clients for her flower farm's first official event. That probably sounded harsh, but it was the truth. Jaime was in charge of handling the clients.

And then the first guests started to arrive for the wedding. Waves of nervousness crashed over Tessa, one right after the other. The bride had never seen the venue but through pictures. Would she like it? Was it what she had in mind? This was one of the most important days in a woman's life. She would remember this day forever. And then there was the groom, albeit he was a vague part

319

of this story. For the first time, Tessa felt the weight of all that this day represented for the bride and groom, and her stomach churned. How did Jaime and Liam do this all the time without getting ulcers?

Tessa breathed in through her nose and slowly out through her mouth, over and over. Calming down, her gaze swept the still-unnamed flower farm. The land that surrounded the greenhouse looked amazing. The dumpster had barely left the property when Dawson, impatient to get started on preparing the soil for spring, had planted a cover crop of clover—or what he called green manure. The unusually warm autumn weather had helped the seeds sprout quickly, and the ground surrounding the greenhouse looked like a carpet of green velvet had been rolled over top. The wedding ceremony would begin as the sun was low in the horizon, and the gentle lighting of the greenhouse glowed a buttery yellow, beckoning people to come in. Welcoming them. Setting the stage for something wonderful to happen.

But it was inside where the magic had happened. Jaime and Liam had transformed the plain, modest glass-sided, glass-roofed greenhouse into a botanical garden. The scene was beyond anything Tessa or Dawson could have imagined. Hanging plants from the roof rafters, large potted plants tucked against the walls that softened the edges of the greenhouse, especially as the sun disappeared. Glass at night could look so cold, but this greenhouse was enveloped in warmth and light. Strands of bulbs draped down from the open rafters. Most of the light came from chandeliers that hung from the center rafter. Warmth came from a heater that had been installed by the electrician yesterday afternoon—not a minute too soon.

The greenhouse had been divided into two sections, fore and back, with the ceremony closest to the entrance, in the front. The dinner reception and dancing had been skillfully hidden behind a wall of fiddle-leaf fig trees in the back. Long rectangular tables and chairs had been brought in for the guests and bridal party, with a dance floor in the center that now held a small round table with a wedding cake.

To Tessa, the venue was breathtaking. Stunning. It still amazed her that Jaime had envisioned the entire winter wonderland scene while it was still so bleak—a basic slab foundation surrounded by brown dirt. And that vision, with a lot of hard work, had come to be!

This morning, while moving in potted plants that had arrived from a supplier in Asheville, she'd shared that thought with Dawson. "Jaime's imagination is way beyond anything I'd ever known in her. And then . . . wait until you see Claire's table arrangements. Or the bridal bouquet. I've never seen anything like it. Full of unusual sprays of foliage that Claire foraged in Sunrise. Things that never, ever would have occurred to me to put into wedding flowers, like silver dollar eucalyptus and hypericum berries. She found them on her way to work and foraged them! They're absolutely gorgeous, Dawson. Sometimes I feel like I'm in the presence of two flower geniuses."

Dawson had been carrying in a potted lemon tree from the truck, while she held a potted hibiscus, and they set them down in a corner of the greenhouse. She wasn't even sure he'd been listening to her, but while seemingly admiring the glossy leaves of the lemon tree, he quietly said that she'd done the same thing when she saw an empty field and imagined it full of flowers. "Three flower geniuses," he said.

She came up to him from behind and put her arms around him. "Thank you, Dawson. Thank you for everything."

He didn't say anything in return, which was typical of him, but he did put his hand on top of hers and squeezed.

twelve

Love is like a beautiful flower which I may not touch, but whose fragrance makes the garden a place of delight just the same.
—*Helen Keller*

JAIME

The wedding guests had arrived and were seated in the greenhouse, waiting patiently for the bride and groom, who were quite late. Jaime tried not to let her mind get away from her—could the bride have fled the scene once again? At the twenty-minute mark past the time the ceremony should've started, she pulled Liam aside. "Has she vanished?"

"Nay," he reassured her. "No doubt they're on their way." But he didn't look as confident as he sounded. "Perhaps, if she's not here in ten minutes, we should offer the guests a bit of libation, though."

"Good idea." So Jaime went to Tessa's Airstream to see if the caterer had brought extra champagne. Inside the tiny space, the caterer and two helpers were preparing trays of appetizers. As soon as the ceremony ended, the reception would begin. It was such a tight space to work in, yet the caterer Liam had found in Highlands seemed to know exactly how to maneuver small spaces. Just as she was about to ask for champagne to be brought to the patient guests, she heard Liam call her name. He was waiting for her right outside the Airstream with a big grin on his handsome face.

"The bride is nearly here. Ready?"

Just then, an old orange Volkswagen bus rumbled up the road and came to a stop in front of the pathway that Dawson had created. Jaime exchanged a look with Liam that said so much. This was the moment of truth. Had they captured the bride's opposite vision? And if so . . . would the bride's mother throw a hissy fit?

Jaime took in a deep breath, bracing herself for whatever reaction she was about to encounter. "I'm as ready as I can be."

"You've been ready for years," he said. "It's showtime." With his hand on Jaime's elbow, they walked over to greet the Volkswagen bus. Something about his warm touch on her elbow gave her a sense of reassurance. Along with a sense of longing. What would happen to them after tonight? Would Liam return to New York City and forget about her again? She shook off those stray thoughts. *Not now, Jaime. Don't start that now.*

Mr. Zimmerman, a jovial man, hopped out of the driver's side and hurried around to slide open the bus door. He smiled at Liam and Jaime, like today was the best day of his life. "Here comes the bride," he said in a thick Bronx accent. "And the groom too."

First out of the bus came a young man who looked like he spent his days surfing. Long, sun-streaked blond hair, deeply tanned, wearing a Tommy Bahama short-sleeved shirt, khaki shorts, and sandals. He paused when he saw the greenhouse and let out one word in a relieved exhale: "Coooool."

Okay, Jaime thought to herself, a smile frozen on her face. *Okay.* The groom seemed happy with the venue. The bride's father seemed happy that the day had arrived. Two down, two to go.

Next came the bride. It took help from both her dad and her groom to help her out of the bus, and she grimaced with each movement, batting their hands away in annoyance. Strangely enough, the irritated look on the bride's face reminded Jaime exactly of the bride's mother, Mrs. Zimmerman. It dawned on Jaime that as desperately as the bride tried to be everything opposite of her mother, she was becoming her mother!

But then the bride saw the luminescent greenhouse. She stopped suddenly, and her face softened, and she burst into tears. She grabbed Liam's hands. "Thank you, thank you."

Happy tears! Thank goodness. Jaime let out a sigh of relief. Three down. One to go.

The last one out of the VW bus was Mrs. Zimmerman. Jaime hadn't seen her since last spring, back in New York City, as the final touches were getting decided for her daughter's original wedding. This woman could put a chill down anyone's spine, and today was no different. She'd been sitting in the passenger seat of the VW, grimly facing forward.

Liam stepped up and opened the door. He whispered something to her, and she whispered back in a loud voice, something about, ". . . and she's wearing red cowboy boots under that wedding dress."

Liam whispered back to her. Jaime wasn't sure what he was saying, but she could tell it was just the right thing to soothe her. Mrs. Zimmerman's shoulders relaxed, and she turned to him with a sheepish look, then a smile. Not a huge smile, but a smile nonetheless.

That man! He had such a way about him.

Liam helped Mrs. Zimmerman climb out of the bus in her formal dress and very high heels. When she noticed Jaime standing there, she glanced at her with a frown.

"Y' must remember m' colleague, Jaime Harper."

"Must I?" Mrs. Zimmerman said sourly. But then her gaze shifted to the greenhouse, shimmering in the late afternoon light, and her whole countenance shifted. "Why, it's a botanical garden. Just like I had planned for her last spring!"

Jaime and Liam looked at each other, shocked. The first wedding venue had been the New York Botanical Garden in the Bronx. As they set to work to transform the greenhouse, they'd completely forgotten the venue of the first wedding. The Opposite Wedding wasn't really opposite at all.

Well, it was what it was. Jaime clasped her hands together. "Liam, would you mind taking Mrs. Zimmerman to her special seat?"

On cue, Liam held out his elbow for Mrs. Zimmerman, and they started down the path to the greenhouse. As soon as they were halfway down the path, Jaime rushed over to the Airstream and told the caterer, "The ceremony begins in two minutes. I'll give you a heads-up as the vows are being exchanged so you can start the reception with champagne for the guests."

Jaime hurried down the path to where the bride waited with her father, outside the greenhouse. She had an odd, uncomfortable look on her face as she gazed at the bridal bouquet in her hands.

Jaime sidled over to Claire to whisper, "The bouquet turned out beautifully."

Claire whispered back, "Then why doesn't the bride look happy?"

Honestly, Jaime didn't know. Maybe . . . it should've been simpler. Three or five long-stemmed sunflowers, perhaps.

The bride's father took a few steps over to Jaime. "Can we move things along here?"

Good grief. Was he kidding? The bridal party had been twenty minutes late, which created all kinds of problems for the caterer, taxed the guests' patience, and stressed the event planners. This family had a history of complicating weddings! But she only smiled at him and deferred to Liam, who had just returned to the wedding party after seating Mrs. Zimmerman.

"Indeed we can, Mr. Zimmerman." He signaled a cue to the banjo player up front and turned to the bride. "Lass, yer a vision to behold." He opened the door. "Yer groom awaits you."

A look of relief filled the bride's face, outshadowed only by her father's relief. He grabbed her arm and started down the aisle, so quickly that the bride stopped in her tracks and whacked him with the beautiful bouquet Claire had made, sending petals of flowers onto the dark green center roll of carpet.

"Daddy!" she shrieked. "Hold your horses! Slow down. I can't move that fast."

And on that shrill note, the wedding ceremony began.

thirteen

In the garden of love, flowers don't die.
—Nitya Prakash

TESSA

Tessa and Dawson remained hovering nervously near the greenhouse until the wedding ceremony was over. She wanted to be available in case Jaime or Claire needed anything brought back from the flower shop. Dawson hung around in case something went horribly wrong with the greenhouse, like a space heater conked out or the electricity went wonky. So far, from where they were standing by the Airstream, this event was a success. The sun was setting, and the dinner service had just started, and this portion of the evening belonged to the caterer. Tessa was starting to relax. When the staff had left the Airstream to deliver dinner plates, Tessa popped inside to get two cups of just-brewed coffee out of the percolating coffeemaker.

She came back out to join Dawson. He was leaning against the Airstream, one ankle crossed over the other, hands in his pockets, a pleased look on his face.

He took the cup she held out for him. "Thanks."

She stood beside him, looking at the greenhouse in the setting sun. "It's amazing, isn't it? All that's happened in just a few weeks." Inside the greenhouse, guests were laughing and enjoying themselves. "I might have imagined fields of flowers, but I had never imagined this." She took a sip of coffee. "Liam wants us to consider keeping this as a venue site and not use it as a greenhouse."

"Yeah," Dawson said. "He told me the same thing."

"But that's ridiculous, right? We need the greenhouse for the flowers. That's what this flower farm is all about."

Dawson remained quiet, which wasn't unusual, but this quiet went on for way too long. She pivoted to face him. "Something's up." A spike of fear trickled through her. Maybe he'd been so insistent about the greenhouse so that he could leave with a clear conscience. The flower farm had a solid base, it had the patronage of Rose's Flower Shop, Tessa had her friends back . . . and now he could get a real job. Elsewhere.

"So . . . I bought those six acres."

"Wait . . . what?" The adjoining six acres to her field?

He pushed off from the trailer. "I know I should've told you, but it was too good a deal to pass up. And this way, if we wanted to keep this greenhouse as a venue site—for weddings or flower workshops or those kinds of things you keep talking about—we could add another greenhouse in the back six acres. This site is best for bringing in the public. Easy access to the road, good parking. And then there's varieties. You wanted year-round flowers and that's going to take more than three acres."

"Dawson . . . hold on a minute. I love the idea of this, but I can't afford that land."

"You don't have to. I bought it."

"You can't afford to buy it."

"I can and I did."

Still confused, she peered at him. "But . . . that would mean . . ." What did it mean?

328

A smile started. "It would mean . . . that you're no longer my boss." He took her coffee cup out of her hand and set both cups on the ground. He took a step closer to her. "It would mean . . . that we're partners." He put his hands on her elbows. "It would mean that we're in this for the long haul." He peered down at her, his eyes landing on her lips. "It would mean I'm all in . . . if you are."

She looked up at him and wrapped her arms around his neck. "All in." She reached up to kiss him, and as his arms circled around her, she realized that she'd never really known what it was to be loved until she was loved by Dawson. Between kisses, she said, "I just came up with a name for our flower farm. A Year of Flowers."

He tightened his arms around her. "I like it. Says it all."

They stayed in an embrace for a long while, so long that Tessa closed her eyes. The minute she did, a lovely feeling came over her. Like a hug from Rose. She opened her eyes with a start, but it was Dawson whose arms held her.

And suddenly a commotion from inside the greenhouse startled them. The caterer bolted out of the greenhouse and ran toward the Airstream. "Get some towels! A blanket! Bring hot water! The bride started line dancing and her water broke! The baby's coming."

fourteen

One day you will look back and see that
all along, you were blooming.
—Morgan Harper Nichols

CLAIRE

Claire sat alone in the waiting room of the Highlands-Cashiers Hospital. Mr. and Mrs. Zimmerman were in the room with their daughter and son-in-law and their yet-to-be-named baby girl, who had been delivered by a Sunrise firefighter in the nick of time—right in the greenhouse. Claire drove the Zimmermans in the Volkswagen bus behind the ambulance. Tessa, Dawson, Jaime, and Liam remained at the site to take care of the guests and clean up. Claire still had the VW bus's keys to give to Mr. Zimmerman and no way to get home. So she was stuck for now.

In the quiet, Claire had time to ponder. She had caught a glimpse of Tessa and Dawson locked in an embrace by the Airstream right before the bride started line dancing and her water broke. And she'd been aware of undercurrents between Jaime and

Liam from the start. She felt left out. She didn't belong. It was a familiar feeling, like a default.

Returning to Sunrise was a good decision, but it also stirred up so much longing for Chris's attention. And he was a magician—always disappearing. Like tonight! He'd told Claire that he would come to the wedding to help out and yet he didn't show up. Nor did he respond to her texts asking for his whereabouts. She felt as if he was always hiding something from her. They'd get a little closer on the weekends, and then *whoosh* . . . he'd vanish again.

She inhaled a deep breath. She wasn't going to let herself go down a well-worn rabbit trail that led to nowhere. These last few months had taught her a few things about herself. She wasn't alone. Even if she felt she was, she wasn't. And she owed that to Chris. He had reminded her that believing in God was one thing. Trusting in him was where all the good stuff came in. That was where the peace lay.

It was good to be here, to be back in the flower shop. It was good to be connected to Jaime and Tessa again. To be forgiven by Rose felt like she was a bird set free from a cage. Yes! That was it exactly. She felt set free from a cage—one of her own making. A cage of insecurities and neediness. A cage of expecting too much from others. Rose, Tessa, Jaime, MaryBeth, Chris. Especially Chris.

Growing tired, she curled up in a chair and closed her eyes.

Just as she started to drift off, a funny feeling came over her, so real that she opened her eyes with a shock. She could've sworn Rose was giving her a hug. But there was no one in the waiting room but Claire.

fifteen

May the flowers remind us why the rain is so necessary.
—Xan Oku

JAIME

Bless their hearts. Even with a baby born in the middle of a wedding reception, and the bride and groom whisked off to the hospital, the guests stayed to party on. It was after eleven o'clock when the last guests left. Jaime had learned a trick from her time at Epic Events: Close the open bar a good hour or so before the formal end to the reception. It always amazed her that shutting off the tap had that kind of effect on a party. Guests drifted away like barn cats.

Liam had finished paying the caterer and locked up the Airstream for Tessa, then came looking for Jaime. She was carrying out the last bag of trash from the greenhouse, so he took it from her and set it with the other bags near the fancy porta potties, waiting to be hauled away in the morning. "Well," he said as he returned to the greenhouse, "who would've thought a bairn would arrive tonight. 'Twas a lovely way to christen Tessa and Dawson's flower farm."

"Definitely a memorable event." She flipped off the lights to the greenhouse and locked the door. For a moment it was pitch black, and then she realized that Liam had come to stand right in front of her, his features visible in the moonlight. Gosh, he smelled good, she thought. Even after a challenging event and a long night, he smelled good.

"'Tis beautiful here."

Did he mean here? Or her? She assumed here, though he was looking at her. Her head rolled back to look at the stars. "There's very little light pollution in the mountains."

"Aye. The bright stars remind me of a Kentucky night sky." He looked up at the stars for a moment, then dropped his head. "I told Dawson and Tessa that they should consider keeping the greenhouse as an event venue. I think there'll be more weddings and parties coming this way."

"Seriously? You think Sunrise could be a go-to place?"

"I do. Highlands is a destination spot for weddings, but 'tis crowded. Sunrise is closer to Asheville, has more of a small-town vibe. It might take some time, but I think there's real possibilities here for Sunrise to become a destination in itself. The lakes, the mountains. It's got everything except enough venues. Rose saw the potential, I think. She brought you all back to see what could happen when y' worked together."

Jaime thought back to the conversation Rose had with them yesterday morning. It felt like days had passed. "Rose said it's like someone has choreographed us."

"Even with seven years' separation?"

"Maybe even more so. It's like we grew in ways that made us better versions of ourselves. The ways we've changed have only benefited us. We're better together."

"So then . . . no regrets about leavin' New York City?"

"This is where I belong."

"I can see that." He reached out to lean a hand on the greenhouse, the other hand in his pants pocket. "Jaime, I'm . . ."

Here it comes, she thought. *The goodbye talk.* Well, she was prepared for it. She tightened her jaw and tilted her head to the side. "Please don't say you're sorry that you need to stay in New York. I realize that's the place you need to be."

"Hold on, lass. I was tryin' to say that I'd like to relocate and move down here. I've been scoutin' out locations and have my eye on office space in Highlands. The plan I've been working on these last few months—when I should've been keeping in touch with you—is to open an Epic Events branch down here. Let Sloane run the New York office and I'll handle the Southern one. There's opportunity here . . . and it's where my roots are." He dropped his arm and reached for her hand. "I'd like to give us a chance to be together, Jaime. If yer willing to take me on."

Was she willing? She'd been in love with this man for years, more so after she worked for him. And these last few weeks, even the last few days, only churned up more feelings. She couldn't believe he was asking her for a commitment. This was her dream! Everything he was telling her was what she'd longed to hear from him . . . but she still had one sizable hitch in her gut. "Liam, will you ever drop your Scottish facade?"

He stiffened. "Why does it matter?"

"I just . . . sometimes I wonder who you really are. A boy from Kentucky or a man from Scotland."

He gazed at her for a long while. "Last we spoke, I took you at yer word when y' said you weren't asking me to change my name or my accent. You just got finished telling me that the time away from Sunrise made you a better version of yourself. 'Tis the same for me, Jaime. My time away from Kentucky allowed me to become the person I wanted to be. 'Tis hard to understand, but lately, when I talk with my granny, speaking in Kentucky dialect feels foreign."

Jaime had to smile. "And what did she say the first time you used your brogue?"

His grin lit up the night. "She loved it. She even cried a bit. It reminded her of her parents who came o'er from Scotland. And then I was in Scotland for a couple months not long ago to do my old college roommate's weddin' and took some time to reflect. I was a wee lad when my great-grandparents came o'er from Scotland the last years of their lives, and I'd forgotten how good it felt to hear stories in their thick brogue, to realize how deep those family roots went." He swept his arms down his body. "This is who I am. This is the man you've known. I'd do anything for you, Jaime, but I can't change who I've become. I don't want to."

As if a lightning bolt struck her, she suddenly understood exactly what he meant. She had changed dramatically from the girl who had left Sunrise on that hot August night. She wouldn't want to be that same girl. He didn't want to be the same boy. She stepped closer to him and placed her hands on his cheeks. "So, basically, you're a Kentucky boy whose rough edges have been sanded down by Scotland."

"Aye." He put his arms around her to draw her close. "And is now a man who's hopelessly in love with a girl from Sunrise."

Closing her eyes, Jaime sank into Liam's embrace. Was this really happening? No sooner had she thought it than the strangest feeling came over her, that deeply loved sense she got whenever she'd been hugged by Rose.

sixteen

All the flowers of all the tomorrows are in the seeds of today.
—Native American proverb

CLAIRE

Claire had nodded off in the hospital waiting room. She felt someone tap her on the arm and woke with a jolt.

Chris was crouched down in front of her, tears streaming down his face. "Claire, she's gone."

She sat up, completely confused. "The baby?" She blinked a few times. "Or the bride?"

"What baby?"

"The bride had a baby." She rubbed her eyes. Was she dreaming?

"That's why you're at the hospital?"

"Yes. I'm waiting to drive her parents back to Sunrise. I forgot to give the bride's father the keys to his Volkswagen bus." She tipped her head. "Why are you here?"

"Rose. I've been with her all day. She was resting most of the day. I knew you were expecting me, but I just didn't feel right about leaving. And then around six, she got herself out of bed and asked me to drive her to the greenhouse. She wanted to see it. So I did. And she loved it. Just loved it. Everything. The whole setting looked magical in the moonlight. I asked her if she wanted to go inside to see the flowers up close, but she said her time was short and she needed me to drive her to the hospital. She passed away about an hour ago."

Shocked, Claire didn't know what to say, what to think. Rose was gone. Gone? How could this be? The shock wore off as suddenly as it came, and tears sheened her vision, blurring her view of him. She was just about to crumble, but in that split second before the first sob escaped, she realized that Chris needed her to be strong, not to fall apart. Later. She could fall apart later, at the flower shop, with Jaime and Tessa.

She slipped down on the floor to perch on her knees, facing him, and took both of his hands in hers. "Rose prepared us for this, Chris. We're going to be okay. We'll get through this." She reached her arms around him, hugging him tight and strong, just like Rose used to. "We're better together."

He buried his face in her curly mess of hair. "We've always been better together," he said, choking up.

She smiled through her tears. "I know." And she did know. Because loving and being loved were two of God's greatest gifts in the entire world. Yes, ma'am, they were.

Author's Note

Thank you to my niece Whitney Woods Kucher. Her life in New York City provided a vivid model for Jaime's tiny apartment. Two true scenes: Whitney's apartment was so small that the shower was in the kitchen. And on the street level of her apartment was a cat adoption agency and a crystal shop.

And a shout-out to my friend Rhonda Raphel, who invited me to join in on her Garden Club's tour of a flower farm right as these novellas were starting to take shape. And a thank-you to my very talented friend Nyna Dolby, who first taught me about flower arranging. I've kept all my notes from your flower events!

A big Rose-style hug to my first draft reader, Lindsey Ross, who provides great flyover feedback of a work in progress. She's so busy, yet she always makes time for my novels.

My daughter-in-law Hayden shared her hometown in the North Carolina mountains with me for this story. She provided all kinds of credible details to set the stage of Sunrise—the smell of firewood in the air, the winding roads, the "everyone knows everyone's business" community. Her input was invaluable. She is a jewel!

As always, I have so much gratitude to the Revell team—Andrea Doering, Brianne Dekker, Karen Steele, Barb Barnes, Kristin Kornoelje, Laura Klynstra, and many others—who make every book as good as it can possibly be.

To the Lord, the Creator of all flowers, *A Year of Flowers* has only heightened my awe and appreciation for your creativity. Imagine what waits for us in Heaven!

Resources

Further reading you might enjoy if you're fond of flowers . . .

Banzakein, Erin, with Jill Jorgensen and Julie Chai. *Floret Farm's A Year in Flowers: Designing Gorgeous Arrangements for Every Season.* San Francisco: Chronicle Books, 2020.

Harampolis, Alethea, and Jill Rizzo. *The Flower Recipe Book.* New York: Artisan, 2013.

Newbery, Georgie. *The Flower Farmer's Year: How to Grow Cut Flowers for Pleasure and Profit.* England: Green Books, 2014.

TURN THE PAGE FOR

a sneak peek

AT SUZANNE'S NEXT ROMANCE,

CAPTURE *the* MOMENT

Coming Summer 2025

one

In every walk with nature one receives far more than he seeks.
—John Muir

Kate Cunningham's eyes widened with awe as the Grand Tetons unfolded before her, a sight so breathtaking that it forced her to pull over to the side of the road. No amount of research could have truly prepared her for the spectacle that lay ahead: a sweeping valley floor pushing right into the steep granite peaks of the Tetons, still covered with snow.

She sat in silence, mesmerized by those peaks, until the awe overwhelmed her and she had to look away. In the meadow in front of her, Kate spotted an elk grazing. The quiet beauty of the scene stirred something within her. Without a moment's hesitation, she leaped out of her car and popped the trunk to retrieve her prized possession—a brand-new Sony Alpha 1, heralded as the epitome of wildlife photography cameras. Working at a zoo to create a portfolio, padding her meager income with gigs from Bar Mitzvahs to weddings, and surviving on a diet of Top Ramen had led her to this moment. Kate was on a mission.

Just as she attached her zoom lens to the camera and focused in on the elk, her eyes widened in amazement as a black bear emerged from the tree line. Following behind her came two cubs.

A flare went off in her heart. She'd barely arrived in the park and she'd already seen more wildlife in two minutes than she'd hoped for in two days! With a mixture of excitement and trepidation, she aimed her lens at the sow and her cubs. As the black bear lumbered away, she looked at the images she'd taken. Good, really good, but not unique. Not noteworthy. Not for *National Geographic*, anyway.

With a vague promise from a *Nat Geo* editor dangling like a tantalizing carrot, Kate had set her sights on capturing a unique photograph of the world's most famous bear—Grizzly Bear 399. The editor, a woman she'd met at the zoo a few weeks ago, had said that if Kate could deliver *that* shot, she would take a serious look at it. But, she said, she would need to see the photograph by the end of May. She handed Kate a piece of paper with her email scribbled down. It was the closest Kate had ever been to a break-through opportunity, and she was determined to seize it. Within her grasp was her dream—to be a wildlife photographer.

Stopping at the Moose Entrance, Kate had learned that Grizzly 399 hadn't emerged from hibernation yet. "Then again, she might be dead," the ranger said in a matter-of-fact way. "She's an old lady, you know."

Oh yeah, Kate knew. She had studied everything there was to know about 399. This bear was iconic, known particularly as a wise and vigilant mother.

The bear's age was the reason that the *Nat Geo* editor said she wanted a close-up picture—everyone assumed this could be the bear's last summer. From what Kate had read, and from the grim remark by the ranger, that was a reasonable assumption. No one expected Grizzly 399 to survive yet another winter. Year after year, she kept surprising them. Kept emerging from her den, often with new cubs. A few years ago, she came out of hibernation with quadruplets—a rare occurrence for a sow. Keeping four cubs well-fed and well-protected was no small feat for a bear of any age.

This summer could be the start of Kate's wildlife photography career. She could sense it—something was coming her way. Something that could change everything.

And if she missed it, she'd be back to the zoo.

She reminded herself that it wouldn't be the worst thing to go back there. It was steady work. She shot pictures of the animals for exhibit signs, as well as for publicity and marketing. Locally, she'd been gaining a bit of recognition after adding quirky captions to the zoo photographs she posted on Instagram. One of her hits was a group of majestic giraffes all looking in unison, with a mischievous monkey photobombing in the background, hanging upside down and looking utterly ridiculous. Kate's caption for the shot: "The relative who never gets mentioned."

She took a few more photographs of the elk, grazing in the meadow. Such a peaceful moment. She was tempted to stay longer, but she wanted to check in at the Jackson Lake Lodge, get something to eat, and plan out her locations for the week. It was one thing to read a guidebook about the national park, it was another thing to be here, surrounded by its vastness. Its grandeur.

Thank you, thank you, thank you, God, for bringing me here.

She put the cap on her camera lens, satisfied. This, she thought, was a good note to end her first day on. A very good note.

℮·ℓ·℮

Grant Cooper, known as Coop in Grand Teton National Park circles, stepped into park headquarters with a pretty strong suspicion as to why he'd been summoned. His boss wanted to chat. Coop couldn't help but find it ironic—District Ranger Tim Rivers, a man not known for his chatty nature, calling him in for a conversation. Then again, Coop wasn't much of a talker either, and that's one reason they got along so well.

Coop lived all year for summer months in the mountains. The rest of the year, he traded his seasonal ranger hat for the role of a high school biology teacher at a private high school in Salt

Lake City, attempting to cram knowledge into the minds of bored teenagers until he ran out of words and patience by May, when the school year ended. Summers, however, were his escape, a time to protect grizzly and black bears and recharge his soul. Bears, especially, held a special place in his heart.

But this summer season, which kicked off recently, had started out on a bad foot. It was a record year for snowfall, with the park entirely socked in. In a regular year, most of the snow was gone by July and August, the heaviest tourist season. But this wasn't a regular year. It was mid-May, and there was still an enormous amount of snow and ice to melt from the mountains, creating dangerous conditions for inexperienced hikers—which, in Coop's eyes, was most of them.

A series of encounters with clueless tourists had left Coop frustrated much earlier in the season than usual. German backpackers disrupted a herd of elk for selfies, a day packer attempted to feed a granola bar to a bear cub, claiming he was "connecting with nature," and the grand finale—a camper had no clue how to put his borrowed-from-his-neighbor-tent together. That was the clincher for Coop. It was a classic tip-off to rangers. When campers had no idea how to erect tents, they had no business hiking in the backcountry.

At that point, Coop's short fuse had heated to the point that these misguided campers complained to park management, which led to this moment in Tim Rivers's small office in the park's headquarters.

Tim sat across from Coop in his perfectly pressed uniform, with a badge gleaming on his chest. On a corner of the desk sat his wide-brimmed hat. He was a quintessential parkie and had been assigned to numerous parks, all over the country. Coop met Tim a few years ago, when he'd given a talk at Coop's high school about a career in the National Park Service. Afterward, Coop introduced himself, explaining that he had spent every summer of his life backpacking in the national parks. It was the main reason he had chosen teaching as a profession. Like everything in life, Coop took teaching seriously, he gave it everything he had, but he wanted his summers free for the wilderness.

Tim convinced Coop to work as a seasonal Jenny Lake Ranger at Grand Teton National Park, sealing the deal when he described the work of a backcountry ranger. Remote. Isolated. "You're already doing it," Tim had said. "You're a seasonal vagabond. Why not earn money and do a little good for the world while you're at it?"

So, for the last two summers, that's exactly what Coop ended up doing. Being a seasonal Jenny Lake Ranger was just the right fit for him, kind of like teaching but with even more passion poured into it. He was all in—maybe even more than that. The gig just clicked for him; his hair got all wild, shaving felt optional, and he took on a rugged, work-hardened look. It was like he turned into the opposite of Mr. Cooper, the biology teacher at the high school who rocked a tie every day. For him, being a seasonal ranger was like hitting the jackpot—a chance to hang out with nature all summer, far from the hustle and bustle of regular life. Far away from entitled teenagers, far away from most human beings. A certain female named Emma, in particular. The Emma Dilemma, he called it.

It had been a perfect job until now.

Sitting in Tim's office, Coop wondered if this was the way his students might feel when summoned to the principal's office. Defensive. Indignant. Misunderstood. "Tim, I was only doing my job. Those tourists were deliberately ignoring rules of the park. Rules that are posted *everywhere*."

"I don't disagree with you, but the park service is under fire to reexamine its training regarding insensitivity."

Coop slapped his palm against his chest. "Tim, how is it insensitive when I'm trying to stop some tourist from getting way too cozy with a wild animal she thinks is just 'the cutest thing'?"

Trying unsuccessfully to swallow a smile, Tim paused and

dropped his chin. When he lifted his head, he was back to business. "Coop, you know as well as I do that the official policy of the NPS is to not make fun of tourists."

Yeah, yeah, yeah. Coop knew.

"Let me ask you a serious question." Tim leaned back in his chair and folded his hands behind his head. "What concerns you more? The people or the animals?"

Coop's eyes narrowed. "Is this a trick question?"

"The tourists reported that you called them idiots."

Did he? He might have. They *were* idiots.

"Clueless," Tim continued, leaning forward to read off the report. "Oblivious. Ignorant. Illiterate."

Yep. Coop might have added a few more adjectives. "Okay, okay. I get it. I'll be more careful." He started to rise from his seat, but Tim shook his head.

"Sally wants to reassign you."

Coop plopped back down in the seat. Great, just great.

If Tim Rivers was a true parkie, Sally Janus was a park lifer. She was acting chief ranger of Grand Teton National Park, but she sure wasn't acting.

Most likely, if you asked someone to describe a female chief ranger, they'd come up with a rather robust woman. Strong, big, fearless. Sally was petite, barely over five feet tall, bright bleached-blond hair, with a squeaky little-girl voice. She reminded Coop of Dolly Parton. Coop found her to be an interesting person. And Tim thought so too, far more so.

Coop knew from Tim that the National Park Service path to career advancement was full of bureaucratic red tape. Qualified rangers competed for the same top positions via a point system. So most of the high-ranking rangers Coop worked with, like Tim and Sally, had earned their points at less popular parks or historical parks, waiting to get appointed to a promotion at a popular park. Or they would take an acting role at a more popular park, like Grand Teton, and wait.

So that's what Sally was currently doing. As acting chief ranger, she was responsible for overseeing all aspects of the park, from law enforcement to resource management. And her word was law in the park.

Great, just great. So . . . he'd been yanked from the backcountry. His mind raced through the dreaded possibilities—Visitor Center duty, trail maintenance. Nope, he couldn't face it. "Tim, if I can't be in the backcountry, I'd rather not be a ranger. I'd rather just spend my summer with a backpack. I quit."

"Too bad. You signed a contract," Tim said, unfazed. "We're not about to lose that sixth sense you have. You're one of the best bear managers I've ever seen. Somehow you know the where-abouts of bears before anyone else. Even the full-time Jenny Lake Rangers. And even if you're not in the backcountry, you'll still be managing bears."

"What?" Coop squinted. "Please tell me you don't mean that I'll be directing traffic for bear jams."

"At times, yes. But Sally mostly wants you to manage the pho-tographers who are angling for the best wildlife shot."

Worse than bear jams. Coop squeezed his eyes shut in frus-tration. "I don't get it," he said, opening his eyes. "How could it possibly help the park's insensitivity problem to assign me to babysit bear paparazzi?"

Tim pointed at him. "For that very reason. We're going to show the world that Grand Teton National Park encourages people and wildlife to coexist. We are going to help wildlife photographers do their work, but safely, from a distance." Growing serious, he leaned forward on his elbows. "Look, I agree with Sally on this. I'd feel better if you were down in the valley too. There's chatter about a poacher who thinks it's time to take 399 as a trophy."

"Is it a credible threat? Seems like every year we hear similar rumblings."

"Not sure." Tim seesawed his hand in the air. "And I'm not sure how many years the old girl has left."

"Then, doesn't it make more sense to keep me in the backcountry? Keeping an eye on her?"

Tim shrugged. "If it makes you feel any better, Sally's replaced you with Gallagher, Baker, and Spencer. Three rangers."

Coop sighed. Three rangers who were more like the Three Stooges. But if Sally had made up her mind to reassign him, there was no way around it. And Tim wasn't going to intervene. Added to her authority was that Tim was sweet on her. His gruff voice got soft and gooey when he talked about Sally. Coop had warned him not to get involved with someone he worked with, especially not a boss, but did he listen? Nope.

Tim pushed an envelope across the desk. "Here's a plus. In that envelope is your key. I was able to get you in park housing near Jackson Lake Lodge. I tried to get you a trailer, but they were all spoken for."

"Those dorms?" Coop groaned. "Tim, I'm not a kid." That meant he would have a roommate. That meant sharing a communal bathroom. That meant the only time he'd be sleeping in the great outdoors was when he had time off. "Are you trying to punish me?"

"All ages live in those dorms. You know that. All genders too. Might end up being good for you. Who knows? Maybe you'll meet the woman of your dreams." He grinned. "My mother used to say there's a match for every flame."

Now Tim was pushing Coop's buttons. This was a touchy subject.

"There's a shoe for every foot." Tim's eyes danced with amusement. "A key for every lock."

With a huff, Coop scooped up the envelope with the key to his dorm room and stormed out to Tim's loud guffaws.

Twenty minutes later, Coop parked his truck in the massive parking lot at Jackson Lake Lodge, swung his backpack over one shoulder, and walked toward the dormitories, frustrated and annoyed. He slid the key into his room's lock, pushing the door wide open. The small room held two twin beds, a couple of desks, three built-in bureau drawers, and a window offering a view of the majestic Tetons.

That was a plus.

Then came the minus.

On the bed closest to the window was a scrawny kid with a mop of unruly long hair, a red bandana tied around his forehead. He had earbuds in, listening to something on his phone. He looked at Coop as curiously as Coop looked at him.

"Aww, man," the kid said, sounding disappointed. "Don't tell me I got stuck with a roommate after all. And they sent in Smokey the Bear? I bet my old man's behind this."

"Hello to you too." Coop unloaded his backpack on the empty bed.

"Sorry. I'm just bummed to have to share my space."

As was Coop. "Shouldn't you be at work?"

"Nope. Done for the day. I'm just sitting here contemplating the existential path of mankind."

In the middle of unzipping his backpack, Coop stopped and turned. "How old are you?"

"Old enough." The kid sat up and slapped his hands on his knees. "Call me Frankie."

"I go by Coop." But if this kid were in Coop's biology class, it would be Mr. Cooper, the only teacher who wore a tie.

"Coop . . . like a chicken coop?"

"Like my last name is Cooper."

"Ah, like Alice Cooper," Frankie said, his tone an odd mix of enthusiasm and cynicism.

"Yeah, something like that," Coop said, suppressing a smile. "A little less makeup." He gave him a sideways glance. "Where are you working this summer?"

"I should be in the Wildlife Brigades."

"Why aren't you?"

"Apparently, you have to be eighteen years old or have *parental permission.*" Frankie said it with a sneer. "But my old man decided I needed some"—he wiggled two fingers for air quotes—"character-building experience." His face contorted into an exaggerated frown. "So, here I am, serving time in the glorious Youth Conservation Program."

"So what exactly are you doing?"

"So far, I've been assigned to cleaning toilets and unclogging bear-proof trash bins." Frankie hopped off the bed with a lackadaisical stretch. "You seem pretty old for the Youth Conservation Program."

"That's because I am." This kid could use a filter on his mouth. "I'm a seasonal ranger. For the last few summers, I've been assigned to the backcountry."

"Now *that* sounds like a worthy and noble occupation." Frankie's eyebrows lifted, his expression serious. "So what happened to turn your luck for this summer?"

"Assigned to manage the valley's wildlife photography. Bears, mostly."

Frankie's eyes widened, then he burst out with a scoff. "Dude, what a comedown. You're the official bear photographers' manager." He couldn't stop chuckling. "Man, you must've done something really stupid."

Coop opened and shut the drawers, finding them full of Frankie's jumbled clothes. "Hey, I'm going to need some space."

"Yeah, yeah. Just empty one out."

"I'll empty two out." Coop scooped up Frankie's clothes and dumped them on the floor. He gave his obnoxious roommate a *look.* "Privileges of age."

Wade Schmit tapped his fingers impatiently on the desk, glancing at the clock every few seconds. He expected punctuality, especially from those who worked under him. Finally, the phone rang, and he picked it up with a swift motion. "Feldmann, you're late."

"Apologies," came the response. "This case requires meticulous planning."

"Any sign of it?"

"Nothing yet."

"Good," Wade said, nodding. He glanced out the window, noting the overgrown grass, and made a mental note to speak to the gardener later. He prided himself on attention to detail, something he expected from everyone who worked for him. "I want a good hunt, Feldmann. Better than good."

"I assure you, sir, I'm doing everything in my power to ensure that."

"Timing is crucial. This needs to happen before it's seen. Within the next two weeks."

"Understood."

"And you're confident you've chosen the right person for the job?"

"Absolutely. As you said, a disgruntled insider makes the perfect turncoat."

Wade leaned back, running a hand over his face. Feldmann's reassurances were comforting, but he needed results. "Keep me updated on every development."

"You can rely on me, Mr. Schmidt."

"Can I?" Wade's skepticism rose a notch. "So far, your efforts seem more focused on negotiations than actual scouting."

"Well, it's this bear, sir. It's the prize everyone wants."

Suzanne Woods Fisher is the award-winning, bestselling author of more than forty books, including *The Moonlight School* and *Anything but Plain*, as well as the Cape Cod Creamery, Three Sisters Island, Nantucket Legacy, Amish Beginnings, The Bishop's Family, The Deacon's Family, and The Inn at Eagle Hill series. She is also the author of several nonfiction books about the Amish, including *Amish Peace* and *Amish Proverbs*. She lives in California. Learn more at SuzanneWoodsFisher.com and follow Suzanne on Facebook @SuzanneWoodsFisherAuthor and X @SuzanneWFisher.

A Note from the Publisher

Dear Reader,

Thank you for selecting a Revell novel! We're so happy to be part of your reading life through this work. Our mission here at Revell is to publish stories that reach the heart. Through friendship, romance, suspense, or a travel back in time, we bring stories that will entertain, inspire, and encourage you. We believe in the power of stories to change our lives and are grateful for the privilege of sharing these stories with you.

We believe in building lasting relationships with readers, and we'd love to get to know you better. If you have any feedback, questions, or just want to chat about your experience reading this book, please email us directly at publisher@revellbooks.com. Your insights are incredibly important to us, and it would be our pleasure to hear how we can better serve you.

We look forward to hearing from you and having the chance to enhance your experience with Revell Books.

The Publishing Team at Revell Books
A Division of Baker Publishing Group
publisher@revellbooks.com

Revell

Welcome to Summer
on Cape Cod

"This story is uplifting and inspirational, emphasizing what is important in life. The small-town setting, humorous banter, colorful characters, and healing make for a wonderful story."

—No Apology Book Reviews on *The Sweet Life*

"Memorable characters, gorgeous Maine scenery, and plenty of family drama. I can't wait to visit Three Sisters Island again!"

—IRENE HANNON,

bestselling author of the beloved Hope Harbor series

Following the lives of three sisters, this contemporary romance series from Suzanne Woods Fisher is sure to delight her fans and draw new ones.

Connect with SUZANNE

SuzanneWoodsFisher.com